LOOK WHO'S T·A·L·K·I·N·G

An Anthology of Voices in the Modern American Short Story

A partial listing of the contents:

Bruce Weber was born in New York City. He graduated from the University of Michigan and received an M.A. from Columbia University. He has been a fiction editor for *Esquire* Magazine and has taught English at the Horace Mann School in Riverdale, New York. His articles on contemporary writers have appeared in a variety of publications. He is currently an editor for *The New York Times Magazine.*

LOOK WHO'S T·A·L·K·I·N·G

An Anthology of Voices in the Modern American Short Story

EDITED BY BRUCE WEBER

WASHINGTON SQUARE PRESS
PUBLISHED BY POCKET BOOKS
New York London Toronto Sydney Tokyo

These stories are works of fiction. Names, characters, places and incidents are either the product of the authors' imaginations or are used fictitiously. Any resemblance to actual events or locales or persons, living or dead, is entirely coincidental.

A WASHINGTON SQUARE PRESS *Original* Publication

A Washington Square Press Publication of
POCKET BOOKS, a division of Simon & Schuster Inc.
1230 Avenue of the Americas, New York, NY 10020

ISBN: 0-671-68723-9

First Washington Square Press printing December 1986

10 9 8 7 6 5 4 3 2

WASHINGTON SQUARE PRESS and WSP colophon are registered trademarks of Simon & Schuster Inc.

Cover design by Susan Bissett

Printed in the U.S.A.

Permissions

"Cathedral" from *Cathedral* by Raymond Carver. Copyright © 1981, 1982, 1983 by Raymond Carver. Reprinted by permission of Alfred A. Knopf, Inc.

"The Writer in the Family" from *Lives of the Poets* by E. L. Doctorow. Copyright © 1984 by E. L. Doctorow. Reprinted by permission of Random House, Inc.

"Rock Springs" by Richard Ford first appeared in *Esquire.* Copyright © 1982 by Richard Ford. Reprinted by permission of the author.

"Hiding" from *Monkeys* by Susan Minot. Copyright © 1986 by Susan Minot. Reprinted by permission of the publisher, E. P. Dutton/Seymour Lawrence, a division of New American Library.

"Wants" from *Enormous Changes at the Last Minute* by Grace Paley. Copyright © 1971 by Grace Paley. Reprinted by permission of Farrar, Straus & Giroux, Inc.

"An Amateur's Guide to the Night" from *An Amateur's Guide to the Night* by Mary Robison. Copyright © 1981, 1982, 1983 by Mary Robison. Reprinted by permission of Alfred A. Knopf, Inc.

"Dead Reckoning" from *Easy in the Islands* by Bob Shacochis. Copyright © 1985 by Bob Shacochis. Reprinted by permission of Crown Publishers, Inc.

1959 by Carson McCullers; copyright renewed 1979 by Floria V. Lasky. Reprinted by permission of Houghton Mifflin Company.

"The Magic Barrel" from *The Magic Barrel* by Bernard Malamud. Copyright 1954, 1958 by Bernard Malamud. Reprinted by permission of Farrar, Straus & Giroux, Inc.

"Kiswana Browne" from *The Women of Brewster Place* by Gloria Naylor. Copyright © 1980, 1982 by Gloria Naylor. Reprinted by permission of Viking Penguin, Inc.

"Everything That Rises Must Converge" from *The Complete Stories of Flannery O'Connor*. Copyright © 1961, 1965 by the Estate of Mary Flannery O'Connor. Reprinted by permission of Farrar, Straus & Giroux, Inc.

"The Jilting of Granny Weatherall" from *Flowering Judas and Other Stories* by Katherine Anne Porter. Copyright 1930, 1958 by Katherine Anne Porter. Reprinted by permission of Harcourt Brace Jovanovich, Inc.

"The Liberation" from *The Collected Stories of Jean Stafford*. Copyright © 1969 by Jean Stafford. Reprinted by permission of Farrar, Straus & Giroux, Inc.

"Almos' a Man" from *Eight Men* by Richard Wright. Copyright 1940 by T. Y. Crowell Company, copyright renewed 1961 by Richard Wright. Reprinted by permission of John Hawkins & Associates, Inc.

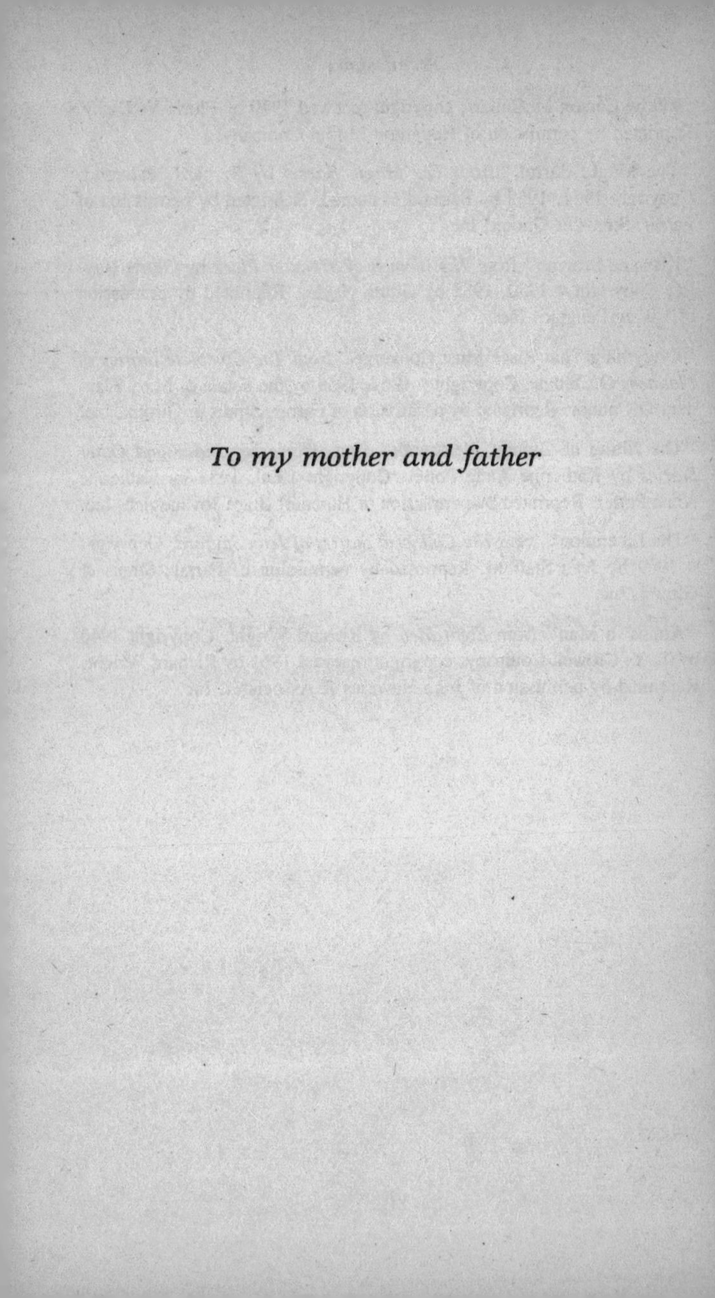

To my mother and father

Acknowledgments

For their constructive comments during the process of putting together this book, I'd like to thank Alice Turner, David Fiorino, John Glusman, Daniel Max and Richard Ford.

Contents

III. THIRD PERSON VOICES

Introduction

> When he was still with us, though, he and my grandfather would trade jokes, and they'd make the telling of the joke last a long long time, which was the best part.
>
> —Mary Robison, "An Amateur's Guide to the Night"

IF YOU ARE like me, then there is someone close to you, someone in your family, maybe, who can't tell a joke worth a damn. With me it is my poor mother, whose fine sense of humor is evident only in that she appreciates being made to laugh. She's quick to pick up on irony, can sense a punchline on the way and enjoys anticipating it, and shows immediate delight when she's surprised by a nifty, climactic twist. But let her try and tell a joke or recount an incident that happened to her or that she witnessed—or tell any story, for that matter—and disaster strikes. She gets excited and nervous. She speaks cautiously as she digs into her memory for the proper order of things. She proceeds with all good intentions, but along the way a crucial detail is forgotten, or a bit of information that ought to remain a mystery is emphatically disclosed, or there is repetition or backtracking or general muddling. Something, anyway. A mess. And whatever laughter was supposed to be elicited by the tale itself instead gets directed at the inept way in which it was told.

While I was growing up, my mother suffered a lot of embarrassment, for this reason, around the family dinner table.

And when the rest of us were through laughing, my brother or I would invariably suggest, "Dad, you tell it," and my father, something of a logician and a practiced wordsmith, would. And we'd all laugh again.

In retrospect, I've come to understand that those twice-told tales at the dinner table were my introduction to the concept of narrative voice. I learned from them for the first time that the pleasure of a story lies not only in the satisfaction that can be derived from a completed tale, but in the process of the telling itself, in how the tale is told. Long before the story is concluded, before its circuit is complete and the fullness of its meaning has a chance to settle in, we, as listeners, react to the teller's voice, to the overall resonance that emanates from qualities like the teller's vocabulary, the rhythms of his sentences, his tone. It is often to the voice of a story, in fact, that we react first. When my mother began one of her earnest, erratic accounts, her breathiness, her halting delivery, her natural befuddlement, all of these immediately influenced my expectations for the story. And when, like Charlie Chaplin laboring with sincerity but incompetence on the assembly line, she lost control and managed to undo all her progress as she went along, I reacted as I do to Chaplin, with delight and sympathy. Then when my father subsequently built his straightforward narrative with lucid diction, subtle inflections, and clever asides, I was carried along by the real momentum generated by his confident telling, and responded accordingly to the mounting tension and its ultimate release in the punch line.

For me, the real point of those dinner jokes is that I enjoyed them twice. Two equally pleasurable, equally genuine responses. For just as to provide a laugh is the aim of a joke teller, so to have one is the aim of a listener. The aim of any story is to evoke a response, I think. And to respond—with joy or sadness, chagrin or satisfaction, sympathy or anger, some human feeling, anyway—is, after all, the paramount reason any of us ever wants to listen to any story in the first place.

The same implied agreement exists between a writer and his readers. Writers write toward a variety of ends, but one wish they all share is to evoke some reaction in the reader. In the most general terms, that's a writer's job. And so it is the reader's to respond, or at least to want to. For without our willing involvement, what is reading but eye strain? And unless we can be moved, then even the most moving story fails.

For many of us, however, responding to a written story with any genuineness or certainty is a problem. Reading a story—because it is done alone and in silence, because the print-filled page has no facial expressions, makes no gestures or sounds, has no body language, because, in short, a written story gives a reader no help in responding to it except for what it offers in the words themselves—is a more difficult task than listening to one. Listening is a passive process, but reading is not; it requires the engagement of our own imaginations. For some people this makes reading intimidating. Too often, as a result, enjoyment goes out the window and puzzlement comes in. Faced with a written story, we clench, become nervous, as if perhaps we're in the presence of secrets. Because there are written lines we can see, we feel the necessity to read between them. It's suddenly imperative to uncover the story's meaning. What's the message of this story? What's the theme? Just what is it this story is trying to say?

I think we mislead ourselves with questions like these. First of all, if a story could be summed up succinctly in a message or a theme, a writer wouldn't have to write a whole story. He could just scribble out the message. But more important, to search for meaning is the writer's work, his difficult business. A reader's business is to respond. Reading is not about tracking down a writer's intention or purpose, as if it were a small, elusive animal; and it isn't even necessary to define a story's accomplishment in order to enjoy it. Yes, of course, there is such a thing as meaning in fiction, the ideas a story fosters and illuminates, but meaning is an ambiguous and arguable thing. Each of us perceives uniquely; we accept or dismiss ideas according to our own lights; thus is the "meaning" of what we read entwined with who we are, thus does it get altered by our changing, growing minds. Meaning is something a reader must journey toward and arrive at, after discourse and thought, and something that can change in our minds even after that. Besides, in reading, as in most journeys, the destination isn't the only thing that matters.

This collection emphasizes a more rudimentary principle. With the lesson of my family dinner table in mind, I've selected the stories each for the use and resonance of its language; that is, its voice, the most accessible property of fiction, the property with which any story engages us first.

Teachers and literary critics often speak of voice as a writer's possession, as in "This new novel represents the debut of a bold voice in American literature"; or, "William Faulkner's dark and penetrating voice is still echoing in the fiction being written today about the South." In this sense, voice refers to the qualities of a writer's intelligence and vision, his values and his priorities, his way of seeing and interpreting the world. To use the term "voice" this way is to distinguish one writer from others, in much the same way we might single out a teacher by what she thinks is important ("She believes in strict discipline in the classroom, more than any other teacher I've ever had"); or a friend by a unique personality quirk ("He's the only guy I know who really cares about clothes"). It's a comprehensive way of speaking, really, which we use to categorize our perceptions and accumulated knowledge for the sake of making useful comparisons.

But if writers themselves can be said to have voices, so can individual stories. The voice of a story resides in its language and communicates with all of language's properties, not just the literal meanings of words and sentences, but with subtler things, too. Rhythms, for example. What are the sentences like? In Ernest Hemingway's "The Battler," they are direct and assertive: "Nick stood up. He was all right. He looked up the track at the lights of the caboose going out of sight around a curve. There was water on both sides of the track, then tamarack swamp." In "Was," by William Faulkner, on the other hand, the sentences are slow to unfold, languorous and complex, disdaining conventional structure, and even occasionally disdaining conventional punctuation. Here is the entire opening paragraph: "Isaac McCaslin, 'Uncle Ike,' past seventy and nearer eighty than he ever corroborated any more, a widower now and uncle to half a county and father to no one''

Vocabulary is another communicative quality. Some voices evoke a seemingly limitless erudition, as if the whole of the English vocabulary were at their disposal; others draw on a more general and familiar pool of words. Some voices employ words so selectively that the reader is drawn by the reverberations of certain choices. In the opening of ''Wants,'' by Grace Paley, the two words *life* and *justified* carry particular weight:

''I saw my ex-husband in the street. I was sitting on the steps of the new library.

''Hello, my life, I said. We had once been married for twenty-seven years, so I felt justified.''

A voice may speak in some specialized language, a regional dialect, perhaps, or with fluency in the expert jargon of some branch of knowledge. Often, in its descriptive phrases or metaphors, a voice will evoke a particular culture or a historical era. In ''Sunshine and Shadow,'' by Ann Beattie, a woman's hat is described as ''a real John Wesley Hardin hat, a favorite left over from the sixties.''

It's often assumed, incorrectly, that a writer chooses his voice, as if a finite number of them were available and the most appropriate one for a story has been selected from a list of concrete alternatives. To the contrary, voice, like character or plot or meaning, is an aspect of fiction, something that lives only in the context of the whole work, existing only because the story does. As readers, we certainly don't need to take note of each peculiarity in the voice in order to enjoy a story, or understand it. Reading isn't listmaking, after all. But voices *are* peculiar—and particular. And it is in the conglomeration of all its small qualities that the voice of any story takes on a singular identity, from which we draw an impression. We can't read with any care at all and not have that be true.

Like everything in a story, the voice is, of course, created by the writer. But to assume that the story's voice is a duplicate of the writer's own is hazardous. In some stories, as in ''Dead Reckoning,'' by Bob Shacochis, for example, in which the male author creates a voice that is unmistakably female, such an effort presents obvious problems. But it is problematic even in stories where the separation between the voice of the writer—the one we'd hear if we met him or her—and the voice of the story may be less in evidence. Remember this is fiction, which presumes invention, and among the things it invents is a narrator, a speaker.

Every work of fiction has a narrator. Some narrators are explicitly personified. Some are not. But the narrator of any tale establishes a relationship with the reader, and this relationship helps explain the nature of the work's particular voice.

"Call me Ishmael," the famous first sentence of Herman Melville's *Moby Dick,* pinpoints right away the narrator's identity, and suggests that the voice of the novel will be shaped by the language as Ishmael uses it. The impression his voice makes on us will help us in forming our opinion of him and the way he views his experiences at sea. John Cheever's "The Enormous Radio" begins, "Jim and Irene Westcott were the kind of people who seem to strike that satisfactory average of income, endeavor, and responsibility that is reached by the statistical reports in college alumni bulletins." Who said that? Who's the wise guy? No one we can name, but the voice of Cheever's narrator has distinct qualities just the same. As the story goes on, the sly remarks continue, poking fun at Jim and Irene; we learn about the characters and their situation through the medium of the speaker's deft and deprecating voice. In other stories, the source of the voice may be initially ambiguous, as it is in Jay McInerney's "It's Six A.M. Do You Know Where You Are?" It begins, "You are not the kind of guy who would be in a place like this at this time of the morning." You? We deduce that the narrator is a character who is addressing himself. But in his voice is an eerie implication of the reader. We feel as if we were being addressed, as if we were supposed to assume for ourselves the identity of the protagonist. The effect is one of uncomfortable intimacy. What if "you" is me? How did I get involved?

The point is that every narrator can be accurately said to have a character. That character's language has features, which, whatever they are, make an impression on us. What we make of that impression constitutes our understanding of the story's "voice."

The stories in this collection are divided by the relationships their narrators forge with the reader. Section one, First Person Voices, contains stories narrated by a character. The teller, in other words, lives in the tale, and we are invited to witness his world. Thus the story's voice will originate in that character's pattern of speech.

Actually, a better way to put it is that we are invited to witness our world as the character sees it. He shares his view of the world with us, and our response to the story depends upon what we think of it. A first person story asks us to have an opinion of the narrator. The way someone speaks reveals clues to his character; in the way first person narrators tell their stories, we're listening for those clues. Is the language formal, using correct grammar and a substantial vocabulary, which might be an indication that the speaker is well educated? Does the narrator speak with an accent or in dialect, hinting at his background? Does he or she repeat key words or phrases, or harp on particular details? That might be an indication of what's on the speaker's mind at the moment. Maybe something is troubling him. Does he misuse words? That raises the question of the speaker's intelligence or whether he might be an insecure person trying to sound impressive.

In section two, Directed Voices, the speaker in each story, as if in assumption that a specific set of ears is listening, aims his narrative at readers as if we were his target. Either by using the "you" address, or by establishing a fictional circumstance for the reader—as, for example, in Ring Lardner's "Haircut," a monologue delivered at us by a barber as if we were his customers, sitting in his chair—the speaker seems to corner the reader, and we take on the role of a captive audience, as if we've been written into the story ourselves.

The voices represented in this section maintain the same personal nature as those in section one. That is, the patterns of language are those spoken by characters. But the relationship between speaker and reader is different. The speaker presumes to be speaking directly to us, and he assumes us to be in the story with him. There's a manipulative edge to these stories; the speaker purports to tell us what to do, or what to think, or how to feel. As a result, there's an initial reflexive edginess on our part. We think: the nerve! But, too, we experience the situation the story describes with a heightened immediacy, a closeness that may be discomforting. The foolishness and gall of the barber in "Haircut," for instance, is something we can't quite laugh at with a wholehearted laugh because we've assumed the role of the customer, sitting there trapped. Our response contains resentment as well as humor.

In the stories in the final section, Third Person Voices, the language emanates from no personified source and is aimed at the reader only by our own inference. Since the identity of the speaker isn't tethered to a single character, the narrator is capable of revealing what an ordinary single mind couldn't possibly know. In a third person narration, we might learn what any given character is thinking at any given moment, or what's going on, meanwhile, across town. By its nature, the narrator in such a story is selective in what it reveals, interpreting the action of the story for us. By whatever indulgence is made in rendering opinions about the characters, and whatever ability he presumes to inform the reader about things that couldn't be simply observed, such a narrator takes on an unassailable wisdom.

What we hear in a third person voice amounts to a guideline, a sly suggestion about how to perceive the characters and interpret their situation. In the language of "The Enormous Radio" we hear the subtle tweaking that the speaker of the story levies at Jim and Irene Westcott. So we're prepared to see the supernatural events of the story as a commentary on their shortcomings, the narrow vision that they've built into their lives. Similarly, the voice of Jean Stafford's "The Liberation" is cool and haughty, the narrator full of pronouncements about the characters, presenting the events of the story with a rigid certainty. In this way, the firm resolve of the main character that surfaces at the story's conclusion is foreshadowed.

No matter what mode of narration is employed, however, the voice of a story provides a reader with his fundamental tool for reading well. The idiosyncrasies of a voice make it possible for us to imagine where it is being emphatic and where confidential, where snide and where genuine, where shrill and where relaxed, where playful and where dead serious. The impression the voice makes on us is how a story lures us toward understanding it. How a story speaks to us creates our response.

In a good story, we can almost hear the voice. It's as if, reading and assimilating the qualities of a voice's language, we're translating the written word into the spoken one, using our eyes to listen; in other words, to read fiction is to look who's talking.

There are anthologies galore whose stories have been selected according to the overt properties they share—Russian short stories, stories by women, short short stories, stories of adventure, experimental fiction. Other anthologies use their selections to trace literary history. Still others divide literature according to the rhetorical methods that authors employ. Many of these collections are helpful guides, introductions to the many definable pockets that exist in the literary tapestry.

Their organizing principles are concerned, however, with the accomplishments of writers, as opposed to the problems of readers. That a story is Faulknerian or nineteenth century or epistolary is not particularly helpful when it comes to a discussion of why a reader might be interested in the characters or with whom a reader's sympathies might lie. Especially for the student reader, there is a misleading implication in the proliferation of these collections, namely that stories are meant to be slotted, urged into categories. Too many students believe that to identify a story as, say, an example of expressionism is to say something conclusive about it; or that to recognize a story as an interior monologue is to understand it, as if living up to a label were what fiction is about.

It's true that all of the stories in this collection are by American writers, and that all were written in this century. They have that in common. But I've applied these restrictions more for the sake of convenience than to supply any literary guidelines. The writers themselves are nonetheless various—living and dead, rural and urban, male and female, black and white, famous and uncelebrated—but even so, the selection was not made in order to showcase the expanse of our native literature or to introduce readers to many of our finest literary artists. For the purpose of this book, the identities of the writers, like their intentions for their work, were of secondary concern.

Rather, I've intended this collection to address the craft of reading, the problem of how to respond. In the notes on the stories to be found at the end of this collection, I've included my own responses, describing briefly, in very general terms, the voice of each story as I hear it, and suggesting how what I hear contributes to what the stories make me think about. The notes are personal, meant only as suggestions. There is not only the potential for disagreement there; it seems to me that my way of reading a given story is just that, mine. But the ideas will perhaps be something to talk about and bicker over, the fact of the matter being that fiction is just about as complicated and inconclusive and impossible to settle with certainty as life is.

In any case, these stories represent a great range, one that I hope is suggestive of the even greater range of possibilities. In provoking the reader to a variety of responses, the stories underscore the strength and wonder of fiction, its own variety, as wide as the limits of imagination, ever expanding, ever accommodating of the new and different voice.

I
FIRST PERSON VOICES

RAYMOND CARVER

Cathedral

THIS BLIND MAN, an old friend of my wife's, he was on his way to spend the night. His wife had died. So he was visiting the dead wife's relatives in Connecticut. He called my wife from his in-laws'. Arrangements were made. He would come by train, a five-hour trip, and my wife would meet him at the station. She hadn't seen him since she worked for him one summer in Seattle ten years ago. But she and the blind man had kept in touch. They made tapes and mailed them back and forth. I wasn't enthusiastic about his visit. He was no one I knew. And his being blind bothered me. My idea of blindness came from the movies. In the movies, the blind moved slowly and never laughed. Sometimes they were led by seeing-eye dogs. A blind man in my house was not something I looked forward to.

That summer in Seattle she had needed a job. She didn't have any money. The man she was going to marry at the end of the summer was in officers' training school. He didn't have any money, either. But she was in love with the guy, and he was in love with her, etc. She'd seen something in the paper: HELP WANTED—*Reading to Blind Man,* and a telephone number. She phoned and went over, was hired on the spot. She'd worked with this blind man all summer. She read stuff to him, case studies, reports, that sort of thing. She helped him organize his little office in the county social-service department. They'd become good friends, my wife and the blind man. How do I know these things? She told me. And she told me something else. On her last day in the office, the blind man asked if he could touch her face. She agreed to this. She told me he touched his fingers to every part of her face, her nose—even her neck! She never forgot it. She even tried to write a poem about it. She was always trying to write a poem. She wrote a poem or two every year, usually after something really important had happened to her.

When we first started going out together, she showed me the poem. In the poem, she recalled his fingers and the way they had moved around over her face. In the poem, she talked about what she had felt at the time, about what went through her mind when the blind man touched her nose and lips. I can remember I didn't think much of the poem. Of course, I didn't tell her that. Maybe I just don't understand poetry. I admit it's not the first thing I reach for when I pick up something to read.

Anyway, this man who'd first enjoyed her favors, the officer-to-be, he'd been her childhood sweetheart. So okay. I'm saying that at the end of the summer she let the blind man run his hands over her face, said goodbye to him, married her childhood etc., who was now a commissioned officer, and she moved away from Seattle. But they'd kept in touch, she and the blind man. She made the first contact after a year or so. She called him up one night from an Air Force base in Alabama. She wanted to talk. They talked. He asked her to send him a tape and tell him about her life. She did this. She sent the tape. On the tape, she told the blind man about her husband and about their life together in the military. She told the blind man she loved her husband but she didn't like it where they lived and she didn't like it that he was a part of the military-industrial thing. She told the blind man she'd written a poem and he was in it. She told him that she was writing a poem about what it was like to be an Air Force officer's wife. The poem wasn't finished yet. She was still writing it. The blind man made a tape. He sent her the tape. She made a tape. This went on for years. My wife's officer was posted to one base and then another. She sent tapes from Moody AFB, McGuire, McConnell, and finally Travis, near Sacramento, where one night she got to feeling lonely and cut off from people she kept losing in that moving-around life. She got to feeling she couldn't go it another step. She went in and swallowed all the pills and capsules in the medicine chest and washed them down with a bottle of gin. Then she got into a hot bath and passed out.

But instead of dying, she got sick. She threw up. Her officer—why should he have a name? he was the childhood sweetheart, and what more does he want?—came home from somewhere, found her, and called the ambulance. In time, she put it all on a tape and sent the tape to the blind man. Over the years, she put all kinds of stuff on tapes and sent the tapes off lickety-split. Next to writing a poem every year, I think it was her chief means of recreation. On one tape, she told the blind man she'd decided to live away from her officer for a time. On another tape, she told him about her divorce. She and I began going out, and of course she told her blind man about it. She told him everything, or so it seemed to me. Once she asked me if I'd like to hear the latest tape from the blind man. This was a year ago. I was on the tape, she said. So I said okay, I'd listen to it. I got us drinks and we settled down in the living room. We made ready to listen. First she inserted the tape into the player and adjusted a couple of dials. Then she pushed a lever. The tape squeaked and someone began to talk in this loud voice. She lowered the volume. After a few minutes of harmless chitchat, I heard my own name in the mouth of this stranger, this blind man I didn't even know! And then this: "From all you've said about him, I can only conclude—" But we were interrupted, a knock at the door, something, and we didn't ever get back to the tape. Maybe it was just as well. I'd heard all I wanted to.

Now this same blind man was coming to sleep in my house.

"Maybe I could take him bowling," I said to my wife. She was at the draining board doing scalloped potatoes. She put down the knife she was using and turned around.

"If you love me," she said, "you can do this for me. If you don't love me, okay. But if you had a friend, any friend, and the friend came to visit, I'd make him feel comfortable." She wiped her hands with the dish towel.

"I don't have any blind friends," I said.

"You don't have *any* friends," she said. "Period. Besides," she said, "goddamn it, his wife's just died! Don't you understand that? The man's lost his wife!"

I didn't answer. She'd told me a little about the blind man's wife. Her name was Beulah. Beulah! That's a name for a colored woman.

"Was his wife a Negro?" I asked.

"Are you crazy?" my wife said. "Have you just flipped or something?" She picked up a potato. I saw it hit the floor, then roll under the stove. "What's wrong with you?" she said. "Are you drunk?"

"I'm just asking," I said.

Right then my wife filled me in with more detail than I cared to know. I made a drink and sat at the kitchen table to listen. Pieces of the story began to fall into place.

Beulah had gone to work for the blind man the summer after my wife had stopped working for him. Pretty soon Beulah and the blind man had themselves a church wedding. It was a little wedding—who'd want to go to such a wedding in the first place?—just the two of them, plus the minister and the minister's wife. But it was a church wedding just the same. It was what Beulah had wanted, he'd said. But even then Beulah must have been carrying the cancer in her glands. After they had been inseparable for eight years—my wife's word, *inseparable*—Beulah's health went into a rapid decline. She died in a Seattle hospital room, the blind man sitting beside the bed and holding on to her hand. They'd married, lived and worked together, slept together—had sex, sure—and then the blind man had to bury her. All this without his having ever seen what the goddamned woman looked like. It was beyond my understanding. Hearing this, I felt sorry for the blind man for a little bit. And then I found myself thinking what a pitiful life this woman must have led. Imagine a woman who could never see herself as she was seen in the eyes of her loved one. A woman who could go on day after day and never receive the smallest compliment from her beloved. A woman whose husband could never read the expression on her face, be it misery or something better. Someone who could wear makeup or not—what difference to him? She could, if she wanted, wear green eye-shadow around one eye, a straight pin in her nostril, yellow slacks and purple shoes, no matter. And then to slip off into death, the blind man's hand on her hand, his blind eyes streaming tears—I'm imagining now—her last thought maybe this: that he never even knew what she looked like, and she on an express to the grave. Robert was left with a small insurance policy and half of a twenty-peso Mexican coin. The other half of the coin went into the box with her. Pathetic.

So when the time rolled around, my wife went to the depot to pick him up. With nothing to do but wait—sure, I blamed him for that—I was having a drink and watching the TV when I heard the car pull into the drive. I got up from the sofa with my drink and went to the window to have a look.

I saw my wife laughing as she parked the car. I saw her get out of the car and shut the door. She was still wearing a smile. Just amazing. She went around to the other side of the car to where the blind man was already starting to get out. This blind man, feature this, he was wearing a full beard! A beard on a blind man! Too much, I say. The blind man reached into the back seat and dragged out a suitcase. My wife took his arm, shut the car door, and, talking all the way, moved him down the drive and then up the steps to the front porch. I turned off the TV. I finished my drink, rinsed the glass, dried my hands. Then I went to the door.

My wife said, "I want you to meet Robert. Robert, this is my husband. I've told you all about him." She was beaming. She had this blind man by his coat sleeve.

The blind man let go of his suitcase and up came his hand.

I took it. He squeezed hard, held my hand, and then he let it go.

"I feel like we've already met," he boomed.

"Likewise," I said. I didn't know what else to say. Then I said, "Welcome. I've heard a lot about you." We began to move then, a little group, from the porch into the living room, my wife guiding him by the arm. The blind man was carrying his suitcase in his other hand. My wife said things like, "To your left here, Robert. That's right. Now watch it, there's a chair. That's it. Sit down right here. This is the sofa. We just bought this sofa two weeks ago."

I started to say something about the old sofa. I'd liked that old sofa. But I didn't say anything. Then I wanted to say something else, small-talk, about the scenic ride along the Hudson. How going *to* New York, you should sit on the right-hand side of the train, and coming *from* New York, the left-hand side.

"Did you have a good train ride?" I said. "Which side of the train did you sit on, by the way?"

"What a question, which side!" my wife said. "What's it matter which side?" she said.

"I just asked," I said.

"Right side," the blind man said. "I hadn't been on a train in nearly forty years. Not since I was a kid. With my folks. That's been a long time. I'd nearly forgotten the sensation. I have winter in my beard now," he said. "So I've been told, anyway. Do I look distinguished, my dear?" the blind man said to my wife.

"You look distinguished, Robert," she said. "Robert," she said. "Robert, it's just so good to see you."

My wife finally took her eyes off the blind man and looked at me. I had the feeling she didn't like what she saw. I shrugged.

I've never met, or personally known, anyone who was blind. This blind man was late forties, a heavy-set, balding man with stooped shoulders, as if he carried a great weight there. He wore brown slacks, brown shoes, a light-brown shirt, a tie, a sports coat. Spiffy. He also had this full beard. But he didn't use a cane and he didn't wear dark glasses. I'd always thought dark glasses were a must for the blind. Fact was, I wished he had a pair. At first glance, his eyes looked like anyone else's eyes. But if you looked close, there was something different about them. Too much white in the iris, for one thing, and the pupils seemed to move around in the sockets without his knowing it or being able to stop it. Creepy. As I stared at his face, I saw the left pupil turn in toward his nose while the other made an effort to keep in one place. But it was only an effort, for that eye was on the roam without his knowing it or wanting it to be.

I said, "Let me get you a drink. What's your pleasure? We have a little of everything. It's one of our pastimes."

"Bub, I'm a Scotch man myself," he said fast enough in this big voice.

"Right," I said. Bub! "Sure you are. I knew it."

He let his fingers touch his suitcase, which was sitting alongside the sofa. He was taking his bearings. I didn't blame him for that.

"I'll move that up to your room," my wife said.

"No, that's fine," the blind man said loudly. "It can go up when I go up."

"A little water with the Scotch?" I said.

"Very little," he said.

"I knew it," I said.

He said, "Just a tad. The Irish actor, Barry Fitzgerald? I'm like that fellow. When I drink water, Fitzgerald said, I drink water. When I drink whiskey, I drink whiskey." My wife laughed. The blind man brought his hand up under his beard. He lifted his beard slowly and let it drop.

I did the drinks, three big glasses of Scotch with a splash of water in each. Then we made ourselves comfortable and talked about Robert's travels. First the long flight from the West Coast to Connecticut, we covered that. Then from Connecticut up here by train. We had another drink concerning that leg of the trip.

I remembered having read somewhere that the blind didn't smoke because, as speculation had it, they couldn't see the smoke they exhaled. I thought I knew that much and that much only about blind people. But this blind man smoked his cigarette down to the nubbin and then lit another one. This blind man filled his ashtray and my wife emptied it.

When we sat down at the table for dinner, we had another drink. My wife heaped Robert's plate with cube steak, scalloped potatoes, green beans. I buttered him up two slices of bread. I said, "Here's bread and butter for you." I swallowed some of my drink. "Now let us pray," I said, and the blind man lowered his head. My wife looked at me, her mouth agape. "Pray the phone won't ring and the food doesn't get cold," I said.

We dug in. We ate everything there was to eat on the table. We ate like there was no tomorrow. We didn't talk. We ate. We scarfed. We grazed that table. We were into serious eating. The blind man had right away located his foods, he knew just where everything was on his plate. I watched with admiration as he used his knife and fork on the meat. He'd cut two pieces of meat, fork the meat into his mouth, and then go all out for the scalloped potatoes, the beans next, and then he'd tear off a hunk of buttered bread and eat that. He'd follow this up with a big drink of milk. It didn't seem to bother him to use his fingers once in a while, either.

We finished everything, including half a strawberry pie. For a few moments, we sat as if stunned. Sweat beaded on our faces. Finally, we got up from the table and left the dirty plates. We didn't look back. We took ourselves into the living room and sank into our places again. Robert and my wife sat on the sofa. I took the big chair. We had us two or three more drinks while they talked about the major things that had come to pass for them in the past ten years. For the most part, I just listened. Now and then I joined in. I didn't want him to think I'd left the room, and I didn't want her to think I was feeling left out. They talked of things that had happened to them—to them!—these past ten years. I waited in vain to hear my name on my wife's sweet lips: "And then my dear husband came into my life"—something like that. But I heard nothing of the sort. More talk of Robert. Robert had done a little of everything, it seemed, a regular blind jack-of-all-trades. But most recently he and his wife had had an Amway distributorship, from which, I gathered, they'd earned their living, such as it was. The blind man was also a ham radio operator. He talked in his loud voice about conversations he'd had with fellow operators in Guam, in the Philippines, in Alaska, and even in Tahiti. He said he'd have a lot of friends there if he ever wanted to go visit those places. From time to time, he'd turn his blind face toward me, put his hand under his beard, ask me something. How long had I been in my present position?

(Three years.) Did I like my work? (I didn't.) Was I going to stay with it? (What were the options?) Finally, when I thought he was beginning to run down, I got up and turned on the TV.

My wife looked at me with irritation. She was heading toward a boil. Then she looked at the blind man and said, "Robert, do you have a TV?"

The blind man said, "My dear, I have two TVs. I have a color set and a black-and-white thing, an old relic. It's funny, but if I turn the TV on, and I'm always turning it on, I turn on the color set. It's funny, don't you think?"

I didn't know what to say to that. I had absolutely nothing to say to that. No opinion. So I watched the news program and tried to listen to what the announcer was saying.

"This is a color TV," the blind man said. "Don't ask me how, but I can tell."

"We traded up a while ago," I said.

The blind man had another taste of his drink. He lifted his beard, sniffed it, and let it fall. He leaned forward on the sofa. He positioned his ashtray on the coffee table, then put the lighter to his cigarette. He leaned back on the sofa and crossed his legs at the ankles.

My wife covered her mouth, and then she yawned. She stretched. She said, "I think I'll go upstairs and put on my robe. I think I'll change into something else. Robert, you make yourself comfortable," she said.

"I'm comfortable," the blind man said.

"I want you to feel comfortable in this house," she said.

"I am comfortable," the blind man said.

After she'd left the room, he and I listened to the weather report and then to the sports roundup. By that time, she'd been gone so long I didn't know if she was going to come back. I thought she might have gone to bed. I wished she'd come back downstairs. I didn't want to be left alone with a blind man. I asked him if he wanted another drink, and he said sure. Then I asked if he wanted to smoke some dope with me. I said I'd just rolled a number. I hadn't, but I planned to do so in about two shakes.

"I'll try some with you," he said.

"Damn right," I said. "That's the stuff."

I got our drinks and sat down on the sofa with him. Then I rolled us two fat numbers. I lit one and passed it. I brought it to his fingers. He took it and inhaled.

"Hold it as long as you can," I said. I could tell he didn't know the first thing.

My wife came back downstairs wearing a pink robe and her pink slippers.

"What do I smell?" she said.

"We thought we'd have us some cannabis," I said.

My wife gave me a savage look. Then she looked at the blind man and said, "Robert, I didn't know you smoked."

He said, "I do now, my dear. There's a first time for everything. But I don't feel anything yet."

"This stuff is pretty mellow," I said. "This stuff is mild. It's dope you can reason with," I said. "It doesn't mess you up."

"Not much it doesn't, bub," he said, and laughed.

My wife sat on the sofa between the blind man and me. I passed her the number. She took it and toked and then passed it back to me. "Which way is this going?" she said. Then she said, "I shouldn't be smoking this. I can hardly keep my eyes open as it is. That dinner did me in. I shouldn't have eaten so much."

"It was the strawberry pie," the blind man said. "That's what did it," he said, and he laughed his big laugh. Then he shook his head.

"There's more strawberry pie," I said.

"Do you want some more, Robert?" my wife said.

"Maybe in a little while," he said.

We gave our attention to the TV. My wife yawned again. She said, "Your bed is made up when you feel like going to bed, Robert. I know you must have had a long day. When you're ready to go to bed, say so." She pulled his arm. "Robert?"

He came to and said, "I've had a real nice time. This beats tapes, doesn't it?"

I said, "Coming at you," and I put the number between

his fingers. He inhaled, held the smoke, and then let it go. It was like he'd been doing it since he was nine years old.

"Thanks, bub," he said. "But I think this is all for me. I think I'm beginning to feel it," he said. He held the burning roach out for my wife.

"Same here," she said. "Ditto. Me, too." She took the roach and passed it to me. "I may just sit here for a while between you two guys with my eyes closed. But don't let me bother you, okay? Either one of you. If it bothers you, say so. Otherwise, I may just sit here with my eyes closed until you're ready to go to bed," she said. "Your bed's made up, Robert, when you're ready. It's right next to our room at the top of the stairs. We'll show you up when you're ready. You wake me up now, you guys, if I fall asleep." She said that and then she closed her eyes and went to sleep.

The news program ended. I got up and changed the channel. I sat back down on the sofa. I wished my wife hadn't pooped out. Her head lay across the back of the sofa, her mouth open. She'd turned so that her robe had slipped away from her legs, exposing a juicy thigh. I reached to draw her robe back over her, and it was then that I glanced at the blind man. What the hell! I flipped the robe open again.

"You say when you want some strawberry pie," I said.

"I will," he said.

I said, "Are you tired? Do you want me to take you up to your bed? Are you ready to hit the hay?"

"Not yet," he said. "No, I'll stay up with you, bub. If that's all right. I'll stay up until you're ready to turn in. We haven't had a chance to talk. Know what I mean? I feel like me and her monopolized the evening." He lifted his beard and he let it fall. He picked up his cigarettes and his lighter.

"That's all right," I said. Then I said, "I'm glad for the company."

And I guess I was. Every night I smoked dope and stayed up as long as I could before I fell asleep. My wife and I hardly ever went to bed at the same time. When I did go to sleep, I had these dreams. Sometimes I'd wake up from one of them, my heart going crazy.

Something about the church and the Middle Ages was on

the TV. Not your run-of-the-mill TV fare. I wanted to watch something else. I turned to the other channels. But there was nothing on them, either. So I turned back to the first channel and apologized.

"Bub, it's all right," the blind man said. "It's fine with me. Whatever you want to watch is okay. I'm always learning something. Learning never ends. It won't hurt me to learn something tonight. I got ears," he said.

We didn't say anything for a time. He was leaning forward with his head turned at me, his right ear aimed in the direction of the set. Very disconcerting. Now and then his eyelids drooped and then they snapped open again. Now and then he put his fingers into his beard and tugged, like he was thinking about something he was hearing on the television.

On the screen, a group of men wearing cowls were being set upon and tormented by men dressed in skeleton costumes and men dressed as devils. The men dressed as devils wore devil masks, horns, and long tails. This pageant was part of a procession. The Englishman who was narrating the thing said it took place in Spain once a year. I tried to explain to the blind man what was happening.

"Skeletons," he said. "I know about skeletons," he said, and he nodded.

The TV showed this one cathedral. Then there was a long, slow look at another one. Finally, the picture switched to the famous one in Paris, with its flying buttresses and its spires reaching up to the clouds. The camera pulled away to show the whole of the cathedral rising above the skyline.

There were times when the Englishman who was telling the thing would shut up, would simply let the camera move around over the cathedrals. Or else the camera would tour the countryside, men in fields walking behind oxen. I waited as long as I could. Then I felt I had to say something. I said, "They're showing the outside of this cathedral now. Gargoyles. Little statues carved to look like monsters. Now I guess they're in Italy. Yeah, they're in Italy. There's paintings on the walls of this one church."

"Are those fresco paintings, bub?" he asked, and he sipped from his drink.

I reached for my glass. But it was empty. I tried to remember what I could remember. "You're asking me are those frescoes?" I said. "That's a good question. I don't know."

The camera moved to a cathedral outside Lisbon. The differences in the Portuguese cathedral compared with the French and Italian were not that great. But they were there. Mostly the interior stuff. Then something occurred to me, and I said, "Something has occurred to me. Do you have any idea what a cathedral is? What they look like, that is? Do you follow me? If somebody says cathedral to you, do you have any notion what they're talking about? Do you know the difference between that and a Baptist church, say?"

He let the smoke dribble from his mouth. "I know they took hundreds of workers fifty or a hundred years to build," he said. "I just heard the man say that, of course. I know generations of the same families worked on a cathedral. I heard him say that, too. The men who began their life's work on them, they never lived to see the completion of their work. In that wise, bub, they're no different from the rest of us, right?" He laughed. Then his eyelids drooped again. His head nodded. He seemed to be snoozing. Maybe he was imagining himself in Portugal. The TV was showing another cathedral now. This one was in Germany. The Englishman's voice droned on. "Cathedrals," the blind man said. He sat up and rolled his head back and forth. "If you want the truth, bub, that's about all I know. What I just said. What I heard him say. But maybe you could describe one to me? I wish you'd do it. I'd like that. If you want to know, I really don't have a good idea."

I stared hard at the shot of the cathedral on the TV. How could I even began to describe it? But say my life depended on it. Say my life was being threatened by an insane guy who said I had to do it or else.

I stared some more at the cathedral before the picture flipped off into the countryside. There was no use. I turned to the blind man and said, "To begin with, they're very tall." I was looking around the room for clues. "They reach way up. Up and up. Toward the sky. They're so big, some of them, they have to have these supports. To help hold them up, so to speak. These supports are called buttresses. They remind me of viaducts, for some reason. But maybe you don't know viaducts, either? Sometimes the cathedrals have devils and such carved into the front. Sometimes lords and ladies. Don't ask me why this is," I said.

He was nodding. The whole upper part of his body seemed to be moving back and forth.

"I'm not doing so good, am I?" I said.

He stopped nodding and leaned forward on the edge of the sofa. As he listened to me, he was running his fingers through his beard. I wasn't getting through to him, I could see that. But he waited for me to go on just the same. He nodded, like he was trying to encourage me. I tried to think what else to say. "They're really big," I said. "They're massive. They're built of stone. Marble, too, sometimes. In those older days, when they built cathedrals, men wanted to be close to God. In those olden days, God was an important part of everyone's life. You could tell this from their cathedral-building. I'm sorry," I said, "but it looks like that's the best I can do for you. I'm just no good at it."

"That's all right, bub," the blind man said. "Hey, listen. I hope you don't mind my asking you. Can I ask you something? Let me ask you a simple question, yes or no. I'm just curious and there's no offense. You're my host. But let me ask if you are in any way religious? You don't mind my asking?"

I shook my head. He couldn't see that, though. A wink is the same as a nod to a blind man. "I guess I don't believe in it. In anything. Sometimes it's hard. You know what I'm saying?"

"Sure, I do," he said.

"Right," I said.

The Englishman was still holding forth. My wife sighed in her sleep. She drew a long breath and went on with her sleeping.

"You'll have to forgive me," I said. "But I can't tell you

what a cathedral looks like. It just isn't in me to do it. I can't do any more than I've done."

The blind man sat very still, his head down, as he listened to me.

I said, "The truth is, cathedrals don't mean anything special to me. Nothing. Cathedrals. They're something to look at on late-night TV. That's all they are."

It was then that the blind man cleared his throat. He brought something up. He took a handkerchief from his back pocket. Then he said, "I get it, bub. It's okay. It happens. Don't worry about it," he said. "Hey, listen to me. Will you do me a favor? I got an idea. Why don't you find us some heavy paper? And a pen. We'll do something. We'll draw one together. Get us a pen and some heavy paper. Go on, bub, get the stuff," he said.

So I went upstairs. My legs felt like they didn't have any strength in them. They felt like they did after I'd done some running. In my wife's room, I looked around. I found some ballpoints in a little basket on her table. And then I tried to think where to look for the kind of paper he was talking about.

Downstairs, in the kitchen, I found a shopping bag with onion skins in the bottom of the bag. I emptied the bag and shook it. I brought it into the living room and sat down with it near his legs. I moved some things, smoothed the wrinkles from the bag, spread it out on the coffee table.

The blind man got down from the sofa and sat next to me on the carpet.

He ran his fingers over the paper. He went up and down the sides of the paper. The edges, even the edges. He fingered the corners.

"All right," he said. "All right, let's do her."

He found my hand, the hand with the pen. He closed his hand over my hand. "Go ahead, bub, draw," he said. "Draw. You'll see. I'll follow along with you. It'll be okay. Just begin now like I'm telling you. You'll see. Draw," the blind man said.

So I began. First I drew a box that looked like a house. It could have been the house I lived in. Then I put a roof on it. At either end of the roof, I drew spires. Crazy.

"Swell," he said. "Terrific. You're doing fine," he said. "Never thought anything like this could happen in your lifetime, did you, bub? Well, it's a strange life, we all know that. Go on now. Keep it up."

I put in windows with arches. I drew flying buttresses. I hung great doors. I couldn't stop. The TV station went off the air. I put down the pen and closed and opened my fingers. The blind man felt around over the paper. He moved the tips of his fingers over the paper, all over what I had drawn, and he nodded.

"Doing fine," the blind man said.

I took up the pen again, and he found my hand. I kept at it. I'm no artist. But I kept drawing just the same.

My wife opened up her eyes and gazed at us. She sat up on the sofa, her robe hanging open. She said, "What are you doing? Tell me, I want to know."

I didn't answer her.

The blind man said, "We're drawing a cathedral. Me and him are working on it. Press hard," he said to me. "That's right. That's good," he said. "Sure. You got it, bub. I can tell. You didn't think you could. But you can, can't you? You're cooking with gas now. You know what I'm saying? We're going to really have us something here in a minute. How's the old arm?" he said. "Put some people in there now. What's a cathedral without people?"

My wife said, "What's going on? Robert, what are you doing? What's going on?"

"It's all right," he said to her. "Close your eyes now," the blind man said to me.

I did it. I closed them just like he said.

"Are they closed?" he said. "Don't fudge."

"They're closed," I said.

"Keep them that way," he said. He said, "Don't stop now. Draw."

So we kept on with it. His fingers rode my fingers as my hand went over the paper. It was like nothing else in my life up to now.

Then he said, "I think that's it. I think you got it," he said. "Take a look. What do you think?"

But I had my eyes closed. I thought I'd keep them that way for a little longer. I thought it was something I ought to do.

"Well?" he said. "Are you looking?"

My eyes were still closed. I was in my house. I knew that. But I didn't feel like I was inside anything.

"It's really something," I said.

E. L. DOCTOROW

The Writer in the Family

IN 1955 MY FATHER died with his ancient mother still alive in a nursing home. The old lady was ninety and hadn't even known he was ill. Thinking the shock might kill her, my aunts told her that he had moved to Arizona for his bronchitis. To the immigrant generation of my grandmother, Arizona was the American equivalent of the Alps, it was where you went for your health. More accurately, it was where you went if you had the money. Since my father had failed in all the business enterprises of his life, this was the aspect of the news my grandmother dwelled on, that he had finally had some success. And so it came about that as we mourned him at home in our stocking feet, my grandmother was bragging to her cronies about her son's new life in the dry air of the desert.

My aunts had decided on their course of action without consulting us. It meant neither my mother nor my brother nor I could visit Grandma because we were supposed to have moved west too, a family, after all. My brother Harold and I didn't mind—it was always a nightmare at the old people's home, where they all sat around staring at us while we tried to make conversation with Grandma. She looked terrible, had numbers of ailments, and her mind wandered. Not seeing her was no disappointment either for my mother, who had never gotten along with the old woman and did not visit when she could have. But what was disturbing was that my aunts had acted in the manner of that side of the family of making government on everyone's behalf, the true citizens by blood and the lesser citizens by marriage. It was exactly this attitude that had tormented by mother all her married life. She claimed Jack's family had never accepted her. She had battled them for twenty-five years as an outsider.

A few weeks after the end of our ritual mourning my Aunt Frances phoned us from her home in Larchmont. Aunt Frances was the wealthier of my father's sisters. Her husband was a lawyer, and both her sons were at Amherst. She had called to say that Grandma was asking why she didn't hear from Jack. I had answered the phone. "You're the writer in the family," my aunt said. "Your father had so much faith in you. Would you mind making up something? Send it to me and I'll read it to her. She won't know the difference."

That evening, at the kitchen table, I pushed my homework aside and composed a letter. I tried to imagine my father's response to his new life. He had never been west. He had never traveled anywhere. In his generation the great journey was from the working class to the professional class. He hadn't managed that either. But he loved New York, where he had been born and lived his life, and he was always discovering new things about it. He especially loved the old parts of the city below Canal Street, where he would find ships' chandlers or firms that wholesaled in spices and teas. He was a salesman for an appliance jobber with accounts all over the city. He liked to bring home rare cheeses or exotic foreign vegetables that were sold only in certain neighborhoods. Once he brought home a barometer, another time an antique ship's telescope in a wooden case with a brass snap.

"Dear Mama," I wrote. "Arizona is beautiful. The sun shines all day and the air is warm and I feel better then I have in years. The desert is not as barren as you would expect, but filled with wildflowers and cactus plants and peculiar crooked trees that look like men holding their arms out. You can see great distances in whatever direction you turn and to the west is a range of mountains maybe fifty miles from here, but in the morning with the sun on them you can see the snow on their crests."

My aunt called some days later and told me it was when she read this letter aloud to the old lady that the full effect of Jack's death came over her. She had to excuse herself and went out in the parking lot to cry. "I wept so," she said. "I felt such terrible longing for him. You're so right, he loved to go places, he loved life, he loved everything."

We began trying to organize our lives. My father had borrowed money against his insurance and there was very little left. Some commissions were still due but it didn't look as if his firm would honor them. There was a couple of thousand dollars in a savings bank that had to be maintained there until the estate was settled. The lawyer involved was Aunt Frances' husband and he was very proper. "The estate!" my mother muttered, gesturing as if to pull out her hair. "The estate!" She applied for a job part-time in the admissions office of the hospital where my father's terminal illness had been diagnosed, and where he had spent some months until they had sent him home to die. She knew a lot of the doctors and staff and she had learned "from bitter experience," as she told them, about the hospital routine. She was hired.

I hated that hospital, it was dark and grim and full of tortured people. I thought it was masochistic of my mother to seek out a job there, but did not tell her so.

We lived in an apartment on the corner of 175th Street and the Grand Concourse, one flight up. Three rooms. I shared the bedroom with my brother. It was jammed with furniture because when my father had required a hospital bed in the last weeks of his illness we had moved some of the living-room pieces into the bedroom and made over the living room for him. We had to navigate bookcases, beds, a gateleg table, bureaus, a record player and radio console, stacks of 78 albums, my brother's trombone and music stand, and so on. My mother continued to sleep on the convertible sofa in the living room that had been their bed before his illness. The two rooms were connected by a narrow hall made even narrower by bookcases along the wall. Off the hall were a small kitchen and dinette and a bathroom. There were lots of appliances in the kitchen—broiler, toaster, pressure cooker, counter-top dishwasher, blender—that my father had gotten through his job, at cost. A treasured phrase in our house: *at cost.* But most of these fixtures went unused because my mother did not care for them. Chromium devices with timers or gauges that required the reading of elaborate instructions were not for her. They were in part responsible for the awful clutter of our lives and now she wanted to get rid of them. "We're being buried," she said. "Who needs them!"

So we agreed to throw out or sell anything inessential. While I found boxes for the appliances and my brother tied the boxes with twine, my mother opened my father's closet and took out his clothes. He had several suits because as a salesman he needed to look his best. My mother wanted us to try on his suits to see which of them could be altered and used. My brother refused to try them on. I tried on one jacket which was too large for me. The lining inside the sleeves chilled my arms and the vaguest scent of my father's being came to me.

"This is way too big," I said.

"Don't worry," my mother said. "I had it cleaned. Would I let you wear it if I hadn't?"

It was the evening, the end of winter, and snow was coming down on the windowsill and melting as it settled. The ceiling bulb glared on a pile of my father's suits and trousers on hangers flung across the bed in the shape of a dead man. We refused to try on anything more, and my mother began to cry.

"What are you crying for?" my brother shouted. "You wanted to get rid of things, didn't you?"

A few weeks later my aunt phoned again and said she thought it would be necessary to have another letter from Jack. Grandma had fallen out of her chair and bruised herself and was very depressed.

"How long does this go on?" my mother said.

"It's not so terrible," my aunt said, "for the little time left to make things easier for her."

My mother slammed down the phone. "He can't even die when he wants to!" she cried. "Even death comes second to

Mama! What are they afraid of, the shock will kill her? Nothing can kill her. She's indestructible! A stake through the heart couldn't kill her!"

When I sat down in the kitchen to write the letter I found it more difficult than the first one. "Don't watch me," I said to my brother. "It's hard enough."

"You don't have to do something just because someone wants you to," Harold said. He was two years older than me and had started at City College; but when my father became ill he had switched to night school and gotten a job in a record store.

"Dear Mama," I wrote. "I hope you're feeling well. We're all fit as a fiddle. The life here is good and the people are very friendly and informal. Nobody wears suits and ties here. Just a pair of slacks and a short-sleeved shirt. Perhaps a sweater in the evening. I have bought into a very successful radio and record business and I'm doing very well. You remember Jack's Electric, my old place on Forty-third Street? Well, now it's Jack's Arizona Electric and we have a line of television sets as well."

I sent that letter off to my Aunt Frances, and as we all knew she would, she phoned soon after. My brother held his hand over the mouthpiece. "It's Frances with her latest review," he said.

"Jonathan? You're a very talented young man. I just wanted to tell you what a blessing your letter was. Her whole face lit up when I read the part about Jack's store. That would be an excellent way to continue."

"Well, I hope I don't have to do this anymore, Aunt Frances. It's not very honest."

Her tone changed. "Is your mother there? Let me talk to her."

"She's not here," I said.

"Tell her not to worry," my aunt said. "A poor old lady who has never wished anything but the best for her will soon die."

I did not repeat this to my mother, for whom it would have been one more in the family anthology of unforgivable remarks. But then I had to suffer it myself for the possible truth it might embody. Each side defended its position with rhetoric, but I, who wanted peace, rationalized the snubs and rebuffs each inflicted on the other, taking no stands, like my father himself.

Years ago his life had fallen into a pattern of business failures and missed opportunities. The great debate between his family on one side, and my mother Ruth on the other, was this: who was responsible for the fact that he had not lived up to anyone's expectations?

As to the prophecies, when spring came my mother's prevailed. Grandma was still alive.

One balmly Sunday my mother and brother and I took the bus to the Beth El cemetery in New Jersey to visit my father's grave. It was situated on a slight rise. We stood looking over rolling fields embedded with monuments. Here and there processions of black cars wound their way through the lanes, or clusters of people stood at open graves. My father's grave was planted with tiny shoots of evergreen but it lacked a headstone. We had chosen one and paid for it and then the stonecutters had gone on strike. Without a headstone my father did not seem to be honorably dead. He didn't seem to me properly buried.

My mother gazed at the plot beside his, reserved for her coffin. "They were always too fine for other people," she said. "Even in the old days on Stanton Street. They put on airs. Nobody was ever good enough for them. Finally Jack himself was not good enough for them. Except to get them things wholesale. Then he was good enough for them."

"Mom, please," my brother said.

"If I had known. Before I ever met him he was tied to his mama's apron strings. And Essie's apron strings were like chains, let me tell you. We had to live where we could be near them for the Sunday visits. Every Sunday, that was my life, a visit to mamaleh. Whatever she knew I wanted, a better apartment, a stick of furniture, a summer camp for the boys, she spoke against it. You know your father, every decision had to be considered and reconsidered. And nothing changed. Nothing ever changed."

She began to cry. We sat her down on a nearby bench. My

brother walked off and read the names on stones. I looked at my mother, who was crying, and I went off after my brother.

"Mom's still crying," I said. "Shouldn't we do something?"

"It's all right," he said. "It's what she came here for."

"Yes," I said, and then a sob escaped from my throat. "But I feel like crying too."

My brother Harold put his arm around me. "Look at this old black stone here," he said. "The way it's carved. You can see the changing fashion in monuments—just like everything else."

Somewhere in this time I began dreaming of my father. Not the robust father of my childhood, the handsome man with healthy pink skin and brown eyes and a mustache and the thinning hair parted in the middle. My dead father. We were taking him home from the hospital. It was understood that he had come back from death. This was amazing and joyous. On the other hand, he was terribly mysteriously damaged, or, more accurately, spoiled and unclean. He was very yellowed and debilitated by his death, and there were no guarantees that he wouldn't soon die again. He seemed aware of this and his entire personality was changed. He was angry and impatient with all of us. We were trying to help him in some way, struggling to get him home, but something prevented us, something we had to fix, a tattered suitcase that had sprung open, some mechanical thing: he had a car but it wouldn't start; or the car was made of wood; or his clothes, which had become too large for him, had caught in the door. In one version he was all bandaged and as we tried to lift him from his wheelchair into a taxi the bandage began to unroll and catch in the spokes of the wheelchair. This seemed to be some unreasonableness on his part. My mother looked on sadly and tried to get him to cooperate.

That was the dream. I shared it with no one. Once when I woke, crying out, my brother turned on the light. He wanted to know what I'd been dreaming but I pretended I didn't remember. The dream made me feel guilty. I felt guilty *in* the dream too because my enraged father knew we didn't want to live with him. The dream represented us taking him home, or trying to, but it was nevertheless understood by all of us that he was to live alone. He was this derelict back from death, but what we were doing was taking him to some place where he would live by himself without help from anyone until he died again.

At one point I became so fearful of this dream that I tried not to go to sleep. I tried to think of good things about my father and to remember him before his illness. He used to call me "matey." "Hello, matey," he would say when he came home from work. He always wanted us to go someplace—to the store, to the park, to a ball game. He loved to walk. When I went walking with him he would say: "Hold your shoulders back, don't slump. Hold your head up and look at the world. Walk as if you meant it!" As he strode down the street his shoulders moved from side to side, as if he was hearing some kind of cakewalk. He moved with a bounce. He was always eager to see what was around the corner.

The next request for a letter coincided with a special occasion in the house. My brother Harold had met a girl he liked and had gone out with her several times. Now she was coming to our house for dinner.

We had prepared for this for days, cleaning everything in sight, giving the house a going-over, washing the dust of disuse from the glasses and good dishes. My mother came home early from work to get the dinner going. We opened the gateleg table in the living room and brought in the kitchen chairs. My mother spread the table with a laundered white cloth and put out her silver. It was the first family occasion since my father's illness.

I liked my brother's girlfriend a lot. She was a thin girl with very straight hair and she had a terrific smile. Her presence seemed to excite the air. It was amazing to have a living breathing girl in our house. She looked around and what she said was: "Oh, I've never seen so many books!" While she and my brother sat at the table my mother was in the kitchen putting the food into serving bowls and I was going from the kitchen to the living room, kidding around like a waiter, with a white cloth over my arm and a high style of service, placing the serving dish of green beans on the table with a flourish. In the kitchen my mother's eyes were sparkling. She looked at me and nodded and mimed the words: "She's adorable!"

My brother suffered himself to be waited on. He was wary of what we might say. He kept glancing at the girl—her name was Susan—to see if we met with her approval. She worked in an insurance office and was taking courses in accounting at City College. Harold was under a terrible strain but he was excited and happy too. He had bought a bottle of Concord-grape wine to go with the roast chicken. He held up his glass and proposed a toast. My mother said: "To good health and happiness," and we all drank, even I. At that moment the phone rang and I went into the bedroom to get it.

"Jonathan? This is your Aunt Frances. How is everyone?"

"Fine, thank you."

"I want to ask one last favor of you. I need a letter from Jack. Your grandma's very ill. Do you think you can?"

"Who is it?" my mother called from the living room.

"OK, Aunt Frances," I said quickly. "I have to go now, we're eating dinner." And I hung up the phone.

"It was my friend Louie," I said, sitting back down. "He didn't know the math pages to review."

The dinner was very fine. Harold and Susan washed the dishes and by the time they were done my mother and I had folded up the gateleg table and put it back against the wall and I had swept the crumbs up with the carpet sweeper. We all sat and talked and listened to records for a while and then my brother took Susan home. The evening had gone very well.

Once when my mother wasn't home my brother had pointed out something: the letters from Jack weren't really necessary. "What is this ritual?" he said, holding his palms up. "Grandma is almost totally blind, she's half deaf and crippled. Does the situation really call for a literary composition? Does it need verisimilitude? Would the old lady know the difference if she was read the phone book?"

"Then why did Aunt Frances ask me?"

"That is the question, Jonathan. Why did she? After all, she could write the letter herself—what difference would it make? And if not Frances, why not Frances' sons, the Amherst students? They should have learned by now to write."

"But they're not Jack's sons," I said.

"That's exactly the point," my brother said. "The idea is *service.* Dad used to bust his balls getting them things wholesale, getting them deals on things. Frances of Westchester really needed things at cost. And Aunt Molly. And Aunt Molly's husband, and Aunt Molly's ex-husband. Grandma, if she needed an errand done. He was always on the hook for something. They never thought his time was important. They never thought every favor he got was one he had to pay back. Appliances, records, watches, china, opera tickets, any goddamn thing. Call Jack."

"It was a matter of pride to him to be able to do things for them," I said. "To have connections."

"Yeah, I wonder why," my brother said. He looked out the window.

Then suddenly it dawned on me that I was being implicated.

"You should use your head more," my brother said.

Yet I had agreed once again to write a letter from the desert and so I did. I mailed it off to Aunt Frances. A few days later, when I came home from school, I thought I saw her sitting in her car in front of our house. She drove a black Buick Roadmaster, a very large clean car with whitewall tires. It was Aunt Frances all right. She blew the horn when she saw me. I went over and leaned in at the window.

"Hello, Jonathan," she said. "I haven't long. Can you get in the car?"

"Mom's not home," I said. "She's working."

"I know that. I came to talk to you."

"Would you like to come upstairs?"

"I can't, I have to get back to Larchmont. Can you get in for a moment, please?"

I got in the car. My Aunt Frances was a very pretty white-haired woman, very elegant, and she wore tasteful clothes. I had always liked her and from the time I was a child she had enjoyed pointing out to everyone that I looked more like her son than Jack's. She wore white gloves and held the steering wheel and looked straight ahead as she talked, as if the car was in traffic and not sitting at the curb.

"Jonathan," she said, "there is your letter on the seat. Needless to say I didn't read it to Grandma. I'm giving it back to you and I won't ever say a word to anyone. This is just between us. I never expected cruelty from you. I never thought you were capable of doing something so deliberately cruel and perverse."

I said nothing.

"Your mother has very bitter feelings and now I see she has poisoned you with them. She has always resented the family. She is a very strong-willed, selfish person."

"No she isn't," I said.

"I wouldn't expect you to agree. She drove poor Jack crazy with her demands. She always had the highest aspirations and he could never fulfill them to her satisfaction. When he still had his store he kept your mother's brother, who drank, on salary. After the war when he began to make a little money he had to buy Ruth a mink jacket because she was so desperate to have one. He had debts to pay but she wanted a mink. He was a very special person, my brother, he should have accomplished something special, but he loved your mother and devoted his life to her. And all she ever thought about was keeping up with the Joneses."

I watched the traffic going up the Grand Concourse. A bunch of kids were waiting at the bus stop at the corner. They had put their books on the ground and were horsing around.

"I'm sorry I have to descend to this," Aunt Frances said. "I don't like talking about people this way. If I have nothing good to say about someone, I'd rather not say anything. How is Harold?"

"Fine."

"Did he help you write this marvelous letter?"

"No."

After a moment she said more softly: "How are you all getting along?"

"Fine."

"I would invite you up for Passover if I thought your mother would accept."

I didn't answer.

She turned on the engine. "I'll say good-bye now, Jonathan. Take your letter. I hope you give some time to thinking about what you've done."

That evening when my mother came home from work I saw that she wasn't as pretty as my Aunt Frances. I usually thought my mother was a good-looking woman, but I saw now that she was too heavy and that her hair was undistinguished.

"Why are you looking at me?" she said.

"I'm not."

"I learned something interesting today," my mother said. "We may be eligible for a V.A. pension because of the time your father spent in the Navy."

That took me by surprise. Nobody had ever told me my father was in the Navy.

"In World War I," she said, "he went to Webb's Naval Academy on the Harlem River. He was training to be an ensign. But the war ended and he never got his commission."

After dinner the three of us went through the closets looking for my father's papers, hoping to find some proof that could be filed with the Veterans Administration. We came up with two things, a Victory medal, which my brother said everyone got for being in the service during the Great War, and an astounding sepia photograph of my father and his shipmates on the deck of a ship. They were dressed in bell-bottoms and T-shirts and armed with mops and pails, brooms and brushes.

"I never knew this," I found myself saying. "I never knew this."

"You just don't remember," my brother said.

I was able to pick out my father. He stood at the end of the row, a thin, handsome boy with a full head of hair, a mustache, and an intelligent smiling countenance.

"He had a joke," my mother said. "They called their training ship the S.S. *Constipation* because it never moved."

Neither the picture nor the medal was proof of anything, but my brother thought a duplicate of my father's service record had to be in Washington somewhere and that it was just a matter of learning how to go about finding it.

"The pension wouldn't amount to much," my mother said. "Twenty or thirty dollars. But it would certainly help."

I took the picture of my father and his shipmates and propped it against the lamp at my bedside. I looked into his youthful face and tried to relate it to the Father I knew. I looked at the picture a long time. Only gradually did my eye connect it to the set of Great Sea Novels in the bottom shelf of the bookcase a few feet away. My father had given that set to me: it was uniformly bound in green with gilt lettering and it included works by Melville, Conrad, Victor Hugo and Captain Marryat. And lying across the top of the books, jammed in under the sagging shelf above, was his old ship's telescope in its wooden case with the brass snap.

I thought how stupid, and imperceptive, and self-centered I had been never to have understood while he was alive what my father's dream for his life had been.

On the other hand, I had written in my last letter from Arizona—the one that had so angered Aunt Frances—something that might allow me, the writer in the family, to soften my judgment of myself. I will conclude by giving the letter here in its entirety.

Dear Mama,

This will be my final letter to you since I have been told by the doctors that I am dying.

I have sold my store at a very fine profit and am sending Frances a check for five thousand dollars to be deposited in your account. My present to you, Mamaleh. Let Frances show you the passbook.

As for the nature of my ailment, the doctors haven't told me what it is, but I know that I am simply dying of the wrong life. I should never have come to the desert. It wasn't the place for me.

I have asked Ruth and the boys to have my body cremated and the ashes scattered in the ocean.

Your loving son,
Jack

RICHARD FORD

Rock Springs

EDNA AND I had started down from Kalispell Heading for Tampa–St. Pete, where I still had some friends from the old glory days who wouldn't turn me into the police. I had managed to scrape with the law in Kalispell over several bad checks—which is a prison crime in Montana. And I knew Edna was already looking at her cards and thinking about a move, since it wasn't the first time I'd been in law scrapes in my life. She herself had already had her own troubles, losing her kids and keeping her ex-husband, Danny, from breaking in her house and stealing her things while she was at work, which was really why I had moved in in the first place, that and needing to give my little daughter, Cheryl, a better shake in things.

I don't know what was between Edna and me, just beached by the same tides when you got down to it. Though love has been built on frailer ground than that, as I well know. And when I came in the house that afternoon, I just asked her if she wanted to go to Florida with me, leave things where they sat, and she said, "Why not? My datebook's not that full."

Edna and I had been a pair eight months, more or less man and wife, some of which time I had been out of work, and some when I'd worked at the dog track as a lead-out and could help with the rent and talk sense to Danny when he came around. Danny was afraid of me because Edna had told him I'd been in prison in Florida for killing a man once, though that wasn't true. I had once been in jail in Tallahassee for stealing tires and had gotten into a fight on the county farm where a man had lost his eye. But I hadn't done the hurting, and Edna just wanted the story worse than it was so Danny wouldn't act crazy and make her have to take her kids back, since she had made a good adjustment to not having them, and I already had Cheryl with me. I'm not a violent person and would never put a man's eye out, much less kill someone. My former wife, Helen, would come all the way from Waikiki Beach to testify to that. We never had violence, and I believe in crossing the street to stay out of trouble's way. Though Danny didn't know that.

But we were half down through Wyoming, going toward I-80 and feeling good about things, when the oil light flashed on in the car I'd stolen, a sign I knew to be a bad one.

I'd gotten us a good car, a cranberry Mercedes I'd stolen out of an ophthalmologist's lot in Whitefish, Montana. I stole it because I thought it would be comfortable over a long haul, because I thought it got good mileage, which it didn't, and because I'd never had a good car in my life, just old Chevy junkers and used trucks back from when I was a kid swamping citrus with Cubans.

The car made us all high that day. I ran the windows up and down, and Edna told us some jokes and made faces. She could be lively. Her features would light up like a beacon and you could see her beauty, which wasn't ordinary. It all made me giddy, and I drove clear down to Bozeman, then straight on through the park to Jackson Hole. I rented us the bridal suite in the Quality Court in Jackson and left Cheryl and her little dog, Duke, sleeping while Edna and I drove to a rib barn and drank beer and laughed till after midnight.

It felt like a whole new beginning for us, bad memories left behind and a new horizon to build on. I got so worked up, I had a tattoo done on my arm that said FAMOUS TIMES, and Edna bought a Bailey hat with an Indian feather band and a little turquoise-and-silver bracelet for Cheryl, and we made love on the seat of the car in the Quality Court parking lot just as the sun was burning up on the Snake River, and everything seemed then like the end of the rainbow.

It was that very enthusiasm, in fact, that made me keep the car one day longer instead of driving it into the river and stealing another one, like I should have done and *had* done before.

Where the car went bad there wasn't a town in sight or even a house, just some low mountains maybe fifty miles away or maybe a hundred, a barbed-wire fence in both directions, hardpan prairie, and some hawks sailing through the evening air seizing insects.

I got out to look at the motor, and Edna got out with Cheryl and the dog to let them have a pee by the car. I checked the water and checked the oil stick, and both of them said perfect.

"What's that light mean, Earl?" Edna said. She had come and stood by the car with her hat on. She was just sizing things up for herself.

"We shouldn't run it," I said. "Something's not right in the oil."

She looked around at Cheryl and Little Duke, who were peeing on the hardtop side by side like two little dolls, then out at the mountains, which were becoming black and lost in the distance. "What're we doing?" she said. She wasn't worried yet, but she wanted to know what I was thinking about.

"Let me try it again," I said.

"That's a good idea," she said, and we all got back in the car.

When I turned the motor over, it started right away and the red light stayed off and there weren't any noises to make you think something was wrong. I let it idle a minute, then pushed the accelerator down and watched the red bulb. But there wasn't any light on, and I started wondering if maybe I hadn't dreamed I saw it, or that it had been the sun catching an angle off the window chrome, or maybe I was scared of something and didn't know it.

"What's the matter with it, Daddy?" Cheryl said from the back seat. I looked back at her, and she had on her turquoise bracelet and Edna's hat set back on the back of her head and that little black-and-white Heinz dog on her lap. She looked like a little cowgirl in the movies.

"Nothing, honey, everything's fine now," I said.

"Little Duke tinkled when I tinkled," Cheryl said, and laughed.

"You're two of a kind," Edna said, not looking back. Edna was usually good with Cheryl, but I knew she was tired now. We hadn't had much sleep, and she had a tendency to get cranky when she didn't sleep. "We oughta ditch this damn car first chance we get," she said.

"What's the first chance we got?" I said, because I knew she'd been at the map.

"Rock Springs, Wyoming," Edna said with conviction. "Thirty miles down this road."

She pointed out ahead. I had wanted all along to drive the car into Florida like a big success story. But I knew Edna was right about it, that we shouldn't take crazy chances. I had kept thinking of it as my car and not the ophthalmologist's, and that was how you got caught in these things.

"Then my belief is we ought to go to Rock Springs and negotiate ourselves a new car," I said. I wanted to stay upbeat, like everything was panning out right.

"That's a great idea," Edna said, and she leaned over and kissed me hard on the mouth.

"That's a great idea," Cheryl said. "Let's pull on out of here right now."

The sunset that day I remember as being the prettiest I'd ever seen. Just as it touched the rim of the horizon, it all at once fired the air into jewels and red sequins the precise likes of which I had never seen before and haven't seen since. The West has it all over everywhere for sunsets, even Florida, where it's supposedly flat but where half the time trees block your view.

"It's cocktail hour," Edna said after we'd driven awhile. "We ought to have a drink and celebrate something." She felt better thinking we were going to get rid of the car. It certainly had dark troubles and was something you'd want to put behind you.

Edna had out a whiskey bottle and some plastic cups and was measuring levels on the glove-box lid. She liked drinking, and she liked drinking in the car, which was something you got used to in Montana, where it wasn't against the law, where, though, strangely enough, a bad check would land you in Deer Lodge Prison for a year.

"Did I ever tell you I once had a monkey?" Edna said, setting my drink on the dashboard where I could reach it when I was ready. Her spirits were already picked up. She was like that, up one minute and down the next.

"I don't think you ever did tell me that," I said. "Where were you then?"

"Missoula," she said. She put her bare feet on the dash and rested the cup on her breasts. "I was waitressing at the Amvets. It was before I met you. Some guy came in one day with a monkey. A spider monkey. And I said, just to be joking, 'I'll roll you for that monkey.' And the guy said, 'Just one roll?' And I said, 'Sure.' He put the monkey down on the bar, picked up the cup, and rolled out boxcars. I picked it up and rolled out three fives. And I just stood there looking at the guy. He was just some guy passing through, I guess a vet. He got a strange look on his face—I'm sure not as strange as the one I had—but he looked kind of sad and surprised and satisfied all at once. I said, 'We can roll again.' But he said, 'No. I never roll twice for anything.' And he sat and drank a beer and talked about one thing and another for a while, about nuclear war and building a stronghold somewhere up in the Bitterroot, whatever it was, while I just watched the monkey, wondering what I was going to do with it when the guy left. And pretty soon he got up and said, 'Well, goodbye, Chipper'; that was this monkey's name, of course. And then he left before I could say anything. And the monkey just sat on the bar all that night. I don't know what made me think of that, Earl. Just something weird. I'm letting my mind wander."

"That's perfectly fine," I said. I took a drink of my drink. "I'd never own a monkey," I said after a minute. "They're too nasty. I'm sure Cheryl would like a monkey, though, wouldn't you, honey?" Cheryl was down on the seat playing with Little Duke. She used to talk about monkeys all the time then. "What'd you ever do with that monkey?" I said, watching the speedometer. We were having to go slower now because the red light kept fluttering on. And all I could do to keep it off was go slower. We were going maybe thirty-five and it was an hour before dark, and I was hoping Rock Springs wasn't far away.

"You really want to know?" Edna said. She gave me a quick, sharp glance, then looked back at the empty desert as if she was brooding over it.

"Sure," I said. I was still upbeat. I figured *I* could worry about breaking down and let other people be happy for a change.

"I kept it a week," she said. She seemed gloomy all of a sudden, as if she saw some aspect of the story she had never seen before. "I took it home and back and forth to the Amvets on my shifts. And it didn't cause any trouble. I fixed a chair up for it to sit on, back of the bar, and people liked it. It made a nice little clicking noise. We changed its name to Mary because the bartender figured out it was a girl. Though I was never really comfortable with it at home. I felt like it watched me too much. Then one day a guy came in, some guy who'd been in Vietnam, still wore a fatigue coat. And he said to me, 'Don't you know that a monkey'll kill you? It's got more strength in its fingers than you got in your whole body.' He said people had been killed in Vietnam by monkeys, bunches of them marauding while you were asleep, killing you and covering you with leaves. I didn't believe a word of it, except that when I got home and got undressed I started looking over across the room at Mary on her chair in the dark watching me. And I got the creeps. And after a while I got up and went out to the car, got a length of clothesline wire, and came back in and wired her to the doorknob through her little silver collar, and went back and tried to sleep. And I guess I must've slept the sleep of the dead—though I don't remember it—because when I got up I found Mary had tupped off her chair back and hanged herself on the wire line. I'd made it too short."

Edna seemed badly affected by that story and slid low in

the seat so she couldn't see over the dash. "Isn't that a shameful story, Earl, what happened to that poor little monkey?"

"I see a town! I see a town!" Cheryl started yelling from the back seat, and right up Little Duke started yapping and the whole car fell into a racket. And sure enough she had seen something I hadn't, which was Rock Springs, Wyoming, at the bottom of a long hill, a little glowing jewel in the desert with I-80 running on the north side and the black desert spread out behind.

"That's it, honey," I said. "That's where we're going. You saw it first."

"We're hungry," Cheryl said. "Little Duke wants some fish, and I want spaghetti." She put her arms around my neck and hugged me.

"Then you'll just get it," I said. "You can have anything you want. And so can Edna and so can Little Duke." I looked over at Edna, smiling, but she was staring at me with eyes that were fierce with anger. "What's wrong?" I said.

"Don't you care anything about that awful thing that happened to me?" she said. Her mouth was drawn tight, and her eyes kept cutting back at Cheryl and Little Duke, as if they had been tormenting her.

"Of course, I do," I said. "I thought that was an awful thing." I didn't want her to be unhappy. We were almost there, and pretty soon we could sit down and have a real meal without thinking somebody might be hunting us.

"You want to know what I did with that monkey?" Edna said.

"Sure I do," I said.

She said, "I put her in a green garbage bag, put it in the trunk of my car, drove to the dump, and threw her in the trash." She was staring at me darkly, as if the story meant something to her that was real important but that only she could see and that the rest of the world was a fool for.

"Well, that's horrible," I said. "But I don't see what else you could do. You didn't mean to kill it. You'd have done it differently if you had. And then you had to get rid of it, and I don't know what else you could have done. Throwing it away might seem unsympathetic to somebody, probably, but not to me. Sometimes that's all you can do, and you can't worry about what somebody else thinks." I tried to smile at her, but the red light was staying on if I pushed the accelerator at all, and I was trying to gauge if we could coast to Rock Springs before the car gave out completely. I looked at Edna again. "What else can I say?" I said.

"Nothing," she said, and stared back at the dark highway. "I should've known that's what you'd think. You've got a character that leaves something out, Earl. I've known that a long time."

"And yet here you are," I said. "And you're not doing so bad. Things could be a lot worse. At least we're all together here."

"Things could always be worse," Edna said. "You could go to the electric chair tomorrow."

"That's right," I said. "And somewhere somebody probably will. Only it won't be you."

"I'm hungry," said Cheryl. "When're we gonna eat? Let's find a motel. I'm tired of this. Little Duke's tired of it too."

Where the car stopped rolling was some distance from the town, though you could see the clear outline of the interstate in the dark with Rock Springs lighting up the sky behind. You could hear the big tractors hitting the spacers in the overpass, revving up for the climb to the mountains.

I shut off the lights.

"What're we going to do now?" Edna said irritably, giving me a bitter look.

"I'm figuring it," I said. "It won't be hard, whatever it is. You won't have to do anything."

"I'd hope not," she said, and looked the other way.

Across the road and across a dry wash a hundred yards was what looked like a huge mobile-home town, with a factory or a refinery of some kind lit up behind it and in full swing. There were lights on in a lot of the mobile homes, and there were cars moving along an access road that ended near the freeway overpass a mile the other way. The lights in the mobile homes seemed friendly to me, and I knew right then what I should do.

"Get out," I said, and opened my door.

"Are we walking?" Edna said.

"We're pushing," I said.

"I'm not pushing," Edna said, and reached up and locked her door.

"All right," I said. "Then you just steer."

"You pushing us to Rock Springs, are you, Earl? It doesn't look like it's more than about three miles," Edna said.

"I'll push," Cheryl said from the back.

"No, hon. Daddy'll push. You just get out with Little Duke and move out of the way."

Edna gave me a threatening look, just as if I'd tried to hit her. But when I got out she slid into my seat and took the wheel, staring angrily ahead straight into the cottonwood scrub.

"Edna can't drive that car," Cheryl said from out in the dark. "She'll run it in the ditch."

"Yes, she can, hon. Edna can drive it as good as I can. Probably better."

"No, she can't," Cheryl said. "No, she can't either." And I thought she was about to cry, but she didn't.

I told Edna to keep the ignition on so it wouldn't lock up and to steer into the cottonwoods with the parking lights on so she could see. And when I started, she steered it straight off into the trees, and I kept pushing until we were twenty yards into the cover and the tires sank in the soft sand and nothing at all could be seen from the road.

"Now where are we?" she said, sitting at the wheel. Her voice was tired and hard, and I knew she could have put a good meal to use. She had a sweet nature, and I recognized that this wasn't her fault but mine. Only I wished she could be more hopeful.

"You stay right here, and I'll go over to that trailer park and call us a cab," I said.

"What cab?" Edna said, her mouth wrinkled as if she'd never heard anything like that in her life.

"There'll be cabs," I said, and tried to smile at her. "There's cabs everywhere."

"What're you going to tell him when he gets here? Our

stolen car broke down and we need a ride to where we can steal another one? That'll be a big hit, Earl."

"I'll talk," I said. "You just listen to the radio for ten minutes and then walk on out to the shoulder like nothing was suspicious. And you and Cheryl act nice. She doesn't need to know about this car."

"Like we're not suspicious enough already, right?" Edna looked up at me out of the lighted car. "You don't think right, did you know that, Earl? You think the world's stupid and you're smart. But that's not how it is. I feel sorry for you. You might've *been* something, but things just went crazy someplace."

I had a thought about poor Danny. He was a vet and crazy as a shit-house mouse, and I was glad he wasn't in for all this. "Just get the baby in the car," I said, trying to be patient. "I'm hungry like you are."

"I'm tired of this," Edna said. "I wish I'd stayed in Montana."

"Then you can go back in the morning," I said. "I'll buy the ticket and put you on the bus. But not till then."

"Just get on with it, Earl," she said, slumping down in the seat, turning off the parking lights with one foot and the radio on with the other.

The mobile-home community was as big as any I'd ever seen. It was attached in some way to the plant that was lighted up behind it, because I could see a car once in a while leave one of the trailer streets, turn in the direction of the plant, then go slowly into it. Everything in the plant was white, and you could see that all the trailers were painted white and looked exactly alike. A deep hum came out of the plant, and I thought as I got closer that it wouldn't be a location I'd ever want to work in.

I went right to the first trailer where there was a light and knocked on the metal door. Kids' toys were lying in the gravel around the little wood steps, and I could hear talking on TV that suddenly went off. I heard a woman's voice talking, and then the door opened wide.

A large Negro woman with a wide, friendly face stood in

the doorway. She smiled at me and moved forward as if she was going to come out, but she stopped at the top step. There was a little Negro boy behind her peeping out from behind her legs, watching me with his eyes half closed. The trailer had that feeling that no one else was inside, which was a feeling I knew something about.

"I'm sorry to intrude," I said. "But I've run up on a little bad luck tonight. My name's Earl Middleton."

The woman looked at me, then out into the night toward the freeway as if what I had said was something she was going to be able to see. "What kind of bad luck?" she said, looking down at me again.

"My car broke down out on the highway," I said. "I can't fix it myself, and I wondered if I could use your phone to call for help."

The woman smiled down at me knowingly. "We can't live without cars, can we?"

"That's the honest truth," I said.

"They're like our hearts," she said firmly, her face shining in the little bulb light that burned beside the door. "Where's your car situated?"

I turned and looked over into the dark, but I couldn't see anything because of where we'd put it. "It's over there," I said. "You can't see it in the dark."

"Who all's with you now?" the woman said. "Have you got your wife with you?"

"She's with my little girl and our dog in the car," I said. "My daughter's asleep or I would have brought them."

"They shouldn't be left in that dark by themselves," the woman said, and frowned. "There's too much unsavoriness out there."

"The best I can do is hurry back," I said. I tried to look sincere, since everything except Cheryl being asleep and Edna being my wife was the truth. The truth is meant to serve you if you'll let it, and I wanted it to serve me. "I'll pay for the phone call," I said. "If you'll bring the phone to the door I'll call from right here."

The woman looked at me again as if she was searching for a truth of her own, then back out into the night. She was maybe in her sixties but I couldn't say for sure. "You're not going to rob me, are you, Mr. Middleton?" she said, and smiled like it was a joke between us.

"Not tonight," I said, and smiled a genuine smile. "I'm not up to it tonight. Maybe another time."

"Then I guess Terrel and I can let you use our phone with Daddy not here, can't we, Terrel? This is my grandson, Terrel Junior, Mr. Middleton." She put her hand on the boy's head and looked down at him. "Terrel won't talk. Though if he did he'd tell you to use our phone. He's a sweet boy." She opened the screen for me to come in.

The trailer was a big one with a new rug and a new couch and a living room that expanded to give the space of a real house. Something good and sweet was cooking in the kitchen, and the trailer felt like it was somebody's comfortable new home instead of just temporary. I've lived in trailers, but they were just snail backs with one room and no toilet, and they always felt cramped and unhappy—though I've thought maybe it might've been me that was unhappy in them.

There was a big Sony TV and a lot of kids' toys scattered on the floor. I recognized a Greyhound bus I'd gotten for Cheryl. The phone was beside a new leather recliner, and the Negro woman pointed for me to sit down and call and gave me the phone book. Terrel began fingering his toys, and the woman sat on the couch while I called, watching me and smiling.

There were three listings for cab companies, all with one number different. I called the numbers in order and didn't get an answer until the last one, which answered with the name of the second company. I said I was on the highway beyond the interstate and that my wife and family needed to be taken to town and I would arrange for a tow later. While I was giving the location, I looked up the name of a tow service to tell the driver in case he asked.

When I hung up, the Negro woman was sitting looking at me with the same look she had been staring with into the dark, a look that seemed to want truth. She was smiling, though. Something pleased her and I reminded her of it.

"This is a very nice home," I said, resting in the recliner, which felt like the driver's seat of the Mercedes and where I'd have been happy to stay.

"This isn't *our* house, Mr. Middleton," the Negro woman said. "The company owns these. They give them to us for nothing. We have our own home in Rockford, Illinois."

"That's wonderful," I said.

"It's never wonderful when you have to be away from home, Mr. Middleton, though we're only here three months, and it'll be easier when Terrel Junior begins his special school. You see, our son was killed in the war, and his wife ran off without Terrel Junior. Though you shouldn't worry. He can't understand us. His little feelings can't be hurt." The woman folded her hands in her lap and smiled in a satisfied way. She was an attractive woman and had on a blue-and-pink floral dress that made her seem bigger than she could've been, just the right woman to sit on the couch she was sitting on. She was good nature's picture, and I was glad she could be, with her little brain-damaged boy, living in a place where no one in his right mind would want to live a minute. "Where do *you* live, Mr. Middleton?" she said politely, smiling in the same sympathetic way.

"My family and I are in transit," I said. "I'm an ophthalmologist, and we're moving back to Florida, where I'm from. I'm setting up practice in some little town where it's warm year-round. I haven't decided where."

"Florida's a wonderful place," the woman said. "I think Terrel would like it there."

"Could I ask you something?" I said.

"You certainly may," the woman said. Terrel had begun pushing his Greyhound across the front of the TV screen, making a scratch that no one watching the set could miss. "Stop that, Terrel Junior," the woman said quietly. But Terrel kept pushing his bus on the glass, and she smiled at me again as if we both understood something sad. Except I knew Cheryl would never damage a television set. She had respect for nice things, and I was sorry for the lady that Terrel didn't. "What did you want to ask?" the woman said.

"What goes on in that plant or whatever it is back there beyond these trailers, where all the lights are on?"

"Gold," the woman said, and smiled.

"It's what?" I said.

"Gold," the Negro woman said, smiling as she had for almost all the time I'd been there. "It's a gold mine."

"They're mining gold back there?" I said, pointing.

"Every night and every day," she said, smiling in a pleased way.

"Does your husband work there?" I said.

"He's the assayer," she said. "He controls the quality. He works three months a year, and we live the rest of the time at home in Rockford. We've waited a long time for this. We've been happy to have our grandson, but I won't say I'll be sorry to have him go. We're ready to start our lives over." She smiled broadly at me and then at Terrel, who was giving her a spiteful look from the floor. "You said you had a daughter," the Negro woman said. "And what's her name?"

"Irma Cheryl," I said. "She's named for my mother."

"That's nice," she said. "And she's healthy, too. I can see it in your face." She looked at Terrel Junior with pity.

"I guess I'm lucky," I said.

"So far you are," she said. "But children bring you grief, the same way they bring you joy. We were unhappy for a long time before my husband got his job in the gold mine. Now, when Terrel starts to school, we'll be kids again." She stood up. "You might miss your cab, Mr. Middleton," she said, walking toward the door, though not to be forcing me out. She was too polite. "If *we* can't see your car, the cab surely won't be able to."

"That's true," I said, and got up off the recliner, where I'd been so comfortable. "None of us have eaten yet, and your food makes me know how hungry we probably all are."

"There are fine restaurants in town, and you'll find them," the Negro woman said. "I'm sorry you didn't meet my husband. He's a wonderful man. He's everything to me."

"Tell him I appreciate the phone," I said. "You saved me."

"You weren't hard to save," the woman said. "Saving people is what we were all put on earth to do. I just passed you on to whatever's coming to you."

"Let's hope it's good," I said, stepping back into the dark.

"I'll be hoping, Mr. Middleton. Terrel and I will both be hoping."

I waved to her as I walked out into the darkness toward the car where it was hidden in the night.

The cab had already arrived when I got there. I could see its little red and green roof lights all the way across the dry wash, and it made me worry that Edna was already saying something to get us in trouble, something about the car or where we'd come from, something that would cast suspicion on us. I thought, then, how I never planned things well enough. There was always a gap between my plan and what happened, and I only responded to things as they came along and hoped I wouldn't get in trouble. I was an offender in the law's eyes. But I always *thought* differently, as if I weren't an offender and had no intention of being one, which was the truth. But as I read on a napkin once, between the idea and the act a whole kingdom lies. And I had a hard time with my acts, which were oftentimes offender's acts, and my ideas, which were as good as the gold they mined there where the bright lights were blazing.

"We're waiting for you, Daddy," Cheryl said when I crossed the road. "The taxicab's already here."

"I see, hon," I said, and gave Cheryl a big hug. The cab-driver was sitting in the driver's seat having a smoke with the lights on inside. Edna was leaning against the back of the cab between the taillights, wearing her Bailey hat. "What'd you tell him?" I said when I got close.

"Nothin'," she said. "What's there to tell?"

"Did he see the car?"

She glanced over in the direction of the trees where we had hid the Mercedes. Nothing was visible in the darkness, though I could hear Little Duke combing around in the underbrush tracking something, his little collar tinkling. "Where're we going?" she said. "I'm so hungry I could pass out."

"Edna's in a terrible mood," Cheryl said. "She already snapped at me."

"We're tired, honey," I said. "So try to be nicer."

"She's never nice," Cheryl said.

"Run go get Little Duke," I said. "And hurry back."

"I guess *my* questions come last here, right?" Edna said.

I put my arm around her. "That's not true," I said.

"Did you find somebody over there in the trailers you'd rather stay with? You were gone long enough."

"That's not a thing to say," I said. "I was just trying to make things look right, so we don't get put in jail."

"So *you* don't, you mean," Edna said and laughed a little laugh I didn't like hearing.

"That's right. So I don't," I said. "I'd be the one in Dutch." I stared out at the big, lighted assemblage of white buildings and white lights beyond the trailer community, plumes of white smoke escaping up into the heartless Wyoming sky, the whole company of buildings looking like some unbelievable castle, humming away in a distorted dream. "You know what all those buildings are there?" I said to Edna, who hadn't moved and who didn't really seem to care if she ever moved anymore ever.

"No. But I can't say it matters, 'cause it isn't a motel and it isn't a restaurant," she said.

"It's a gold mine," I said, staring at the gold mine, which, I knew now from walking to the trailer, was a greater distance from us than it seemed, though it seemed huge and near, up against the cold sky. I thought there should've been a wall around it with guards instead of just the lights and no fence. It seemed as if anyone could go in and take what they wanted, just the way I had gone up to that woman's trailer and used the telephone, though that obviously wasn't true.

Edna began to laugh then. Not the mean laugh I didn't like, but a laugh that had something caring behind it, a full laugh that enjoyed a joke, a laugh she was laughing the first time I laid eyes on her, in Missoula in the Eastgate bar in 1979, a laugh we used to laugh together when Cheryl was still with her mother and I was working steady at the track and not stealing cars or passing bogus checks to merchants. A better time all around. And for some reason it made me laugh just hearing her, and we both stood there behind the cab in the dark, laughing at the gold mine in the desert, me with my arm around her and Cheryl out rustling up Little Duke and the cabdriver smoking in the cab and our stolen Mercedes-Benz, which I'd had such hopes for in Florida, stuck up to its axle in sand, where I'd never get to see it again.

"I always wondered what a gold mine would look like when I saw it," Edna said, still laughing, wiping a tear from her eye.

"Me too," I said. "I was always curious about it."

"We're a couple of fools, ain't we, Earl?" she said, unable to quit laughing completely. "We're two of a kind."

"It might be a good sign, though," I said.

"How could it be?" she said. "It's not our gold mine. There aren't any drive-up windows." She was still laughing.

"We've seen it," I said, pointing. "That's it right there. It may mean we're getting closer. Some people never see it at all."

"In a pig's eyes, Earl," she said. "You and me see it in a pig's eye."

And she turned and got into the cab to go.

The cabdriver didn't ask anything about our car or where it was, to mean he'd noticed something queer. All of which made me feel like we had made a clean break from the car and couldn't be connected with it until it was too late, if ever. The driver told us a lot about Rock Springs while he drove, that because of the gold mine a lot of people had moved there in just six months, people from all over, including New York, and that most of them lived out in the trailers. Prostitutes from New York City, who he called "B-girls," had come into town, he said, on the prosperity tide, and Cadillacs with New York plates cruised the little streets every night, full of Negroes with big hats who ran the women. He told us that everybody who got in his cab now wanted to know where the women were, and when he got our call he almost didn't come because some of the trailers were brothels operated by the mine for engineers and computer people away from home. He said he got tired of running back and forth out there just for vile business. He said that *60 Minutes* had even done a program about Rock Springs and that a blowup had resulted in Cheyenne, though nothing could be done unless the prosperity left town. "It's prosperity's fruit," the driver said. "I'd rather be poor, which is lucky for me."

He said all the motels were sky-high, but since we were a family he could show us a nice one that was affordable. But I told him we wanted a first-rate place where they took animals, and the money didn't matter because we had had a hard day and wanted to finish on a high note. I also knew that it was in the little nowhere places that the police look for you and find you. People I'd known were always being arrested in cheap hotels and tourist courts with names you'd never heard of before. Never in Holiday Inns or Travelodges.

I asked him to drive us to the middle of town and back out again so Cheryl could see the train station, and while we were there I saw a pink Cadillac with New York plates and a TV aerial being driven slowly by a Negro in a big hat down a narrow street where there were just bars and a Chinese restaurant. It was an odd sight, nothing you could ever expect.

"There's your pure criminal element," the cabdriver said, and seemed sad. "I'm sorry for people like you to see a thing like that. We've got a nice town here, but there're some that want to ruin it for everybody. There used to be a way to deal with trash and criminals, but those days are gone forever."

"You said it," Edna said.

"You shouldn't let it get *you* down," I said to the cabdriver. "There's more of you than them. And there always will be. You're the best advertisement this town has. I know Cheryl will remember you and not *that* man, won't you, honey?" But Cheryl was asleep by then, holding Little Duke in her arms on the taxi seat.

The driver took us to the Ramada Inn on the interstate, not far from where we'd broken down. I had a small pain of regret as we drove under the Ramada awning that we hadn't driven up in a cranberry-colored Mercedes but instead in a beat-up old Chrysler taxi driven by an old man full of complaints. Though I knew it was for the best. We were better off without that car, better, really, in any other car but that one, where the signs had turned bad.

I registered under another name and paid for the room in

cash so there wouldn't be any questions. On the line where it said "Representing" I wrote "ophthalmologist" and put "M.D." after the name. It had a nice look to it, even though it wasn't my name.

When we got to the room, which was in the back where I'd asked for it, I put Cheryl on one of the beds and Little Duke beside her so they'd sleep. She'd missed dinner, but it only meant she'd be hungry in the morning, when she could have anything she wanted. A few missed meals don't make a kid bad. I'd missed a lot of them myself and haven't turned out completely bad.

"Let's have some fried chicken," I said to Edna when she came out of the bathroom. "They have good fried chicken at the Ramadas, and I noticed the buffet was still up. Cheryl can stay right here, where it's safe, till we're back."

"I guess I'm not hungry anymore," Edna said. She stood at the window staring out into the dark. I could see out the window past her some yellowish foggy glow in the sky. For a moment I thought it was the gold mine out in the distance lighting the night, though it was only the interstate.

"We could order up," I said. "Whatever you want. There's a menu on the phone book. You could just have a salad."

"You go ahead," she said. "I've lost my hungry spirit." She sat on the bed beside Cheryl and Little Duke and looked at them in a sweet way and put her hand on Cheryl's cheek just as if she'd had a fever. "Sweet little girl," she said. "Everybody loves you."

"What do you want to do?" I said. "I'd like to eat. Maybe *I'll* order up some chicken."

"Why don't you do that?" she said. "It's your favorite." And she smiled at me from the bed.

I sat on the other bed and dialed room service. I asked for chicken, garden salad, potato, and a roll, plus a piece of hot apple pie and ice tea. I realized I hadn't eaten all day. When I put down the phone I saw that Edna was watching me, not in a hateful way or a loving way, just in a way that seemed to say she didn't understand something and was going to ask me about it.

"When did watching me get so entertaining?" I said, and

smiled at her. I was trying to be friendly. I knew how tired she must be. It was after nine o'clock.

"I was just thinking how much I hated being in a motel without a car that was mine to drive. Isn't that funny? I started feeling like that last night when that purple car wasn't mine. That purple car just gave me the willies, I guess, Earl."

"One of those cars *outside* is yours," I said. "Just stand right there and pick it out."

"I know," she said. "But that's different, isn't it?" She reached and got her blue Bailey hat, put it on her head, and set it way back like Dale Evans. She looked sweet. "I used to like to go to motels, you know," she said. "There's something secret about them and free—I was never paying, of course. But you felt safe from everything and free to do what you wanted because you'd made the decision to be there and paid that price, and all the rest was the good part. Fucking and everything, you know." She smiled at me in a good-natured way.

"Isn't that the way this is?" I said. I was sitting on the bed, watching her, not knowing what to expect her to say next.

"I don't guess it is, Earl," she said, and stared out the window. "I'm thirty-two and I'm going to have to give up on motels. I can't keep that fantasy going anymore."

"Don't you like this place?" I said, and looked around at the room. I appreciated the modern paintings and the lowboy bureau and the big TV. It seemed like a plenty nice enough place to me, considering where we'd been already.

"No, I don't," Edna said with real conviction. "There's no use in my getting mad at you about it. It isn't your fault. You do the best you can for everybody. But every trip teaches you something. And I've learned I need to give up on motels before some bad thing happens to me. I'm sorry."

"What does that mean?" I said, because I really didn't know what she had in mind to do, though I should've guessed.

"I guess I'll take that ticket you mentioned," she said, and got up and faced the window. "Tomorrow's soon enough. We haven't got a car to take me anyhow."

"Well, that's a fine thing," I said, sitting on the bed, feeling like I was in a shock. I wanted to say something to her, to argue with her, but I couldn't think what to say that seemed right. I didn't want to be mad at her, but it made me mad.

"You've got a right to be mad at me, Earl," she said, "but I don't think you can really blame me." She turned around and faced me and sat on the windowsill, her hands on her knees. Someone knocked on the door. I just yelled for them to set the tray down and put it on the bill.

"I guess I *do* blame you," I said. I was angry. I thought about how I could have disappeared into that trailer community and hadn't, had come back to keep things going, had tried to take control of things for everybody when they looked bad.

"Don't. I wish you wouldn't," Edna said, and smiled at me like she wanted me to hug her. "Anybody ought to have their choice in things if they can. Don't you believe that, Earl? Here I am out here in the desert where I don't know anything, in a stolen car, in a motel room under an assumed name, with no money of my own, a kid that's not mine, and the law after me. And I have a choice to get out of all of it by getting on a bus. What would you do? I know exactly what you'd do."

"You think you do," I said. But I didn't want to get into an argument about it and tell her all I could've done and didn't do. Because it wouldn't have done any good. When you get to the point of arguing, you're past the point of changing anybody's mind, even though it's supposed to be the other way, and maybe for some classes of people it is, just never mine.

Edna smiled at me and came across the room and put her arms around me where I was sitting on the bed. Cheryl rolled over and looked at us and smiled, then closed her eyes, and the room was quiet. I was beginning to think of Rock Springs in a way I knew I would always think of it, a lowdown city full of crimes and whores and disappointments, a place where a woman left me, instead of a place where I got things on the straight track once and for all, a place I saw a gold mine.

"Eat your chicken, Earl," Edna said. "Then we can go to bed. I'm tired, but I'd like to make love to you anyway. None of this is a matter of not loving you, you know that."

* * *

Sometime late in the night, after Edna was asleep, I got up and walked outside into the parking lot. It could've been anytime because there was still the light from the interstate frosting the low sky and the big red Ramada sign humming motionlessly in the night and no light at all in the east to indicate it might be morning. The lot was full of cars all nosed in, most of them with suitcases strapped to their roofs and their trunks weighed down with belongings the people were taking someplace, to a new home or a vacation resort in the mountains. I had laid in bed a long time after Edna was asleep, watching the Atlanta Braves on cable television, trying to get my mind off how I'd feel when I saw that bus pull away the next day, and how I'd feel when I turned around and there stood Cheryl and Little Duke and no one to see about them but me alone, and that the first thing I had to do was get hold of some automobile and get the plates switched, then get them some breakfast and get us all on the road to Florida, all in the space of probably two hours, since that Mercedes would certainly look less hid in the daytime than the night, and word travels fast. I've always taken care of Cheryl myself as long as I've had her with me. None of the women ever did; most of them didn't even seem to like her, though they took care of me in a way so that I could take care of her. And I knew that once Edna left, all that was going to get harder. Though what I wanted most to do was not think about it just for a little while, try to let my mind go limp so it could be strong for the rest of what there was. I thought that the difference between a successful life and an unsuccessful one, between me at that moment and all the people who owned the cars that were nosed in to their proper places in the lot, maybe between me and that woman out in the trailers by the gold mine, was how well you were able to put things like this out of your mind and not be bothered by them, and maybe, too, by how many troubles like this one you had to face in a lifetime. Through luck or design they had all faced fewer troubles, and by their own characters, they forgot them faster. And that's what I wanted for me. Fewer troubles, fewer memories of trouble.

I walked over to a car, a Pontiac with Ohio tags, one of the ones with bundles and suitcases strapped to the top and a lot more in the trunk, by the way it was riding. I looked inside the driver's window. There were maps and paperback books and sunglasses and the little plastic holders for cans that hang on the window wells. And in the back there were kids' toys and some pillows and a cat box with a cat sitting in it staring at me like I was the face of the moon. It all looked familiar to me, the very same things I would have in my car if I had a car. Nothing seemed surprising, nothing different. Though I had a funny sensation at that moment and turned and looked up at the windows along the back of the Ramada Inn. All were dark except two. Mine and another one. And I wondered, because it seemed funny, what would you think a man was doing if you saw him in the middle of the night looking in the windows of cars in the parking lot of the Ramada Inn? Would you think he was trying to get his head cleared? Would you think he was trying to get ready for a day when trouble would come down on him? Would you think his girlfriend was leaving him? Would you think he had a daughter? Would you think he was anybody like you?

SUSAN MINOT

Hiding

OUR FATHER DOESN'T go to church with us but we're all downstairs in the hall at the same time, bumbling, getting ready to go. Mum knuckles the buttons of Chicky's snowsuit till he's knot-tight, crouching, her heels lifted out of the backs of her shoes, her nylons creased at the ankles. She wears a black lace veil that stays on her hair like magic. Sherman ripples by, coat flapping, and Mum grabs him by the hood, reeling him in, and zips him up with a pinch at his chin. Gus stands there with his bottom lip out, waiting, looking like someone's smacked him except not that hard. Even though he's nine, he still wants Mum to do him up. Delilah comes half-hurrying down the stairs, late, looking like a ragamuffin with her skirt slid down to her hips and her hair all slept on wrong. Caitlin says, "It's about time." Delilah sweeps along the curve of the banister, looks at Caitlin who's all ready to go herself with her pea jacket and her loafers and bare legs, and tells her, "You're going to freeze." Everyone's in a bad mood because we just woke up.

Dad's outside already on the other side of the French doors, waiting for us to go. You can tell it's cold out there by his white breath blowing by his cheek in spurts. He just stands on the porch, hands shoved in his black parka, feet pressed together, looking at the crusty snow on the lawn. He doesn't wear a hat but that's because he barely feels the cold. Mum's the one who's warm-blooded. At skiing, she'll take you in when your toes get numb. You sit there with hot chocolate and a carton of french fries and the other mothers and she rubs your foot to get the circulation back. Down on the driveway the car is warming up and the exhaust goes straight up, disappearing in thin white curls.

"Okay, Monkeys," says Mum, filing us out the door. Chicky starts down the steps one red boot at a time till Mum whisks him up under a wing. The driveway is wrinkled over with ice so we take little shuffle steps across it, blinking at how bright it is, still only half-awake. Only the station wagon can fit everybody. Gus and Sherman scamper in across the huge backseat. Caitlin's head is the only one that shows over the front. (Caitlin is the oldest and she's twelve. I'm next, then Delilah, then the boys.) Mum rubs her thumbs on the steering wheel so that her gloves are shiny and round at the knuckles. Dad is doing things like checking the gutters, waiting till we leave. When we finally barrel down the hill, he turns and goes back into the house which is big and empty now and quiet.

We keep our coats on in church. Except for the O'Shaunesseys, we have the most children in one pew. Dad only comes on Christmas and Easter, because he's not Catholic. A lot of times you only see the mothers there. When Dad stays at home, he does things like cuts prickles in the woods or tears up thorns, or rakes leaves for burning, or just stands around on the other side of the house by the lilacs, surveying his garden, wondering what to do next. We usually sit up near the front and there's a lot of kneeling near the end. One time Gus got his finger stuck in the diamond-shaped holes of the heating vent and Mum had to yank it out. When the man comes around for the collection, we each put in a nickel or a dime and the handle goes by like a rake. If Mum drops in a five-dollar bill, she'll pluck out a couple of bills for her change.

The church is huge. Out loud in the dead quiet, a baby blares out DAH-DEE. We giggle and Mum goes *Ssshhh* but smiles too. A baby always yells at the quietest part. Only the girls are old enough to go to Communion; you're not allowed to chew it. The priest's neck is peeling and I try not to look. "He leaves me cold," Mum says when we leave, touching her forehead with a fingertip after dipping it into the holy water.

On the way home, we pick up the paper at Cage's and a bag of eight lollipops—one for each of us, plus Mum and Dad, even though Dad never eats his. I choose root beer. Sherman crinkles his wrapper, flicking his eyes around to see if anyone's looking. Gus says, "Sherman, you have to wait till after breakfast." Sherman gives a fierce look and shoves it in his mouth. Up in front, Mum, flicking on the blinker, says, "Take that out," with eyes in the back of her head.

Depending on what time of year it is, we do different things on the weekends. In the fall we might go to Castle Hill and stop by the orchard in Ipswich for cider and apples and red licorice. Castle Hill is closed after the summer so there's nobody else there and it's all covered with leaves. Mum goes up to the windows on the terrace and tries to peer in, cupping her hands around her eyes and seeing curtains. We do things like roll down the hills, making our arms stiff like mummies, or climb around on the marble statues which are really cold, or balance along the edge of the fountains without falling. Mum says *Be careful* even though there's no water in them, just red leaves plastered against the sides. When Dad notices us he yells *Get down.*

One garden has a ghost, according to Mum. A lady used to sneak out and meet her lover in the garden behind the grape trellis. Or she'd hide in the garden somewhere and he'd look for her and find her. But one night she crept out and he didn't come and didn't come and finally when she couldn't stand it any longer, she went crazy and ran off the cliff and killed herself and now her ghost comes back and keeps waiting. We creep into the boxed-in place smelling the yellow berries and the wet bark and Delilah jumps—"What was that?"—trying to scare us. Dad shakes the wood to see if it's rotten. We run ahead and hide in a pile of leaves. Little twigs get in your mouth and your nostrils; we hold still underneath listening to the brittle ticking leaves. When we hear Mum and Dad get close, we burst up to surprise them, all the leaves fluttering down, sputtering from the dust and tiny grits that get all over your face like grey ash, like Ash Wednesday. Mum and Dad just keep walking. She brushes a pine needle from his collar and he jerks his head, thinking of something else, probably that it's a fly. We follow them back to the car in a line all scruffy with leaf scraps.

After church, we have breakfast because you're not allowed to eat before. Dad comes in for the paper or a sliver of bacon. One thing about Dad, he has the weirdest taste. Spam is his favorite thing or this cheese that no one can stand the smell of. He barely sits down at all, glancing at the paper with his feet flat down on either side of him, ready to get up any minute to go back outside and sprinkle white fertilizer on the lawn. After, it looks like frost.

This Sunday we get to go skating at Ice House Pond. Dad drives. "Pipe down," he says into the back seat. Mum faces him with white fur around her hood. She calls him Uncs, short for Uncle, a kind of joke, I guess, calling him Uncs while he calls her Mum, same as we do. We are making a racket.

"Will you quit it?" Caitlin elbows Gus.

"What? I'm not doing anything."

"Just taking up all the room."

Sherman's in the way back. "How come Chicky always gets the front?"

"Cause he's the baby." Delilah is always explaining everything.

"I en not a baby," says Chicky without turning around.

Caitlin frowns at me. "Who said you could wear my scarf?"

I ask into the front seat, "Can we go to the Fairy Garden?" even though I know we won't.

"Why couldn't Rummy come?"

Delilah says, "Because Dad didn't want him to."

Sherman wants to know how old Dad was when he learned how to skate.

Dad says, "About your age." He has a deep voice.

"Really?" I think about that for a minute, about Dad being Sherman's age.

"What about Mum?" says Caitlin.

This isn't his department so he just keeps driving. Mum shifts her shoulders more toward us but still looks at Dad.

"When I was a little girl on the Boston Common." Her teeth are white and she wears fuchsia lipstick. "We used to have skating parties."

Caitlin leans close to Mum's fur hood, crossing her arms into a pillow. "What? With dates?"

Mum bats her eyelashes. "Oh sure. Lots of beaux." She smiles, acting like a flirt. I look at Dad but he's concentrating on the road.

We saw one at a football game once. He had a huge mustard overcoat and bow tie and a pink face like a ham. He bent down to shake our tiny hands, half-looking at Mum the whole time. Dad was someplace else getting the tickets. His name was Hank. After he went, Mum put her sunglasses on her head and told us she used to watch him play football at BC. Dad never wears a tie except to work. One time Gus got lost. We waited until the last people had trickled out and the stadium was practically empty. It had started to get dark and the headlights were crisscrossing out of the parking field. Finally Dad came back carrying him, walking fast, Gus's head bobbing around and his face all blotchy. Dad rolled his eyes and made a kidding groan to Mum and we laughed because Gus was always getting lost. When Mum took him, he rammed his head onto her shoulder and hid his face while we walked back to the car, and under Mum's hand you could see his back twitching, trying to hide his crying.

We have Ice House Pond all to ourselves. In certain places the ice is bumpy and if you glide on it going *Aauuuuhhhh* in a low tone, your voice wobbles and vibrates. Every once in a while, a crack shoots across the pond, echoing just beneath the surface, and you feel something drop in the hollow of your back. It sounds like someone's jumped off a steel wire and left it twanging in the air.

I try to teach Delilah how to skate backwards, but she's flopping all over the ice, making me laugh, with her hat lopsided and her mittens dangling out of her sleeves. When Gus falls, he just stays there, polishing the ice with his mitten.

Dad sees him and says, "I don't care if my son is a violin player," kidding.

Dad played hockey in college and was so good his name is on a plaque that's right as you walk into the Harvard rink. He can go really fast. He takes off—*whooosh*—whizzing, circling at the edge of the pond, taking long strides, then gliding, chopping his skates, crossing over in little jumps. He goes zipping by and we watch him: his hands behind him in a tight clasp, his face as calm as if he were just walking along, only slightly forward. When he sweeps a corner, he tips in, then rolls into a hunch, and starts the long side-pushing again. After he stops, his face is red and the tears leak from the sides of his eyes and there's a white smudge around his mouth like frostbite. Sherman, copying, goes chopping forward on collapsed ankles and it sounds like someone sharpening knives.

Mum practices her 3s from when she used to figure skate. She pushes forward on one skate, turning in the middle like a petal flipped suddenly in the wind. We always make her do a spin. First she does backwards crossovers, holding her wrists like a tulip in her fluorescent pink parka, then stops straight up on her toes, sucking in her breath and dips, twisted, following her own tight circle, faster and faster, drawing her feet together. Whirring around, she lowers into a crouch, ventures out one balanced leg, a twirling whirlpool, hot pink, rises again, spinning, into a blurred pillar or a tornado, her arms going above her head and her hands like the eye of a needle. Then suddenly: stop. Hiss of ice shavings, stopped. We clap our mittens. Her hood has slipped off and her hair is spread across her shoulders like when she's reading in bed, and she takes white breaths with her teeth showing and her pink mouth smiling. She squints over our heads. Dad is way off at the car, unlacing his skates on the tailgate but he doesn't turn. Mum's face means that it's time to go.

Chicky stands in the front seat leaning against Dad. Our parkas crinkle in the cold car. Sherman has been chewing on his thumb and it's a pointed black witch's hat. A rumble goes through the car like a monster growl and before we back up Dad lifts Chicky and sets him leaning against Mum instead.

The speed bumps are marked with yellow stripes and it's

like sea serpents have crawled under the tar. When we bounce, Mum says, "Thank-you-Ma'am" with a lilt in her voice. If it was only Mum, the radio would be on and she'd turn it up on the good ones. Dad snaps it off because there's enough racket already. He used to listen to opera when he got home from work but not anymore. Now we give him hard hugs and he changes upstairs then goes into the TV room to the same place on the couch, propping his book on his crossed knees and reaching for his drink without looking up. At supper, he comes in for a handful of onion-flavored bacon crisps or a dish of miniature corn-on-the-cobs pickled. Mum keeps us in the kitchen longer so he can have a little peace and quiet. Ask him what he wants for Christmas and he'll say *No more arguing*. When Mum clears our plates, she takes a bite of someone's hot dog or a quick spoonful of peas before dumping the rest down the pig.

In the car, we ask Dad if we can stop at Shucker's for candy. When he doesn't answer, it means *No*. Mum's eyes mean *Not today*. She says, "It's treat night anyway." Treats are ginger ale and vanilla ice cream.

On Sunday nights we have treats and BLTs and get to watch Ted Mack and Ed Sullivan. There are circus people on almost every time, doing cartwheels or flips or balancing. We stand up in our socks and try some of it. Delilah does an imitation of Elvis by making jump rope handles into a microphone. Girls come on with silver shoes and their stomachs showing and do clappity tap dances. "That's a cinch," says Mum behind us.

"Let's see you then," we say and she goes over to the brick in front of the fireplace to show us. She bangs the floor with her sneakers, pumping and kicking, thudding her heels in smacks, not like clicking at all, swinging her arms out in front of her like she's wading through the jungle. She speeds up, staring straight at Dad who's reading his book, making us laugh even harder. He's always like that. Sometimes for no reason, he'll snap out of it going, "What? What? What's all this? What's going on?" as if he emerged from a dark tunnel, looking like he does when we wake him up and he hasn't put on his glasses yet, sort of angry. He sits there before dinner, popping black olives into his mouth one at a time, eyes never leaving his book. His huge glass mug is from college and in the lamplight you can see the liquid separate. One layer is beer, the rest is gin. Even smelling it makes you gag.

Dad would never take us to Shucker's for candy. With him, we do things outside. If there's a storm we go down to the rocks to see the waves—you have to yell—and get sopped. Or if Mum needs a nap, we go to the beach. In the spring it's wild and windy as anything, which I love. The wind presses against you and you kind of choke but in a good way. Sherman and I run, run, run! Couples at the end are so far away you can hardly tell they're moving. Rummy races around with other dogs, flipping his rear like a goldfish, snapping at the air, or careening in big looping circles across the beach. Caitlin jabs a stick into the wet part and draws flowers. Chicky smells the seaweed by smushing it all over his face. Delilah's dark bangs jitter across her forehead like magnets and she yells back to Gus lagging behind. Dad looks at things far away. He points out birds—a great blue heron near the breakers as thin as a safety pin or an osprey in the sky, tilting like a paper cutout. We collect little things. Delilah holds out a razor shell on one sandy palm for Dad to take and he says *Uh-huh* and calls Rummy. When Sherman, grinning, carries a dead seagull to him, Dad says, "Cut that out." Once in Maine, I found a triangle of blue and white china and showed it to Dad. "Ah, yes, a bit of crockery," he said.

"Do you think it's from the Indians?" I whispered. They had made the arrowheads we found on the beach.

"I think it's probably debris," he said and handed it back to me. According to Mum, debris is the same thing as litter, as in Don't Be a Litter Bug.

When we get home from skating, it's already started to get dark. Sherman runs up first and beats us to the door but can't open it himself. We are all used to how warm it was in the car so everybody's going *Brrrr,* or *Hurry up,* banging our feet on the porch so it thunders. The sky is dark blue glass and the railing seems whiter and the fur on Mum's hood glows. From the driveway Dad yells, "I'm going downtown. Be right back," slamming the door and starting the car again.

Delilah yells, "Can I come?" and Gus goes, "Me too!" as we watch the car back up.

"Right back," says his deep voice through the crack in the window and he rounds the side of the house.

"How come he didn't stop on the way home?" asks Caitlin, sticking out her chin.

"Yah," said Delilah. "How come?" We look at Mum.

She kicks the door with her boot. "In we go, Totsies," she says instead of answering and drops someone's skate on the porch because she's carrying so much stuff.

Gus gets in a bad mood, standing by the door with his coat on, not moving a muscle. His hat has flaps over his ears. Delilah flops onto the hall sofa, her neck bent, ramming her chin into her chest. "Why don't you take off your coat and stay awhile?" she says, drumming her fingers as slow as a spider on her stomach.

"I don't have to."

"Yah," Sherman butts in. "Who says you're the boss?" He's lying on the marble tile with Rummy, scissor-kicking his legs like windshield wipers.

"No one," says Delilah, her fingers rippling along.

On the piano bench, Caitlin is picking at her split ends. We can hear Mum in the kitchen putting the dishes away.

Banging on the piano fast because she knows it by heart, Caitlin plays "Walking in a Winter Wonderland." Delilah sits up and imitates her behind her back, shifting her hips from side to side, making us all laugh. Caitlin whips around, "What?"

"Nothing." But we can't help laughing.

"Nothing what?" says Mum coming around the corner, picking up mittens and socks from the floor, snapping on the lights.

Delilah stiffens her legs. "We weren't doing anything," she says.

We make room for Mum on the couch and huddle. Gus perches at the edge, sideways.

"When's Dad coming back?" he says.

"You know your father," says Mum vaguely, smoothing Delilah's hair on her lap, daydreaming at the floor but thinking about something. When Dad goes to the store, he only gets one thing, like a can of black bean soup or watermelon rind.

"What shall we play?" says Sherman, strangling Rummy in a hug.

"Yah. Yah. Let's do something," we say and turn to Mum.

She narrows her eyes into spying slits. "All rightee. I might have a little idea."

"What?" we all shout, excited. "What?" Mum hardly ever plays with us because she has to do everything else.

She rises, slowly, lifting her eyebrows, hinting, "You'll see."

"What?" says Gus and his bottom lip loosens nervously.

Delilah's dark eyes flash like jumping beans. "Yah, Mum. What?"

"Just come with me," says Mum in a singsong and we scamper after her. At the bottom of the stairs, she crouches in the middle of us. Upstairs behind her, it's dark.

"Where are we going?" asks Caitlin and everybody watches Mum's face, thinking of the darkness up there.

"Hee hee hee," she says in her witch voice. "We're going to surprise your father, play a little trick."

"What?" asks Caitlin again, getting ready to worry but Mum's already creeping up the stairs so we follow, going one mile per hour like her, not making a peep even though there's no one in the house to hear us.

Suddenly she wheels around. "We're going to hide," she cackles.

"Where?" we all want to know, sneaking along like burglars.

Her voice is hushed. "Just come with me."

At the top of the stairs it is dark and we whisper.

"How about your room?" says Delilah. "Maybe under the bed."

"No," says Sherman breathlessly. "In the fireplace." We all laugh because we could never fit in there.

Standing in the hall, Mum opens the door to the linen closet and pulls the light string. "How about right here?" The light falls across our faces. On the shelves are stacks of bed covers and rolled puffs, red and white striped sheets and pink towels, everything clean and folded and smelling of soap.

All of a sudden Caitlin gasps, "Wait—I hear the car!"

Quickly we all jumble and scramble around, bumbling and knocking and trying to cram ourselves inside. Sherman makes whimpering noises like an excited dog. *Sshhhh*, we say or *Hurry Hurry*, or *Wait*. I knee up to a top shelf and Sherman gets a boost after me and then Delilah comes grunting up. We play in here sometimes. Gus and Chicky crawl into the shelf underneath, wedging themselves in sideways. Caitlin half-sits on molding with her legs dangling and one hand braced against the door frame. When the rushing settles, Mum pulls out the light and hikes herself up on the other ledge. Everyone is off the ground then, and quiet.

Delilah giggles. Caitlin says *Ssshhhh* and I say *Come on* in a whisper. Only when Mum says *Hush* do we all stop and listen. Everyone is breathing; a shelf creaks. Chicky knocks a towel off and it hits the ground like a pillow. Gus says, "I don't hear anything." *Sshhh*, we say. Mum touches the door and light widens and we listen. Nothing.

"False alarm," says Sherman.

Our eyes start to get used to the dark. Next to me Delilah gurgles her spit.

"What do you think he'll do?" whispers Caitlin. We all smile, curled up in the darkness with Mum thinking how fooled he'll be, coming back and not a soul anywhere, standing in the hall with all the lights glaring not hearing a sound.

"Where will he think we've gone?" We picture him looking around for a long time, till finally we all pour out of the closet.

"He'll find out," Mum whispers. Someone laughs at the back of his throat, like a cricket quietly ticking.

Delilah hisses, "Wait—"

"Forget it," says Caitlin who knows it's a false alarm.

"What will he do?" we ask Mum.

She's in the darkest part of the closet, on the other side of the light slant. We hear her voice. "We'll see."

"My foot's completely fallen asleep," says Caitlin.

"Kick it," says Mum's voice.

"Ssshhh," lisps Chicky and we laugh at him copying everybody.

Gus's muffled voice comes from under the shelf. "My head's getting squished."

"Move it," says Delilah.

"Quiet!"

And then we really do hear the car.

"Silence, Monkeys," says Mum and we all hush, holding our breaths. The car hums up the hill.

The motor dies and the car shuts off. We hear the door crack, then clip shut. Footsteps bang up the echoing porch, loud, toe-hard and scuffing. The glass panes rattle when the door opens, resounding in the empty hall, and then the door slams in the dead quiet, reverberating through the whole side of the house. Someone in the closet squeaks like a hamster. Downstairs there isn't a sound.

"Anybody home?" he bellows, and we try not to giggle.

Now what will he do? He strides across the deep hall, going by the foot of the stairs, obviously wondering where everybody's gone, stopping at the hooks to hang up his parka.

"What's he doing?" whispers Caitlin to herself.

"He's by the mitten basket," says Sherman. We all have smiles, our teeth like watermelon wedges, grinning in the dark.

He yells toward the kitchen, "Hello?" and we hunch our shoulders to keep from laughing, holding onto something tight like our toes or the shelf, or biting the side of our mouths.

He starts back into the hall.

"He's getting warmer," whispers Mum's voice, far away. We all wait for his footsteps on the stairs.

But he stops by the TV room doorway. We hear him rustling something, a paper bag, taking out what he's bought, the bag crinkling, setting something down on the hall table, them crumpling up the bag and pitching it in the wastebasket. Gus says, "Why doesn't he—?" *Ssshhh,* says Mum like spitting and we all freeze. He moves again—his footsteps turn and bang on the hollow threshold into the TV room where the rug pads the sound.

Next we hear the TV click on, the sound swelling and the dial switching *tick-ah tikka tikka tick* till it lands on a crowd roar, a football game. We can hear the announcer's voice and the hissbreath behind it of cheering.

Then it's the only sound in the house.

"What do we do now?" says Delilah only half-whispering. Mum slips down from her shelf and her legs appear in the light, touching down.

Still hushed, Sherman goes, "Let's keep hiding."

The loud thud is from Caitlin jumping down. She uses her regular voice. "Forget it. I'm sick of this anyway." Everyone starts to rustle. Chicky panics, "I can't get down" as if we're about to desert him.

"Stop being such a baby," says Delilah, disgusted.

Mum doesn't say anything, just opens the door all the way. Past the banister in the hall it is yellow and bright. We climb out of the closet, feet-feeling our way down backwards, bumping out one at a time, knocking down blankets and washcloths by mistake. Mum guides our backs and checks our landings. We don't leave the narrow hallway. The light from downstairs shines up through the railing and casts shadows on the wall—bars of light and dark like a fence. Standing in it we have stripes all over us. *Hey look,* we say whispering, with the football drone in the background, even though this isn't anything new—we always see this, holding out your arms and seeing the stripes. Lingering near the linen closet we wait. Mum picks up the tumbled things, restacking the stuff we knocked down, folding things, clinching a towel with her chin, smoothing it over her stomach and then matching the corners left and right, like crossing herself, patting everything into neat piles. The light gets like this every night after we've gone to bed and we creep into the hall to listen to Mum and Dad downstairs. The bands of shadows go across our nightgowns and pajamas and we press our foreheads against the railing trying to hear the mumbling of what Mum and Dad are saying down there. Then we hear the deep boom of Dad clearing his throat and look up at Mum. Though she is turned away, we can still see the wince on her face like when you are waiting to be hit or right after you have been. So we keep standing there, our hearts pounding, waving our hands through the flickered stripes, suddenly interested the way you get when it's time to take a bath and you are mesmerized by something. We're stalling, waiting for Mum to finish folding, waiting to see what she's going to do next because we don't want to go downstairs yet, where Dad is, without her.

GRACE PALEY

Wants

I SAW MY ex-husband in the street. I was sitting on the steps of the new library.

Hello, my life, I said. We had once been married for twenty-seven years, so I felt justified.

He said, What? What life? No life of mine.

I said, O.K. I don't argue when there's real disagreement. I got up and went into the library to see how much I owed them.

The librarian said $32 even and you've owed it for eighteen years. I didn't deny anything. Because I don't understand how time passes. I have had those books. I have often thought of them. The library is only two blocks away.

My ex-husband followed me to the Books Returned desk. He interrupted the librarian, who had more to tell. In many ways, he said, as I look back, I attribute the dissolution of our marriage to the fact that you never invited the Bertrams to dinner.

That's possible, I said. But really, if you remember: first, my father was sick that Friday, then the children were born, then I had those Tuesday-night meetings, then the war began. Then we didn't seem to know them any more. But you're right. I should have had them to dinner.

I gave the librarian a check for $32. Immediately she trusted me, put my past behind her, wiped the record clean, which is just what most other municipal and/or state bureaucracies will *not* do.

I checked out the two Edith Wharton books I had just returned because I'd read them so long ago and they are more apropos now than ever. They were *The House of Mirth* and *The Children*, which is about how life in the United States in New York changed in twenty-seven years fifty years ago.

A nice thing I do remember is breakfast, my ex-husband said. I was surprised. All we ever had was coffee. Then I remembered there was a hole in the back of the kitchen closet which opened into the apartment next door. There, they always ate sugar-cured smoked bacon. It gave us a very grand feeling about breakfast, but we never got stuffed and sluggish.

That was when we were poor, I said.

When were we ever rich? he asked.

Oh, as time went on, as our responsibilities increased, we didn't go in need. You took adequate financial care, I reminded him. The children went to camp four weeks a year and in decent ponchos with sleeping bags and boots, just like everyone else. They looked very nice. Our place was warm in winter, and we had nice red pillows and things.

I wanted a sailboat, he said. But you didn't want anything.

Don't be bitter, I said. It's never too late.

No, he said with a great deal of bitterness. I may get a sailboat. As a matter of fact I have money down on an eighteen-foot two-rigger. I'm doing well this year and can look forward to better. But as for you, it's too late. You'll always want nothing.

He had had a habit throughout the twenty-seven years of making a narrow remark which, like a plumber's snake, could work its way through the ear down the throat, halfway to my heart. He would then disappear, leaving me choking with equipment. What I mean is, I sat down on the library steps and he went away.

I looked through *The House of Mirth*, but lost interest. I felt extremely accused. Now, it's true, I'm short of requests and absolute requirements. But I do want *something*.

I want, for instance, to be a different person. I want to be the woman who brings these two books back in two weeks. I want to be the effective citizen who changes the school system and addresses the Board of Estimate on the troubles of this dear urban center.

I *had* promised my children to end the war before they grew up.

I wanted to have been married forever to one person, my ex-husband or my present one. Either has enough character for a whole life, which as it turns out is really not such a long time. You couldn't exhaust either man's qualities or get under the rock of his reasons in one short life.

Just this morning I looked out the window to watch the street for a while and saw that the little sycamores the city had dreamily planted a couple of years before the kids were born had come that day to the prime of their lives.

Well! I decided to bring those two books back to the library. Which proves that when a person or an event comes along to jolt or appraise me I *can* take some appropriate action, although I am better known for my hospitable remarks.

MARY ROBISON

An Amateur's Guide to the Night

STARS WERE SOMETHING, since I'd found out which was which. I was smiling at Epsilon Lyrae through the front windshield of my date's Honda Civic—my date, a much older man who, I would've bet, had washed his curly hair with Herbal Essence. Behind us, in the little back seat, my date's friend was kissing my mom.

I could see Epsilon, and two weeks before, when I biked all the way to a veterans' cemetery outside Terre Haute, I had been able to separate Epsilon's quadruple stars—the yellows and the blues—with just my binoculars. I had been way up on the hill there, making a smeary-red glow in the night with my flashlight. The beam had red cellophane taped on it, so I wouldn't desensitize my night vision, which always took an hour to get working well. My star chart and the sky had made sense entirely then, and though it was stinging cold for late spring, I stayed awhile.

It was cold now, or our dates would have walked us away from the car for some privacy.

Mom was with the cuter guy, Kevin. She always got the lookers, even though she was just five feet tall. She wore platform shoes all the time because of it. That was her answer.

My problem was my hair. It was so stick-straight that I had had it cut like the model Esmé—a bad mistake.

I could here Mom telling her date, "I woke up this morning and the car was gone."

"Sounds like a blues song," he said.

And now she was saying, "It's time for our beddy-bye. Sis has classes tomorrow."

Mom and I passed for sisters. We did it all the time. I was an old seventeen. She was young for thirty-five. We would double-date—not just with these two. We saw all kinds of men. Never for very long, though. Three dates was about the record, because Mom would decide by the second evening out that there was something fishy—that her fellow was married, or running from somebody.

So it was perfectly fine with me. But I knew she hadn't pulled the plug on the evening because of my school, or the hour. I was late for school almost every day. Mom would say, "Why don't you wait and go in at noon? That would look better, not like we overslept, but more like you were ill. I'll write a note that says so."

As for studying, it was my practice to wait until the night before a test to read the books I was supposed to have read.

And I was used to a late schedule because of my waitress job, and the stars, and the late movies. If there was a scary movie on, one with a mummy or a prowler, say, Mom had to watch it, and she made me stay up to watch it with her.

"Thanks for the Greek food and for riding us around. Thank you for the beer," we said to our dates. We had been let out on our front sidewalk.

"Next time we won't take you to such a dive," said one of the men.

"Adios!" I called to them. I threw an arm around Mom.

"Until never," she said, as she waved.

We lived about ten miles north of Terre Haute—me, my mom, and my grandfather. We rented a stone house that was a regular Indiana-type house, on Burnside Boulevard, in a town called Phoenicia.

"Greater Metropolitan Phoenicia," my grandfather liked to

say, the joke being that the whole town was really just two rows of shopping blocks on either side of I88.

Grandpa was up, in the living room. We were all night owls. He was having tea, and he had on the robe that was embroidered with dandelions, in honor of spring, I suppose.

"Girls," he greeted us. "Something called *The Creeper* on Channel Nine. Starring an Onslow Stevens. Nineteen forty-eight. Sounds like your sort of poison."

"Did you tell Lindy about our croquettes?" Mom asked him, and laughed. She tossed her handbag onto the couch and pushed up the sleeves of her sweater.

"I forgot all about telling Lindy about the croquettes. That totally slipped from my mind," Grandpa said.

"Well, honey they poisoned Pop's chicken croquettes. They got his *dinner,*" Mom said to me.

"A narrow escape," Grandpa said.

Lately it had been poison Mom talked about, and who knew if she was kidding? She also talked about "light pills" a great deal.

"This *Creeper* that's on—it says in the *Messenger*—he's half man, half cat-beast," Grandpa said.

"Ooh," Mom said, interested.

I asked them, "Would you like to go out in the back yard with me? I'll set up my telescope and show you some stuff."

I had a Frankus reflector telescope I bought with my waitress money. It wasn't perfect. I got it cheap. It did have motor drive, however, and a stabile equatorial mount, cradle rings, and engraved setting circles.

Mom and Grandpa said no, as always. Not that they could have told the difference between Ursa Minor and Hunting Dogs, but I wanted them, just once, to see how I could pull down Jupiter.

It was late the next night, Friday. I was in my uniform and shoes, just off from work. The big concern, whenever someone giant-stepped over my legs, which were propped up on the coffee table, was to protect my expensive support hose.

The job I had was on the dinner shift, five to eleven, at the Steak Chateau, Friday and Saturday evenings. Waitressing and bussing tables—I did both—could really wear you down. That evening I had been stiffed by a group of five adult people. That means no tip; a lot of juggling and running for nothing. Also, I had forgotten to charge one man for his chef's salad, and guess who got to pay for it.

Allen Tashman and Jay Gordon, accountants, were there at our place for popcorn and the Friday-night movie—one called *White Zombie*. They were there when I got home. Allen, the wimpy one, natch, I managed to talk into the back yard.

"Over that mass of shrubs by the garage. See?"

"I see," he said.

"The big Joe is Capella, eye of the Charioteer. And the Pleiades is hanging around somewhere in the same vicinity—there you go. Six little clots."

"Whoopee," he said.

But I loved telling them that stuff, although sometimes I was guessing, or making it up. I was just a C student in school.

"Hey, Lindy, by the way," Allen said, "are people stealing cars, that you know of?"

"Sis?" I asked. Mom and I were pretending to be sisters again.

"Yeah, she told me she thinks there's a car-theft ring in Phoenicia going on."

"Maybe there is," I said.

"She told me to park deep in the driveway and not out by the curb. Have you heard about it? A bunch of cars missing, from this neighborhood, way out here?"

"It's strange," I said, as if it could have been possible.

"I think your sister's crazy sometimes," Allen said.

I didn't bother to get the telescope. Oddly enough on a *clear* night such as that, a star would have "boiled" in the viewfinder. The stars were too bright, was the problem. They were swimming in their own illumination.

We were talking about breakfast, which nobody wanted to fix. The weekend was over and it was Monday morning, getting on toward nine o'clock. I had intended to shake out of bed early, to see Venus in the west as a morning star. But Mom did something to my alarm clock.

She had been sleeping with me, the nights she got to sleep, in the same room, in the same bed.

She may have bashed my clock.

She probably reached over me and cuffed it.

So we were running behind. But I knew if I didn't eat breakfast I'd get queasy. "Make me an egg, please, Grandpa?"

"Poof, you're an egg. *I* made the coffee," he said.

"Mom, then. Please?"

She said, "Lindy, I can't, honey. I've got to look for my pills. Have either of you seen them anywhere, I wonder?"

"Not I, said the pig," said my grandfather.

"Sorry," I said.

"That's peculiar. Didn't I leave them with the vitamins?" Mom said. "This is important, you two."

"Nobody's got your medicine. Your medicine's not here," Grandpa said, causing Mom to be defensive.

"Never mind. I remember where they are," she said.

I doubted it, I really did. I doubted such things as "light pills" existed. Whenever she brought them up, I pictured something like a planet, boiling white—a radiant pill. I pictured Mom swallowing those! At the pharmacy, when she was haunting them, fretting around the prescription desk, they told her they didn't know what she was talking about, but if they did have such pills, she'd need a doctor's order.

"Just eat a banana. You'll be tardy again, Lindy," Grandpa said to me. "Harriet, they're going to fire you so fast if you waltz in late."

"I quit, Pop. They didn't like me there, so I quit," Mom said.

That was the first we had heard of it.

Mom was a comptometer operator, and even though her mind was usually wandering over in Andromeda, she was one of the fastest operators in the state. She could get another job.

Grandpa had enough money for us, so that wasn't the worry. He had been a successful tailor, had even had his own shop. His only fault had been that he sometimes forgot to tie off his threads—so eventually, some of the clothes he made fell apart a little bit, or so he said.

The problem I saw was that Mom really needed to keep occupied.

Grandpa and she were still debating over who was going to fix breakfast when I stuffed my backpack and left for school.

Our landlady—she was nice—was on the cement porch steps next door where she lived. "Hey, Carl Sagan! Give me a minute!" she called, and I obliged. She said, "A Mrs. H. of Phoenicia asks: 'Why was there a ring around the moon last night?' "

"Ice crystals," I told her, thinking that was probably wrong.

"Goodness, I didn't realize it was that chilly," she said.

"Very high up," I said, still guessing.

It wasn't just our landlady. A lot of neighbors knew me, and knew what a star fiend I was. They'd stop me and ask questions, like, "When is it we're getting Halley's Comet again?" Or, "What'd you make of the Saturn pictures?"

I never had to worry about security. When I was younger, for instance, when my mom wanted to go out, she would drop me way down the street at the movie theater. Then, a few times, either because I had sat through a second showing in order to resee my favorite parts, or because Mom accidentally forgot and didn't pick me up, I had to walk home in the dark. I didn't think a thing of it. There were these chummy neighbors all along the way.

"Can't we get out of here? When can we go?" Mom was asking me.

It was a couple days later, a Wednesday afternoon. I had been extended on the sofa, my head sandwiched between throw pillows so I wouldn't have to hear her carp. Our ironing board was set up—a nosy storky bird—aimed at me and waiting for me to press my uniform and something to wear to school the next day.

"Come on, Lindy," Mom urged me. "I need for you to explain to them."

She meant at the pharmacy.

Her good looks were going, I decided. Her brown hair was faded, and since she had quit work, she hadn't been changing her clothes often enough. I planned to iron a fresh something for her, and see if she'd wear it.

"Do you have to do that? Before we can leave?" she said, whining almost. I was testing the nozzle of the spray-starcher can.

"What would happen if you didn't get some pills?" I asked her.

"I'd run out," she said, and shrugged.

First I did the collar on my uniform, which was a gingham check and not French-looking, as it ought to have been for a place called the "Chateau" anything.

"And then what would happen? After you ran out?" I asked Mom.

"Honey," she said, and with a sigh, "I just should have told you. I should've told you *and* Pop. I have a little tumor. Like a tumor, and it's high up in my brain. I can't sleep well because of it, and I need sleep, or it'll worsen and be too diminishing, you see. But the pills fix me right up, is all they do. They give me a recharge. That's how you can think of it. So I don't need to sleep as much."

I finished ironing my uniform. I folded it and put it into a shopping bag so I could take it to school with me on Friday and keep it in my locker. Friday was going to be hell, I knew. There was a school tea planned for the morning, and in the afternoon I would graduate. Friday evening, the Chateau Jimmy was expecting to get crowds and crowds of seniors and their families.

Grandpa came in from the kitchen. His glasses were on from reading his newspaper. He wiggled a hand through the wrinkled clothes in my laundry basket, which rested on the couch.

"Tell him about your brain tumor, Mom," I said.

"Yeah, brain tumor," Grandpa said. "It's sinusitis. It's just from goldenrod."

It was like him to say that. If I ever had a headache, I got it from combing my hair too roughly, or parting it on the wrong side, according to him. He sat down in his chair. It was a maize color, and had heavy arms. "How does one called

The Magician sound? It's the Fright Theatre feature this weekend."

I was thinking Grandpa was a happier man when my father was around. I could completely forget about my father, these days, unless I was reminded. He had moved to Toledo, several years before, with his company. He had remarried. When he was still with us, though, he and my grandfather would trade jokes, and they'd make the *telling* of the joke last a long long time, which was the funniest part. Springs and summers, they would take Mom to the trotting races over at Geronimo Downs. They'd go almost nightly, in a white and red convertible they had between them.

It was Thursday, the morning before graduation. I was cutting school, since it was nothing, just a rehearsal, and getting class rings and individual awards at an assembly—class artist, class-reunion secretary—not anything that involved me. I planned to show up after lunch and maybe pick up my cap and gown.

Mom and I were on the Shopper's Special, a bus that ran from Phoenicia to Terre Haute on weekdays. I hoped Mom was going to get her hair done, or buy an outfit for tomorrow, but she hadn't said she would. The other shoppers on the Special were a couple of lumpy women and a leather man in golfing clothes, and a guy in a maroon suit who had Mom's whole attention.

The bus shuddered at a light. Its engine noise and the tremor in the hard seat and the clear early sun were all getting to me, making me drowsy.

The maroon suit was behind a Chicago newspaper. Mom glanced back at him. "What do you think *he* does?" she asked me.

"Could be anything," I said.

"No, kiddo. That's a plainclothesman. You can tell."

"He could be," I said.

"He is. I believe he's on here for us."

I was very used to this talk, but today I didn't feel like hearing it. "Please," I said to Mom.

"Forget it," she said.

She looked young again. "Don't act up, girls," the bus driver had teased us when we got on in Phoenicia.

"I can do something," I said to Mom. "I can name the fifteen brightest stars. Want me to? I can give them in order of brightness."

Mom seemed stunned by the offer and her face slackened. The concern went out of her eyes. She looked twelve. "Can you do something like that? Did you have to learn it in school, or on your own?"

"*I* did it. Here we go. They are Sirius, Canopus, Alpha Centauri, Arcturus, Vega," I told her, and right on through to old reddish Antares.

Mom was both smiling and grave, like a person hearing a favorite poem.

"Mom," I said, after a minute, "before commencement tomorrow, there's the Senior Tea. It's just cookies and junk, but I told them maybe you'd help serve. They wanted parents to be guards for the tables, just so nobody takes a hundred cookies instead of one or two."

She was surprised, I could tell. I wondered if she was flattered that I wanted her to be there.

"Honey, I couldn't do *that,*" she said, as though I had asked her to leap over our garage, or jog to Kansas. "I couldn't do that."

The trip to Terre Haute was all the way beside a river. Sometimes, the river was just a large ditch and sometimes it was an actual wild river. Today, it was full to the banks, and we were rolling along in the bus at the same rate as the current.

In the corner of my sight, I saw Mom fussing with the jumbo purse she had brought. I peeked down into it, and there were her toothbrush and plastic soap box and her cloth hair-curlers. So I knew she was thinking of getting off at Platte and seeing if they had a bed for her at the Institute there. I thought maybe her Dr. Goff, whom she saw, had decided she ought to check in for a bit again. Or, more probably it was her idea.

The hospital *was* Mom's idea, I finally learned from Grandpa, but it turned out they didn't have space for her, or they didn't think she needed to get in right then.

She wasn't at my graduation ceremony, which was just as well, in one way—I didn't do a great job, since I had missed rehearsal. During the sitting moments, I wondered about her, though, and I decided that graduation had been one of the chief things upsetting her. She was scared of the "going forward into the world" parts of the commencement speeches.

Grandpa lied to me. He said he was certain Mom was there, just back in one of the cooler seats, under the buck-eye trees. Graduation was outside, see. He said Mom wanted shade.

Late that night, we were all three watching the Fright Theatre feature. A girl in the movie was married to a man who changed into a werewolf and attacked people. Sooner or later, you knew he was going to go after the girl.

"That poor woman," Mom kept saying.

"She's got it tough, all right," Grandpa said. "Trying to keep her husband in Alpo."

I was exhausted from work. I was nibbling the black kernels and oily salt from the bottom of the popcorn bowl.

"She has to make sure he's got all his shots. He's got to be wormed. Here she comes now, going to give him a flea collar," Grandpa said.

I liked being as dragged out as I was. My new apricot robe that Grandpa had made for me was across my legs, keeping them warm. My other graduation gifts, from Mom—really Grandpa—were all telescope related.

There was a pause in the movie for a commercial. "Take a reading on this," Grandpa said. He flipped a big white card to me. The card said, "Happy Graduation, Good Luck in Your Future." It had come from my dad.

I was still looking at the signature, *Your father,* when the movie started back up again. "What if Dad were back living with us?" I asked Grandpa and Mom.

"It would cut down on your mom's dating," Grandpa said.

Mom, concentrating on the television, said, "Uh oh, full moon!"

"But just suppose Dad were to somehow come back here and live with us," I said to Mom. I had put down the card and was pulling on my short hair a little.

"He better not," she said.

"You're damn right, he better not," Grandpa said.

I was surprised. He even sounded angry. I guessed I had been wrong, thinking Grandpa missed having Dad as a crony so much.

I stuffed a pillow behind my head and sat back and listened to the creepy music from the television and to a moth that was stupidly banging on the window screen. It would take a lot for my dad to understand us, and the way we three did things, I thought. He would have to do some thinking.

"Ah, this couch feels good!" I said. "I could lie here forever."

I didn't know whether or not Mom had heard me. But she was beaming, either way. She pointed to the TV screen, where the werewolf lay under a bush, becoming a person again. She said, "Shh."

BOB SHACOCHIS

Dead Reckoning

When I dropped out of Old Dominion, I took the first job I could find, flipping hamburgers in a fast-food place near one of the marinas in Ocean View. My education wasn't helping me one way or another, and it was time to do something that would enrich my life—as if anybody's life is like a loaf of bread you can press vitamins into. I was ambitious, I thought, but not strong. Working in a place like that seemed a fitting penance to endure until I figured myself out. Dumb, I know. Not the inspired thinking that really changes lives. I would come home greasy and exhausted, my hair unhealthy and smelling like onions. I felt like a floozy. Occasionally I would find enough energy to barhop and sleep with men I didn't know very well. You've heard stories like this, I'm sure. But it was the best time, the right place to lose hold of myself. If you don't do it when you're young, then I think you must get stuck forever being perfect and unreal.

The bleakness just kept increasing until they switched me to a morning shift. It was the end of March—the azaleas and dogwoods tried to make me appreciate that although I think spring is a phony season, hardly there at all before winter forgets what it's doing and summer bears down with its heat and humidity. I hated waking up early at first because I could never seem to spend the night decently. No matter how much

I worked on myself in front of the bathroom mirror, my eyes still looked dulled, my mouth decadent, my skin subterranean, my pride—my thick blond hair—unmanageable, an expression of how untied I was. I'd bicycle down Oceanside to the hamburger joint and start heating up the grease. From the very first day this guy would come in every morning around eleven to get a cup of black coffee, a bag of french fries, which he'd soak in vinegar, and a piece of apple pie. Sometimes I'd take his order, sometimes Janine would. Janine obviously knew the guy. She'd ask, "How's it going?" He would look serious and say something like, "No turnbuckles. I can't find the right turnbuckles," or, "I'd like to know just how the hell anybody can afford teak?" Then he'd march off to one of the tables, unroll the big piece of graph paper he always had tucked under his arm, spread his order out on the diagrams and scratches, and study them while he ate, doodling atop the doodles he had made the day before. The plans were so coffee-stained and sticky I don't see how he got the boat built.

It was clear that he cared as much about food as I did about my job. His name was Davis and he was, whenever he came into the place, filthy. His jeans were caked with epoxy, his T-shirt looked like a painter's palette. He wore tennis shoes that could have been chewed on by a shark and he had the worst fingernails I've ever seen on anybody. They were smashed and black and jagged, with enough dirt beneath them to occupy a geologist. I liked his body, though. For all the junk he ate he was handsomely lean, and yet his arms were so muscular they seemed swollen. He never bothered to comb his rusty hair, but it was too short then to give him the wild Leif Ericsson look he has now. If I had created him I would have had more sympathy for his face. Davis had a face you expect to see scars on, like a tally of what's been paid, but he only had a little one, a thin white line that italicized his left eye. I don't know how he got it. His skin was much redder than his hair, his features so abrupt—he looked like a man whose element was fire, who could only be happy with the world ablaze, which was odd, because he loved the sea more than anything else. He was not a romantic figure; his appearance was too haggard—scary—for that. I was attracted to him nevertheless. I was intrigued, glance by glance.

He walked in one day after I had gone through a long, depressing evening in a bar with Janine, that old scene, not caring how much I drank, half wild from this great reservoir of ambivalent desire I felt was in me. By eleven I was a zombie; it took me a second to realize Davis was standing across the counter from me and talking.

"What?" I said wearily, pushing the hair out of my eyes, hating the oily touch of it. I just wanted to go home and sleep for a year.

"You look terrible," he said.

"Thanks. So do you," I told him. "You always do, you know that." He smiled, and the smile was more than I imagined it would be.

"So you built a boat?" I already knew he had but I asked him anyway.

"Yeah. Finishing up. She goes in the water in three or four days."

"Need a crew?" I blurted out. I had not really intended to speak that sentence, only to test out the feeling on myself.

"Oh?" he said suspiciously, the grayness of his eyes bearing down on me, critical, but not by the same standard as the guys in the bars. "Do you sail?"

"Sure," I answered. "Well, a little bit anyway." The only boat I had ever been in or on was a canoe. I was more of the horseback, hiking type—I'd grown up in the Blue Ridge Mountains outside of Charlottesville. Nothing strange or special about me; I was an ordinary girl.

"Well," said Davis slowly, as if he wasn't sure he was being smart. "If the sailmaker gets off his butt we'll go out on the bay some Saturday. Next week. Maybe."

It did not take three or four days for Davis to get his boat in the water—it took him more than a month. The entire time he acted mad or preoccupied so I stopped talking to him about it. Then one afternoon he showed up as I was getting off work and took me sailing, more or less.

Davis was a master craftsman, and a wry bastard of a perfectionist. It had taken him four and a half years to build

Impetuous—a gaff-rigged sloop, thirty-two feet long, and double-ended, her black hull ferrocement. The design was seventy years old and somehow, even though the boat was brand new, Davis had succeeded in giving her an ambiance of graceful age, as if she had been day sailing the Chesapeake since before our parents were born. Everything aboard was not bright and polished and packaged, but quiet, comfortable, and loved. Under full sail *Impetuous* was breathtaking, something bigger in my life than had ever been there before.

A lot of time passed, though, before I learned these details about the boat, learned what gaff-rigging meant and that *Impetuous* had it. When I first went aboard I didn't know stem from stern, didn't have a nautical fact in my head. And I couldn't have guessed how stubborn a true perfectionist can be. I ran my hand along the beautiful woodwork in the cockpit. Davis frowned. "It's not right. Doesn't drain right." Every time I made a compliment, he would say something to undercut it. That's the way he is: it's one of his characteristics I strive to ignore.

That first day on *Impetuous* was like petitioning to join a club that you desperately want to belong to, even though the club's only function is to confuse and harass people who fit your description.

"Let's do it," said Davis. I'm sure I must have looked like a silly belle, eyelids fluttery, clapping my hands, my heart so certain I was meant for this.

I asked him what he wanted me to do. He wanted me to sit in the cockpit and be prepared to take the tiller when he told me to. I felt a nice warmth in my blood that came from being with Davis, and absolutely no apprehension about what was going to take place. I sat down innocently on the edge of the cockpit, my legs crossed comfortably, my fingers resting on the shaft of the tiller, feeling as grand as if I had the best seat in the house at the most spectacular show ever to hit town. And it started out like that. Davis, magician and sorcerer, salty and seaworthy, huffed and grunted and raised the mainsail, dazzling me with its white immensity, its thunderous rustling. It shone like snow and swelled as big as a mountainside. It was wonderful.

He began to winch up the anchor and call instructions back to me. Then he started yelling, curses like knots tied into the weave of my fantasy. I began to feel unworthy, a moron, a bug. "Starboard, damn it, starboard." When he saw I didn't understand he yelled *Steer right, for Chrissakes!* so I swung the tiller right as far as I could, the boat began to circle the wrong way, and he screamed at me, "To the right, goddammit, what's wrong with you?" I felt terrible, but how was I to know that when you pushed the tiller right the boat went left? We ran aground there in the anchorage—serious taboo for a prideful sailor, an elemental failure, like a farmer who can't plow his rows straight. Somebody had to come pull us off because Davis had no money left over to put an engine in the boat. His yelling frightened me, but in the days ahead I got better. I don't know why he gave me the chance but he did, and I took it.

One Saturday in June we were out in the middle of the Chesapeake, a day of sluggish weather, no pressures. When the sun started to fade and drain into the haze of the far shore, we headed back in but the wind died before we were halfway there. We drifted in the humid evening light until the water shallowed enough to set an anchor out. Night closed us in gently and we lit the kerosene running lamps and hung them in the rigging. Out there in the middle of nowhere they looked cheerful and secure. I felt as if everything bad in my life had remained onshore and everything good was out on the water with me. We went below, shared a can of tuna fish with saltines and drank warm beer. On the quilt-covered bunk we lay in each other's arms until morning, whispering. Oh, he was so full of chivalry, this Davis; he could be tender and patient when he wanted to. I thought to myself I'd fall far in love with him someday. Maybe he'd fall in love with me, too, although I'm not certain what made me think that, unless it was that I was a woman willing to tolerate him, his quick shouting, the pick pick pick of his perfectionism, his demanding (and hypnotic) presence. I kept quiet and mostly tried to please him. It was just the right thing to do. I finally wanted something. I finally felt that something was worth the effort. I was that clear about Davis and the boat.

* * *

Davis was in the Navy, he had been for six years. His current tour was up in July and he wasn't going to reenlist this time. He served night duty as a radio technician. During the daytime he sweated over *Impetuous.* I don't know when he slept. He had joined the military because he was bored and because he was poor. That's how he came in, and that's how he was going out. The boat had taken all his money. Routine had neutralized his job. Now he planned to sail around the world, the hard way, through the Strait of Magellan, across the Pacific without a landfall to New Zealand, around the Cape of Good Hope—all of this without a motor to depend on. "So what?" he lectured me. "How long do you think engines have been on boats?" The first leg of the voyage would take him to the Grenadine Islands in the Caribbean, where he had already arranged to charter the boat out for the winter season. Enough money would come in this way to pay for food and whatever else was needed.

"Can I go with you?" I asked. He glared at the hesitation in my voice and I wondered if I were crazy. Then I said, "Take me with you, Davis."

"I don't think you can handle it," he said. "It can get pretty rough."

"Yes, I can," I insisted. I hadn't the slightest idea of what he meant by rough. "You just can't go off and leave me," I said. "I want to be with you."

He didn't have an answer right away, but he did say yes. I withdrew what savings I had from my bank and bought a small diesel engine for the boat. He never really was a purist about it. He just didn't have enough money himself. It took about three weeks to get it in and running properly. *Impetuous* felt more like home to me after that. (But oh, the back talk I was to endure from that engine, the diesel muttering, and Davis muttering—a woman muttered against.)

Davis got his walking papers from the Navy, I moved out of my apartment, and we lived together on board. The Coast Guard offered courses in navigation and Davis wanted me to sign up even though we weren't going to be around long enough for me to be certified. The books weren't easy to comprehend and the instructor cared very little for women, but I enjoyed working with the equations and learned what I could. Now on our day sails we steered the boat out of the bay into the ocean. It was more rigorous but didn't seem impossible. The perpetual heaving made me sick but Davis said that was normal and I would get used to it. In the meantime without Dramamine I had no more equilibrium than a sedated duck.

Davis decided that Cape Hatteras, the graveyard of the Atlantic, might be too drastic an initiation for me, so we were going to follow the Intracoastal Waterway to the top of the Florida Keys, then do the long haul to Puerto Rico, replenish our supplies there, leave the Atlantic for the Caribbean Sea, island-hopping our way to the cluster of Grenadines. We had to be in Bequia by November 15 for our first charter group, three medics whom Davis played softball with on the base. On the map it all looked charmingly simple, islands like stepping-stones from one continent to another. I quit my job and phoned my parents. They said no and I said good-bye. We left Norfolk the first week in August.

The Intracoastal Waterway, I discovered, is a party circuit for weekend warriors. The three weeks we spent on it lulled me into the notion that traveling by sailboat was like driving a sleek but clumsy bus from one good time to the next. The developed stretches along the canals reeked of money and Southern idleness; in some marinas I felt the yachtsmen's disdainful eyes on *Impetuous*, as if she were an old Chevy wagon in a parking lot full of Mercedes and Porsches. We sneaked through Miami in the middle of the night into the free anchorage at Dinner Key. Our generator malfunctioned, costing us six days waiting for the new part to be hunted down. Davis stayed angry minute by minute; all he wanted was to get out on the sea where he didn't have to depend on other people. When the generator was fixed and we thought we could leave, Betty, a hurricane prowling Barbados, made us think again. We sat under sunny skies for another week until Betty blew herself out on the thumb of the Yucatan. On a Friday morning in September we motored out Government Cut, raised our sails, and surged into the Gulf Stream.

There is much to say about the voyage but only one thing

that really matters: by the third day out from land I thought Davis had it in his mind to kill us. I honestly did. "You're navigating, you know," he'd told me days before in Miami. I'd said okay, accepting the task casually because I knew perfectly well he was a better navigator than I was and would catch any of my mistakes. At Monty's Raw Bar, I drank beer and munched conch fritters, leisurely charting out our course, an agent who had never actually left the travel office and therefore had no idea what the tickets, the reservations, the itinerary, represented.

We headed south-southeast through the Straits of Florida. My unsteady stomach was pacified by Dramamine; I felt brave and twice as alive as I ever had been. The Gulf Stream was calm, the wind well mannered but *there,* always there. After four hours on watch, Davis turned the boat over to me for two. Everywhere I looked the world was blue. I was alone with my man and that was it, that was all that was left of the planet.

When the sun went down I started worrying like an old lady. I had the sensation of being blind, moving too fast, out of control. We were in the shipping lanes and I imagined one of the big tankers crunching right through us. They have so many lights that at night on the sea they show up like cities rocking in a void. You can't see where you're going; you have to have faith, and faith was something I was beginning to lose. I stood watch from ten till midnight and from four to six. My grip on the tiller seemed to be my only hold on life. I stared at the compass as if it were a crystal ball. Everything I needed to know was spinning around under the faintly lit dome, and yet I felt I hadn't the power to read it correctly. I felt this grave loneliness—more than anything else I wanted Davis to wake up and be next to me, wanted to touch him, have him reassure me. Davis and the sun both came up at the same time. I was cold and afraid, crying inside from the responsibility that cut into me like the blade of an ax. Davis looked relaxed—strong and liberated. He brought me a cup of hot coffee, said he was proud of me. Everything's going to be okay, I thought then. Everything's all right.

* * *

The second day we were becalmed. The ocean never appears more endless than when the wind stops and the surface slows like gelatin. I studied the charts. How much were we losing to the current? How much drift did I have to compensate for? At noon I raised the sextant in my sore hands and shot a fix on the sun. I computed and drew lines and checked the books, eventually marking a little *x* on the edge of the Grand Bahama Bank.

"I think we're right here," I told Davis, spreading the chart out on the hot deck in front of him.

"What do you mean, you think?" he answered me. "Don't think, just know."

"It's hard to know for sure, Davis," I said. "Don't get upset."

"I'm not upset," he said. "But your well-being depends on knowing, not thinking you know. Aren't I right?"

I went back down to the cabin and tried to work out the position again. I was doing the best I could. By sundown the radio was broadcasting storm warnings. Davis seemed to look forward to the bad weather gathering out there in front of us, invisible only to our sense of sight. He was hungry so I cooked him spaghetti for his supper, throwing up into a bucket after five minutes of smelling the sauce heating on the stove.

On my first watch of the night the clouds absorbed the range of stars above us. Davis came up at midnight to take the helm. Nothing had changed, but I was so keyed up I thought I could hear the forces gathering out there in the darkness ahead, like armies beyond the next rise. Exhausted, I went below and collapsed on the bunk, pulling the quilt over my head. I don't know how long I slept but I was awakened violently, thrown out of bed across the beam of the boat, shanghaied and suddenly at war. From very far away Davis was shouting at me to come on deck. *Impetuous* was experiencing a bucking and pitching that didn't make sense to my body. I had to crawl to where Davis was. The boat had heeled severely in the wind; the oceanic floodwaters churned over half the deck. The rain and blackness were impossible to see through, the noise horrendous, a ripping apart of the soft world that floated us. I had to take the tiller while Davis reefed the mainsail and dropped the jib. I remember this—the terror blooming in my throat, making me a blind animal; the pain as the storm raced through the sky and ocean, transferred to the boat and centered, like electricity, into the tiller as I fought against it; and the extreme loneliness again, as if the universe could offer no truer moment than this, ever.

Davis screamed at me hysterically: "You stupid-ass bitch, get her into the wind, goddammit, put her up into it. Dumb fucking cunt." It was no time to be sensitive, I suppose.

We lost the jib. It blew out, its clean geometrical precision exploding into tatters before I could command the boat to come about. He seemed to blame me for that. "We almost lost the boat," he said. "No boat—no more me, no more you. You have to react quicker, you have to be on top of it, you have to be ten times stronger than you think you are. When you think you've reached your limit, that's when you really have to start pushing ahead."

I didn't want to hear it. "You bastard, Davis," I told him. "I'm not tough. I know you want me to be. I'm trying, I honestly am, but I'm not tough. I'm just afraid."

The rest of the night I refused to leave his side. The seas were huge, invisible until they crashed down onto us. The boat shuddered continuously with their impact, lurching as the water swept across the deck. The cement hull made an eerie humming sound. Even with Dramamine I kept puking. To comfort me, Davis tied a rope between us, from waist to waist. I could not tolerate the thought of being separated from him, being alone in the sea, struggling for however long it took me to give in. Davis ate amphetamines and battled against the weather. Eyes blazing, he seemed well suited for the horror of it. By morning the wind was not as renegade. The waves still held their size though, each one a rushing continent about to bury *Impetuous*.

"Davis, let's head into port somewhere and wait until this passes," I pleaded. "I can't take it."

"There's nothing nearby but Cuba and we can't go there and there's no need to run away," he said. "This isn't something we can walk away from. Boats teach you to stick with your trouble until it's over."

"Please don't lecture me," I said quietly, my one courageous moment. Mostly I was so fundamentally shocked—by the power of the water, by Davis, by the taste I had of my life's end—that I just closed up completely.

"We're beating it," Davis said, surveying the slab of purple clouds overhead. "The worst has passed."

He was right about the weather—we would not have to go through a night like that again. But the worst was not over for me. The cloud cover remained for six days; a front had stalled on top of us. There would be occasional rents of blue sky, progressively bigger and longer as the days went by, but for six days I could not get a satisfactory noontime fix on the sun.

"Davis," I said hopelessly, "I don't know where we are. You've got to help me navigate."

"That's your responsibility, isn't it?"

"But I don't know where we are," I said. I couldn't keep my tears back anymore.

"Find out," he said without emotion.

"Why, Davis, why won't you help me?"

"Learn to depend on yourself." I couldn't stand the holy, self-satisfied look on his face when he said that. "If something happens to me you should be able to take over. Otherwise you shouldn't be here."

"Maybe I shouldn't be here."

He didn't reply and I hated him. I had to rely on dead reckoning, which is a system of estimating where you're going based on where you've just been. It's primarily guesswork, especially if as the days go by you're less and less certain where you've been. I studied and studied the chart, worked it all out over and over again, but kept arriving at different answers. By the seventh day I couldn't think straight.

"Davis," I begged, "I still don't know where we are. Please, let's just head due south. We should be able to sight the coast of Haiti by nightfall. I think so, anyway. If not we're in a lot of trouble."

None of this made the impression I expected. "No," he said. "Get us to Puerto Rico."

I became paralyzed with my own inability to change things, hardly speaking to Davis over the next two days. On the tenth day I told him I wanted to get off the boat. He laughed at me. "Where you gonna go?" he said.

"I can't stand it anymore. I'm out of Dramamine and sick all the time. I'm fed up with everything always moving, moving, moving. Every inch of my body is black and blue. I can't even brush my teeth."

"I told you not to leave anything lying around on deck. This isn't the Chesapeake Bay. There's no margin of error here. Stop acting like it's my fault we can't brush our teeth."

At breakfast on the eleventh day I said, "Davis, let's just stop for a day or two. We've got to be pretty close to the eastern tip of the Dominican Republic. I need a rest from all this. Then we can go on."

"Find Puerto Rico," he said, again, pointing to the scope of the horizon. "Find the Mona Passage. Get us into the Caribbean."

I was too battered to implore or argue any longer. The following day, at midafternoon, I commanded with very little confidence, "Steer due east. We'll mark the west coast of the island and take it down and around to Ponce." As the sun set behind us we still sailed forward into an empty seascape.

"It's not there," I told Davis sadly. "We should have crashed into it by now. I knew it wouldn't be there. You're letting me kill the two of us, Davis. And I don't understand why."

I could not go on watch that night, I felt so utterly defeated. I resigned myself to hell and Davis knew that but didn't do a damn thing to comfort me. At sunrise I came up on deck and stared blankly at him. His face seemed raw and worn out. He had eaten a bagful of amphetamines during the past four days to keep going—the Navy's secret weapon, he called them.

"I'm sorry I can't do anything," I said. "I'm sorry for everything."

"You can," he answered. "Take the tiller while I wash up."

He disappeared for five minutes and then was back up, letting the boom swing out over the starboard gunwale.

"What are you doing?" I asked him. My shorts were damp and itchy. All of a sudden I couldn't sit still.

"What does it look like? Change your course to one-sixty."

"Why?"

"Don't ask me why, just do it. Stop feeling so sorry for yourself and take a look around."

Sargasso weed was scattered everywhere in gold lines along the surface. The blueness had become subtly richer, less opaque, less threatening. It appeared to be, despite my gloom, a gorgeous day. I could see other boats, a fishing fleet, trawlers stiffly waving their tall arms, on the horizon in front of us. After a minute all this information sank in.

"My God, are we near land?"

"Can't you smell it?" Once he said it I could. It smelled like newly broken soil, fresh and safe.

"Where's Puerto Rico?"

"Stand up and look."

I popped up but had to turn around before I could find what it was I needed to see—a hazy gray smudge, and below it green hills, the white and red lines of rooftops. I didn't understand.

"Davis, how can that be it?"

"That's it all right. We passed it during the night."

I started to shriek—not at Davis, but at myself. How could that be? The island was on the wrong side of the boat; it should have been off our port stern. I looked back at Davis, a crazy woman, my voice shaky.

"We're supposed to stop. Why aren't we stopping?"

"It's too late. We missed our turn."

"Don't joke with me, Davis. I'm too upset. Just tell me what's going on."

"What's going on, lady, is that your navigation has been wrong for the last six days. Ever since Cuba your course has been too slow and too high and too easterly. What's going on is that you have passed the Antilles and are on your way to fucking Africa."

That is our history. That is where we have been. Why couldn't Davis have told me, why couldn't he have spared me the extent of my suffering? He knew all along, had been keeping our course secretly on a second chart, verifying it with a radio direction finder I didn't even know was aboard. What did I learn, except to despise his coldheartedness and hate my own acquiescence? Hardship builds character, he was always reminding me. Well, not when the odds are bad and nobody's lifting a finger to help. So that's where we've been, and yet, knowing our tracks, I could not accurately predict where we were going. Davis had hurt me and I wanted to leave him. We reached St. Croix that night and docked at Frederiksted. He wished only to order a new jib and proceed immediately to Nevis to wait for it to be flown down. St. Croix was too American, he felt, and he didn't want to hang around until the sail was ready. He didn't bother to ask me what I wanted. When we got off *Impetuous* for the first time in twelve days I thought I had made up my mind.

"I'm going home," I said.

"That's your decision," he answered calmly, meeting my eye without the customary arrogance the sail had given him. "But I wish you'd stay."

"How can you expect me to believe that! After what you did to me out there."

He took hold of my arm as we walked to a café. "It won't happen again. It won't happen because now you know how bad it can get. You have no illusions."

"You're such a shit."

"That's right."

"Why can't you lighten up on me, Davis?"

"Stay with me until Nevis. Nevis will give you what you want."

"What do I want?"

"You want everything to be beautiful and perfect and easy."

"What do you think I am, damn it? That's not true. I'm just trying to survive. Can't you see that?" Davis rolled his eyes when I said "survive" as if it were the biggest cliché. His attention was already someplace else on the busy street. But something in me couldn't stop, was compelled to go on. I was back at sea with him the next day.

Nevis was indeed beautiful—a perfect island, a perfect paradise, if you could relieve it of its history and its bittersweet poverty. Alexander Hamilton was born there, the son of a Scottish aristocrat. America's saint of the well-to-do, he lost his blue blood defending the manliest of virtues, his honor, or *Honor,* I guess he would have said, the imprudent fellow. I can't think of the island without seeing him lounging around as a young blade, a pretty boy who wore a sherbet-colored velvet coat and silk stockings and shoes with red wooden heels, a sword always knocking against his leg. He must have loved it. I know Davis would have. Davis, the picaroon.

The sail over from St. Croix took thirty hours, thirty hours under flawless conditions, but I could not release myself from my paranoia to enjoy it the way I should have. I fell for the island, though. It was my reward, my redemption song. After going through what I had, I felt I deserved a place like this; I felt as if I owned Nevis. We dove in clear turquoise water, poked around the reefs like two lazy turtles, bathed naked, bathed on beaches as empty as the moon. Soaking in mineral springs, I stopped focusing on what was wrong with Davis and again saw what was good. We hiked into lush mountains to a waterfall too cold to swim in. Clouds encircled us on our way down. For a while I felt once more that dread sensation of being lost, but we were on land, sweet land, and it passed without effect. In Charlestown we sat in palm-thatched bars and yakked with the locals, drank moonshine rum, ate curried goat stew. We walked and we walked and we walked, hand in hand, sailors ashore on legs still wobbly from the sea.

Each morning we would row our dinghy in from the anchorage to the public dock, busy in a slow way with stevedores and children, the dirty concrete piled with lumber and cases of glistening bottled beer, lumpy sacks of vegetables, hands of bananas, slaughtered animals, all steaming in the tropic sun. We wandered through the quayside markets and stalls, buying fruit from the hucksters and hot loaves of bread from an old woman who cooked them in a Dutch oven over an open fire. The bread was delicious, the days exalted, unlike any I had ever known. And yet Nevis questioned me, burdened my heart with its children—preschool beggars with big eyes, kids growing up on the hot streets. Most of the population was poor, but not pathetically so. Some people lived in scrap shacks, but most owned small two-room wooden houses with rusted tin roofs and no plumbing. In these latitudes that's not as stricken as it sounds. The worst of it was they couldn't get ahead no matter how hard they tried. In Nevis people had enough to carry on, sometimes a little more. Other than that they were stuck. Everybody but the merchants seemed terminally unemployed, although it was common for families to have a little garden or a piece of land in the hills where they could pick mangoes and grow sweet potatoes or tether a cow. Only the shop owners and civil servants could afford to dress the way they wanted; otherwise people wore clothes that were ill-fitting or torn, the zippers always busted, but rarely dirty. That's how it was in Nevis, my first true touch of paradise. I've been to better places since, but mostly I've been to worse.

The little kids in the countryside were shy and withdrawn, very formal when you did get them talking. They would say yes, sir, yes, missus, good day to you. In Charlestown, though, the kids begged whenever a white person appeared. Davis hated them.

"That's what tourism does," he said.

The first morning we bought bread from the old woman, a black boy—he was probably ten or eleven years old—was there. His feet were bare, as ours were, and he wore a pair of shorts cut off from shiny black pants and a white T-shirt with one of the shoulders ripped out. He watched us buy bread and then approached with his hand out in front of him. I looked down because I thought he wanted to show us something.

"Mistah," he said to Davis, "please fah a dime. Me muddah dead ahnd me faddah blind."

Davis ignored him.

"Can't we give him something?" I asked.

"No way," Davis said. "All these people think every white person in the world is a Rockefeller. I work for my money and I don't have enough of it, either. I'm not giving it away."

I dug into my pocket to find a coin for the boy. Davis grabbed my wrist. "Don't," he said. "If you give to him you're going to have to give something to every kid on the road watching you right now. How can you justify giving to him and not to the others?"

Since I didn't have an answer for that I gave in to Davis. "Is this your son?" I asked the bread lady. She grimaced and ground her loose jaw, shook her head, scolding me. "I doan raise no rude pickahninny."

Each morning after that the boy was there, and each time he'd wait until after we had purchased our bread and then he would say to Davis, "Mistah, please fah a dime. Me muddah dead ahnd me faddah blind." I tried to close my eyes to it. He was such a handsome little boy though, long-lashed eyes, an elegantly boned face, brilliant teeth, sticklike arms and legs that he was striving to grow into. I wish that my perspective on him wasn't distorted by what Davis saw. The boy was not sullen; there was a gay spirit about him that I couldn't dismiss.

I didn't want to leave Nevis but I understood that *Impetuous* would have to leave soon if she were going to make her deadline in the Grenadines. As our time on the island shortened I felt the tension between Davis and me rekindle. I still wasn't positive that I wanted to continue on with him. He wasn't pressing me for an answer, at least not verbally, but the pressure was there anyway.

On what turned out to be our final morning in Nevis we went to the bread lady to buy our breakfast. The beggar kid was there, too, but this time he had a pack of his brethren behind him. For moral support, I supposed. They were all in raggy clothes, all pretty and smooth like beach pebbles, the way black children are. Some of them just looked curious, some attempted to look very tough or serious. Davis paid for the bread. The black kid stuck out his hand. It was the longest-running show on Nevis.

"Mistah, please fah a dime. Me muddah dead ahnd me faddah blind."

Maybe it was because of the audience, the knowledge that his message would be heard by many ears, or maybe it was because he already knew this would be our last day here, since the new jib had arrived, and therefore he could say good-bye to the island by bringing to a conclusion his ritual with the kid, but Davis finally conceded to talk to him.

"What's your name?"

"Willessly," the boy readily answered, pleased for the opportunity. He had a languid, musical voice that sounded like the middle range of notes on a clarinet.

"Your mother's dead, right?"

"Yes, mahn."

"Your father's blind?"

"Yes."

"Look here, Willessly. If I were you I wouldn't smile when I say that."

Giggling erupted among Willessly's comrades. His bright smile only increased. Davis glared down at them all. Willessly wouldn't withdraw his hand.

"Me hungry, mahn. Please fah a piece ah bread."

"Jesus, he's so good-natured about it," I whispered to Davis. "Why don't you give him some? There's plenty."

"You don't get it, do you?" he said, turning on me. His look was empty of everything I thought it should be full of—the intimacy we had established in Norfolk, cultivated in the garden of Nevis. "It would be a sign of weakness. When you give to people like this, they're not grateful, they don't respect you. What happens is they hate you. They think you're a fool for giving in to them."

"But, Davis, he's just a little boy."

"Me hungry, mahn."

"Let's go," Davis said, stuffing the loaves into his haversack. "Go eat a coconut," he said to Willessly. The audience of kids thought this statement was extremely funny. They laughed, not at us but at Willessly, teasing and taunting him. A game was being played here but I couldn't tell what it was. There we stood in the tiny square of the marketplace, the stalls abundant with a rainbow of fruits and vegetables, the air luscious with the smells of spices, of frying coconut oil and garlic and cumin, the scents of frangipani and lime. Palm trees sprouted up everywhere against the cloudless sky like exaggerated flowers. Calypso music screeched from several radios in the nearby buildings.

"Me hungry, mahn." Willessly bent down, scraped up a handful of dirt and put it in his mouth. The black kids responded as if this act were inspired.

"Look de boy dere goin ahll out."

"He mahd. Him dizzy."

"Oh, sweet Lahd, him eat de dirt now."

And a shrill little-girl's voice sang, "Momma goin beat you, Willessly. Momma goin strike."

"Let's go," Davis said. He spun me around and we started walking away down a grassy alley that led to the water. I looked over my shoulder. Willessly was spitting out the dirt. He wiped his mouth with the bottom of his T-shirt, leaving muddy streaks on the overbleached whiteness, and followed us.

We walked along the beach away from town. I could hear the kids behind us having a grand time.

The ocean on this side of Nevis was like a mountain lake, serene and glassy, bluer than the sky. As you walked along the shore, the water was so transparent you could easily spot fish. Long skinny fish like Willessly, fat clown fish, fish dressed for carnival, sleek hot-rod fish. The bay was crescent-shaped and we stopped in the middle of it to eat our food, a shadowy grove of sea grape and palms behind us, the cool sea in front. We sat in the sand and stripped down to our bathing suits. Willessly advanced on us. Somewhere he had gotten hold of a baby. Maybe the infant had been with the kids all along and I just hadn't seen her. He toted her haphazardly, his arms wrapped under her arms and around her chest, the rest of her dangling loose, facing us, her cheeks like bowls of chocolate pudding.

"You want to buy dis baby?" he asked Davis.

Davis squinted at him. "How much?"

"Twenty dollahs U.Ess."

"Get lost," Davis said, chewing his bread.

"She too dahk fah you? I cahn get you a clear-skin one, ya know."

Davis didn't bother to answer. The kid handed the baby over to one of the girls backing him up. Willessly spoke directly to me for the first time. "You husbahnd doan like blahck peoples." It was no accusation; there was no bitterness.

"No," I said nervously. "No, I don't think that's true. You shouldn't say that."

"Yes, it's true." He insisted upon it in such a friendly, straightforward way, his dark eyes playful but firm, that I smiled. "He doan care fah de color ah shit."

"What?"

"God made black peoples from his own shit," he said, holding out his thin arm as if the evidence were there.

That's the most terrible sentence I ever heard anyone speak, let alone a child. I think my heart shrank and burrowed into my stomach when he said it.

"Who told you that?" Davis snapped.

"Me muddah."

"Your mother's dead."

"Yes."

"You *are* full of shit, you little bastard."

"Davis, don't say that."

"Where's your pride, boy?" he demanded.

Willessly had a quizzical look on his face, a veteran player determining his opponent's newest strategy. He rubbed his snotty nose, went over to his group of friends and came right back to us.

"You want to buy dis?" He held out an old swim fin, its rubber cracked and faded.

"No," Davis said. "I want you to get out of here right now."

"You want to buy dis?" Willessly now had in his small hands a conch shell that looked as though it had been lying in the sun for years, all but a trace of its inner pinkness burned away.

"Go away. I told you I don't want to buy anything."

"Lady, you want dis?" I shook my head no.

"I give it to you. Fah free." He thrust the shell into my lap. I thanked him and he retreated back to the group.

I stretched out in the sand, letting the sunshine cook me. If you'd taken a picture of us it would have made a nice postcard, I guess, another enticing image for a travel brochure. The kids were in the water, splashing and laughing with no thought for keeping their clothes dry. The baby was left by herself propped in the bone-colored sand. A schooner under full sail edged by close offshore. The jungle soared behind us, climbing the volcano to a height that could no longer support it. And here was this rugged fellow beside me, my man, ready to kick the world's ass.

After an hour or so we started back to Charlestown, the kids still tagging behind us. We planned to catch the morning bus—not a bus, really, but an old flatbed truck with benches nailed down to it—to the windward side of the island. Davis was going to skin-dive for lobster on the barrier reef; I had heard about some women in one of the villages over there who still made pottery the same way the Arawak Indians used to, and I wanted to watch them.

We stopped in a rum shop near the corner where we were supposed to pick up the transportation. It was dark inside and smelled like rancid butter. An old phonograph played reggae music, intolerably scratchy and loud. We had not entered into this shop before. It was full of black men who stood along the counter or sat balefully against the wall. The atmosphere was oppressive. For the first time I felt we were unwanted here, that we were resented. All our immunities were canceled: We were not tourists spending money. We were just there sharing the island.

Willessly followed us in, the other kids crowded around the doorway. Davis bought a can of Tennant's ale and some Aristocrisp peanuts that came packaged in old Heineken bottles. The peanuts were grown and roasted in St. Vincent, the mother island of the Grenadines. Davis loved them, said they were better than any you could get in the States. He shook some out of the green bottle into his mouth, crunched on them, took a gulp of his ale.

"You want anything?"

"No," I said. "Just to leave."

"Mistah, buy me a Coke," Willessly said. He had not retired his smile. I decided I liked him a lot. He didn't care that Davis was deaf.

"I'm real tired of you annoying me," Davis said. I thought he was going to challenge the boy to a fight from the way he spoke.

"Please fah a ground nut," Willessly persisted.

"Piss off."

"I'm going," I said. "We'll miss our ride."

I started toward the door. Faces creased with malice loomed up at me, thick, gagging smells, unhealthy air. The shop seemed more crowded than when we first came in. I had to push through people, all men, their muscles tight, their eyes reddened with an appetite foreign to me. Someone began to hiss, *psst.* The sound was ominous but it only made me feel hard. The younger men scowled at me and called out, "Busy, busy." In the islands, a "busy" women is a whore. I wasn't going to let it penetrate me; my determination to handle it all coolly just kept building. I should have been afraid but if I was I can't remember. I was being bumped around. I looked back for Davis and felt a hand grab and pinch one of my tits. That did it for me. I felt walled off by sharks on one side, this righteous lion on the other, me and the kid in the middle trying to stay alive. There was this teenager in front of me, cocky and leering. He winked at me and snarled with laughter. His teeth were dirty and he wore a red beret that was puffed up with the wool of his hair. I knew he was the one who'd grabbed me. I reacted without even considering the consequence. I punched him in the ear.

"Wha I do?" he protested, his high voice wounded, a charade of injustice received, waving his hands in front of him. "Wha I do? I doan do a dahmn ting. Dis bitch womahn crazee."

"Don't tell me that, man," I screamed at him. "Get out of my way."

He stepped aside and I passed out the door through a chorus of snickers, Davis and Willessly in my wake. I felt as if I had blood all over me and that that entitled me to anything I wanted. I kept on screaming.

"Davis, goddammit, give the kid a peanut."

I waited with my hands on my hips. Davis didn't do anything. Actually, he finished off his ale and chucked the can into the gutter.

"If you don't give the kid some peanuts, I swear to God I'm going to go back to the boat right now, unlock the shotgun and write you a good-bye letter on the sails in buckshot."

"Okay, okay," Davis said reluctantly, although I believe he had a private desire to see me play out my rage. He called Willessly over. "Here," he said. He gave him a peanut—one lousy peanut. I would have smashed the bottle out of Davis's hand if it hadn't been for the way Willessly responded.

He held the peanut up in the air like a trophy. He jumped up in the dirt street, displaying the tiny gold nut to his friends. They each examined it enviously. He went from one to the other until they had all seen it.

"What I tell you," he called out to them. "What I tell you, Mahcus? You owe me, mahn, I tellin you now, I ahm de best."

They weren't concerned with us anymore. I watched as they tramped back toward the marketplace, Willessly in front of them, walking backward, full of bravura, ten feet tall, the peanut still raised triumphantly between his thumb and index finger.

"You see that," Davis said. "All he wanted to do was make a fool out of me."

"All you wanted to do," I told him, matching his awful smirk, "was teach him a lesson he didn't need to be taught."

That evening, under a waxing moon and sharp northeasterly breeze, we took up anchor and sailed away. I knew that going out to sea would not be an act of war this time, and I saw, like Eve, that paradise had become just another place to leave behind. I felt good about that, because I could tell myself that across the waters, with the winds and sometimes against them, somewhere there would be another. I could move ahead without even thinking about it. And to hell with Davis.

EUDORA WELTY

Why I Live at the P.O.

I WAS GETTING along fine with Mama, Papa-Daddy and Uncle Rondo until my sister Stella-Rondo just separated from her husband and came back home again. Mr. Whitaker! Of course I went with Mr. Whitaker first, when he first appeared here in China Grove, taking "Pose Yourself" photos, and Stella-Rondo broke us up. Told him I was one-sided. Bigger on one side than the other, which is a deliberate, calculated falsehood: I'm the same. Stella-Rondo is exactly twelve months to the day younger than I am and for that reason she's spoiled.

She's always had anything in the world she wanted and then she'd throw it away. Papa-Daddy gave her this gorgeous Add-a-Pearl necklace when she was eight years old and she threw it away playing baseball when she was nine, with only two pearls.

So as soon as she got married and moved away from home the first thing she did was separate! From Mr. Whitaker! This photographer with the popeyes she said she trusted. Came home from one of those towns up in Illinois and to our complete surprise brought this child of two.

Mama said she like to made her drop dead for a second. "Here you had this marvelous blonde child and never so much as wrote your mother a word about it," says Mama. "I'm thoroughly ashamed of you." But of course she wasn't.

Stella-Rondo just calmly takes off this *hat,* I wish you could see it. She says, "Why, Mama, Shirley-T.'s adopted, I can prove it."

"How?" says Mama, but all I says was, "H'm!" There I was over the hot stove, trying to stretch two chickens over five people and a completely unexpected child into the bargain, without one moment's notice.

"What do you mean—'H'm!'?" says Stella-Rondo, and Mama says, "I heard that, Sister."

I said that oh, I didn't mean a thing, only that whoever Shirley-T. was, she was the spit-image of Papa-Daddy if he'd cut off his beard, which of course he'd never do in the world. Papa-Daddy's Mama's papa and sulks.

Stella-Rondo got furious! She said, "Sister, I don't need to tell you you got a lot of nerve and always did have and I'll thank you to make no future reference to my adopted child whatsoever."

"Very well," I said. "Very well, very well. Of course I noticed at once she looks like Mr. Whitaker's side too. That frown. She looks like a cross between Mr. Whitaker and Papa-Daddy."

"Well, all I can say is she isn't."

"She looks exactly like Shirley Temple to me," says Mama, but Shirley-T. just ran away from her.

So the first thing Stella-Rondo did at the table was turn Papa-Daddy against me.

"Papa-Daddy," she says. He was trying to cut up his meat. "Papa-Daddy!" I was taken completely by surprise. Papa-Daddy is about a million years old and's got his long-long beard. "Papa-Daddy, Sister says she fails to understand why you don't cut off your beard."

So Papa-Daddy l-a-y-s down his knife and fork! He's real rich. Mama says he is, he says he isn't. So he says, "Have I heard correctly? You don't understand why I don't cut off my beard?"

"Why," I says, "Papa-Daddy, of course I understand. I did not say any such of a thing, the idea!"

He says, "Hussy!"

I says, "Papa-Daddy, you know I wouldn't any more want

you to cut off your beard than the man in the moon. It was the farthest thing from my mind! Stella-Rondo sat there and made that up while she was eating breast of chicken."

But he says, "So the postmistress fails to understand why I don't cut off my beard. Which job I got you through my influence with the government. 'Bird's nest'—is that what you call it?"

Not that it isn't the next to smallest P.O. in the entire state of Mississippi.

I says, "Oh, Papa-Daddy," I says, "I didn't say any such of a thing. I never dreamed it was a bird's nest, I have always been grateful though this is the next to smallest P.O. in the state of Mississippi, and I do not enjoy being referred to as a hussy by my own grandfather."

But Stella-Rondo says, "Yes, you did say it too. Anybody in the world could of heard you, that had ears."

"Stop right there," says Mama, looking at *me*.

So I pulled my napkin straight back through the napkin ring and left the table.

As soon as I was out of the room Mama says, "Call her back, or she'll starve to death," but Papa-Daddy says, "This is the beard I started growing on the Coast when I was fifteen years old." He would of gone on till nightfall if Shirley-T. hadn't lost the Milky Way she ate in Cairo.

So Papa-Daddy says, "I am going out and lie in the hammock, and you can all sit here and remember my words: I'll never cut off my beard as long as I live, even one inch, and I don't appreciate it in you at all." Passed right by me in the hall and went straight out and got in the hammock.

It would be a holiday. It wasn't five minutes before Uncle Rondo suddenly appeared in the hall in one of Stella-Rondo's flesh-colored kimonos, all cut on the bias, like something Mr. Whitaker probably thought was gorgeous.

"Uncle Rondo!" I says. "I didn't know who that was! Where are you going?"

"Sister," he says, "get out of my way, I'm poisoned."

"If you're poisoned stay away from Papa-Daddy," I says. "Keep out of the hammock. Papa-Daddy will certainly beat you on the head if you come within forty miles of him. He thinks I deliberately said he ought to cut off his beard after he got me the P.O., and I've told him and told him and told him, and he acts like he just don't hear me. Papa-Daddy must of gone stone deaf."

"He picked a fine day to do it then," says Uncle Rondo, and before you could say "Jack Robinson" flew out in the yard.

What he'd really done, he'd drunk another bottle of that prescription. He does it every single Fourth of July as sure as shooting, and it's horribly expensive. Then he falls over in the hammock and snores. So he insisted on zigzagging right on out to the hammock, looking like a half-wit.

Papa-Daddy woke up with this horrible yell and right there without moving an inch he tried to turn Uncle Rondo against me. I heard every word he said. Oh, he told Uncle Rondo I didn't learn to read till I was eight years old and he didn't see how in the world I ever got the mail put up at the P.O., much less read it all, and he said if Uncle Rondo could only fathom the lengths he had gone to to get me that job! And he said on the other hand he thought Stella-Rondo had a brilliant mind and deserved credit for getting out of town. All the time he was just lying there swinging as pretty as you please and looping out his beard, and poor Uncle Rondo was *pleading* with him to slow down the hammock, it was making him as dizzy as a witch to watch it. But that's what Papa-Daddy likes about a hammock. So Uncle Rondo was too dizzy to get turned against me for the time being. He's Mama's only brother and is a good case of a one-track mind. Ask anybody. A certified pharmacist.

Just then I heard Stella-Rondo raising the upstairs window. While she was married she got this peculiar idea that it's cooler with the windows shut and locked. So she has to raise the window before she can make a soul hear her outdoors.

So she raises the window and says, *"Oh!"* You would have thought she was mortally wounded.

Uncle Rondo and Papa-Daddy didn't even look up, but kept right on with what they were doing. I had to laugh.

I flew up the stairs and threw the door open! I says, "What

in the wide world's the matter, Stella-Rondo? You mortally wounded?"

"No," she says, "I am not mortally wounded but I wish you would do me the favor of looking out that window there and telling me what you see."

So I shade my eyes and look out the window.

"I see the front yard," I says.

"Don't you see any human beings?" she says.

"I see Uncle Rondo trying to run Papa-Daddy out of the hammock," I says. "Nothing more. Naturally, it's so suffocating-hot in the house, with all the windows shut and locked, everybody who cares to stay in their right mind will have to go out and get in the hammock before the Fourth of July is over."

"Don't you notice anything different about Uncle Rondo?" asks Stella-Rondo.

"Why, no, except he's got on some terrible-looking flesh-colored contraption I wouldn't be found dead in, is all I can see," I says.

"Never mind, you won't be found dead in it, because it happens to be part of my trousseau, and Mr. Whitaker took several dozen photographs of me in it," says Stella-Rondo. "What on earth could Uncle Rondo *mean* by wearing part of my trousseau out in the broad open daylight without saying so much as 'Kiss my foot,' *knowing* I only got home this morning after my separation and hung my negligee up on the bathroom door, just as nervous as I could be?"

"I'm sure I don't know, and what do you expect me to do about it?" I says. "Jump out the window?"

"No, I expect nothing of the kind. I simply declare that Uncle Rondo looks like a fool in it, that's all," she says. "It makes me sick to my stomach."

"Well, he looks as good as he can," I says. "As good as anybody in reason could." I stood up for Uncle Rondo, please remember. And I said to Stella-Rondo, "I think I would do well not to criticize so freely if I were you and came home with a two-year-old child I had never said a word about, and no explanation whatever about my separation."

"I asked you the instant I entered this house not to refer

one more time to my adopted child, and you gave me your word of honor you would not,'' was all Stella-Rondo would say, and started pulling out every one of her eyebrows with some cheap Kress tweezers.

So I merely slammed the door behind me and went down and made some green-tomato pickle. Somebody had to do it. Of course Mama had turned both the niggers loose; she always said no earthly power could hold one anyway on the Fourth of July, so she wouldn't even try. It turned out that Jaypan fell in the lake and came within a very narrow limit of drowning.

So Mama trots in. Lifts up the lid and says, ''H'm! Not very good for your Uncle Rondo in his precarious condition, I must say. Or poor little adopted Shirley-T. Shame on you!''

That made me tired. I says, ''Well, Stella-Rondo had better thank her lucky stars it was her instead of me came trotting in with that very peculiar-looking child. Now if it had been me that trotted in from Illinois and brought a peculiar-looking child of two, I shudder to think of the reception I'd of got, much less controlled the diet of an entire family.''

''But you must remember, Sister, that you were never married to Mr. Whitaker in the first place and didn't go up to Illinois to live,'' says Mama, shaking a spoon in my face. ''If you had I would of been just as overjoyed to see you and your little adopted girl as I was to see Stella-Rondo, when you wound up with your separation and came on back home.''

''You would not,'' I says.

''Don't contradict me, I would,'' says Mama.

But I said she couldn't convince me though she talked till she was blue in the face. Then I said, ''Besides, you know as well as I do that that child is not adopted.''

''She most certainly is adopted,'' says Mama, stiff as a poker.

I says, ''Why Mama, Stella-Rondo had her just as sure as anything in this world, and just too stuck up to admit it.''

''Why, Sister,'' said Mama. ''Here I thought we were going to have a pleasant Fourth of July, and you start right out not believing a word your own baby sister tells you!''

"Just like Cousin Annie Flo. Went to her grave denying the facts of life," I remind Mama.

"I told you if you ever mentioned Annie Flo's name I'd slap your face," says Mama, and slaps my face.

"All right, you wait and see," I says.

"I," says Mama, "*I* prefer to take my children's word for anything when it's humanly possible." You ought to see Mama, she weighs two hundred pounds and has real tiny feet.

Just then something perfectly horrible occurred to me.

"Mama," I says, "can that child talk?" I simply had to whisper! "Mama, I wonder if that child can be—you know—in any way? Do you realize," I says, "that she hasn't spoken one single, solitary word to a human being up to this minute? This is the way she looks," I says, and I looked like this.

Well, Mama and I just stood there and stared at each other. It was horrible!

"I remember well that Joe Whitaker frequently drank like a fish," says Mama. "I believed to my soul he drank *chemicals.*" And without another word she marches to the foot of the stairs and calls Stella-Rondo.

"Stella-Rondo? O-o-o-o-o! Stella-Rondo!"

"What?" says Stella-Rondo from upstairs. Not even the grace to get up off the bed.

"Can that child of yours talk?" asks Mama.

Stella-Rondo says, "Can she what?"

"Talk! Talk!" says Mama. "Burdyburdyburdyburdy!"

So Stella-Rondo yells back, "Who says she can't talk?"

"Sister says so," says Mama.

"You didn't have to tell me, I know whose word of honor don't mean a thing in this house," says Stella-Rondo.

And in a minute the loudest Yankee voice I ever heard in my life yells out, "OE'm Pop-OE the Sailor-r-r-r Ma-a-an!" and then somebody jumps up and down in the upstairs hall. In another second the whole house would of fallen down.

"Not only talks, she can tap-dance!" calls Stella-Rondo. "Which is more than some people I won't name can do."

"Why, the little precious darling thing!" Mama says, so surprised. "Just as smart as she can be!" Starts talking baby talk right there. Then she turns on me. "Sister, you ought to be thoroughly ashamed! Run upstairs this instant and apologize to Stella-Rondo and Shirley-T."

"Apologize for what?" I says. "I merely wondered if the child was normal, that's all. Now that she's proved she is, why, I have nothing further to say."

But Mama just turned on her heel and flew out, furious. She ran right upstairs and hugged the baby. She believed it was adopted. Stella-Rondo hadn't done a thing but turn her against me from upstairs while I stood there helpless over the hot stove. So that made Mama, Papa-Daddy and the baby all on Stella-Rondo's side.

Next, Uncle Rondo.

I must say that Uncle Rondo has been marvelous to me at various times in the past and I was completely unprepared to be made to jump out of my skin, the way it turned out. Once Stella-Rondo did something perfectly horrible to him—broke a chain letter from Flanders Field—and he took the radio back he had given her and gave it to me. Stella-Ronda was furious! For six months we all had to call her Stella instead of Stella-Rondo, or she wouldn't answer. I always thought Uncle Rondo had all the brains of the entire family. Another time he sent me to Mammoth Cave, with all expenses paid.

But this would be the day he was drinking that prescription, the Fourth of July.

So at supper Stella-Rondo speaks up and says she thinks Uncle Rondo ought to try to eat a little something. So finally Uncle Rondo said he would try a little cold biscuits and ketchup, but that was all. So *she* brought it to him.

"Do you think it wise to disport with ketchup in Stella-Rondo's flesh-colored kimono?" I says. Trying to be considerate! If Stella-Rondo couldn't watch out for her trousseau, somebody had to.

"Any objections?" asked Uncle Rondo, just about to pour out all the ketchup.

"Don't mind what she says, Uncle Rondo," says Stella-Rondo. "Sister has been devoting this solid afternoon to sneering out my bedroom window at the way you look."

"What's that?" says Uncle Rondo. Uncle Rondo has got

the most terrible temper in the world. Anything is liable to make him tear the house down if it comes at the wrong time.

So Stella-Rondo says, "Sister says, 'Uncle Rondo certainly does look like a fool in that pink kimono!' "

Do you remember who it was really said that?

Uncle Rondo spills out all the ketchup and jumps out of his chair and tears off the kimono and throws it down on the dirty floor and puts his foot on it. It had to be sent all the way to Jackson to the cleaners and re-pleated.

"So that's your opinion of your Uncle Rondo, is it?" he says. "I look like a fool, do I? Well, that's the last straw. A whole day in this house with nothing to do, and then to hear you come out with a remark like that behind my back!"

"I didn't say any such thing, Uncle Rondo," I says, "and I'm not saying who did, either. Why, I think you look all right. Just try to take care of yourself and not talk and eat at the same time," I says. "I think you better go lie down."

"Lie down my foot," says Uncle Rondo. I ought to of known by that he was fixing to do something perfectly horrible.

So he didn't do anything that night in the precarious state he was in—just played Casino with Mama and Stella-Rondo and Shirley-T. and gave Shirley-T. a nickel with a head on both sides. It tickled her nearly to death, and she called him "Papa." But at 6:30 A.M. the next morning, he threw a whole five-cent package of some unsold one-inch firecrackers from the store as hard as he could into my bedroom and they every one went off. Not one bad one in the string. Anybody else, there'd be one that wouldn't go off.

Well, I'm just terribly susceptible to noise of any kind, the doctor has always told me I was the most sensitive person he had ever seen in his whole life, and I was simply prostrated. I couldn't eat! People tell me they heard it as far as the cemetery, and old Aunt Jep Peterson, that had been holding her own so good, thought it was Judgment Day and she was going to meet her whole family. It's usually so quiet here.

And I'll tell you it didn't take me any longer than a minute to make up my mind what to do. There I was with the whole entire house on Stella-Rondo's side and turned against me. If I have anything at all I have pride.

So I just decided I'd go straight down to the P.O. There's plenty of room there in the back, I says to myself.

Well! I made no bones about letting the family catch on to what I was up to. I didn't try to conceal it.

The first thing they knew, I marched in where they were all playing Old Maid and pulled the electric oscillating fan out by the plug, and everything got real hot. Next I snatched the pillow I'd done the needlepoint on right off the davenport from behind Papa-Daddy. He went "Ugh!" I beat Stella-Rondo up the stairs and finally found my charm bracelet in her bureau drawer under a picture of Nelson Eddy.

"So that's the way the land lies," says Uncle Rondo. There he was, piecing on the ham. "Well, Sister, I'll be glad to donate my army cot if you got any place to set it up, providing you'll leave right this minute and let me get some peace." Uncle Rondo was in France.

"Thank you kindly for the cot and 'peace' is hardly the word I would select if I had to resort to firecrackers at 6:30 A.M. in a young girl's bedroom," I says back to him. "And as to where I intend to go, you seem to forget my position as postmistress of China Grove, Mississippi," I says. "I've always got the P.O."

Well, that made them all sit up and take notice.

I went out front and started digging up some four-o'clocks to plant around the P.O.

"Ah-ah-ah!" says Mama, raising the window. "Those happen to be my four-o'clocks. Everything planted in that star is mine. I've never known you to make anything grow in your life."

"Very well," I says. "But I take the fern. Even you, Mama, can't stand there and deny that I'm the one watered that fern. And I happened to know where I can send in a box top and get a packet of one thousand mixed seeds, no two the same kind, free."

"Oh, where?" Mama wants to know.

But I says, "Too late. You 'tend to your house, and I'll 'tend to mine. You hear things like that all the time if you know how to listen to the radio. Perfectly marvelous offers. Get anything you want free."

So I hope to tell you I marched in and got that radio, and they could of all bit a nail in two, especially Stella-Rondo, that it used to belong to, and she well knew she couldn't get it back, I'd sue for it like a shot. And I very politely took the sewing-machine motor I helped pay the most on to give Mama for Christmas back in 1929, and a good big calendar, with the first-aid remedies on it. The thermometer and the Hawaiian ukulele certainly were rightfully mine, and I stood on the step-ladder and got all my watermelon-rind preserves and every fruit and vegetable I'd put up, every jar. Then I began to pull the tacks out of the bluebird wall vases on the archway to the dining room.

"Who told you you could have those, Miss Priss?" says Mama, fanning as hard as she could.

"I bought 'em and I'll keep track of 'em," I says. "I'll tack 'em up and I'll keep track of 'em," I says. "I'll tack 'em up one on each side the post office window, and you can see 'em when you come to ask me for your mail, if you're so dead to see 'em."

"Not I! I'll never darken the door to that post office again if I live to be a hundred," Mama says. "Ungrateful child! After all the money we spent on you at the Normal."

"Me either," says Stella-Rondo. "You just let my mail lie there and *rot,* for all I care. I'll never come and relieve you of a single, solitary piece."

"I should worry," I says. "And who you think's going to sit down and write you all those big fat letters and postcards, by the way? Mr. Whitaker? Just because he was the only man ever dropped down in China Grove and you got him—unfairly—is he going to sit down and write you a lengthy correspondence after you come home giving no rhyme nor reason whatsoever for your separation and no explanation for the presence of that child? I may not have your brilliant mind, but I fail to see it."

So Mama says, "Sister, I've told you a thousand times that Stella-Rondo simply got homesick, and this child is far too big to be hers," and she says, "Now, why don't you all just sit down and play Casino?"

Then Shirley-T. sticks out her tongue at me in this perfectly horrible way. She has no more manners than the man in the moon. I told her she was going to cross her eyes like that some day and they'd stick.

"It's too late to stop me now," I says. "You should have tried that yesterday. I'm going to the P.O. and the only way you can possibly see me is to visit me there."

So Papa-Daddy says, "You'll never catch me setting foot in that post office, even if I should take a notion into my head to write a letter some place." He says, "I won't have you reachin' out of that little old window with a pair of shears and cuttin' off any beard of mine. I'm too smart for you!"

"We all are," says Stella-Rondo.

But I said, "If you're so smart, where's Mr. Whitaker?"

So then Uncle Rondo says, "I'll thank you from now on to stop reading all the orders I get on postcards and telling everybody in China Grove what you think is the matter with them," but I says, "I draw my own conclusions and will continue in the future to draw them." I says, "If people want to write their inmost secrets on penny postcards, there's nothing in the wide world you can do about it, Uncle Rondo."

"And if you think we'll ever *write* another postcard you're sadly mistaken," says Mama.

"Cutting off your nose to spite your face then," I says. "But if you're all determined to have no more to do with the U.S. mail, think of this: What will Stella-Rondo do now, if she wants to tell Mr. Whitaker to come after her?"

"Wah!" says Stella-Rondo. I knew she'd cry. She had a conniption fit right there in the kitchen.

"It will be interesting to see how long she holds out," I says. "And now—I am leaving."

"Good-bye," says Uncle Rondo.

"Oh, I declare," says Mama, "to think a family of mine should quarrel on the Fourth of July, or the day after, over Stella-Rondo leaving old Mr. Whitaker and having the sweetest little adopted child! It looks like we'd all be glad!"

"Wah!" says Stella-Rondo, and has a fresh conniption fit.

"*He* left *her*—you mark my words," I says. "That's Mr. Whitaker. I know Mr. Whitaker. After all, I knew him first. I said from the beginning he'd up and leave her. I foretold every single thing that's happened."

"Where did he go?" asks Mama.

"Probably to the North Pole, if he knows what's good for him," I says.

But Stella-Rondo just bawled and wouldn't say another word. She flew to her room and slammed the door.

"Now look what you've gone and done, Sister," says Mama. "You go apologize."

"I haven't got time, I'm leaving," I says.

"Well, what are you waiting around for?" asks Uncle Rondo.

So I just picked up the kitchen clock and marched off, without saying "Kiss my foot" or anything and never did tell Stella-Rondo good-bye.

There was a nigger girl going along on a little wagon right in front.

"Nigger girl," I says, "come help me haul these things down the hill, I'm going to live in the post office."

Took her nine trips in her express wagon. Uncle Rondo came out on the porch and threw her a nickel.

And that's the last I've laid eyes on any of my family or my family laid eyes on me for five solid days and nights. Stella-Rondo may be telling the most horrible tales in the world about Mr. Whitaker, but I haven't heard them. As I tell everybody, I draw my own conclusions.

But oh, I like it here. It's ideal, as I've been saying. You see, I've got everything cater-cornered, the way I like it. Hear the radio? All the war news. Radio, sewing-machine, book ends, ironing board and that great big piano lamp—peace, that's what I like. Butter-bean vines planted all along the front where the strings are.

Of course, there's not much mail. My family are naturally the main people in China Grove, and if they prefer to vanish from the face of the earth, for all the mail they get or the mail they write, why, I'm not going to open my mouth. Some of the folks here in town are taking up for me and some turned against me. I know which is which. There are always people who will quit buying stamps just to get on the right side of Papa-Daddy.

But here I am, and here I'll stay. I want the world to know I'm happy.

And if Stella-Rondo should come to me this minute, on bended knees, and *attempt* to explain the incidents of her life with Mr. Whitaker, I'd simply put my fingers in both my ears and refuse to listen.

II
DIRECTED VOICES

RING LARDNER

Haircut

I GOT ANOTHER barber that comes over from Carterville and helps me out Saturdays, but the rest of the time I can get along all right alone. You can see for yourself that this ain't no New York City and besides that, the most of the boys works all day and don't have no leisure to drop in here and get themselves prettied up.

You're a newcomer, ain't you? I thought I hadn't seen you round before. I hope you like it good enough to stay. As I say, we ain't no New York City or Chicago, but we have pretty good times. Not as good, though, since Jim Kendall got killed. When he was alive, him and Hod Meyers used to keep this town in an uproar. I bet they was more laughin' done here than any town its size in America.

Jim was comical, and Hod was pretty near a match for him. Since Jim's gone, Hod tries to hold his end up just the same as ever, but it's tough goin' when you ain't got nobody to kind of work with.

They used to be plenty fun in here Saturdays. This place is jam-packed Saturdays, from four o'clock on. Jim and Hod would show up right after their supper, round six o'clock. Jim would set himself down in that big chair, nearest the blue spittoon. Whoever had been settin' in that chair, why they'd get up when Jim come in and give it to him.

You'd of thought it was a reserved seat like they have sometimes in a theayter. Hod would generally always stand or walk up and down, or some Saturdays, of course, he'd be settin' in this chair part of the time, gettin' a haircut.

Well, Jim would set there a w'ile without openin' his mouth only to spit, and then finally he'd say to me, "Whitey,"—my right name, that is, my right first name, is Dick, but everybody round here calls me Whitey—Jim would say, "Whitey, your nose looks like a rosebud tonight. You must of been drinkin' some of your aw de cologne."

So I'd say, "No, Jim, but you look like you'd been drinkin' somethin' of that kind or somethin' worse."

Jim would have to laugh at that, but then he'd speak up and say, "No, I ain't had nothin' to drink, but that ain't sayin' I wouldn't like somethin'. I wouldn't even mind if it was wood alcohol."

Then Hod Meyers would say, "Neither would your wife." That would set everybody to laughin' because Jim and his wife wasn't on very good terms. She'd of divorced him only they wasn't no chance to get alimony and she didn't have no way to take care of herself and the kids. She couldn't never understand Jim. He *was* kind of rough, but a good fella at heart.

Him and Hod had all kinds of sport with Milt Sheppard. I don't suppose you've seen Milt. Well, he's got an Adam's apple that looks more like a mushmelon. So I'd be shavin' Milt and when I'd start to shave down here on his neck, Hod would holler, "Hey, Whitey, wait a minute! Before you cut into it, let's make up a pool and see who can guess closest to the number of seeds."

And Jim would say, "If Milt hadn't of been so hoggish, he'd of ordered a half a cantaloupe instead of a whole one and it might not of stuck in his throat."

All the boys would roar at this and Milt himself would force a smile, though the joke was on him. Jim certainly was a card!

There's his shavin' mug, settin' on the shelf, right next to Charley Vail's. "Charles M. Vail." That's the druggist. He comes in regular for his shave, three times a week. And Jim's is the cup next to Charley's. "James H. Kendall." Jim won't need no shavin' mug no more, but I'll leave it there just the same for old time's sake. Jim certainly was a character!

Years ago, Jim used to travel for a canned goods concern over in Carterville. They sold canned goods. Jim had the whole northern half of the State and was on the road five days out of every week. He'd drop in here Saturdays and tell his experiences for that week. It was rich.

I guess he paid more attention to playin' jokes than makin' sales. Finally the concern let him out and he come right home here and told everybody he'd been fired instead of sayin' he'd resigned like most fellas would of.

It was a Saturday and the shop was full and Jim got up out of that chair and says, "Gentlemen, I got an important announcement to make. I been fired from my job."

Well, they asked him if he was in earnest and he said he was and nobody could think of nothin' to say till Jim finally broke the ice himself. He says, "I been sellin' canned goods and now I'm canned goods myself."

You see, the concern he'd been workin' for was a factory that made canned goods. Over in Carterville. And now Jim said he was canned himself. He was certainly a card!

Jim had a great trick that he used to play w'ile he was travelin'. For instance, he'd be ridin' on a train and they'd come to some little town like, well, like, we'll say, like Benton. Jim would look out the train window and read the signs on the stores.

For instance, they'd be a sign, "Henry Smith, Dry Goods." Well, Jim would write down the name and the name of the town and when he got to wherever he was goin' he'd mail back a postal card to Henry Smith at Benton and not sign no name to it, but he'd write on the card, well, somethin' like "Ask your wife about that book agent that spent the afternoon last week," or "Ask your Missus who kept her from gettin' lonesome the last time you was in Carterville." And he'd sign the card, "A Friend."

Of course, he never knew what really come of none of these jokes, but he could picture what *probably* happened and that was enough.

Jim didn't work very steady after he lost his position with

the Carterville people. What he did earn, doin' odd jobs round town, why he spent pretty near all of it on gin and his family might of starved if the stores hadn't of carried them along. Jim's wife tried her hand at dressmakin', but they ain't nobody goin' to get rich makin' dresses in this town.

As I say, she'd of divorced Jim, only she seen that she couldn't support herself and the kids and she was always hopin' that some day Jim would cut out his habits and give her more than two or three dollars a week.

They was a time when she would go to whoever he was workin' for and ask them to give her his wages, but after she done this once or twice, he beat her to it by borrowin' most of his pay in advance. He told it all round town, how he had outfoxed his Missus. He certainly was a caution!

But he wasn't satisfied with just outwittin' her. He was sore the way she had acted, tryin' to grab off his pay. And he made up his mind he'd get even. Well, he waited till Evans's Circus was advertised to come to town. Then he told his wife and two kiddies that he was goin' to take them to the circus. The day of the circus, he told them he would get the tickets and meet them outside the entrance to the tent.

Well, he didn't have no intentions of bein' there or buyin' tickets or nothin'. He got full of gin and laid round Wright's poolroom all day. His wife and the kids waited and waited and of course he didn't show up. His wife didn't have a dime with her, or nowhere else, I guess. So she finally had to tell the kids it was all off and they cried like they wasn't never goin' to stop.

Well, it seems, w'ile they was cryin', Doc Stair came along and he asked what was the matter, but Mrs. Kendall was stubborn and wouldn't tell him, but the kids told him and he insisted on takin' them and their mother in the show. Jim found this out afterwards and it was one reason why he had it in for Doc Stair.

Doc Stair come here about a year and a half ago. He's a mighty handsome young fella and his clothes always look like he has them made to order. He goes to Detroit two or three times a year and w'ile he's there he must have a tailor take his measure and then make him a suit to order. They cost pretty near twice as much, but they fit a whole lot better than if you just bought them in a store.

For a w'ile everybody was wonderin' why a young doctor like Doc Stair should come to a town like this where we already got old Doc Gamble and Doc Foote that's both been here for years and all the practice in town was always divided between the two of them.

Then they was a story got round that Doc Stair's gal had throwed him over, a gal up in the Northern Peninsula somewheres, and the reason he come here was to hide himself away and forget it. He said himself that he thought they wasn't nothin' like general practice in a place like ours to fit a man to be a good all round doctor. And that's why he'd came.

Anyways, it wasn't long before he was makin' enough to live on, though they tell me that he never dunned nobody for what they owed him, and the folks here certainly has got the owin' habit, even in my business. If I had all that was comin' to me for just shaves alone, I could go to Carterville and put up at the Mercer for a week and see a different picture every night. For instance, they's old George Purdy—but I guess I shouldn't ought to be gossipin'.

Well, last year, our coroner died, died of the flue. Ken Beatty, that was his name. He was the coroner. So they had to choose another man to be coroner in his place and they picked Doc Stair. He laughed at first and said he didn't want it, but they made him take it. It ain't no job that anybody would fight for and what a man makes out of it in a year would just about buy seeds for their garden. Doc's the kind, though, that can't say no to nothin' if you keep at him long enough.

But I was goin' to tell you about a poor boy we got here in town—Paul Dickson. He fell out of a tree when he was about ten years old. Lit on his head and it done somethin' to him and he ain't never been right. No harm in him, but just silly. Jim Kendall used to call him cuckoo; that's a name Jim had for anybody that was off their head, only he called people's head their bean. That was another of his gags, callin' head bean and callin' crazy people cuckoo. Only poor Paul ain't crazy, but just silly.

You can imagine that Jim used to have all kinds of fun with Paul. He'd send him to the White Front Garage for a left-handed monkey wrench. Of course they ain't no such a thing as a left-handed monkey wrench.

And once we had a kind of a fair here and they was a baseball game between the fats and the leans and before the game started Jim called Paul over and sent him way down to Schrader's hardware store to get a key for the pitcher's box.

They wasn't nothin' in the way of gags that Jim couldn't think up, when he put his mind to it.

Poor Paul was always kind of suspicious of people, maybe on account of how Jim had kept foolin' him. Paul wouldn't have much to do with anybody only his own mother and Doc Stair and a girl here in town named Julie Gregg. That is, she ain't a girl no more, but pretty near thirty or over.

When Doc first come to town, Paul seemed to feel like here was a real friend and he hung around Doc's office most of the w'ile; the only time he wasn't there was when he'd go home to eat or sleep or when he seen Julie Gregg doin' her shoppin'.

When he looked out Doc's window and seen her, he'd run downstairs and join her and tag along with her to the different stores. The poor boy was crazy about Julie and she always treated him mighty nice and made him feel like he was welcome, though of course it wasn't nothin' but pity on her side.

Doc done all he could to improve Paul's mind and he told me once that he really thought the boy was gettin' better, that they was times when he was as bright and sensible as anybody else.

But I was goin' to tell you about Julie Gregg. Old Man Gregg was in the lumber business, but got to drinkin' and lost the most of his money and when he died, he didn't leave nothin' but the house and just enough insurance for the girl to skimp along on.

Her mother was a kind of a half invalid and didn't hardly ever leave the house. Julie wanted to sell the place and move somewheres else after the old man died, but the mother said she was born here and would die here. It was tough on Julie, as the young people round this town—well, she's too good for them.

She's been away to school and Chicago and New York and different places and they ain't no subject she can't talk on, where you take the rest of the young folks here and you mention anything to them outside of Gloria Swanson or Tommy Meighan and they think you're delirious. Did you see Gloria in Wages of Virtue? You missed somethin'!

Well, Doc Stair hadn't been here more than a week when he come in one day to get shaved and I recognized who he was as he had been pointed out to me, so I told him about my old lady. She's been ailin' for a couple of years and either Doc Gamble or Doc Foote, neither one, seemed to be helpin' her. So he said he would come out and see her, but if she was able to get out herself, it would be better to bring her to his office where he could make a completer examination.

So I took her to his office and w'ile I was waitin' for her in the reception room, in come Julie Gregg. When somebody comes in Doc Stair's office, they's a bell that rings in his inside office so as he can tell they's somebody to see him.

So he left my old lady inside and come out to the front office and that's the first time him and Julie met and I guess it was what they call love at first sight. But it wasn't fifty-fifty. This young fella was the slickest lookin' fella she'd ever seen in this town and she went wild over him. To him she was just a young lady that wanted to see the doctor.

She'd came on about the same business I had. Her mother had been doctorin' for years with Doc Gamble and Doc Foote and without no results. So she'd heard they was a new doc in town and decided to give him a try. He promised to call and see her mother that same day.

I said a minute ago that it was love at first sight on her part. I'm not only judgin' by how she acted afterwards but how she looked at him that first day in his office. I ain't no mind reader, but it was wrote all over her face that she was gone.

Now Jim Kendall, besides bein' a jokesmith and a pretty good drinker, well, Jim was quite a lady-killer. I guess he run pretty wild durin' the time he was on the road for them Carterville people, and besides that, he'd had a couple little affairs of the heart right here in town. As I say, his wife could of divorced him, only she couldn't.

But Jim was like the majority of men, and women, too, I guess. He wanted what he couldn't get. He wanted Julie Gregg and worked his head off tryin' to land her. Only he'd of said bean instead of head.

Well, Jim's habits and his jokes didn't appeal to Julie and of course he was a married man, so he didn't have no more chance than, well, than a rabbit. That's an expression of Jim's himself. When somebody didn't have no chance to get elected or somethin', Jim would always say they didn't have no more chance than a rabbit.

He didn't make no bones about how he felt. Right in here, more than once, in front of the whole crowd, he said he was stuck on Julie and anybody that could get her for him was welcome to his house and his wife and kids included. But she wouldn't have nothin' to do with him; wouldn't even speak to him on the street. He finally seen he wasn't gettin' nowheres with his usual line so he decided to try the rough stuff. He went right up to her house one evenin' and when she opened the door he forced his way in and grabbed her. But she broke loose and before he could stop her, she run in the next room and locked the door and phoned to Joe Barnes. Joe's the marshal. Jim could hear who she was phonin' to and he beat it before Joe got there.

Joe was an old friend of Julie's pa. Joe went to Jim the next day and told him what would happen if he ever done it again.

I don't know how the news of this little affair leaked out. Chances is that Joe Barnes told his wife and she told somebody else's wife and they told their husband. Anyways, it did leak out and Hod Meyers had the nerve to kid Jim about it, right here in this shop. Jim didn't deny nothin' and kind of laughed it off and said for us all to wait; that lots of people had tried to make a monkey out of him, but he always got even.

Meanw'ile everybody in town was wise to Julie's bein' wild mad over the Doc. I don't suppose she had any idear how her face changed when him and her was together; of course she couldn't of, or she'd of kept away from him. And she didn't know that we was all noticin' how many times she made excuses to go up to his office or pass it on the other side of the street and look up in his window to see if he was there. I felt sorry for her and so did most other people.

Hod Meyers kept rubbin' it into Jim about how the Doc had cut him out. Jim didn't pay no attention to the kiddin' and you could see he was plannin' one of his jokes.

One trick Jim had was the knack of changin' his voice. He could make you think he was a girl talkin' and he could mimic any man's voice. To show you how good he was along this line, I'll tell you the joke he played on me once.

You know, in most towns of any size, when a man is dead and needs a shave, why the barber that shaves him soaks him five dollars for the job; that is, he don't soak *him*, but whoever ordered the shave. I just charge three dollars because personally I don't mind much shavin' a dead person. They lay a whole lot stiller than live customers. The only thing is that you don't feel like talkin' to them and you get kind of lonesome.

Well, about the coldest day we ever had here, two years ago last winter, the phone rung at the house w'ile I was home to dinner and I answered the phone and it was a woman's voice and she said she was Mrs. John Scott and her husband was dead and would I come out and shave him.

Old John had always been a good customer of mine. But they live seven miles out in the country, on the Streeter road. Still I didn't see how I could say no.

So I said I would be there, but would have to come in a jitney and it might cost three or four dollars besides the price of the shave. So she, or the voice, it said that was all right, so I got Frank Abbott to drive me out to the place and when I got there, who should open the door but old John himself! He wasn't no more dead than, well, than a rabbit.

It didn't take no private detective to figure out who had played me this little joke. Nobody could of thought it up but Jim Kendall. He certainly was a card!

I tell you this incident just to show you how he could disguise his voice and make you believe it was somebody else talkin'. I'd of swore it was Mrs. Scott had called me. Anyways, some woman.

Well, Jim waited till he had Doc Stair's voice down pat; then he went after revenge.

He called Julie up on a night when he knew Doc was over in Carterville. She never questioned but what it was Doc's voice. Jim said he must see her that night; he couldn't wait no longer to tell her somethin'. She was all excited and told him to come to the house. But he said he was expectin' an important long distance call and wouldn't she please forget her manners for once and come to his office. He said they couldn't nothin' hurt her and nobody would see her and he just *must* talk to her a little w'ile. Well, poor Julie fell for it.

Doc always keeps a night light in his office, so it looked to Julie like they was somebody there.

Meanw'ile Jim Kendall had went to Wright's poolroom, where they was a whole gang amusin' themselves. The most of them had drank plenty of gin, and they was a rough bunch even when sober. They was always strong for Jim's jokes and when he told them to come with him and see some fun they give up their card games and pool games and followed along.

Doc's office is on the second floor. Right outside his door they's a flight of stairs leadin' to the floor above. Jim and his gang hid in the dark behind these stairs.

Well, Julie come up to Doc's door and rung the bell and they was nothin' doin'. She rung it again and rung it seven or eight times. Then she tried the door and found it locked. Then Jim made some kind of a noise and she heard it and waited a minute, and then she says, "Is that you, Ralph?" Ralph is Doc's first name.

They was no answer and it must of came to her all of a sudden that she'd been bunked. She pretty near fell downstairs and the whole gang after her. They chased her all the way home, hollerin', "Is that you, Ralph?" and "Oh, Ralphie, dear, is that you?" Jim says he couldn't holler it himself, as he was laughin' too hard.

Poor Julie! She didn't show up here on Main Street for a long, long time afterward.

And of course Jim and his gang told everybody in town, everybody but Doc Stair. They was scared to tell him, and he might of never knowed only for Paul Dickson. The poor cuckoo, as Jim called him, he was here in the shop one night when Jim was still gloatin' yet over what he'd done to Julie. And Paul took in as much of it as he could understand and he run to Doc with the story.

It's a cinch Doc went up in the air and swore he'd make Jim suffer. But it was a kind of a delicate thing, because if it got out that he had beat Jim up, Julie was bound to hear of it and then she'd know that Doc knew and of course knowin' that he knew would make it worse for her than ever. He was goin' to do somethin', but it took a lot of figurin'.

Well, it was a couple days later when Jim was here in the shop again, and so was the cuckoo. Jim was goin' duck-shootin' the next day and had came in lookin' for Hod Meyers to go with him. I happened to know that Hod had went over to Carterville and wouldn't be home till the end of the week. So Jim said he hated to go alone and he guessed he would call it off. Then poor Paul spoke up and said if Jim would take him he would go along. Jim thought a w'ile and then he said, well, he guessed a half-wit was better than nothin'.

I suppose he was plottin' to get Paul out in the boat and play some joke on him, like pushin' him in the water. Anyways, he said Paul could go. He asked him had he ever shot a duck and Paul said no, he'd never even had a gun in his hands. So Jim said he could set in the boat and watch him and if he behaved himself, he might lend him his gun for a couple of shots. They made a date to meet in the mornin' and that's the last I seen of Jim alive.

Next mornin', I hadn't been open more than ten minutes when Doc Stair come in. He looked kind of nervous. He asked me had I seen Paul Dickson. I said no, but I knew where he was, out duck-shootin' with Jim Kendall. So Doc says that's what he had heard, and he couldn't understand it because Paul had told him he wouldn't never have no more to do with Jim as long as he lived.

He said Paul had told him about the joke Jim had played on Julie. He said Paul had asked him what he thought of the joke and the Doc had told him that anybody that would do a thing like that ought not to be let live.

I said it had been a kind of a raw thing, but Jim just couldn't resist no kind of a joke, no matter how raw. I said I thought he was all right at heart, but just bubblin' over with mischief. Doc turned and walked out.

At noon he got a phone call from old John Scott. The lake where Jim and Paul had went shootin' is on John's place. Paul had come runnin' up to the house a few minutes before and said they'd been an accident. Jim had shot a few ducks and then give the gun to Paul and told him to try his luck. Paul hadn't never handled a gun and he was nervous. He was shakin' so hard that he couldn't control the gun. He let fire and Jim sunk back in the boat, dead.

Doc Stair, bein' the coroner, jumped in Frank Abbott's flivver and rushed out to Scott's farm. Paul and old John was down on the shore of the lake. Paul had rowed the boat to shore, but they'd left the body in it, waitin' for Doc to come.

Doc examined the body and said they might as well fetch it back to town. They was no use leavin' it there or callin' a jury, as it was a plain case of accidental shootin'.

Personally I wouldn't never leave a person shoot a gun in the same boat I was in unless I was sure they knew somethin' about guns. Jim was a sucker to leave a new beginner have his gun, let alone a half-wit. It probably served Jim right, what he got. But still we miss him round here. He certainly was a card!

Comb it wet or dry?

JAY McINERNEY

It's Six A.M. Do You Know Where You Are?

You are not the kind of guy who would be at a place like this at this time of the morning. But you are here, and you cannot say that the terrain is entirely unfamiliar, although the details are a little fuzzy. You are at a nightclub talking to a girl with a shaved head. The club is either the Bimbo Box or the Lizard Lounge. It might all come a little clearer if you could slip into the bathroom and do a little more Bolivian Marching Powder. There is a small voice inside of you insisting that this epidemic lack of clarity is the result of too much of that already, but you are not yet willing to listen to that voice. The night has already turned on that imperceptible pivot where two A.M. changes to six A.M. You know that moment has come and gone, but you are not yet willing to concede that you have crossed the line beyond which all is gratuitous damage and the palsy of unravelled nerve endings. Somewhere back there it was possible to cut your losses, but you rode past that moment on a comet trail of white powder and now you are trying to hang onto that rush. Your brain at this moment is composed of brigades of tiny Bolivian soldiers. They are tired and muddy from their long march through the night. There are holes in their boots and they are hungry. They need to be fed. They need the Bolivian Marching Powder.

Something vaguely tribal about this scene—pendulous jewelry, face paint, ceremonial headgear and hairstyles. You feel that there is also a certain Latin theme, which is more than the fading buzz of marimbas in your brain.

You are leaning back against a post which may or may not be structural with regard to the building, but which feels essential for the maintenance of an upright position. The bald girl is saying this used to be a good place to come before the assholes discovered it. You do not want to be talking to this bald girl, or even listening to her, which is all you're doing, but you don't have your barge pole handy, and just at the moment you don't want to test the powers of speech or locomotion.

How did you get here? It was your friend, Tad Allagash, who powered you in here, and now he has disappeared. Tad is the kind of guy who certainly would be at a place like this at this time of the morning. He is either your best self or your worst self, you're not sure which. Earlier in the evening it seemed clear that he was your best self. You started on the Upper East Side with champagne and unlimited prospects, strictly observing the Allagash rule of perpetual motion: one drink per stop. Tad's mission in life is to have more fun than anyone else in New York City, and this involves a lot of moving around, since there is always the likelihood that you are missing something, that where you aren't is more fun than where you are. You are awed by this strict refusal to acknowledge any goal higher than the pursuit of pleasure. You want to be like that. You also think that he is shallow and dangerous. His friends are all rich and spoiled, like the cousin from Memphis you met earlier in the evening who would not accompany you below Fourteenth Street because he said he didn't have a lowlife visa. This cousin had a girlfriend with cheekbones to break your heart, and you knew she was the real thing when she absolutely refused to acknowledge your presence. She possessed secrets—about islands, about horses—which you would never know.

You have traveled from the meticulous to the slime. The girl with the shaved head has a scar tattooed on her scalp. It looks like a long, sutured gash. You tell her it is very realistic. She takes this as a compliment and thanks you. You meant as opposed to romantic. "I could use one of those right over my heart," you say.

"You want I can give you the name of the guy did it. You'd be surprised how cheap." You don't tell her that nothing would surprise you now. Her voice, for instance, which is like the New Jersey State Anthem played through an electric shaver.

The bald girl is emblematic of the problem. What the problem is is that for some reason you think you are going to meet the kind of girl who is not the kind of girl who would be at a place like this at this time of the morning. When you meet her you are going to tell her that what you really want is a house in the country with a garden. New York, the club scene, bald women—you're tired of all that. Your presence here is only a matter of conducting an experiment in limits, reminding yourself of what you aren't. You see yourself as the kind of guy who wakes up early on Sunday morning and steps out to pick up *The Times* and croissants. You take a cue from the Arts and Leisure section and decide to check out some exhibition—costumes of the Hapsburg Court at the Met, say, or Japanese lacquerware of the Muromachi period at the Asia Society. Maybe you will call that woman you met at the publishing party Friday night, the party you did not get sloppy drunk at, the woman who is an editor at a famous publishing house even though she looks like a fashion model. See if she wants to check out the exhibition and maybe do an early dinner. You will wait until eleven A.M. to call her, because she may not be an early riser, like you. She may have been out a little late, at a nightclub, say. It occurs to you that there is time for a couple of sets of tennis before the museum. You wonder if she plays, but then, of course she would.

When you meet the girl who wouldn't etcetera, you will tell her that you are slumming, visiting your own six A.M. Lower East Side of the soul on a lark, stepping nimbly between the piles of garbage to the marimba rhythms in your head.

On the other hand, any beautiful girl, specifically one with a full head of hair, would help you stave off this creeping sense of mortality. You remember the Bolivian Marching Powder and realize you're not down yet. First you have to get rid of this bald girl because she is doing bad things to your mood.

In the bathroom there are no doors on the stalls, which makes it tough to be discreet. But clearly, you are not the only person here to take on fuel. Lots of sniffling going on. The windows in here are blacked over, and for this you are profoundly grateful.

Hup, two. Three, four. The Bolivian soldiers are back on their feet. They are off and running in formation. Some of them are dancing, and you must do the same.

Just outside the door you spot her: tall, dark, and alone, half-hiding behind a pillar at the edge of the dance floor. You approach laterally, moving your stuff like a bad spade through the slalom of a synthesized conga rhythm. She jumps when you touch her shoulder.

"Dance?"

She looks at you as if you had just suggested instrumental rape. "I do not speak English," she says, when you ask again.

"Français?"

She shakes her head. Why is she looking at you that way, like there are tarantulas nesting in your eye sockets?

"You are by any chance from Bolivia? Or Peru?"

She is looking around for help now. Remembering a recent encounter with a young heiress's bodyguard at Danceteria—or was it New Berlin?—you back off, hands raised over your head.

The Bolivian soldiers are still on their feet, but they have stopped singing their marching song. You realize that we are at a crucial juncture with regard to morale. What we need is a good pep talk from Tad Allagash, but he is not to be found. You try to imagine what he would say. *Back on the horse. Now we're* really *going to have some fun.* Something like that. You suddenly realize that he has already slipped out with some rich hose queen. He is back at her place on Fifth Ave., and they are doing some of her off-the-boat-quality drugs. They are scooping it out of tall Ming vases and snorting it off of each other's naked bodies. You hate Tad Allagash.

Go home. Cut your losses.

Stay. Go for it.

You are a republic of voices tonight. Unfortunately, the republic is Italy. All these voices are waving their arms and screaming at each other. There's an *ex cathedra* riff coming down from the Vatican: *Repent. There's still time. Your body is the temple of the Lord and you have defiled it.* It is, after all, Sunday morning, and as long as you have any brain cells left there will always be this resonant patriarchal basso echoing down the marble vaults of your churchgoing childhood to remind you that this is the Lord's day. What you need is another overpriced drink to drown it out. But a search of pockets yields only a dollar bill and change. You paid ten to get in here. Panic is gaining on you.

You spot a girl at the edge of the dance floor who looks like your last chance for earthly salvation against the creeping judgment of Sunday morning. You know for a fact that if you go out into the morning alone, without even your sunglasses, which you have forgotten (because who, after all, plans on these travesties), that the harsh, angling light will turn you to flesh and bone. Mortality will pierce you through the retina. But there she is in her pegged pants, a kind of doo-wop retro ponytail pulled off to the side, great lungs, as eligible a candidate as you could hope to find this late in the game. The sexual equivalent of fast food.

She shrugs and nods when you ask her to dance. You like the way she moves, half-tempo, the oiled ellipses of her hips and shoulders. You get a little hip and ass contact. After the second song she says she's tired. She's on the edge of bolting when you ask her if she needs a little pick-me-up.

"You've got some blow?" she says.

"Monster," you say.

She takes your arm and leads you into the Ladies'. There's another guy in the stall beside yours so it's okay. After a couple of spoons she seems to like you just fine and you are feeling very likable yourself. A couple more. This girl is all nose. When she leans forward for the spoon the front of her shirt falls open in a way you can't help noticing. You wonder if this is her way of thanking you.

Oh yes.

"I love drugs," she says, as you march towards the bar.

"It's something we have in common," you say.

"Have you ever noticed how all the good words start with D? D and L."

You try to think about this. You're not quite sure what she's driving at. The Bolivians are singing their marching song but you can't quite make out the words.

"You know? Drugs. Delight. Decadence."

"Debauchery," you say, catching the tune now.

"Dexedrine."

"Delectable. Deranged. Debilitated."

"And L. Lush and luscious."

"Languorous."

"Lazy."

"Libidinous."

"What's that?" she says.

"Horny."

"Oh," she says, and casts a long, arching look over your shoulder. Her eyes glaze in a way that reminds you precisely of the closing of a sandblasted glass shower door. You can see that the game is over, though you're not sure which rule you broke. Possibly she finds "H" words offensive. She is scanning the dance floor for a man with a compatible vocabulary. You have more: *down* and *depressed; lost* and *lonely.* It's not that you are really going to miss this girl who thinks that *decadence* and *dexedrine* are the high points of the language of the Kings James and Lear, but the touch of flesh, the sound of another human voice. . . . You know that there is a special purgatory waiting out there for you, a desperate half-sleep which is like a grease fire in the brain pan.

The girl half-waves as she disappears into the crowd. There is no sign of the other girl, the girl who would not be here. There is no sign of Tad Allagash. The Bolivians are mutinous. You can't stop the voices.

Here you are again.

All messed up and no place to go.

It is worse even than you expected, stepping out into the morning. The light is like a mother's reproach. The sidewalk sparkles cruelly. Visibility unlimited. The downtown warehouses look serene and rested in this beveled light. A cab passes uptown and you start to wave, then realize you have no money. The cab stops. You jog over and lean in the window.

"I guess I'll walk after all."

"Ass hole." He leaves rubber.

You start north, holding your hand over your eyes. There is a bum sleeping on the sidewalk, swathed in garbage bags. He lifts his head as you pass. "God bless you and forgive your sins," he says. You wait for the cadge, but that's all he says. You wish he hadn't said it.

As you turn away, what is left of your olfactory equipment sends a message to your brain. The smell of fresh bread. Somewhere they are baking bread. You see bakery trucks loading in front of a loft building on the next block. You watch as bags of rolls are carried out onto the loading dock by a man with a tattooed forearm. This man is already at work, so that regular people will have fresh bread for their morning tables. The righteous people who sleep at night and eat eggs for breakfast. It is Sunday morning and you have not eaten since . . . when? Friday night. As you approach, the smell of the bread washes over you like a gentle rain. You inhale deeply, filling your lungs with it. Tears come to your eyes, and you are filled with such a rush of tenderness and pity that you stop beside a lamppost and hang on for support.

You remember another Sunday morning in your old apartment on Cornelia Street when you woke to the smell of bread from the bakery downstairs. There was the smell of bread every morning, but this is the one you remember. You turned to see your wife sleeping beside you. Her mouth was open and her hair fell down across the pillow to your shoulder. The tanned skin of her shoulder was the color of bread fresh from the oven. Slowly, and with a growing sense of exhilaration, you remembered who you were. You were the boy and she was the girl, your college sweetheart. You weren't famous yet, but you had the rent covered, you had your favorite restaurant where the waitresses knew your name and you could bring your own bottle of wine. It all seemed to be just the way you had pictured it when you had discussed plans for marriage and New York. The apartment with the pressed tin ceiling, the claw-footed bath, the windows that didn't quite fit the frame. It seemed almost as if you had wished for that very place. You leaned against your wife's shoulder. Later you would get up quietly, taking care not to wake her, and go downstairs for croissants and the *Sunday Times*, but for a long time you lay there breathing in the mingled scents of bread, hair and skin. You were in no hurry to get up. You knew it was a moment you wanted to savor. You didn't know how soon it would be over, that within a year she would go back to Michigan to file for divorce.

You approach the man on the loading dock. He stops working and watches you. You feel that there is something wrong with the way your legs are moving.

"Bread." This is what you say to him. You meant to say something more, but this is as much as you can get out.

"What was your first clue?" he says. He is a man who has served his country, you think, a man with a family somewhere outside the city. Small children. Pets. A garden.

"Could I have some? A roll or something?"

"Get out of here."

The man is about your size, except for the belly, which you don't have. "I'll trade you my jacket," you say. It is one hundred percent raw silk from Paul Stuart. You take it off, show him the label.

"You're crazy," the man says. Then he looks back into the warehouse. He picks up a bag of hard rolls and throws them at your feet. You hand him the jacket. He checks the label, sniffs the jacket, then tries it on.

You tear the bag open and the smell of warm dough rushes over you. The first bite sticks in your throat and you almost gag. You will have to go slowly. You will have to learn everything all over again.

LORRIE MOORE

The Kid's Guide to Divorce

PUT EXTRA SALT on the popcorn because your mom'll say that she needs it because the part where Inger Berman almost dies and the camera does tricks to elongate her torso sure gets her every time.

Think: Geeze, here she goes again with the Kleenexes.

She will say thanks honey when you come slowly, slowly around the corner in your slippers and robe, into the living room with Grandma's old used-to-be-salad-bowl piled high. I made it myself, remind her, and accidentally drop a few pieces on the floor. Mittens will bat them around with his paws.

Mmmmm, good to replenish those salts, she'll munch and smile soggily.

Tell her the school nurse said after a puberty movie once that salt is bad for people's hearts.

Phooey, she'll say. It just makes it thump, that's all. Thump, thump, thump—oh look! She will talk with her mouth full of popcorn. Cary Grant is getting her out of there. Did you unplug the popper?

Pretend you don't hear her. Watch Inger Berman look elongated; wonder what it means.

You'd better check, she'll say.

Groan. Make a little *tsk* noise with your tongue on the roof of your mouth. Run as fast as you can because the next commercial's going to be the end. Unplug the popper. Bring Mittens back in with you because he is mewing by the refrigerator. He'll leave hair on your bathrobe. Dump him in your mom's lap.

Hey baby, she'll coo at the cat, scratching his ears. Cuddle close to your mom and she'll reach around and scratch one of your ears too, kissing your cheek. Then she'll suddenly lean forward, reaching toward the bowl on the coffee table, carefully so as not to disturb the cat. I always think he's going to realize faster than he does, your mom will say between munches, hand to hand to mouth. Men can be so dense and frustrating. She will wink at you.

Eye the tube suspiciously. All the bad guys will let Cary Grant take Inger Berman away in the black car. There will be a lot of old-fashioned music. Stand and pull your bathrobe up on the sides. Hang your tongue out and pretend to dance like a retarded person at a ball. Roll your eyes. Waltz across the living room with exaggerated side-to-side motions, banging into furniture. Your mother will pretend not to pay attention to you. She will finally say in a flat voice: How wonderful, gee, you really send me.

When the music is over, she will ask you what you want to watch now. She'll hand you the *TV Guide.* Look at it. Say: The Late, Late Chiller. She'll screw up one of her eyebrows at you, but say *please, please* in a soft voice and put your hands together like a prayer. She will smile back and sigh, okay.

Switch the channel and return to the sofa. Climb under the blue afghan with your mother. Tell her you like this beginning cartoon part best where the mummy comes out of the coffin and roars, *CHILLER!!* Get up on one of the arms of the sofa and do an imitation, your hands like claws, your elbows stiff, your head slumped to one side. Your mother will tell you to sit back down. Snuggle back under the blanket with her.

When she says, Which do you like better, the mummy or the werewolf, tell her the werewolf is scary because he goes out at night and does things that no one suspects because in the day he works in a bank and has no hair.

What about the mummy? she'll ask, petting Mittens.

Shrug your shoulders. Fold in your lips. Say: The mummy's just the mummy.

With the point of your tongue, loosen one of the chewed, pulpy kernels in your molars. Try to swallow it, but get it caught in your throat and begin to gasp and make horrible retching noises. It will scare the cat away.

Good God, be careful, your mother will say, thwacking you on the back. Here, drink this water.

Try groaning root beer, root beer, like a dying cowboy you saw on a commercial once, but drink the water anyway. When you are no longer choking, your face is less red, and you can breathe again, ask for a Coke. Your mom will say: I don't think so; Dr. Atwood said your teeth were atrocious.

Tell her Dr. Atwood is for the birds.

What do you mean by that? she will exclaim.

Look straight ahead. Say: I dunno.

The mummy will be knocking down telephone poles, lifting them up, and hurling them around like Lincoln Logs.

Wow, all wrapped up and no place to go, your mother will say.

Cuddle close to her and let out a long, low, admiring *Neato.*

The police will be in the cemetery looking for a monster. They won't know whether it's the mummy or the werewolf, but someone will have been hanging out there leaving little smoking piles of bones and flesh that even the police dogs get upset and whine at.

Say something like gross-out, and close your eyes.

Are you sure you want to watch this?

Insist that you are not scared.

There's a rock concert on Channel 7, you know.

Think about it. Decide to try Channel 7, just for your mom's sake. Somebody with greasy hair who looks like Uncle Jack will be saying something boring.

Your mother will agree that he does look like Uncle Jack. A little.

A band with black eyeshadow on will begin playing their guitars. Stand and bounce up and down like you saw Julie Steinman do once.

God, why do they always play them down at their crotches? your mom will ask.

Don't answer, simply imitate them, throwing your hair back and fiddling bizarrely with the crotch of your pajama bottoms. Your mother will slap you and tell you you're being fresh.

Act hurt. Affect a slump. Pick up a magazine and pretend you're reading it. The cat will rejoin you. Look at the pictures of the food.

Your mom will try to pep you up. She'll say: Look! Pat Benatar! Let's dance.

Tell her you think Pat Benatar is stupid and cheap. Say nothing for five whole minutes.

When the B-52's come on, tell her you think *they're* okay.

Smile sheepishly. Then the two of you will get up and dance like wild maniacs around the coffee table until you are sweating, whooping to the oo-ah-oo's, jumping like pogo sticks, acting like space robots. Do razz-ma-tazz hands like your mom at either side of your head. During a commercial, ask for an orange soda.

Water or milk, she will say, slightly out of breath, sitting back down.

Say shit, and when she asks what did you say, sigh: Nothing.

Next is Rod Stewart singing on a roof somewhere. Your mom will say: He's sort of cute.

Tell her Julie Steinman saw him in a store once and said he looked really old.

Hmmmm, your mother will say.

Study Rod Stewart carefully. Wonder if you could make your legs go like that. Plan an imitation for Julie Steinman.

When the popcorn is all gone, yawn. Say: I'm going to bed now.

Your mother will look disappointed, but she'll say, okay, honey. She'll turn the TV off. By the way, she'll ask hesitantly like she always does. How did the last three days go?

Leave out the part about the lady and the part about the beer. Tell her they went all right, that he's got a new silver dartboard and that you went out to dinner and this guy named Hudson told a pretty funny story about peeing in the hamper. Ask for a 7-Up.

JOHN O'HARA

Pal Joey

DEAR PAL TED:

Well at last I am getting around to knocking off a line or two to let you know how much I apprisiate it you sending me that wire on opening nite. Dont think because I didnt answer before I didnt apprisiate it because that is far from the case. But I guess you know that because if you knew when I was opening you surely must be aware how busy Ive been ever since opening nite. I figure you read in *Variety* what date I was opening in which case I figure you have seen the write ups since then telling how busy Ive been and believe me its no exagerton.

Well maybe it seems a long time since opening nite and in a way it does to me too. It will only be five weeks this coming Friday but it seems longer considering all that has happened to your old pal Joey. Its hard to believe that under two months ago Joey was strictly from hunger as they say but I was. The last time I saw you (August) remember the panic was on. I figured things would begin to break a little better around August but no. A couple spots where I figured I would fit in didnt open at all on acct of bankroll trouble and that was why I left town and came out this way. I figured you live in a small town in Michigan and you can stay away from the hot spots because there arent any and that way you save money. I was correct but I sure didnt figure the panic would stay on as long as it did. I finely sold the jalloppy and hocked my diamond ring the minute I heard there would be a chance down this way. I never was in Ohio before but maybe I will never be any place else. At least I like it enough to remain here the remainder of my life but of course if NBC is listening in Im only kidding.

Well I heard about this spot through a little mouse I got to know up in Michigan. She told me about this spot as it is her home town altho spending her vacation every year in Michigan. I was to a party one nite (private) and they finely got me to sing a few numbers for them and the mouse couldn't take her eyes off me. She sat over in one corner of the room not paying any attenton to the dope she was with until finely it got so even he noticed it and began making cracks but loud. I burned but went on singing and playing but he got too loud and I had to stop in the middle of a number and I said right at him if he didnt like it why didnt he try himself. Perhaps he could do better. The others at the party got sore at him and told him to pipe down but that only made him madder and the others told me to go ahead and not pay any attention to him. So I did. Then when I got finished with a few more numbers I looked around and the heel wasnt there but the mouse was. She didnt give me a hand but I could tell she was more impress than some that were beating their paws off. So I went over to her and told her I was sorry if it embarrassed her me calling attention to her dope boy friend but she said he wasnt a boy friend. I said well I figured that. I said she looked as if she could do better than him and she said, "you for instance" and I said well yes. We laughed and got along fine and I took her home. She was staying with her grandmother and grandfather, two respectible old married people that lived there all their life. They were too damn respectible for me. They watched her like a hawk and one oclock was the latest she could be out. That to me is the dumbest way to treat that kind of a mouse. If its going to happen it can happen before nine oclock and if it isnt going to happen it isnt going to no matter if you stay out till nine oclock the next morning. But whats the use of being old if you cant be dumb? So anyway Nan told me about this spot down here and knew the asst mgr of the hotel where the spot is and she said she would give me a send in and if I didnt hold them up for too much of the ready she was sure I could get the job. I sing and play every afternoon in the cocktail bar and at night I relieve the band in the ballroom. Anyway I figured I would have to freshen up the old wardrobe so I had to get rid of the jalloppy and hock my diamond ring. I made the trip to Ohio with Nan in her own jalloppy which isnt exactly a jalloppy I might add. Its a 37 Plymouth conv coop. It took us three days to go from Mich. to Ohio but Ill thank you not to ask any questions about my private life.

This asst mgr auditioned me when we finely arrived and I knew right away I was in because he asked me for a couple of old numbers like Everybody Step and Swanee and a Jerry Kern medley and he was a Carmichael fan. Everything he asked me for I gave him and of course I put up a nice appearance being sunburned and a white coat from the proseeds of selling the jalloppy and hocking the ring. I rehearsed with the band altho Collins the leader hates my guts and finely I talked this asst mgr into letting me do a single irregardless of the band and he did.

Well you might say I ran the opening nite. I m.c'd and they had a couple kids from a local dancing school doing tap, one of them not bad altho no serious competition for Ginger Rogers. They were only on for the first week. They also had another mouse who was with the band, living with the drummer. She tried to be like Maxine. Well she wasnt even colored, thats how much like Maxine she was. The local 400 turned out for the opening nite and inside a week I was besieged with offers to entertain at private parties which I do nearly every Sunday as the bar and ballroom are not open Sunday or at least I do not work. In additon to the job at the hotel and the private parties you probably have read about the radio job. I went on sustaining the first week and by the end of the second week I got myself a nice little commercial. I am on just before the local station hooks up with NBC Blue Network five nites a week but I dont think you can catch me in New York. Not yet! My sponsor is the Acme Credit Jewellery

Company but I only have eight more weeks to go with them then I am free to negosiate with a better sponsor. Still Im not complaining. Your old pal Joey is doing all right for himself. I get a due bill at the hotel and what they pay me in additon aint hay. I also have the radio spot and the private parties. I went for a second hand Lasalle coop and I am thinking of joining the country club. I go there all the time with some of the local 400 so I figure I might as well join but will wait till I make sure I am going to stay here. I get my picture in the paper and write ups so much that I dont even bother to put them in my scrap book any more.

The crowd at the club are always ribbing me about it and accuse me of having the reporters on my payroll but I just tell them no, not the reporters, the editors. I am a little sore at one of the papers because the local Winchell links my name constantly with the name of a very sweet kid that I go to the club and play golf with. Not that it isnt true. We see each other all the time and she comes to the hotel practically every nite with a party and when Im through for the nite we usely take a ride out to a late spot out in the country. Her father is president of the second largest bank. It is the oldest. The biggest bank was formally two banks but they merged. Her name is Jean Spencer and a sweeter kid never lived. I really go for her. But this local Winchell took a personal dislike to me and made a couple cracks about us. One was "That personality boy at a downtown hotel has aired the femme that got him the job and is now trying to move into society." Me trying to move in to society! Society moved in on me is more like it. Jean was burned because she was afraid her father might see the item and when I meet her father I dont want him to have the wrong impression. I think the colyumist got the item from my ex-friend Nan. I didnt see much of her when I was rehearsing and the afternoon of opening nite she called up and said she wanted to come but what the hell could I do? Ask for a big table when they were getting $5 a head cover charge? I was glad enough to get the job without asking too many favors. Then a week or so later she called up and asked me could I let her have $50. I aksed her what for and she hung up. Well if she didnt even want to do me the curtesy to tell me what for I wasnt going to follow her around begging her to take it. But I gave it a few days thought and decided to let her have it but when I phoned her they said she quit her job and left town. I understand from Schall the asst mgr that she sold her Plymouth and went to N.Y. Her name is Nan Hennessey so if you run into her anywhere youll know her. She could be worse, that is worse on the eye, a little dumb tho.

Well pally, they will be billing me for stealing all their writing paper if I dont quit this. Just to show you I dont forget I inclose $30. Ill let you have the rest as soon as possible. Any time I can help you out the same way just let me know and you can count on me. I guess you kissed that fifty goodbye but that isnt the way I do things. But I guess you know that, hey pal?

All the best from
Pal Joey

III
THIRD PERSON VOICES

CONRAD AIKEN

Silent Snow, Secret Snow

JUST WHY IT should have happened, or why it should have happened just when it did, he could not, of course, possibly have said; nor perhaps could it even have occurred to him to ask. The thing was above all a secret, something to be preciously concealed from Mother and Father; and to that very fact it owed an enormous part of its deliciousness. It was like a peculiarly beautiful trinket to be carried unmentioned in one's trouser-pocket—a rare stamp, an old coin, a few tiny gold links found trodden out of shape on the path in the park, a pebble of carnelian, a sea shell distinguishable from all others by an unusual spot or stripe—and, as if it were anyone of these, he carried around with him everywhere a warm and persistent and increasingly beautiful sense of possession. Nor was it only a sense of possession—it was also a sense of protection. It was as if, in some delightful way, his secret gave him a fortress, a wall behind which he could retreat into heavenly seclusion. This was almost the first thing he had noticed about it—apart from the oddness of the thing itself—and it was this that now again, for the fiftieth time, occurred to him, as he sat in the little schoolroom. It was the half hour for geography. Miss Buell was revolving with one finger, slowly, a huge terrestrial globe which had been placed on her desk. The green and yellow continents passed and repassed, questions were asked and answered, and now the little girl in front of him, Deirdre, who had a funny little constellation of freckles on the back of her neck, exactly like the Big Dipper, was standing up and telling Miss Buell that the equator was the line that ran round the middle.

Miss Buell's face, which was old and grayish and kindly, with gray stiff curls beside the cheeks, and eyes that swam very brightly, like little minnows, behind thick glasses, wrinkled itself into a complication of amusements.

"Ah! I see. The earth is wearing a belt, or a sash. Or someone drew a line round it!"

"Oh, no—not that—I mean—"

In the general laughter, he did not share, or only a very little. He was thinking about the Arctic and Antarctic regions, which of course, on the globe, were white. Miss Buell was now telling them about the tropics, the jungles, the steamy heat of equatorial swamps, where the birds and butterflies, and even the snakes, were like living jewels. As he listened to these things, he was already, with a pleasant sense of half-effort, putting his secret between himself and the words. Was it really an effort at all? For effort implied something voluntary, and perhaps even something one did not especially want; whereas this was distinctly pleasant, and came almost of its own accord. All he needed to do was to think of that morning, the first one, and then of all the others—

But it was all so absurdly simple! It had amounted to so little. It was nothing, just an idea—and just why it should have become so wonderful, so permanent, was a mystery—a very pleasant one, to be sure, but also, in an amusing way, foolish. However, without ceasing to listen to Miss Buell, who had now moved up to the north temperate zones, he deliberately invited his memory of the first morning. It was only a moment or two after he had waked up—or perhaps the moment itself. But was there, to be exact, an exact moment? Was one awake all at once? or was it gradual? Anyway, it was after he had stretched a lazy hand up towards the headrail, and yawned, and then relaxed again among his warm covers, all the more grateful on a December morning, that the thing had happened. Suddenly, for no reason, he had thought of the postman, he remembered the postman. Perhaps there was nothing so odd in that. After all, he heard the postman almost every morning in his life—his heavy boots could be heard clumping round the corner at the top of the little cobbled hill-street, and knock at each door, the crossings and re-crossings of the street, till finally the clumsy steps came stumbling across to the very door, and the tremendous knock came which shook the house itself.

(Miss Buell was saying "Vast wheat-growing areas in North America and Siberia."

Dierdre had for the moment placed her left hand across the back of her neck.)

But on this particular morning, the first morning, as he lay there with his eyes closed, he had for some reason *waited* for the postman. He wanted to hear him come round the corner. And that was precisely the joke—he never did. He never came. He never had come—*round the corner*—again. For when at last the steps *were* heard, they had already, he was quite sure, come a little down the hill, to the first house; and even so, the steps were curiously different—they were softer, they had a new secrecy about them, they were muffled and indistinct; and while the rhythm of them was the same, it now said a new thing—it said peace, it said remoteness, it said cold, it said sleep. And he had understood the situation at once—nothing could have seemed simpler—there had been snow in the night, such as all winter he had been longing for; and it was this which had rendered the postman's first footsteps inaudible, and the later ones faint. Of course! How lovely! And even now it must be snowing—it was going to be a snowy day—the long white ragged lines were drifting and sifting across the street, across the faces of the old houses, whispering and hushing, making little triangles of white in the corners between cobblestones, seething a little when the wind blew them over the ground to a drifted corner; and so it would be all day, getting deeper and deeper and silenter and silenter.

(Miss Buell was saying "Land of perpetual snow.")

All this time, of course (while he lay in bed), he had kept his eyes closed, listening to the nearer progress of the postman, the muffled footsteps thumping and slipping on the snow-sheathed cobbles; and all the other sounds—the double knocks, a frosty far-off voice or two, a bell ringing thinly and softly as if under a sheet of ice—had the same slightly abstracted quality, as if removed by one degree from actuality—as if everything in the world had been insulated by snow. But when at last, pleased, he opened his eyes, and turned them towards the window, to see for himself this long-desired and now so clearly imagined miracle—what he saw instead was brilliant sunlight on a roof; and when, astonished, he jumped out of bed and stared down into the street, expecting to see the cobbles obliterated by the snow, he saw nothing but the bare bright cobbles themselves.

Queer, the effect this extraordinary surprise had had upon him—all the following morning he had kept with him a sense as of snow falling about him, a secret screen of new snow between himself and the world. If he had not dreamed such a thing—and how could he have dreamed it while awake?—how else could one explain it? In any case, the delusion had been so vivid as to affect his entire behavior. He could not now remember whether it was on the first or the second morning—or was it even the third?—that his mother had drawn attention to some oddness in his manner.

"But my darling—" she had said at the breakfast table—"what has come over you? You don't seem to be listening . . ."

And how often that very thing had happened since!

(Miss Buell was now asking if anyone knew the difference between the North Pole and the Magnetic Pole. Deirdre was holding up her flickering brown hand, and he could see the four white dimples that marked the knuckles.)

Perhaps it hadn't been either the second or third morning—or even the fourth or fifth. How could he be sure? How could he be sure just when the delicious *progress* had become clear? Just when it had really *begun*? The intervals weren't very precise. . . . All he now knew was, that at some point or other—perhaps the second day, perhaps the sixth—he had noticed that the presence of the snow was a little more insistent, the sound of it clearer; and, conversely, the sound of the postman's footsteps more indistinct. Not only could he not hear the steps come round the corner, he could not even hear them at the first house. It was below the first house that he heard them; and then, a few days later, it was below the second house that he heard them; and a few days later again, below the third. Gradually, gradually, the snow was becoming heavier, the sound of its seething louder, the cobblestones more and more muffled. When he found, each morning, on going to the window, after the ritual of listening that the roofs and cobbles were as bare as ever, it made no difference. This was, after all, what rewarded him: the thing was his own, belonged to no one else. No one else knew about it, not even his mother and father. There, outside, were the bare cobbles; and here, inside, was the snow. Snow growing heavier each day, muffling the world, hiding the ugly, and deadening increasingly—above all—the steps of the postman.

"But my darling—" she had said at the luncheon table—"what has come over you? You don't seem to listen when people speak to you. That's the third time I've asked you to pass your plate. . . ."

How was one to explain this to Mother? or to Father? There was, of course, nothing to be done about it: nothing. All one could do was to laugh embarrassedly, pretend to be a little ashamed, apologize, and take a sudden and somewhat disingenuous interest in what was being done or said. The cat had stayed out all night. He had a curious swelling on his left cheek—perhaps somebody had kicked him, or a stone had struck him. Mrs. Kempton was or was not coming to tea. The house was going to be house cleaned, or "turned out," on Wednesday instead of Friday. A new lamp was provided for his evening work—perhaps it was eyestrain which accounted for this new and so peculiar vagueness of his—Mother was looking at him with amusement as she said this, but with something else as well. A new lamp? A new lamp. Yes Mother, No Mother, Yes Mother. School is going very well. The geometry is very easy. The history is very dull. The geography is very interesting—particularly when it takes one to the North Pole. Why the North Pole? Oh, well, it would be fun to be an explorer. Another Peary or Scott or Shackleton. And then abruptly he found his interest in the talk at an end, stared at the pudding on his plate, listened, waited, and began once more—ah how heavenly, too, the first beginnings—to hear or feel—for could he actually hear it?—the silent snow, the secret snow.

(Miss Buell was telling them about the search for the Northwest Passage, about Hendrik Hudson, the Half Moon.)

This had been, indeed, the only distressing feature of the new experience: the fact that it so increasingly had brought him into a kind of mute misunderstanding, or even conflict, with his father and mother. It was as if he were trying to lead a double life. On the one hand he had to be Paul Hasleman, and keep up the appearance of being that person—dress, wash, and answer intelligently when spoken to—; on the other, he had to explore this new world which had been opened to him. Nor could there be the slightest doubt—not the slightest—that the new world was the profounder and more wonderful of the two. It was irresistible. It was miraculous. Its beauty was simply beyond anything—beyond speech as beyond thought—utterly incommunicable. But how then, between the two worlds, of which he was thus constantly aware, was he to keep a balance? One must get up, one must go to breakfast, one must talk with Mother, go to school, do one's lessons—and, in all this, try not to appear too much of a fool. But if all the while one was also trying to extract the full deliciousness of another and quite separate existence, one which could not easily (if at all) be spoken of—how was one to manage? How was one to explain? Would it be safe to explain? Would it be absurd? Would it merely mean that he would get into some obscure kind of trouble?

These thoughts came and went, came and went, as softly and secretly as the snow; they were not precisely a disturbance, perhaps they were even a pleasure; he liked to have them; their presence was something palpable, something he could stroke with his hand, without closing his eyes, and without ceasing to see Miss Buell and the school room and the globe and the freckles on Deirdre's neck; nevertheless he did in a sense cease to see, or to see the obvious external world, and substituted for this vision of snow, the sound of snow, and the slow, almost soundless, approach of the postman.

Yesterday, it had been only at the sixth house that the postman had become audible; the snow was much deeper now, it was falling more swiftly and heavily, the sound of its setting was more distinct, more soothing, more persistent. And this morning, it had been—as nearly as he could figure—just above the seventh house—perhaps only a step or two above: at most, he had heard two or three footsteps before the knock had sounded. . . . And with each such narrowing of the sphere, each nearer approach of the limit at which the postman was first audible, it was odd how sharply was increased the amount of illusion which had to be carried into the ordinary business of daily life. Each day, it was harder to get out of bed, to go to the window, to look out at the—as always—perfectly empty and snowless street. Each day it was more difficult to go through the perfunctory motions of greeting Mother and Father at breakfast, to reply to their questions, to put his books together and go to school. And at school, how extraordinarily hard to conduct with success simultaneously the public life and the life that was secret. There were times when he longed—positively ached—to tell everyone about it—to burst out with it—only to be checked almost at once by a far-off feeling as of some faint absurdity which was inherent in it—but *was* it absurd?—and more importantly by a sense of mysterious power in his very secrecy. Yes: it must be kept secret. That, more and more, became clear. At whatever cost to himself, whatever pain to others—

(Miss Buell looked straight at him, smiling, and said, "Perhaps we'll ask Paul. I'm sure Paul will come out of his daydream long enough to be able to tell us. Won't you, Paul." He rose slowly from his chair, resting one hand on the brightly varnished desk, and deliberately stared through the snow towards the blackboard. It was an effort, but it was amusing to make it. "Yes," he said slowly, "it was what we now call the Hudson River. This he thought to be the Northwest Passage. He was disappointed." He sat down again, and as he did so Deirdre half turned in her chair and gave him a shy smile, of approval and admiration.)

At whatever pain to others.

This part of it was very puzzling, very puzzling. Mother

was very nice, and so was Father. Yes, that was all true enough. He wanted to be nice to them, to tell them everything—and yet, was it really wrong of him to want to have a secret place of his own?

At bedtime, the night before, Mother had said, "If this goes on, my lad, we'll have to see a doctor, we will! We can't have our boy—" But what was it she had said? "Live in another world"? "Live so far away"? The word "far" had been in it, he was sure, and then Mother had taken up a magazine again and laughed a little, but with an expression which wasn't mirthful. He had felt sorry for her. . . .

The bell rang for dismissal. The sound came to him through long curved parallels of falling snow. He saw Deirdre rise, and had himself risen almost as soon—but not quite as soon—as she.

II

On the walk homeward, which was timeless, it pleased him to see through the accompaniment, or counterpoint, of snow, the items of mere externality on his way. There were many kinds of bricks in the sidewalks, and laid in many kinds of pattern. The garden walls too were various, some of wooden palings, some of plaster, some of stone. Twigs of bushes leaned over the walls; the little hard green winterbuds of lilac, on gray stems, sheathed and fat; other branches very thin and fine and black and desiccated. Dirty sparrows huddled in the bushes, as dull in color as dead fruit left in leafless trees. A single starling creaked on a weather vane. In the gutter, beside a drain, was a scrap of torn and dirty newspaper, caught in a little delta of filth: the word ECZEMA appeared in large capitals, and below it was a letter from Mrs. Amelia D. Cravath, 2100 Pine Street, Fort Worth, Texas, to the effect that after being a sufferer for years she had been cured by Caley's Ointment. In the little delta, beside the fan-shaped and deeply runneled continent of brown mud, were lost twigs, descended from their parent trees, dead matches, a rusty horse-chestnut burr, a small concentration of sparkling gravel on the lip of the sewer, a fragment of eggshell, a streak of yellow sawdust which had been wet and was now dry and congealed, a brown pebble, and a broken feather. Further on was a cement sidewalk, ruled into geometrical parallelograms, with a brass inlay at one end commemorating the contractors who had laid it, and, halfway across, an irregular and random series of dog-tracks, immortalized in synthetic stone. He knew these well, and always stepped on them; to cover the little hollows with his own foot had always been a queer pleasure; today he did it once more, but perfunctorily and detachedly, all the while thinking of something else. That was a dog, a long time ago, who had made a mistake and walked on the cement while it was still wet. He had probably wagged his tail, but that hadn't been recorded. Now, Paul Hasleman, aged twelve, on his way home from school, crossed the same river, which in the meantime had frozen into rock. Homeward through the snow, the snow falling in bright sunshine. Homeward?

Then came the gateway with the two posts surmounted by egg-shaped stones which had been cunningly balanced on their ends, as if by Columbus, and mortared in the very act of balance: a source of perpetual wonder. On the brick wall just beyond, the letter H had been stenciled, presumably for some purpose. H? H.

The green hydrant, with a little green-painted chain attached to the brass screw-cap.

The elm tree, with the great gray wound in the bark, kidney-shaped, into which he always put his hand—to feel the cold but living wood. The injury, he had been sure, was due to the gnawings of a tethered horse. But now it deserved only a passing palm, a merely tolerant eye. There were more important things. Miracles. Beyond the thoughts of trees, mere elms. Beyond the thoughts of sidewalks, mere stone, mere brick, mere cement. Beyond the thoughts even of his own shoes, which trod these sidewalks obediently, bearing a burden—far above—of elaborate mystery. He watched them. They were not very well polished; he had neglected them, for a very good reason: they were one of the many parts of the increasing difficulty of the daily return to daily life, the morning struggle. To get up, having at last opened one's eyes, to go to the window, and discover no snow, to wash, to dress, to descend the curving stairs to breakfast—

At whatever pain to others, nevertheless, one must persevere in severance, since the incommunicability of the experience demanded it. It was desirable of course to be kind to Mother and Father, especially as they seemed to be worried, but it was also desirable to be resolute. If they should decide—as appeared likely—to consult the doctor, Doctor Howells, and have Paul inspected, his heart listened to through a kind of dictaphone, his lungs, his stomach—well, that was all right. He would go through with it. He would give them answer for question, too—perhaps such answers as they hadn't expected? No. That would never do. For the secret world must, at all cost, be preserved.

The bird-house in the apple-tree was empty—it was the wrong time of year for wrens. The little round black door had lost its pleasure. The wrens were enjoying other houses, other nests, remoter trees. But this too was a notion which he only vaguely and grazingly entertained—as if, for the moment, he merely touched an edge of it; there was something further on, which was already assuming a sharper importance; something which already teased at the corners of his eyes, teasing also at the corner of his mind. It was funny to think that he so wanted this, so awaited it—and yet found himself enjoying this momentary dalliance with the bird-house, as if for a quite deliberate postponement and enhancement of the approaching pleasure. He was aware of his delay, of his smiling and detached and now almost uncomprehending gaze at the little bird-house; he knew what he was going to look at next: it was his own little cobbled hill-street, his own house, the little river at the bottom of the hill, the grocer's shop with the cardboard man in the window—and now, thinking of all this, he turned his head, still smiling, and looking quickly right and left through the snow-laden sunlight.

And the mist of snow, as he had foreseen, was still on it—a ghost of snow falling in the bright sunlight, softly and steadily floating and turning and pausing, soundlessly meeting the snow that covered, as with a transparent mirage, the bare bright cobbles. He loved it—he stood still and loved it. Its beauty was paralyzing—beyond all words, all experience, all dream. No fairy-story he had ever read could be compared with it—none had ever given him this extraordinary combination of ethereal loveliness with a something else, unnameable, which was just faintly and deliciously terrifying. What was this thing? As he thought of it, he looked upward toward his own bedroom window, which was open—and it was as if he looked straight into the room and saw himself lying half awake in his bed. There he was—at this very instant he was still perhaps actually there—more truly there than standing here at the edge of the cobbled hill-street, with one hand lifted to shade his eyes against the snow-sun. Had he indeed ever left his room, in all this time? since that very first morning? Was the whole progress still being enacted there, was it still the same morning, and himself not yet wholly awake? And even now, had the postman not yet come round the corner? . . .

This idea amused him, and automatically, as he thought of it, he turned his head and looked toward the top of the hill. There was, of course, nothing there—nothing and no one. The street was empty and quiet. And all the more because of its emptiness it occurred to him to count the houses—a thing which, oddly enough, he hadn't before thought of doing. Of course, he had known there weren't many—many, that is, on his own side of the street, which were the ones that figured in the postman's progress—but nevertheless it came to him as something of a shock to find that there were precisely *six*, above his own house—his own house was the seventh.

Six!

Astonished, he looked at his own house—looked at the door, on which was the number thirteen—and then realized that the whole thing was exactly and logically and absurdly what he ought to have known. Just the same, the realization gave him abruptly, and even a little frighteningly, a sense of hurry. He was being hurried—he was being rushed. For—he knit his brows—he couldn't be mistaken—it was just above the *seventh* house, his *own* house, that the postman had first been audible this very morning. But in that case—in that case—did it mean that tomorrow he would hear nothing? The knock he had heard must have been the knock of their own door. Did it mean—

and this was an idea which gave him a really extraordinary feeling of surprise—that he would never hear the postman again?—that tomorrow morning the postman would already have passed the house, in a snow by then so deep as to render his footsteps completely inaudible? That he would have made his approach down the snow-filled street so soundless, so secretly, that he, Paul Hasleman, there lying in bed, would not have waked in time, or, waking, would have heard nothing?

But how could that be? unless even the knocker should be muffled in the snow—frozen tight, perhaps? . . . But in that case—

A vague feeling of disappointment came over him; a vague sadness, as if he felt himself deprived of something which he had long looked forward to, something much prized. After all this, all this beautiful progress, the slow delicious advance of the postman through the silent and secret snow, the knock creeping closer each day, and the footsteps nearer, the audible compass of the world thus daily narrowed, narrowed, narrowed, as the snow soothingly and beautifully encroached and deepened, after all this, was he to be defrauded of the one thing he had so wanted—to be able to count, as it were, the last two or three solemn footsteps, as they finally approached his own door? Was it all going to happen, at the end, so suddenly? or indeed, had it already happened? with no slow and subtle gradations of menace, in which he could luxuriate?

He gazed upward again, toward his own window which flashed in the sun: and this time almost with a feeling that it would be better if he *were* still in bed, in that room; for in that case this must still be the first morning, and there would be six more mornings to come—or, for that matter, seven or eight or nine—how could he be sure?—or even more.

III

After supper, the inquisition began. He stood before the doctor, under the lamp, and submitted silently to the usual thumpings and tappings.

"Now will you please say 'Ah!'?"

"Ah!"

"Now again please, if you don't mind."

"Ah."

"Say it slowly, and hold it if you can—"

"Ah-h-h-h-h-h—"

"Good."

How silly all this was. As if it had anything to do with his throat! Or his heart or lungs!

Relaxing his mouth, of which the corners, after all this absurd stretching, felt uncomfortable, he avoided the doctor's eyes, and stared towards the fireplace, past his mother's feet (in gray slippers) which projected from the green chair, and his father's feet (in brown slippers) which stood neatly side by side on the hearth rug.

'Hm. There is certainly nothing wrong there . . ."

He felt the doctor's eyes fixed upon him, and, as if merely to be polite, returned the look, but with a feeling of justifiable evasiveness.

"Now, young man, tell me,—do you feel all right?"

"Yes, sir, quite all right."

"No headaches? no dizziness?"

"No, I don't think so."

"Let me see. Let's get a book, if you don't mind—yes, thank you, that will do splendidly—and now, Paul, if you'll just read it, holding it as you would normally hold it—"

He took the book and read:

"And another praise have I to tell for this the city our mother, the gift of a great god, a glory of the land most high; the might of horses, the might of young horses, the might of the sea. . . . For thou, son of Cronus, our lord Poseidon, hast throned herein this pride, since in these roads first thou didst show forth the curb that cures the rage of steeds. And the shapely oar, apt to men's hands, hath a wondrous speed on the brine, following the hundred-footed Nereids. . . . O land that art praised above all lands, now is it for thee to make those bright praises seen in deeds."

He stopped, tentatively, and lowered the heavy book.

"No—as I thought—there is certainly no superficial sign of eye-strain."

Silence thronged the room, and he was aware of the focused scrutiny of the three people who confronted him . . .

"We could have his eyes examined—but I believe it is something else."

"What could it be?" This was his father's voice.

"It's only this curious absent-minded—" This was his mother's voice.

In the presence of the doctor, they both seemed irritatingly apologetic.

"I believe it is something else. Now Paul—I would like very much to ask you a question or two. You will answer them, won't you—you know I'm an old, old friend of yours, eh? That's right! . . ."

His back was thumped twice by the doctor's fat fist,—then the doctor was grinning at him with false amiability, while with one finger-nail he was scratching the top button of his waistcoat. Beyond the doctor's shoulder was the fire, the fingers of flame making light prestidigitation against the sooty fireback, the soft sound of their random flutter the only sound.

"I would like to know—is there anything that worries you?"

The doctor was again smiling, his eyelids low against the little black pupils, in each of which was a tiny white bead of light. Why answer him? why answer him at all? "At whatever pain to others"—but it was all a nuisance, this necessity for resistance, this necessity for attention: it was as if one had been stood up on a brilliantly lighted stage, under a great round blaze of spotlight; as if one were merely a trained seal, or a performing dog, or a fish, dipped out of an aquarium and held up by the tail. It would serve them right if he were merely to bark or growl. And meanwhile, to miss these last few precious hours, these hours of which every minute was more beautiful than the last, more menacing—? He still looked, as if from a great distance, at the beads of light in the doctor's eyes, at the fixed false smile, and then, beyond, once more at his mother's slippers, his father's slippers, the soft flutter of the fire. Even here, even amongst these hostile presences, and in this arranged light, he could see the snow, he could hear it—it was in the corners of the room, where the shadow was deepest, under the sofa, behind the half-opened door which led to the dining room. It was gentler here, softer, its seethe the quietest of whispers, as if, in deference to a drawing room, it had quite deliberately put on its "manners"; it kept itself out of sight, obliterated itself, but distinctly with an air of saying, "Ah, but just wait! Wait till we are alone together! Then I will begin to tell you something new! Something white! something cold! something sleepy! something of cease, and peace, and the long bright curve of space! Tell them to go away. Banish them. Refuse to speak. Leave them, go upstairs to your room, turn out the light and get into bed—I will go with you, I will be waiting for you, I will tell you a better story than Little Kay of the Skates, or The Snow Ghost—I will surround your bed, I will close the windows, pile a deep drift against the door, so that none will ever again be able to enter. Speak to them! . . ." It seemed as if the little hissing voice came from a slow white spiral of falling flakes in the corner by the front window—but he could not be sure. He felt himself smiling, then, and said to the doctor, but without looking at him, looking beyond him still—

"Oh, no, I think not—"

"But are you sure, my boy?"

His father's voice came softly and coldly then—the familiar voice of silken warning. . . .

"You needn't answer at once, Paul—remember we're trying to help you—think it over and be quite sure, won't you?"

He felt himself smiling again, at the notion of being quite sure. What a joke! As if he weren't so sure that reassurance was no longer necessary, and all this cross-examination a ridiculous farce, a grotesque parody! What could they know about it? These gross intelligences, these humdrum minds so bound to the usual, the ordinary? Impossible to tell them about it! Why, even now, even now, with the proof so abundant, so formidable, so imminent, so appallingly present here in this very room, could they believe it?—could even his mother believe it? No—it was only too plain that if anything were said about it, the merest hint given, they would be incredulous—they would laugh—they would say "Absurd!"—think things about him which weren't true. . . .

"Why no, I'm not worried—why should I be?"

He looked then straight at the doctor's low-lidded eyes, looked from one of them to the other, from one bead of light to the other, and gave a little laugh.

The doctor seemed to be disconcerted by this. He drew back in his chair, resting a fat white hand on either knee. The smile faded slowly from his face.

"Well, Paul!" he said, and paused gravely, "I'm afraid you don't take this quite seriously enough. I think you perhaps don't quite realize—don't quite realize—" He took a deep quick breath, and turned, as if helplessly, at a loss for words, to the others. But Mother and Father were both silent—no help was forthcoming.

"You must surely know, be aware, that you have not been quite yourself, of late? don't you know that? . . ."

It was amusing to watch the doctor's renewed attempt at a smile, a queer disorganized look, as of confidential embarrassment.

"I feel all right, sir," he said, and again gave the little laugh.

"And we're trying to help you." The doctor's tone sharpened.

"Yes sir, I know. But why? I'm all right. I'm just *thinking*, that's all."

His mother made a quick movement forward, resting a hand on the back of the doctor's chair.

"Thinking?" she said. "But my dear, about what?"

This was a direct challenge—and would have to be directly met. But before he met it, he looked again into the corner by the door, as if for reassurance. He smiled again at what he saw, at what he heard. The little spiral was still there, still softly whirling, like the ghost of a white kitten chasing the ghost of a white tail, and making as it did so the faintest of whispers. It was all right! If only he could remain firm, everything was going to be all right.

"Oh, about anything, about nothing,—*you* know the way you do!"

"You mean—day-dreaming?"

"Oh, no—thinking!"

"But thinking about *what*?"

"Anything."

He laughed a third time—but this time, happening to glance upward towards his mother's face, he was appalled at the effect his laughter seemed to have upon her. Her mouth had opened in an expression of horror. . . . This was too bad! Unfortunate! He had known it would cause pain, of course—but he hadn't expected it to be quite so bad as this. Perhaps—perhaps if he just gave them a tiny gleaming hint—?

"About the snow," he said.

"What on earth!" This was his father's voice. The brown slippers came a step nearer on the hearth-rug.

"But, my dear, what do you mean!" This was his mother's voice.

The doctor merely stared.

"Just *snow,* that's all. I like to think about it."

"Tell us about it, my boy."

"But that's all it is. There's nothing to tell. *You* know what snow is?"

This he said almost angrily, for he felt that they were trying to corner him. He turned sideways so as no longer to face the doctor, and the better to see the inch of blackness between the window-sill and the lowered curtain,—the cold inch of beckoning and delicious night. At once he felt better, more assured.

"Mother—can I go to bed, now, please? I've got a headache."

"But I thought you said—"

"It's just come. It's all these questions—! Can I, Mother?"

"You can go as soon as the doctor has finished."

"Don't you think this thing ought to be gone into thoroughly, and *now*?" This was Father's voice. The brown slippers again came a step nearer, the voice was the well-known "punishment" voice, resonant and cruel.

"Oh, what's the use, Norman—"

Quite suddenly, everyone was silent. And without precisely facing them, nevertheless he was aware that all three of them were watching him with an extraordinary intensity—staring hard at him—as if he had done something monstrous, or was himself some kind of monster. He could hear the soft irregular flutter of the flames; the cluck-click-cluck-click of the clock; far and faint, two sudden spurts of laughter from the kitchen, as quickly cut off as begun; a murmur of water in the pipes; and then, the silence seemed to deepen, to spread out, to become world-long and world-wide, to become timeless and shapeless, and to center inevitably and rightly, with a slow and sleepy but enormous concentration of all power, on the beginning of a new sound. What this new sound was going to be, he knew perfectly well. It might begin with a hiss, but it would end with a roar—there was no time to lose—he must escape. It mustn't happen here—

Without another word, he turned and ran up the stairs.

IV

Not a moment too soon. The darkness was coming in long white waves. A prolonged sibilance filled the night—a great seamless seethe of wild influence went abruptly across it—a cold low humming shook the windows. He shut the door and flung off his clothes in the dark. The bare black floor was like a little raft tossed in waves of snow, almost overwhelmed, washed under whitely, up again, smothered in curled billows of feather. The snow was laughing: it spoke from all sides at once: it pressed closer to him as he ran and jumped exulting into his bed.

"Listen to us!" it said. "Listen! We have come to tell you the story we told you about. You remember? Lie down. Shut your eyes, now—you will no longer see much—in this white darkness who could see, or want to see? We will take the place of everything. . . . Listen—"

A beautiful varying dance of snow began at the front of the room, came forward and then retreated, flattened out toward the floor, then rose fountain-like to the ceiling, swayed, recruited itself from a new stream of flakes which poured laughing in through the humming window, advanced again, lifted long white arms. It said peace, it said remoteness, it said cold—it said—

But then a gash of horrible light fell brutally across the room from the opening door—the snow drew back hissing—something alien had come into the room—something hostile. This thing rushed at him, clutched at him, shook him—and he was not merely horrified, he was filled with such a loathing as he had never known. What was this? this cruel disturbance? this act of anger and hate? It was as if he had to reach up a hand toward another world for any understanding of it,—an effort of which he was only barely capable. But of that other world he still remembered just enough to know the exorcising words. They tore themselves from his other life suddenly—

"Mother! Mother! Go away! I hate you!"

And with that effort, everything was solved, everything became all right: the seamless hiss advanced once more, the long white wavering lines rose and fell like enormous whispering sea-waves, the whisper becoming louder, the laughter more numerous.

"Listen!" it said. "We'll tell you the last, the most beautiful and secret story—shut your eyes—it is a very small story—a story that gets smaller and smaller—it comes inward instead of opening like a flower—it is a flower becoming a seed—a little cold seed—do you hear? we are leaning closer to you—"

The hiss was now becoming a roar—the whole world was a vast moving screen of snow—but even now it said peace, it said remoteness, it said cold, it said sleep.

ANN BEATTIE

Sunshine and Shadow

THE WOODS JAKE and Laura Ann were walking in were a few miles from his aunt's house, in a remote corner of Pennsylvania. His aunt was in Key Biscayne for the winter. The night before, they had trained the car headlights on the stump where she kept a jar with the house key hidden inside. Leaving New York had been a sudden whim; all day he had been thinking about the farm, and when he had mentioned it late at night to Laura Ann she had sprung out of bed and begun dressing, half seriously, half mocking. This was a just punishment for so much fretfulness. He had already complained that he wanted a garage that didn't cheat him. That he wished the damned cleaner would smile less and lose his clothes less often. And snow falling on a Friday night—what was the point, when alternate-side-of-the-street parking couldn't be suspended?

"Come on," she had said. "We act like old people. Let's go to Pennsylvania. It'll be beautiful in the morning with the sun on the snow." It was as predictable as her amazed smile: when she took up things he had halfheartedly instigated, he would then go along with them, gradually convincing himself that he was doing her a favor. He found himself standing as she pulled her baggy jeans over the thermal long johns she slept in and searched through the sweaters in their closet. She took out the blue turtleneck. Then she stood in front of the mirror, parting her hair, sticking in a shiny, star-shaped clip to keep it out of her face. The first time he had brought her to his aunt's house, ten years before, their last spring vacation from college, she had been such a city slicker that walking through the woods she had asked what the red and aqua tubes were that she saw scattered in the bushes, not knowing they were shotgun shells.

In the morning they walked through the woods, jeans tucked into their rubber fishing boots. In front of them, heaped in the junkyard they had cut through as a shortcut, were broken pieces of a carrousel: saddles without stirrups and huge horse heads with frosty eyes and broken teeth. As she raised the camera to focus, he noticed her diamond wedding band sparkling. The brim of her hat was pulled low; it was a real John Wesley Hardin hat, a favorite left over from the sixties.

"Bracket it," he said.

She moved the camera away from her eye. "Did I ever tell you about bracketing?" she said.

"I read it in a book, I suppose."

She inched up on the horse heads, as if they might move. She crouched in the snow. It was quiet; the click disturbed the woods like a shot.

He loved her amazed smile—the way he could announce some unexpected piece of information and arouse her curiosity. She couldn't believe that he would know a thing like that—retain a term that didn't even apply to something he *did*. . . . When he met her she had been the eager, bright student of literature, whose professor embarrassed her when she gave an interpretation of a book in a class and he asked whether she would also climb a ladder by using the spaces between rungs.

They had brought water with them from the city, because his aunt had turned off the water before she left for the winter. It had been a long, tiring day. He drank a glass of cold water, savoring it like brandy, and he stood looking out the living-room window, into the back field. It was Saturday night and she was reading old magazines, pacing around the house, sitting close to the Franklin stove. She walked away from him at the window, and he was ten feet or so away from her, but he felt the distance, that something missing he couldn't put his finger on. He decided it was fatigue: they were both tired from walking so far in the snow. They were listening to one of his aunt's collection of great old records that his aunt did not realize were great. A scratchy "Pennies From Heaven" was playing, and in his mind he played saxophone in the background, his fingers tapping out the notes on the cold windowpane. When he moved his head nose-close to the window he could see the cement driveway, full of cracks and gullies, the part of the driveway where his mother had run a hose into the car and killed herself with carbon monoxide. The spring before, he had noticed that the driveway was now so overgrown that a wild rosebush had sent up dozens of runners.

He saw Laura Ann's reflection in the window, and though he couldn't see the details of her face, he knew them so well that they were as vivid imagined as seen: those large doe eyes, full of wonder. Now there was nothing to indicate that she didn't forgive him for his having had an affair with her friend except those eyes, sad even above a smile. He pressed his forehead to the window and looked at the black, star-covered sky. When he was a child, a friend had told him that the stars were sky stones. It probably explained a lot that he had never gotten any misinformation about sex—only about the stars.

The quilt on top of the blanket was called Sunshine and Shadow. It had been on this bed as long as he could remember, but it was only lately, in the city, when quilts became fashionable, that he had found out the name of the pattern. It was a quilt begun by his grandmother and finished by his mother and his aunt. He had stared at it when he was a child: squares of differing sizes, alternately light and dark—a diamond pattern radiating from the smallest gray square in the center. He had hypnotized himself into dizziness studying the pattern and come to no conclusions, the way he had stared at inanimate objects years ago when he was tripping. Whatever revelations he had were long gone; he couldn't paraphrase them, so he didn't know how to talk about them. He could remember things he had thought about, but he couldn't remember his conclusions. Or, if he could, they no longer seemed to have any context.

Laura Ann was lying next to him in bed, breathing quietly, deep in sleep. The light was coming up. The star-shaped barrette had almost worked its way loose; her long, curly hair was spread around her on the pillow like a Vargas girl's in *Playboy*, but instead of being picture-pretty, her face was puffy from sleep. He kissed the tip of a curl and wondered if he loved her. On a trip to Pennsylvania a year ago, they had built a snowman, and while he chipped away, trying to make it anatomically correct below its snow belly, she had worked equally hard to pile on breasts. Somewhere in the woods, behind the junkyard, until it melted, there had been a hermaphroditic snowman.

He put his cheek against her hair, trying to think about all the strange, funny times he had had with Laura Ann, trying to forget his ex-lover. Awake, Laura Ann was often as quiet about things as she was now, in sleep, but not deliberately secretive. She had begun a course in photography during her lunch hour. He had seen the little gray plastic film container on a table and asked about it. She was going to study photography, she had said simply. Just another thing she had considered, and acted on, without ever mentioning it. His anger had been childish, saying that photography made everything into potential art, that there were easy shots sure to succeed. "You're not the first one to come up with that," she had said.

What she had not said was that knowing odd facts could be an equally cheap trick: why Bill Monroe fired Richard Greene; who made the first chocolate-chip cookie; the way to get dried wax off of candlesticks. He had always remembered odd facts, trying to outshine his brother, Derek, who operated in a fog and always came out in the clear. He rolled over and remembered advice from his shrink: Don't fall asleep thinking bad thoughts about yourself. He remembered apologizing to Laura Ann for condemning photography by showing an interest in her recent prints, and the irregular black borders around them. "You chisel out the negative holder," she had said, holding her first finger an inch above the thumb so that he could see the imaginary negative holder. "You print it exactly the way it was shot. Then there's no way you can cheat."

Before he had gone to California the previous spring, he had tried to clear his head about what he wanted. When Derek called from Los Angeles and threw around phrases like "in the money" or "out of the money," discussing closing transactions and sure ways to beat the system, all he could think of was that silliness in *Bonnie and Clyde* when Bonnie and Clyde go to the movies and watch Ginger Rogers and the chorus singing "We're in the Money" in *Gold Diggers of 1933*. Now his brother was in California with a teenage girlfriend, driving a silver Porsche and practically living on undercooked pasta. He visited him and was amazed at his brother's life—that Derek and Liz sat on the sofa and bent over a small, square pin with a picture of Elvis Costello on it and snorted coke off of Elvis's face the way millions of middle-class people sat down for an evening cocktail.

He came back to New York with huaraches from Olvera Street and ten pints of the best-tasting strawberries he had ever eaten. He remembered standing on the other side of the X-ray machine at the airport, watching the fuzzy stacks of strawberries pass through. Thinking about The Situation, he had drunk too much wine and smoked too much with his brother, and he had fixated on one little aspect of Mary or Laura Ann: Laura Ann's hair versus Mary's wide-set eyes. Taking an overview? Laura Ann, naked, long and smooth-skinned; Mary, her sexy adolescent thinness, her flat breasts. Mary had given him an ultimatum: Decide or forget it. Laura Ann, who didn't know he was having an affair then, had given him a soft leather traveling bag.

When he returned that summer, the city looked grim. Few places to see the sky, buildings crowding each other. He looked out the window of the cab and saw a sharp-nosed gargoyle above the door of a building; he saw bums curled with their backs to buildings, sleeping expressionlessly, as if they had just shared some intimacy with the sidewalk. He thought about calling Mary, but didn't. She had an answering machine, and he didn't want to risk hearing Mary's voice that was not Mary's voice.

His last thought before he went to sleep now made him smile: as he had passed a man walking his golden retriever, the man had said to the dog, "I don't believe you, Morty. You pissed on the one sign of life in that treebox."

Laura Ann knew Mary. Those tearful late-night phone calls she had made months ago weren't to some mystery lover, as he had at first suspected, but to Mary. And then the phone calls stopped and she began to be nice to him again. "You pretend to be so casual," she said. "It's a good cover-up, but I know what's underneath. I know how you spend hours with your calculator meticulously going over your bank statement. I know that you'll even read a bad book to the end. I know how you make love."

The last time he saw Mary, she was sitting at a table inside the Empire Diner when he was walking by. She didn't see him. On his way back from his cash machine, he walked into the Empire. They were squirting Windex on the table where Mary and her friends had been. He went to the phone at the end of the counter and said what he'd wanted to say for a long time. "If I love anybody, I love you, Laura Ann. Admit that you've never forgiven me. I don't want to come back and walk into that strain again."

"You wouldn't come back if you didn't want to," she said.

The woman at the piano bobbed her shoulders as she played "Fascinatin' Rhythm." A man in a gorilla suit walked in and began talking to one of the waiters, gesturing with his paw. A chauffeur, arms crossed, waited outside by a long white Cadillac.

"You love me," she said. Then, in a near whisper: "The way I cheat and chip dried food off the plates when I'm setting the table. The way I rub your shoulders. My perfume."

"Your voice," he said.

"I'm exhausted." She sighed. "Don't take it personally if I've gone to sleep when you come home."

The counterman was talking in a huddle with a waitress. "I *told* him that we don't take reservations. 'You show up, that's when we take your name,' I said to him. 'You come back with four other people, we'll give you the back table.' I was just doing my job."

Jake searched through his wallet and took out a business card. He dialed another number.

"This is Doctor Garfield," Garfield's voice said. "I'm not available at this time. Please leave your message at the tone, or call me at my home in an emergency." Garfield gave his home number, and there was a beep. Listening to the silence that followed, Jake thought: Alexander Graham Bell would never have believed that it would come to this.

Walking back to the apartment, he thought about what he had always been sure he loved: the fields in Pennsylvania, acres of them, stretching away from his aunt's farm, so flat and green. And the porch swing, missing the middle board, that he sat on to watch sunsets. The tangled mounds of peas that he tied around thick stakes in the garden, trying to keep them growing upward. The summer his uncle ripped the honeysuckle off the porch and poured poison on the ground—the stub where the vine had begun. The porch, where the honeysuckle used to crisscross the screen, the floor transformed into complicated patterns of lace when the sunlight shone through the leaves. And the time he begged to be dressed in the neighbor's bee-keeping suit, the big spaceman helmet with netting over the front covering his head and face, and then the unexpected, horrible dread he had felt as bees swarmed around him and crawled on the suit. He had stayed rooted to the spot, paying no attention to the neighbor, who shouted from his tractor in the not-too-far distance that it was all right—there wasn't any way he could hurt the bees. It was a million times worse than being zipped into the stiff yellow rain slicker and sent off to school. In the field, he had been petrified. Finally, the neighbor's voice had reached him and he knew he had to move, and he *did* move, trying hopelessly to shrug away the bees. Then he managed to turn his back on the hives, and eventually, as he walked, they disappeared behind him. He was at that point of life where he realized he wasn't supposed to cry anymore, but he was on the verge of tears when he sat eating toast in the neighbor's kitchen, toast soggy with butter and spread with thick, dark honey, hardly able to swallow because his throat was so constricted. Later, watching television, looking at the way astronauts floated toward each other to connect in space, he would think about the way he must have looked. There had been one acid trip, one of the last, when he had felt that same heavy disembodiment—that he was grounded, and he had to move, but it was impossible, and if he had taken off, he would have drifted not far from the ground, at a peculiar tilt, like the old man walking through air in the Chagall painting. This realization—and this present life of confusion—was a long way from his thoughts, when he had rocked in a swing missing a board, on the front porch of a house in Pennsylvania.

She was, as she had said she would be, in bed. She didn't open her eyes, although he thought that she had heard him walk in. If she had, this particular night, those steady green eyes might have had the power Kryptonite had on Superman. He was always struggling to think that he didn't need her. That love didn't mean need. That crazy conflict acid produced, of having your senses touched sharply, yet knowing you were powerless to respond. Even before acid, that sudden, strength-sucking anxiety—the fear, standing in front of the big white boxes of bees swarming in and out.

What strength it took just to lie there, eyelids lightly closed, nothing to suggest that the way she looked, curled on the bed, was a position difficult to maintain. He knew that if he asked her in the morning, she would look at him with exasperation and say that she had been asleep.

He sat at the foot of the bed. She had not pulled the shade. The streetlight, streaming light through the curtains, blotched her body—luminous shapes that were almost a triangle, almost a circle. If she had opened her eyes and seen him sitting there, smiling fondly, whatever he told her about being unsure of whether they should stay together would be discounted. Her version of it would be that he thought about her so much and stared so often because he was in love. It would be like the story the neighbor told his aunt and uncle all summer: how he had loved those bees, how he had been mesmerized by them. And how, being a gentle boy, he had not wanted to make a move if it might possibly hurt them.

JOHN CHEEVER

The Enormous Radio

JIM AND IRENE Westcott were the kind of people who seem to strike that satisfactory average of income, endeavor, and respectability that is reached by the statistical reports in college alumni bulletins. They were the parents of two young children, they had been married nine years, they lived on the twelfth floor of an apartment house near Sutton Place, they went to the theatre on an average of 10.3 times a year, and they hoped someday to live in Westchester. Irene Westcott was a pleasant, rather plain girl with soft brown hair and a wide, fine forehead upon which nothing at all had been written, and in the cold weather she wore a coat of fitch skins dyed to resemble mink. You could not say that Jim Westcott looked younger than he was, but you could at least say of him that he seemed to feel younger. He wore his graying hair cut very short, he dressed in the kind of clothes his class had worn at Andover, and his manner was earnest, vehement, and intentionally naïve. The Westcotts differed from their friends, their classmates, and their neighbors only in an interest they shared in serious music. They went to a great many concerts—although they seldom mentioned this to anyone—and they spent a good deal of time listening to music on the radio.

Their radio was an old instrument, sensitive, unpredictable, and beyond repair. Neither of them understood the mechanics of radio—or of any of the other appliances that surrounded them—and when the instrument faltered, Jim would strike the side of the cabinet with his hand. This sometimes helped. One Sunday afternoon, in the middle of a Schubert quartet, the music faded away altogether. Jim struck the cabinet repeatedly, but there was no response; the Schubert was lost to them forever. He promised to buy Irene a new radio, and on Monday when he came home from work he told her that he had got one. He refused to describe it, and said it would be a surprise for her when it came.

The radio was delivered at the kitchen door the following afternoon, and with the assistance of her maid and the handyman Irene uncrated it and brought it into the living room. She was struck at once with the physical ugliness of the large gumwood cabinet. Irene was proud of her living room, she had chosen its furnishings and colors as carefully as she chose her clothes, and now it seemed to her that the new radio stood among her intimate possessions like an aggressive intruder. She was confounded by the number of dials and switches on the instrument panel, and she studied them thoroughly before she put the plug into a wall socket and turned the radio on. The dials flooded with a malevolent green light, and in the distance she heard the music of a piano quintet. The quintet was in the distance for only an instant; it bore down upon her with a speed greater than light and filled the apartment with the noise of music amplified so mightily that it knocked a china ornament from a table to the floor. She rushed to the instrument and reduced the volume. The violent forces that were snared in the ugly gumwood cabinet made her uneasy. Her children came home from school then, and she took them to the Park. It was not until later in the afternoon that she was able to return to the radio.

The maid had given the children their suppers and was supervising their baths when Irene turned on the radio, reduced the volume, and sat down to listen to a Mozart quintet that she knew and enjoyed. The music came through clearly. The new instrument had a much purer tone, she thought, than the old one. She decided that tone was most important and that she could conceal the cabinet behind a sofa. But as soon as she had made her peace with the radio, the interference began. A crackling sound like the noise of a burning powder fuse began to accompany the singing of the strings. Beyond the music, there was a rustling that reminded Irene unpleasantly of the sea, and as the quintet progressed, these noises were joined by many others. She tried all the dials and switches but nothing dimmed the interference, and she sat down, disappointed and bewildered, and tried to trace the flight of the melody. The elevator shaft in her building ran beside the living-room wall, and it was the noise of the elevator that gave her a clue to the character of the static. The rattling of the elevator cables and the opening and closing of the elevator doors were reproduced in her loudspeaker, and, realizing that the radio was sensitive to electrical currents of all sorts, she began to discern through the Mozart the ringing of telephone bells, the dialing of phones, and the lamentation of a vacuum cleaner. By listening more carefully, she was able to distinguish doorbells, elevator bells, electric razors, and Waring mixers, whose sounds had been picked up from the apartments that surrounded hers and transmitted through her loudspeaker. The powerful and ugly instrument, with its mistaken sensitivity to discord, was more than she could hope to master, so she turned the thing off and went into the nursery to see her children.

When Jim Westcott came home that night, he went to the radio confidently and worked the controls. He had the same sort of experience Irene had had. A man was speaking on the station Jim had chosen, and his voice swung instantly from the distance into a force so powerful that it shook the apartment. Jim turned the volume control and reduced the voice. Then, a minute or two later, the interference began. The ringing of telephones and doorbells set in, joined by the rasp of the elevator doors and the whir of cooking appliances. The character of the noise had changed since Irene had tried the radio earlier; the last of the electric razors were being unplugged, the vacuum cleaners had all been returned to their closets, and the static reflected that change in pace that overtakes the city after the sun goes down. He fiddled with the knobs but couldn't get rid of the noises, so he turned the radio off and told Irene that in the morning he'd call the people who had sold it to him and give them hell.

The following afternoon, when Irene returned to the apartment from a luncheon date, the maid told her that a man had come and fixed the radio. Irene went into the living room before she took off her hat or her furs and tried the instrument. From the loudspeaker came a recording of the "Missouri Waltz." It reminded her of the thin, scratchy music from an old-fashioned phonograph that she sometimes heard across the lake where she spent her summers. She waited until the waltz had finished, expecting an explanation of the recording, but there was none. The music was followed by silence, and then the plaintive and scratchy record was repeated. She turned the dial and got a satisfactory burst of Caucasian music—the thump of bare feet in the dust and the rattle of coin jewelry—but in the background she could hear the ringing of bells and a confusion of voices. Her children came home from school then, and she turned off the radio and went to the nursery.

When Jim came home that night, he was tired, and he took a bath and changed his clothes. Then he joined Irene in the living room. He had just turned on the radio when the maid announced dinner, so he left it on, and he and Irene went to the table.

Jim was too tired to make even a pretense of sociability, and there was nothing about the dinner to hold Irene's interest, so her attention wandered from the food to the deposits of silver polish on the candlesticks and from there to the music in the other room. She listened for a few minutes to a Chopin prelude and then was surprised to hear a man's voice break in. "For Christ's sake, Kathy," he said, "do you always have to play the piano when I get home?" The music stopped abruptly. "It's the only chance I have," a woman said. "I'm at the office all day." "So am I," the man said. He added something obscene about an upright piano, and slammed a door. The passionate and melancholy music began again.

"Did you hear that?" Irene asked.

"What?" Jim was eating his dessert.

"The radio. A man said something while the music was still going on—something dirty."

"It's probably a play."

"I don't think it *is* a play," Irene said.

They left the table and took their coffee into the living room. Irene asked Jim to try another station. He turned the knob. "Have you seen my garters?" a man asked. "Button me up," a woman said. "Have you seen my garters?" the man said again. "Just button me up and I'll find your garters," the woman said. Jim shifted to another station. "I wish you wouldn't leave apple cores in the ashtrays," a man said. "I hate the smell."

"This is strange," Jim said.

"Isn't it?" Irene said.

Jim turned the knob again. " 'On the coast of Coromandel where the early pumpkins blow,' " a woman with a pronounced English accent said, " 'in the middle of the woods lived the Yonghy-Bonghy-Bò. Two old chairs, and half a candle, one old jug without a handle . . .' "

"My God!" Irene cried. "That's the Sweeneys' nurse."

" 'These were all his worldly goods,' " the British voice continued.

"Turn that thing off," Irene said. "Maybe they can hear *us.*" Jim switched the radio off. "That was Miss Armstrong, the Sweeneys' nurse," Irene said. "She must be reading to the little girl. They live in 17-B. I've talked with Miss Armstrong in the Park. I know her voice very well. We must be getting other people's apartments."

"That's impossible," Jim said.

"Well, that was the Sweeneys' nurse," Irene said hotly. "I know her voice. I know it very well. I'm wondering if they can hear us."

Jim turned the switch. First from a distance and then nearer, nearer, as if borne on the wind, came the pure accents of the Sweeneys' nurse again: " *'Lady Jingly! Lady Jingly!'* " she said, " *'sitting where the pumpkins blow, will you come and be my wife?* said the Yonghy-Bonghy-Bò . . .' "

Jim went over to the radio and said "Hello" loudly into the speaker.

" *'I am tired of living singly,'* " the nurse went on, " *'on this coast so wild and shingly, I'm a-weary of my life; if you'll come and be my wife, quite serene would be my life . . .' "*

"I guess she can't hear us," Irene said. "Try something else."

Jim turned to another station, and the living room was filled with the uproar of a cocktail party that had overshot its mark. Someone was playing the piano and singing the "Whiffenpoof Song," and the voices that surrounded the piano were vehement and happy. "Eat some more sandwiches," a woman shrieked. There were screams of laughter and a dish of some sort crashed to the floor.

"Those must be the Fullers, in 11-E," Irene said. "I knew they were giving a party this afternoon. I saw her in the liquor store. Isn't this too divine? Try something else. See if you can get those people in 18-C."

The Westcotts overheard that evening a monologue on salmon fishing in Canada, a bridge game, running comments on home movies of what had apparently been a fortnight at Sea Island, and a bitter family quarrel about an overdraft at the bank. They turned off their radio at midnight and went to bed, weak with laughter. Sometime in the night, their son began to call for a glass of water and Irene got one and took it to his room. It was very early. All the lights in the neighborhood were extinguished, and from the boy's window she could see the empty street. She went into the living room and tried the radio. There was some faint coughing, a moan, and then a man spoke. "Are you all right, darling?" he asked. "Yes," a woman said wearily. "Yes, I'm all right, I guess," and then she added with great feeling, "But, you know, Charlie, I don't feel like myself any more. Sometimes there are about fifteen or twenty minutes in the week when I feel like myself. I don't like to go to another doctor, because the doctor's bills are so awful already, but I just don't feel like myself, Charlie. I just never feel like myself." They were not young, Irene thought. She guessed from the timbre of their voices that they were middle-aged. The restrained melancholy of the dialogue and the draft from the bedroom window made her shiver, and she went back to bed.

* * *

The following morning, Irene cooked breakfast for the family—the maid didn't come up from her room in the basement until ten—braided her daughter's hair, and waited at the door until her children and her husband had been carried away in the elevator. Then she went into the living room and tried the radio. "I don't want to go to school," a child screamed. "I hate school. I won't go to school. I hate school." "You will go to school," an enraged woman said. "We paid eight hundred dollars to get you into that school and you'll go if it kills you." The next number on the dial produced the worn record of the "Missouri Waltz." Irene shifted the control and invaded the privacy of several breakfast tables. She overheard demonstrations of indigestion, carnal love, abysmal vanity, faith, and despair. Irene's life was nearly as simple and sheltered as it appeared to be, and the forthright and sometimes brutal language that came from the loudspeaker that morning astonished and troubled her. She continued to listen until her maid came in. Then she turned off the radio quickly, since this insight, she realized, was a furtive one.

Irene had a luncheon date with a friend that day, and she left her apartment at a little after twelve. There were a number of women in the elevator when it stopped at her floor. She stared at their handsome and impassive faces, their furs, and the cloth flowers in their hats. Which one of them had been to Sea Island? she wondered. Which one had overdrawn her bank account? The elevator stopped at the tenth floor and a woman with a pair of Skye terriers joined them. Her hair was rigged high on her head and she wore a mink cape. She was humming the "Missouri Waltz."

Irene had two Martinis at lunch, and she looked searchingly at her friend and wondered what her secrets were. They had intended to go shopping after lunch, but Irene excused herself and went home. She told the maid that she was not to be disturbed; then she went into the living room, closed the doors, and switched on the radio. She heard, in the course of the afternoon, the halting conversation of a woman entertaining her aunt, the hysterical conclusion of a luncheon party, and a hostess briefing her maid about some cocktail guests. "Don't give the best Scotch to anyone who hasn't white hair," the hostess said. "See if you can get rid of that liver paste before you pass those hot things, and could you lend me five dollars? I want to tip the elevator man."

As the afternoon waned, the conversations increased in intensity. From where Irene sat, she could see the open sky above the East River. There were hundreds of clouds in the sky, as though the south wind had broken the winter into pieces and were blowing it north, and on her radio she could hear the arrival of cocktail guests and the return of children and businessmen from their schools and offices. "I found a good-sized diamond on the bathroom floor this morning," a woman said. "It must have fallen out of that bracelet Mrs. Dunston was wearing last night." "We'll sell it," a man said. "Take it down to the jeweler on Madison Avenue and sell it. Mrs. Dunston won't know the difference, and we could use a couple of hundred bucks . . ." " 'Oranges and lemons, say the bells of St. Clement's,' " the Sweeneys' nurse sang. " 'Halfpence and farthings, say the bells of St. Martin's. When will you pay me? say the bells at old Bailey . . .' " "It's not a hat," a woman cried, and at her back roared a cocktail party. "It's not a hat, it's a love affair. That's what Walter Florell said. He said it's not a hat, it's a love affair," and then, in a lower voice, the same woman added, "Talk to somebody, for Christ's sake, honey, talk to somebody. If she catches you standing here not talking to anybody, she'll take us off her invitation list, and I love these parties."

The Westcotts were going out for dinner that night, and when Jim came home, Irene was dressing. She seemed sad and vague, and he brought her a drink. They were dining with friends in the neighborhood, and they walked to where they were going. The sky was broad and filled with light. It was one of those splendid spring evenings that excite memory and desire, and the air that touched their hands and faces felt very soft. A Salvation Army band was on the corner playing "Jesus is Sweeter." Irene drew on her husband's arm and held him there for a minute, to hear the music. "They're really such nice people, aren't they?" she said. "They have such nice faces. Actually, they're so much nicer than a lot of the people we know." She took a bill from her purse and walked over and dropped it into the tambourine. There was in her face, when she returned to her husband, a look of radiant melancholy that he was not familiar with. And her conduct at the dinner party that night seemed strange to him, too. She interrupted her hostess rudely and stared at the people across the table from her with an intensity for which she would have punished her children.

It was still mild when they walked home from the party, and Irene looked up at the spring stars. " 'How far that little candle throws its beams,' " she exclaimed. " 'So shines a good deed in a naughty world.' " She waited that night until Jim had fallen asleep, and then went into the living room and turned on the radio.

Jim came home at about six the next night. Emma, the maid, let him in, and he had taken off his hat and was taking off his coat when Irene ran into the hall. Her face was shining with tears and her hair was disordered. "Go up to 16-C, Jim!" she screamed. "Don't take off your coat. Go up to 16-C. Mr. Osborn's beating his wife. They've been quarreling since four o'clock, and now he's hitting her. Go up there and stop him."

From the radio in the living room, Jim heard screams, obscenities, and thuds. "You know you don't have to listen to this sort of thing," he said. He strode into the living room and turned the switch. "It's indecent," he said. "It's like looking in windows. You know you don't have to listen to this sort of thing. You can turn it off."

"Oh, it's so horrible, it's so dreadful," Irene was sobbing. "I've been listening all day, and it's so depressing."

"Well, if it's so depressing, why do you listen to it? I bought this damned radio to give you some pleasure," he said. "I paid a great deal of money for it. I thought it might make you happy. I wanted to make you happy."

"Don't, don't, don't, don't quarrel with me," she moaned, and laid her head on his shoulder. "All the others have been quarreling all day. Everybody's been quarreling. They're all worried about money. Mrs. Hutchinson's mother is dying of cancer in Florida and they don't have enough money to send her to the Mayo Clinic. At least, Mr. Hutchinson says they don't have enough money. And some woman in this building is having an affair with the handyman—with that hideous handyman. It's too disgusting. And Mrs. Melville has heart trouble and Mr. Hendricks is going to lose his job in April and Mrs. Hendricks is horrid about the whole thing and that girl who plays the 'Missouri Waltz' is a whore, a common whore, and the elevator man has tuberculosis and Mr. Osborn has been beating Mrs. Osborn." She wailed, she trembled with grief and checked the stream of tears down her face with the heel of her palm.

"Well, why do you have to listen?" Jim asked again. "Why do you have to listen to this stuff if it makes you so miserable?"

"Oh, don't, don't, don't," she cried. "Life is too terrible, too sordid and awful. But we've never been like that, have we, darling? Have we? I mean, we've always been good and decent and loving to one another, haven't we? And we have two children, two beautiful children. Our lives aren't sordid, are they, darling? Are they?" She flung her arms around his neck and drew his face down to hers. "We're happy, aren't we, darling? We are happy, aren't we?"

"Of course we're happy," he said tiredly. He began to surrender his resentment. "Of course we're happy. I'll have that damned radio fixed or taken away tomorrow." He stroked her soft hair. "My poor girl," he said.

"You love me, don't you?" she asked. "And we're not hypercritical or worried about money or dishonest, are we?"

"No, darling," he said.

A man came in the morning and fixed the radio. Irene turned it on cautiously and was happy to hear a California-wine commercial and a recording of Beethoven's Ninth Symphony, including Schiller's "Ode to Joy." She kept the radio on all day and nothing untoward came from the speaker.

A Spanish suite was being played when Jim came home. "Is everything all right?" he asked. His face was pale, she thought. They had some cocktails and went in to dinner to the "Anvil Chorus" from *Il Trovatore*. This was followed by Debussy's "La Mer."

"I paid the bill for the radio today," Jim said. "It cost four hundred dollars. I hope you'll get some enjoyment out of it."

"Oh, I'm sure I will," Irene said.

"Four hundred dollars is a good deal more than I can afford," he went on. "I wanted to get something that you'd enjoy. It's the last extravagance we'll be able to indulge in this year. I see that you haven't paid your clothing bills yet. I saw them on your dressing table." He looked directly at her. "Why did you tell me you'd paid them? Why did you lie to me?"

"I just didn't want you to worry, Jim," she said. She drank some water. "I'll be able to pay my bills out of this month's allowance. There were the slipcovers last month, and that party."

"You've got to learn to handle the money I give you a little more intelligently, Irene," he said. "You've got to understand that we don't have as much money this year as we had last. I had a very sobering talk with Mitchell today. No one is buying anything. We're spending all our time promoting new issues, and you know how long that takes. I'm not getting any younger, you know. I'm thirty-seven. My hair will be gray next year. I haven't done as well as I'd hoped to do. And I don't suppose things will get any better."

"Yes, dear," she said.

"We've got to start cutting down," Jim said. "We've got to think of the children. To be perfectly frank with you, I worry about money a great deal. I'm not at all sure of the future. No one is. If anything should happen to me, there's the insurance, but that wouldn't go very far today. I've worked awfully hard to give you and the children a comfortable life," he said bitterly. "I don't like to see all my energies, all of my youth, wasted in fur coats and radios and slipcovers and—"

"Please, Jim," she said. "Please. They'll hear us."

"*Who'll hear us?* Emma can't hear us."

"The radio."

"Oh, I'm sick!" he shouted. "I'm sick to death of your apprehensiveness. The radio can't hear us. Nobody can hear us. And what if they can hear us? Who cares?"

Irene got up from the table and went into the living room.

Jim went to the door and shouted at her from there. "Why are you so Christly all of a sudden? What's turned you overnight into a convent girl? You stole your mother's jewelry before they probated her will. You never gave your sister a cent of that money that was intended for her—not even when she needed it. You made Grace Howland's life miserable, and where was all your piety and your virtue when you went to that abortionist? I'll never forget how cool you were. You packed your bag and went off to have that child murdered as if you were going to Nassau. If you'd had any reasons, if you'd had any good reasons—"

Irene stood for a minute before the hideous cabinet, disgraced and sickened, but she held her hand on the switch before she extinguished the music and the voices, hoping that the instrument might speak to her kindly, that she might hear the Sweeneys' nurse. Jim continued to shout at her from the door. The voice on the radio was suave and noncommittal. "An early-morning railroad disaster in Tokyo," the loudspeaker said, "killed twenty-nine people. A fire in a Catholic hospital near Buffalo for the care of blind children was extinguished early this morning by nuns. The temperature is forty-seven. The humidity is eighty-nine."

WILLIAM FAULKNER

Was

1

ISAAC MCCASLIN, 'UNCLE Ike,' past seventy and nearer eighty than he ever corroborated any more, a widower now and uncle to half a county and father to no one

this was not something participated in or even seen by himself, but by his elder cousin, McCaslin Edmonds, grandson of Isaac's father's sister and so descended by the distaff, yet notwithstanding the inheritor, and in his time the bequestor, of that which some had thought then and some still thought should have been Isaac's, since his was the name in which the title to the land had first been granted from the Indian patent and which some of the descendants of his father's slaves still bore in the land. But Isaac was not one of these:—a widower these twenty years, who in all his life had owned but one object more than he could wear and carry in his pockets and his hands at one time, and this was the narrow iron cot and the stained lean mattress which he used camping in the woods for deer and bear or for fishing or simply because he loved the woods; who owned no property and never desired to since the earth was no man's but all men's, as light and air and weather were; who lived still in the cheap frame bungalow in Jefferson which his wife's father gave them on their marriage and which his wife had willed to him at her death and which he had pretended to accept, acquiesce to, to humor her, ease her going but which was not his, will or not, chancery dying wishes mortmain possession or whatever, himself merely holding it for his wife's sister and her children who had lived in it with him since his wife's death, holding himself welcome to live in one room of it as he had during his wife's time or she during her time or the sister-in-law and her children during the rest of his and after

not something he had participated in or even remembered except from the hearing, the listening, come to him through and from his cousin McCaslin born in 1850 and sixteen years his senior and hence, his own father being near seventy when Isaac, an only child, was born, rather his brother than cousin and rather his father than either, out of the old time, the old days

2

When he and Uncle Buck ran back to the house from discovering that Tomey's Turl had run again, they heard Uncle Buddy cursing and bellowing in the kitchen, then the fox and the dogs came out of the kitchen and crossed the hall into the dogs' room and they heard them run through the dogs' room into his and Uncle Buck's room then they saw them cross the hall again into Uncle Buddy's room and heard them run through Uncle Buddy's room into the kitchen again and this time it sounded like the whole kitchen chimney had come down and Uncle Buddy bellowing like a steamboat blowing and this time the fox and the dogs and five or six sticks of firewood all came out of the kitchen together with Uncle Buddy in the middle of them hitting at everything in sight with another stick. It was a good race.

When he and Uncle Buck ran into their room to get Uncle Buck's necktie, the fox had treed behind the clock on the mantel. Uncle Buck got the necktie from the drawer and kicked the dogs off and lifted the fox down by the scruff of the neck and shoved it back into the crate under the bed and they went to the kitchen, where Uncle Buddy was picking the breakfast up out of the ashes and wiping it off with his apron. "What in damn's hell do you mean," he said, "turning that damn fox out with the dogs all loose in the house?"

"Damn the fox," Uncle Buck said. "Tomey's Turl has broke out again. Give me and Cass some breakfast quick. We might just barely catch him before he gets there."

Because they knew exactly where Tomey's Turl had gone, he went there every time he could slip off, which was about twice a year. He was heading for Mr Hubert Beauchamp's place just over the edge of the next county, that Mr Hubert's sister, Miss Sophonsiba (Mr Hubert was a bachelor too, like Uncle Buck and Uncle Buddy) was still trying to make people call Warwick after the place in England that she said Mr Hubert was probably the true earl of only he never even had enough pride, not to mention energy, to take the trouble to establish his just rights. Tomey's Turl would go there to hang around Mr Hubert's girl, Tennie, until somebody came and got him. They couldn't keep him at home by buying Tennie from Mr Hubert because Uncle Buck said he and Uncle Buddy had so many niggers already that they could hardly walk around on their own land for them, and they couldn't sell Tomey's Turl to Mr Hubert because Mr Hubert said he not only wouldn't buy Tomey's Turl, he wouldn't have that damn white half-McCaslin on his place even as a free gift, not even if Uncle Buck and Uncle Buddy were to pay board and keep for him. And if somebody didn't go and get Tomey's Turl right away, Mr Hubert would fetch him back himself, bringing Miss Sophonsiba, and they would stay for a week or longer, Miss Sophonsiba living in Uncle Buddy's room and Uncle Buddy moved clean out of the house, sleeping in one of the cabins in the quarters where the niggers used to live in his great-grandfather's time until his great-grandfather died and Uncle Buck and Uncle Buddy moved all the niggers into the big house which his great-grandfather had not had time to finish, and not even doing the cooking while they were there and not even coming to the house any more except to sit on the front gallery after supper, sitting in the darkness between Mr Hubert and Uncle Buck until after a while even Mr Hubert would give up telling how many more head of niggers and acres of land he would add to what he would give Miss Sophonsiba when she married, and go to bed. And one midnight last summer Uncle Buddy just happened by accident to be awake and hear Mr Hubert drive out of the lot and by the time he waked them and they got Miss Sophonsiba up and dressed and the team put to the wagon and caught Mr Hubert, it was almost daylight. So it was always he and Uncle Buck who went to fetch Tomey's Turl because Uncle Buddy never went anywhere, not even to town and not even to fetch Tomey's Turl from Mr Hubert's, even though they all knew that Uncle Buddy could have risked it ten times as much as Uncle Buck could have dared.

They ate breakfast fast. Uncle Buck put on his necktie while they were running toward the lot to catch the horses. The only time he wore the necktie was on Tomey's Turl's account and he hadn't even had it out of the drawer since that night last summer when Uncle Buddy had waked them in the dark and said, "Get up out of that bed and damn quick." Uncle Buddy didn't own a necktie at all; Uncle Buck said Uncle Buddy wouldn't take that chance even in a section like theirs, where ladies were so damn seldom thank God that a man could ride for days in a straight line without having to dodge a single one. His grandmother (she was Uncle Buck's and Uncle Buddy's sister; she had raised him following his mother's death. That was where he had got his christian name: McCaslin, Carothers McCaslin Edmonds) said that Uncle Buck and Uncle Buddy both used the necktie just as another way of daring people to say they looked like twins, because even at sixty they would still fight anyone who claimed he could not tell them apart; whereupon his father had answered that any man who ever played poker once with Uncle Buddy would never mistake him again for Uncle Buck or anybody else.

Jonas had the two horses saddled and waiting. Uncle Buck didn't mount a horse like he was any sixty years old either, lean and active as a cat, with his round, close-cropped white head and his hard little gray eyes and his white-stubbed jaw, his foot in the iron and the horse already moving, already running at the open gate when Uncle Buck came into the seat. He scrabbled up too, onto the shorter pony, before Jonas could boost him up, clapping the pony with his heels into its own stiff, short-coupled canter, out the gate after Uncle Buck, when Uncle Buddy (he hadn't even noticed him) stepped out from the gate and caught the bit. "Watch him," Uncle Buddy said. "Watch Theophilus. The minute anything begins to look wrong, you ride to hell back here and get me. You hear?"

"Yes, sir," he said. "Lemme go now. I wont even ketch Uncle Buck, let alone Tomey's Turl—"

Uncle Buck was riding Black John, because if they could just catch sight of Tomey's Turl at least one mile from Mr Hubert's gate, Black John would ride him down in two minutes. So when they came out on the long flat about three miles from Mr Hubert's, sure enough, there was Tomey's Turl on the Jake mule about a mile ahead. Uncle Buck flung his arm out and back, reining in, crouched on the big horse, his little round head and his gnarled neck thrust forward like a cooter's. "Stole away!" he whispered. "You stay back where he wont see you and flush. I'll circle him through the woods and we will bay him at the creek ford."

He waited until Uncle Buck had vanished into the woods. Then he went on. But Tomey's Turl saw him. He closed in too fast; maybe he was afraid he wouldn't be there in time to see him when he treed. It was the best race he had ever seen. He had never seen old Jake go that fast, and nobody had ever known Tomey's Turl to go faster than his natural walk, even riding a mule. Uncle Buck whooped once from the woods, running on sight, then Black John came out of the trees, driving, soupled out flat and level as a hawk, with Uncle Buck right up behind his ears now and yelling so that they looked exactly like a big black hawk with a sparrow riding it, across the field and over the ditch and across the next field, and he was running too; the mare went out before he even knew she was ready, and he was yelling too. Because, being a nigger, Tomey's Turl should have jumped down and run for it afoot as soon as he saw them. But he didn't; maybe Tomey's Turl had been running off from Uncle Buck for so long that he had even got used to running away like a white man would do it. And it was like he and old Jake had added Tomey's Turl's natural walking speed to the best that old Jake had ever done in his life, and it was just exactly enough to beat Uncle Buck to the ford. Because when he and the pony arrived, Black John was blown and lathered and Uncle Buck was down, leading him around in a circle to slow him down, and they could already hear Mr Hubert's dinner horn a mile away.

Only, for a while Tomey's Turl didn't seem to be at Mr Hubert's either. The boy was still sitting on the gatepost, blowing the horn—there was no gate there; just two posts and a nigger boy about his size sitting on one of them, blowing a fox-horn; this was what Miss Sophonsiba was still reminding people was named Warwick even when they had already known for a long time that's what she aimed to have it called, until when they wouldn't call it Warwick she wouldn't even seem to know what they were talking about and it would sound as if she and Mr Hubert owned two separate plantations covering the same area of ground, one on top of the other. Mr Hubert was sitting in the spring-house with his boots off and his feet in the water, drinking a toddy. But nobody there had seen Tomey's Turl; for a time it looked like Mr Hubert couldn't even place who Uncle Buck was talking about. "Oh, that nigger," he said at last. "We'll find him after dinner."

Only it didn't seem as if they were going to eat either. Mr Hubert and Uncle Buck had a toddy, then Mr Hubert finally sent to tell the boy on the gate post he could quit blowing, and he and Uncle Buck had another toddy and Uncle Buck still saying, "I just want my nigger. Then we got to get on back toward home."

"After dinner," Mr Hubert said. "If we dont start him somewhere around the kitchen, we'll put the dogs on him. They'll find him if it's in the power of mortal Walker dogs to do it."

But at last a hand began waving a handkerchief or something white through the broken place in an upstairs shutter. They went to the house, crossing the back gallery, Mr Hubert warning them again, as he always did, to watch out for the rotted floor-board he hadn't got around to having fixed yet. Then they stood in the hall, until presently there was a jangling and swishing noise and they began to smell the perfume, and Miss Sophonsiba came down the stairs. Her hair was roached under a lace cap; she had on her Sunday dress and beads and a red ribbon around her throat and a little nigger girl carrying her fan and he stood quietly a little behind Uncle Buck, watching her lips until they opened and he could see the roan tooth. He had never known anyone before with a roan tooth and he remembered how one time his grandmother and his father were talking about Uncle Buddy and Uncle Buck and his grandmother said that Miss Sophonsiba had matured into a fine-looking woman once. Maybe she had. He didn't know. He wasn't but nine.

"Why, Mister Theophilus," she said. "And McCaslin," she said. She had never looked at him and she wasn't talking to him and he knew it, although he was prepared and balanced to drag his foot when Uncle Buck did. "Welcome to Warwick."

He and Uncle Buck dragged their foot. "I just come to get my nigger," Uncle Buck said. "Then we got to get on back home."

Then Miss Sophonsiba said something about a bumblebee, but he couldn't remember that. It was too fast and there was too much of it, the earrings and beads clashing and jingling like little trace chains on a toy mule trotting and the perfume stronger too, like the earrings and beads sprayed it out each time they moved and he watched the roan-colored tooth flick and glint between her lips; something about Uncle Buck was a bee sipping from flower to flower and not staying long anywhere and all that stored sweetness to be wasted on Uncle Buddy's desert air, calling Uncle Buddy Mister Amodeus like she called Uncle Buck Mister Theophilus, or maybe the honey was being stored up against the advent of a queen and who was the lucky queen and when? "Ma'am?" Uncle Buck said. Then Mr Hubert said:

"Hah. A buck bee. I reckon that nigger's going to think he's a buck hornet, once he lays hands on him. But I reckon what Buck's thinking about sipping right now is some meat gravy and biscuit and a cup of coffee. And so am I."

They went into the dining room and ate and Miss Sophonsiba said how seriously now neighbors just a half day's ride apart ought not to go so long as Uncle Buck did, and Uncle

Buck said Yessum, and Miss Sophonsiba said Uncle Buck was just a confirmed roving bachelor from the cradle born and this time Uncle Buck even quit chewing and looked and said, Yes, ma'am, he sure was, and born too late at it to ever change now but at least he could thank God no lady would ever have to suffer the misery of living with him and Uncle Buddy, and Miss Sophonsiba said ah, that maybe Uncle Buck just aint met the woman yet who would not only accept what Uncle Buck was pleased to call misery, but who would make Uncle Buck consider even his freedom a small price to pay, and Uncle Buck said, "Nome. Not yet."

Then he and Mr Hubert and Uncle Buck went out to the front gallery and sat down. Mr Hubert hadn't even got done taking his shoes off again and inviting Uncle Buck to take his off, when Miss Sophonsiba came out the door carrying a tray with another toddy on it. "Damnit, Sibbey," Mr Hubert said. "He's just et. He dont want to drink that now." But Miss Sophonsiba didn't seem to hear him at all. She stood there, the roan tooth not flicking now but fixed because she wasn't talking now, handing the toddy to Uncle Buck until after a while she said how her papa always said nothing sweetened a Missippi toddy like the hand of a Missippi lady and would Uncle Buck like to see how she use to sweeten her papa's toddy for him? She lifted the toddy and took a sip of it and handed it again to Uncle Buck and this time Uncle Buck took it. He dragged his foot again and drank the toddy and said if Mr Hubert was going to lay down, he would lay down a while too, since from the way things looked Tomey's Turl was fixing to give them a long hard race unless Mr Hubert's dogs were a considerable better than they used to be.

Mr Hubert and Uncle Buck went into the house. After a while he got up too and went around to the back yard to wait for them. The first thing he saw was Tomey's Turl's head slipping along above the lane fence. But when he cut across the yard to turn him, Tomey's Turl wasn't even running. He was squatting behind a bush, watching the house, peering around the bush at the back door and the upstairs windows, not whispering exactly but not talking loud either: "Whut they doing now?"

"They're taking a nap now," he said. "But never mind that; they're going to put the dogs on you when they get up."

"Hah," Tomey's Turl said. "And nem you mind that neither. I got protection now. All I needs to do is to keep Old Buck from ketching me unto I gets the word."

"What word?" he said. "Word from who? Is Mr Hubert going to buy you from Uncle Buck?"

"Huh," Tomey's Turl said again. "I got more protection than whut Mr Hubert got even." He rose to his feet. "I gonter tell you something to remember: anytime you wants to git something done, from hoeing out a crop to getting married, just get the womenfolks to working at it. Then all you needs to do is set down and wait. You member that."

Then Tomey's Turl was gone. And after a while he went back to the house. But there wasn't anything but the snoring coming out of the room where Uncle Buck and Mr Hubert were, and some more light-sounding snoring coming from upstairs. He went to the spring-house and sat with his feet in the water as Mr Hubert had been doing, because soon now it would be cool enough for a race. And sure enough, after a while Mr Hubert and Uncle Buck came out onto the back gallery, with Miss Sophonsiba right behind them with the toddy tray only this time Uncle Buck drank his before Miss Sophonsiba had time to sweeten it, and Miss Sophonsiba told them to get back early, that all Uncle Buck knew of Warwick was just dogs and niggers and now that she had him, she wanted to show him her garden that Mr Hubert and nobody else had any sayso in. "Yessum," Uncle Buck said. "I just want to catch my nigger. Then we got to get on back home."

Four or five niggers brought up the three horses. They could already hear the dogs waiting still coupled in the lane, and they mounted and went on down the lane, toward the quarters, with Uncle Buck already out in front of even the dogs. So he never did know just when and where they jumped Tomey's Turl, whether he flushed out of one of the cabins or not. Uncle Buck was away out in front on Black John and they hadn't even cast the dogs yet when Uncle Buck roared, "Gone away! I godfrey, he broke cover then!" and Black John's feet clapped four times like pistol shots while he was gathering to go out, then he and Uncle Buck vanished over the hill like they had run at the blank edge of the world itself. Mr Hubert was roaring too: "Gone away! Cast them!" and they all piled over the crest of the hill just in time to see Tomey's Turl away out across the flat, almost to the woods, and the dogs streaking down the hill and out onto the flat. They just tongued once and when they came boiling up around Tomey's Turl it looked like they were trying to jump up and lick him in the face until even Tomey's Turl slowed down and he and the dogs all went into the woods together, walking, like they were going home from a rabbit hunt. And when they caught up with Uncle Buck in the woods, there was no Tomey's Turl and no dogs either, nothing but old Jake about a half an hour later, hitched in a clump of bushes with Tomey's Turl's coat tied on him for a saddle and near a half bushel of Mr Hubert's oats scattered around on the ground that old Jake never even had enough appetite left to nuzzle up and spit back out again. It wasn't any race at all.

"We'll get him tonight though," Mr Hubert said. "We'll bait for him. We'll throw a picquet of niggers and dogs around Tennie's house about midnight, and we'll get him."

"Tonight, hell," Uncle Buck said. "Me and Cass and that nigger all three are going to be half way home by dark. Aint one of your niggers got a fyce or something that will trail them hounds?"

"And fool around here in the woods for half the night too?" Mr Hubert said. "When I'll bet you five hundred dollars that all you got to do to catch that nigger is to walk up to Tennie's cabin after dark and call him?"

"Five hundred dollars?" Uncle Buck said. "Done! Because me and him neither one are going to be anywhere near Tennie's house by dark. Five hundred dollars!" He and Mr Hubert glared at one another.

"Done!" Mr Hubert said.

So they waited while Mr Hubert sent one of the niggers back to the house on old Jake and in about a half an hour the nigger came back with a little bob-tailed black fyce and a new bottle of whisky. Then he rode up to Uncle Buck and held something out to him wrapped in a piece of paper. "What?" Uncle Buck said.

"It's for you," the nigger said. Then Uncle Buck took it and unwrapped it. It was the piece of red ribbon that had been on Miss Sophonsiba's neck and Uncle Buck sat there on Black John, holding the ribbon like it was a little water moccasin only he wasn't going to let anybody see he was afraid of it, batting his eyes fast at the nigger. Then he stopped batting his eyes.

"What for?" he said.

"She just sont hit to you," the nigger said. "She say to tell you 'success'."

"She said what?" Uncle Buck said.

"I dont know, sir," the nigger said. "She just say 'success'."

"Oh," Uncle Buck said. And the fyce found the hounds. They heard them first, from a considerable distance. It was just before sundown and they were not trailing, they were making the noise dogs make when they want to get out of something. They found what that was too. It was a ten-foot-square cotton-house in a field about two miles from Mr Hubert's house and all eleven of the dogs were inside it and the door wedged with a chunk of wood. They watched the dogs come boiling out when the nigger opened the door, Mr Hubert sitting his horse and looking at the back of Uncle Buck's neck.

"Well, well," Mr Hubert said. "That's something, anyway. You can use them again now. They dont seem to have no more trouble with your nigger than he seems to have with them."

"Not enough," Uncle Buck said. "That means both of them. I'll stick to the fyce."

"All right," Mr Hubert said. Then he said, "Hell, 'Filus, come on. Let's go eat supper. I tell you, all you got to do to catch that nigger is—"

"Five hundred dollars," Uncle Buck said.

"What?" Mr Hubert said. He and Uncle Buck looked at each other. They were not glaring now. They were not joking each other either. They sat there in the beginning of twilight, looking at each other, just blinking a little. "What five hundred dollars?'' Mr Hubert said. ''That you wont catch that nigger in Tennie's cabin at midnight tonight?''

''That me or that nigger neither aint going to be near nobody's house but mine at midnight tonight.'' Now they did glare at each other.

''Five hundred dollars,'' Mr Hubert said. ''Done.''

''Done,'' Uncle Buck said.

''Done,'' Mr Hubert said.

''Done,'' Uncle Buck said.

So Mr Hubert took the dogs and some of the niggers and went back to the house. Then he and Uncle Buck and the nigger with the fyce went on, the nigger leading old Jake with one hand and holding the fyce's leash (it was a piece of gnawed plowline) with the other. Now Uncle Buck let the fyce smell Tomey's Turl's coat; it was like for the first time now the fyce found out what they were after and they would have let him off the leash and kept up with him on the horses, only about that time the nigger boy began blowing the fox-horn for supper at the house and they didn't dare risk it.

Then it was full dark. And then—he didn't know how much later nor where they were, how far from the house, except that it was a good piece and it had been dark for good while and they were still going on, with Uncle Buck leaning down from time to time to let the fyce have another smell of Tomey's Turl's coat while Uncle Buck took another drink from the whisky bottle—they found that Tomey's Turl had doubled and was making a long swing back toward the house. ''I godfrey, we've got him,'' Uncle Buck said. ''He's going to earth. We'll cut back to the house and head him before he can den.'' So they left the nigger to cast the fyce and follow him on old Jake, and he and Uncle Buck rode for Mr Hubert's, stopping on the hills to blow the horses and listen to the fyce down in the creek bottom where Tomey's Turl was still making his swing.

But they never caught him. They reached the dark quarters; they could see lights still burning in Mr Hubert's house and somebody was blowing the fox-horn again and it wasn't any boy and he had never heard a fox-horn sound mad before either, and he and Uncle Buck scattered out on the slope below Tennie's cabin. Then they heard the fyce, not trailing now but yapping, about a mile away, then the nigger whooped and they knew the fyce had faulted. It was at the creek. They hunted the banks both ways for more than an hour, but they couldn't straighten Tomey's Turl out. At last even Uncle Buck gave up and they started back toward the house, the fyce riding too now, in front of the nigger on the mule. They were just coming up the lane to the quarters; they could see on along the ridge to where Mr Hubert's house was all dark now, when all of a sudden the fyce gave a yelp and jumped down from old Jake and hit the ground running and yelling every jump, and Uncle Buck was down too and had snatched him off the pony almost before he could clear his feet from the irons, and they ran too, on past the dark cabins toward the one where the fyce had treed. "We got him!" Uncle Buck said. "Run around to the back. Dont holler; just grab up a stick and knock on the back door, loud."

Afterward, Uncle Buck admitted that it was his own mistake, that he had forgotten when even a little child should have known: not ever to stand right in front of or right behind a nigger when you scare him; but always to stand to one side of him. Uncle Buck forgot that. He was standing facing the front door and right in front of it, with the fyce right in front of him yelling fire and murder every time it could draw a new breath; he said the first he knew was when the fyce gave a shriek and whirled and Tomey's Turl was right behind it. Uncle Buck said he never even saw the door open; that the fyce just screamed once and ran between his legs and then Tomey's Turl ran right clean over him. He never even bobbled; he knocked Uncle Buck down and then caught him before he fell without even stopping, snatched him up under one arm, still running, and carried him along for about ten feet, saying, "Look, out of here, old Buck. Look out of here, old Buck," before he threw him away and went on. By that time they couldn't even hear the fyce any more at all.

Uncle Buck wasn't hurt; it was only the wind knocked out of him where Tomey's Turl had thrown him down on his back. But he had been carrying the whisky bottle in his back pocket, saving the last drink until Tomey's Turl was captured, and he refused to move until he knew for certain if it was just whisky and not blood. So Uncle Buck laid over on his side easy, and he knelt behind him and raked the broken glass out of his pocket. Then they went on to the house. They walked. The nigger came up with the horses, but nobody said anything to Uncle Buck about riding again. They couldn't hear the fyce at all now. "He was going fast, all right," Uncle Buck said. "But I dont believe that even he will catch that fyce, I godfrey, what a night."

"We'll catch him tomorrow," he said.

"Tomorrow, hell," Uncle Buck said. "We'll be at home tomorrow. And the first time Hubert Beauchamp or that nigger either one set foot on my land, I'm going to have them arrested for trespass and vagrancy."

The house was dark. They could hear Mr Hubert snoring good now, as if he had settled down to road-gaiting at it. But they couldn't hear anything from upstairs, even when they were inside the dark hall, at the foot of the stairs. "Likely hers will be at the back," Uncle Buck said. "Where she can holler down to the kitchen without having to get up. Besides, an unmarried lady will sholy have her door locked with strangers in the house." So Uncle Buck eased himself down onto the bottom step, and he knelt and drew Uncle Buck's boots off. Then he removed his own and set them against the wall, and he and Uncle Buck mounted the stairs, feeling their way up and into the upper hall. It was dark too, and still there was no sound anywhere except Mr Hubert snoring below, so they felt their way along the hall toward the front of the house, until they felt a door. They could hear nothing beyond the door, and when Uncle Buck tried the knob, it opened. "All right," Uncle Buck whispered. "Be quiet." They could see a little now, enough to see the shape of the bed and the mosquito-bar. Uncle Buck threw down his suspenders and unbuttoned his trousers and went to the bed and eased himself carefully down onto the edge of it, and he knelt again and drew Uncle Buck's trousers off and he was just removing his own when Uncle Buck lifted the mosquito-bar and raised his feet and rolled into the bed. That was when Miss Sophonsiba sat up on the other side of Uncle Buck and gave the first scream.

3

When he reached home just before dinner time the next day, he was just about worn out. He was too tired to eat, even if Uncle Buddy had waited to eat dinner first; he couldn't have stayed on the pony another mile without going to sleep. In fact, he must have gone to sleep while he was telling Uncle Buddy, because the next thing he knew it was late afternoon and he was lying on some hay in the jolting wagon-bed, with Uncle Buddy sitting on the seat above him exactly the same way he sat a horse or sat in his rocking chair before the kitchen hearth while he was cooking, holding the whip exactly as he held the spoon or fork he stirred and tasted with. Uncle Buddy had some cold bread and meat and a jug of buttermilk wrapped in damp towsacks waiting when he waked up. He ate, sitting in the wagon in almost the last of the afternoon. They must have come fast, because they were not more than two miles from Mr Hubert's. Uncle Buddy waited for him to eat. Then he said, "Tell me again," and he told it again: how he and Uncle Buck finally found a room without anybody in it, and Uncle Buck sitting on the side of the bed saying, "O godfrey, Cass. O godfrey, Cass," and then they heard Mr Hubert's feet on the stairs and watched the light come down the hall and Mr Hubert came in, in his nightshirt, and walked over and set the candle on the table and stood looking at Uncle Buck.

"Well, 'Filus," he said. "She's got you at last."

"It was an accident," Uncle Buck said. "I swear to godfrey—"

"Hah," Mr Hubert said. "Dont tell me. Tell her that."

"I did," Uncle Buck said. "I did tell her. I swear to god—"

"Sholy," Mr Hubert said. "And just listen." They listened a minute. He had been hearing her all the time. She was nowhere near as loud as at first; she was just steady. "Dont you want to go back in there and tell her again it was an accident, that you never meant nothing and to just excuse you and forget about it? All right."

"All right what?" Uncle Buck said.

"Go back in there and tell her again," Mr Hubert said. Uncle Buck looked at Mr Hubert for a minute. He batted his eyes fast.

"Then what will I come back and tell you?" he said.

"To me?" Mr Hubert said. "I would call that a horse of another color. Wouldn't you?"

Uncle Buck looked at Mr Hubert. He batted his eyes fast again. Then he stopped again. "Wait," he said. "Be reasonable. Say I did walk into a lady's bedroom, even Miss Sophonsiba's; say, just for the sake of the argument, there wasn't no other lady in the world but her and so I walked into hers and tried to get in bed with her, would I have took a nine-year-old boy with me?"

"Reasonable is just what I'm being," Mr Hubert said. "You come into bear-country of your own free will and accord. All right; you were a grown man and you knew it was bear-country and you knew the way back out like you knew the way in and you had your chance to take it. But no. You had to crawl into the den and lay down by the bear. And whether you did or didn't know the bear was in it dont make any difference. So if you got back out of that den without even a claw-mark on you, I would not only be unreasonable, I'd be a damned fool. After all, I'd like a little peace and quiet and freedom myself, now I got a chance for it. Yes, sir. She's got you, 'Filus, and you know it. You run a hard race and you run a good one, but you skun the hen-house one time too many."

"Yes," Uncle Buck said. He drew his breath in and let it out again, slow and not loud. But you could hear it. "Well," he said. "So I reckon I'll have to take the chance then."

"You already took it," Mr Hubert said. "You did that when you came back here." Then he stopped too. Then he batted his eyes, but only about six times. Then he stopped and looked at Uncle Buck for more than a minute. "What chance?" he said.

"That five hundred dollars," Uncle Buck said.

"What five hundred dollars?" Mr Hubert said. He and Uncle Buck looked at one another. Now it was Mr Hubert that batted his eyes again and then stopped again. "I thought you said you found him in Tennie's cabin."

"I did," Uncle Buck said. "What you bet me was I would catch him there. If there had been ten of me standing in front of that door, we wouldn't have caught him." Mr Hubert blinked at Uncle Buck, slow and steady.

"So you aim to hold me to that fool bet," he said.

"You took your chance too," Uncle Buck said. Mr Hubert blinked at Uncle Buck. Then he stopped. Then he went and took the candle from the table and went out. They sat on the edge of the bed and watched the light go down the hall and heard Mr Hubert's feet on the stairs. After a while they began to see the light again and they heard Mr Hubert's feet coming back up the stairs. Then Mr Hubert entered and went to the table and set the candle down and laid a deck of cards by it.

"One hand," he said. "Draw. You shuffle, I cut, this boy deals. Five hundred dollars against Sibbey. And we'll settle this nigger business once and for all too. If you win, you buy Tennie; if I win, I buy that boy of yours. The price will be the same for each one: three hundred dollars."

"Win?" Uncle Buck said. "The one that wins buys the niggers?"

"Wins Sibbey, damn it!" Mr Hubert said. "Wins Sibbey! What the hell else are we setting up till midnight arguing about? The lowest hand wins Sibbey and buys the niggers."

"All right," Uncle Buck said. "I'll buy the damn girl then and we'll call the rest of this foolishness off."

"Hah," Mr Hubert said again. "This is the most serious foolishness you ever took part in in your life. No. You said you wanted your chance, and now you've got it. Here it is, right here on this table, waiting on you."

So Uncle Buck shuffled the cards and Mr Hubert cut them. Then he took up the deck and dealt in turn until Uncle Buck and Mr Hubert had five. And Uncle Buck looked at his hand a long time and then said two cards and he gave them to him, and Mr Hubert looked at his hand quick and said one card and he gave it to him and Mr Hubert flipped his discard onto the two which Uncle Buck had discarded and slid the new card into his hand and opened it out and looked at it quick again and closed it and looked at Uncle Buck and said, "Well? Did you help them threes?"

"No," Uncle Buck said.

"Well I did," Mr Hubert said. He shot his hand across the table so that the cards fell face-up in front of Uncle Buck and they were three kings and two fives, and said, "By God, Buck McCaslin, you have met your match at last."

"And that was all?" Uncle Buddy said. It was late then, near sunset; they would be at Mr Hubert's in another fifteen minutes.

"Yes, sir," he said, telling that too: how Uncle Buck waked him at daylight and he climbed out a window and got the pony and left, and how Uncle Buck said that if they pushed him too close in the meantime, he would climb down the gutter too and hide in the woods until Uncle Buddy arrived.

"Hah," Uncle Buddy said. "Was Tomey's Turl there?"

"Yes, sir," he said. "He was waiting in the stable when I got the pony. He said, 'Aint they settled it yet?' "

"And what did you say?" Uncle Buddy said.

"I said, 'Uncle Buck looks like he's settled. But Uncle Buddy aint got here yet.' "

"Hah," Uncle Buddy said.

And that was about all. They reached the house. Maybe Uncle Buck was watching them, but if he was, he never showed himself, never came out of the woods. Miss Sophonsiba was nowhere in sight either, so at least Uncle Buck hadn't quite given up; at least he hadn't asked her yet. And he and Uncle Buddy and Mr Hubert ate supper and they came in from the kitchen and cleared the table, leaving only the lamp on it and the deck of cards. Then it was just like last night, except that Uncle Buddy had no necktie and Mr Hubert wore clothes now instead of a nightshirt and it was a shaded lamp on the table instead of a candle, and Mr Hubert sitting at his end of the table with the deck in his hands, riffling the edges with his thumb and looking at Uncle Buddy. Then he tapped the edges even and set the deck out in the middle of the table, under the lamp, and folded his arms on the edge of the table and leaned forward a little on the table, looking at Uncle Buddy, who was sitting at his end of the table with his hands in his lap, all one gray color, like an old gray rock or a stump with gray moss on it, that still, with his round white head like Uncle Buck's but he didn't blink like Uncle Buck and he was a little thicker than Uncle Buck, as if from sitting down so much watching food cook, as if the things he cooked had made him a little thicker than he would have been and the things he cooked with, the flour and such, had made him all one same quiet color.

"Little toddy before we start?" Mr Hubert said.

"I dont drink," Uncle Buddy said.

"That's right," Mr Hubert said. "I knew there was something else besides just being woman-weak that makes 'Filus seem human. But no matter." He batted his eyes twice at Uncle Buddy. "Buck McCaslin against the land and niggers you have heard me promise as Sophonsiba's dowry on the day she marries. If I beat you, 'Filus marries Sibbey without any dowry. If you beat me, you get 'Filus. But I still get the three hundred dollars 'Filus owes me for Tennie. Is that correct?"

"That's correct," Uncle Buddy said.

"Stud," Mr Hubert said. "One hand. You to shuffle, me to cut, this boy to deal."

"No," Uncle Buddy said. "Not Cass. He's too young. I dont want him mixed up in any gambling."

"Hah," Mr Hubert said. "It's said that a man playing cards with Amodeus McCaslin aint gambling. But no matter." But he was still looking at Uncle Buddy; he never even turned his head when he spoke: "Go to the back door and holler. Bring the first creature that answers, animal mule or human, that can deal ten cards."

So he went to the back door. But he didn't have to call because Tomey's Turl was squatting against the wall just outside the door, and they returned to the dining-room where Mr Hubert still sat with his arms folded on his side of the table and Uncle Buddy sat with his hands in his lap on his side and the deck of cards face-down under the lamp between them. Neither of them even looked up when he and Tomey's Turl entered. "Shuffle," Mr Hubert said. Uncle Buddy shuffled and set the cards back under the lamp and put his hands back into his lap and Mr Hubert cut the deck and folded his arms back onto the table-edge. "Deal," he said. Still neither he nor Uncle Buddy looked up. They just sat there while Tomey's Turl's saddle-colored hands came into the light and took up the deck and dealt, one card face-down to Mr Hubert and one face-down to Uncle Buddy, and one face-up to Mr Hubert and it was a king, and one face-up to Uncle Buddy and it was a six.

"Buck McCaslin against Sibbey's dowry," Mr Hubert said. "Deal." And the hand dealt Mr Hubert a card and it was a three, and Uncle Buddy a card and it was a two. Mr Hubert looked at Uncle Buddy. Uncle Buddy rapped once with his knuckles on the table.

"Deal," Mr Hubert said. And the hand dealt Mr Hubert a card and it was another three, and Uncle Buddy a card and it was a four. Mr Hubert looked at Uncle Buddy's cards. Then he looked at Uncle Buddy and Uncle Buddy rapped on the table again with his knuckles.

"Deal," Mr Hubert said, and the hand dealt him an ace and Uncle Bobby a five and now Mr Hubert just sat still. He didn't look at anything or move for a whole minute; he just sat there and watched Uncle Buddy put one hand onto the table for the first time since he shuffled and pinch up one corner of his face-down card and look at it and then put his hand back into his lap. "Check," Mr Hubert said.

"I'll bet you them two niggers," Uncle Buddy said. He didn't move either. He sat there just like he sat in the wagon or on a horse or in the rocking chair he cooked from.

"Against what?" Mr Hubert said.

"Against the three hundred dollars Theophilus owes you for Tennie, and the three hundred you and Theophilus agreed on for Tomey's Turl," Uncle Buddy said.

"Hah," Mr Hubert said, only it wasn't loud at all this time, nor even short. Then he said "Hah. Hah. Hah" and not loud either. Then he said, "Well." Then he said, "Well, well." Then he said: "We'll check up for a minute. If I win, you take Sibbey without dowry and the two niggers, and I dont owe 'Filus anything. If you win—"

"—Theophilus is free. And you owe him the three hundred dollars for Tomey's Turl," Uncle Buddy said.

"That's just if I call you," Mr Hubert said. "If I dont call you, 'Filus wont owe me nothing and I wont owe 'Filus nothing, unless I take that nigger which I have been trying to explain to you and him both for years that I wont have on my place. We will be right back where all this foolishness started from, except for that. So what it comes down to is, I either got to give a nigger away, or risk buying one that you done already admitted you cant keep at home." Then he stopped talking. For about a minute it was like he and Uncle Buddy had both gone to sleep. Then Mr Hubert picked up his face-down card and turned it over. It was another three, and Mr Hubert sat there without looking at anything at all, his fingers beating a tattoo, slow and steady and not very loud, on the table. "H'm," he said. "And you need a trey and there aint but four of them and I already got three. And you just shuffled. And I cut afterward. And if I call you, I will have to buy that nigger. Who dealt these cards, Amodeus?" Only he didn't wait to be answered. He reached out and tilted the lamp-shade, the light moving up Tomey's Turl's arms that were supposed to be black but were not quite white, up his Sunday shirt that was supposed to be white but wasn't quite either, that he put on every time he ran away just as Uncle Buck put on the necktie each time he went to bring him back, and on to his face; and Mr Hubert sat there, holding the lamp-shade and looking at Tomey's Turl. Then he tilted the shade back down and took up his cards and turned them face-down and pushed them toward the middle of the table. "I pass, Amodeus," he said.

4

He was still too worn out for sleep to sit on a horse, so this time he and Uncle Buddy and Tennie all three rode in the wagon, while Tomey's Turl led the pony from old Jake. And when they got home just after daylight, this time Uncle Buddy never even had time to get breakfast started and the fox never even got out of the crate, because the dogs were right there in the room. Old Moses went right into the crate with the fox, so that both of them went right on through the back end of it. That is, the fox went through, because when Uncle Buddy opened the door to come in, old Moses was still wearing most of the crate around his neck until Uncle Buddy kicked it off of him. Sothey just made one run, across the front gallery and around the house and they could hear the fox's claws when he went scrabbling up the lean-pole, onto the roof—a fine race while it lasted, but the tree was too quick.

"What in damn's hell do you mean," Uncle Buddy said, "casting that damn thing with all the dogs right in the same room?"

"Damn the fox," Uncle Buck said. "Go on and start breakfast. It seems to me I've been away from home a whole damn month."

ERNEST HEMINGWAY

The Battler

NICK STOOD UP. He was all right. He looked up the track at the lights of the caboose going out of sight around a curve. There was water on both sides of the track, then tamarack swamp.

He felt of his knee. The pants were torn and the skin was barked. His hands were scraped and there were sand and cinders driven up under his nails. He went over to the edge of the track, down the little slope to the water and washed his hands. He washed them carefully in the cold water, getting the dirt out from the nails. He squatted down and bathed his knee.

That lousy crut of a brakeman. He would get him some day. He would know him again. That was a fine way to act.

"Come here, kid," he said. "I got something for you."

He had fallen for it. What a lousy kid thing to have done. They would never suck him in that way again.

"Come here, kid, I got something for you." Then *wham* and he lit on his hands and knees beside the track.

Nick rubbed his eye. There was a big bump coming up. He would have a black eye, all right. It ached already. That son of a crutting brakeman.

He touched the bump over his eye with his fingers. Oh, well, it was only a black eye. That was all he had gotten out of it. Cheap at the price. He wished he could see it. Could not see it looking into the water, though. It was dark and he was a long way off from anywhere. He wiped his hands on his trousers and stood up, then climbed the embankment to the rails.

He started up the track. It was well ballasted and made easy walking, sand and gravel packed between the ties, solid walking. The smooth road-bed like a causeway went on ahead through the swamp. Nick walked along. He must get to somewhere.

Nick had swung on to the freight train when it slowed down for the yards outside of Walton Junction. The train, with Nick on it, had passed through Kalkaska as it started to get dark. Now he must be nearly to Mancelona. Three or four miles of swamp. He stepped along the track, walking so he kept on the ballast between the ties, the swamp ghostly in the rising mist. His eye ached and he was hungry. He kept on hiking, putting the miles of track back of him. The swamp was all the same on both sides of the track.

Ahead there was a bridge. Nick crossed it, his boots ringing hollow on the iron. Down below the water showed black between the slits of ties. Nick kicked a loose spike and it dropped into the water. Beyond the bridge were hills. It was high and dark on both sides of the track. Up the track Nick saw a fire.

He came up the track towards the fire carefully. It was off to one side of the track, below the railway embankment. He had only seen the light from it. The track came out through a cut and where the fire was burning the country opened out and fell away into woods. Nick dropped carefully down the embankment and cut into the woods to come up to the fire through the trees. It was a beechwood forest and the fallen beechnut burrs were under his shoes as he walked between the trees. The fire was bright now, just at the edge of the trees. There was a man sitting by it. Nick waited behind the tree and watched. The man looked to be alone. He was sitting there with his head in his hands looking at the fire. Nick stepped out and walked into the fire-light.

The man sat there looking into the fire. When Nick stopped quite close to him he did not move.

"Hello!" Nick said.

The man looked up.

"Where did you get the shiner?" he said.

"A brakeman busted me."

"Off the through freight?"

"Yes."

"I saw the bastard," the man said. "He went through here 'bout an hour and a half ago. He was walking along the top of the cars slapping his arms and singing."

"The bastard!"

"It must have made him feel good to bust you," the man said seriously.

"I'll bust him."

"Get him with a rock some time when he's going through," the man advised.

"I'll get him."

"You're a tough one, aren't you?"

"No," Nick answered.

"All you kids are tough."

"You got to be tough," Nick said.

"That's what I said."

The man looked at Nick and smiled. In the firelight Nick saw that his face was misshapen. His nose was sunken, his eyes were slits, he had queer-shaped lips. Nick did not perceive all this at once, he only saw the man's face was queerly formed and mutilated. It was like putty in color. Dead looking in the firelight.

"Don't you like my pan?" the man asked.

Nick was embarrassed.

"Sure," he said.

"Look here!" the man took off his cap.

He had only one ear. It was thickened and tight against the side of his head. Where the other ear should have been there was a stump.

"Ever see one like that?"

"No," said Nick. It made him a little sick.

"I could take it," the man said. "Don't you think I could take it, kid?"

"You bet!"

"They all bust their hands on me," the little man said. "They couldn't hurt me."

He looked at Nick. "Sit down," he said. "Want to eat?"

"Don't bother," Nick said. "I'm going on to the town."

"Listen!" the man said. "Call me Ad."

"Sure!"

"Listen," the little man said. "I'm not quite right."

"What's the matter?"

"I'm crazy."

He put on his cap. Nick felt like laughing.

"You're all right," he said.

"No, I'm not. I'm crazy. Listen, you ever been crazy?"

"No," Nick said. "How does it get you?"

"I don't know," Ad said. "When you got it you don't know about it. You know me, don't you?"

"No."

"I'm Ad Francis."

"Honest to God?"

"Don't you believe it?"

"Yes."

Nick knew it must be true.

"You know how I beat them?"

"No," Nick said.

"My heart's slow. It only beats forty a minute. Feel it."

Nick hesitated.

"Come on," the man took hold of his hand. "Take hold of my wrist. Put your fingers there."

The little man's wrist was thick and the muscles bulged above the bone. Nick felt the slow pumping under his fingers.

"Got a watch?"

"No."

"Neither have I," Ad said. "It ain't any good if you haven't got a watch."

Nick dropped his wrist.

"Listen," Ad Francis said. "Take ahold again. You count and I'll count up to sixty."

Feeling the slow hard throb under his fingers Nick started to count. He heard the little man counting slowly, one, two, three, four, five, and on—aloud.

"Sixty," Ad finished. "That's a minute. What did you make it?"

"Forty," Nick said.

"That's right," Ad said happily. "She never speeds up."

A man dropped down the railroad embankment and came across the clearing to the fire.

"Hello, Bugs!" Ad said.

"Hello!" Bugs answered. It was a Negro's voice. Nick knew from the way he walked that he was a Negro. He stood with his back to them bending over the fire. He straightened up.

"This is my pal Bugs," Ad said. "He's crazy, too."

"Glad to meet you," Bugs said. "Where you say you're from?"

"Chicago," Nick said.

"That's a fine town," the Negro said. "I didn't catch your name."

"Adams. Nick Adams."

"He says he's never been crazy, Bugs," Ad said.

"He's got a lot coming to him," the Negro said. He was unwrapping a package by the fire.

"When are we going to eat, Bugs?" the prize-fighter asked.

"Right away."

"Are you hungry, Nick?"

"Hungry as hell."

"Hear that, Bugs?"

"I hear most of what goes on."

"That ain't what I asked you."

"Yes. I heard what the gentleman said."

Into a skillet he was laying slices of ham. As the skillet grew hot the grease sputtered and Bugs, crouching on long nigger legs over the fire, turned the ham and broke eggs into the skillet, tipping it from side to side to baste the eggs with the hot fat.

"Will you cut some bread out of that bag, Mister Adams?" Bugs turned from the fire.

"Sure."

Nick reached in the bag and brought out a loaf of bread. He cut six slices. Ad watched him and leaned forward.

"Let me take your knife, Nick," he said.

"No, you don't," the Negro said. "Hang on to your knife, Mister Adams."

The prize-fighter sat back.

"Will you bring me the bread, Mister Adams?" Bugs asked. Nick brought it over.

"Do you like to dip your bread in the ham fat?" the Negro asked.

"You bet!"

"Perhaps we'd better wait until later. It's better at the finish of the meal. Here."

The Negro picked up a slice of ham and laid it on one of the pieces of bread, then slid an egg on top of it.

"Just close that sandwich, will you, please, and give it to Mister Francis."

Ad took the sandwich and started eating.

"Watch out how that egg runs," the Negro warned. "This is for you, Mister Adams. The remainder for myself."

Nick bit into the sandwich. The Negro was sitting opposite him beside Ad. The hot fried ham and eggs tasted wonderful.

"Mister Adams is right hungry," the Negro said. The little man whom Nick knew by name as a former champion fighter was silent. He had said nothing since the Negro had spoken about the knife.

"May I offer you a slice of bread dipped right in the hot ham fat?" Bugs said.

"Thanks a lot."

The little white man looked at Nick.

"Will you have some, Mister Adolph Francis?" Bugs offered from the skillet.

Ad did not answer. He was looking at Nick.

"Mister Francis?" came the nigger's soft voice.

Ad did not answer. He was looking at Nick.

"I spoke to you, Mister Francis," the nigger said softly.

Ad kept on looking at Nick. He had his cap down over his eyes. Nick felt nervous.

"How the hell do you get that way?" came out from under the cap sharply at Nick.

"Who the hell do you think you are? You're a snotty bastard. You come in here where nobody asks you and eat a man's food and when he asks to borrow a knife you get snotty."

He glared at Nick, his face was white and his eyes almost out of sight under his cap.

"You're a hot sketch. Who the hell asked you to butt in here?"

"Nobody."

"You're damn right nobody did. Nobody asked you to stay either. You come in here and act snotty about my face and smoke my cigars and drink my liquor and then talk snotty. Where the hell do you think you get off?"

Nick said nothing. Ad stood up.

"I'll tell you, you yellow-livered Chicago bastard. You're going to get your can knocked off. Do you get that?"

Nick stepped back. The little man came towards him slowly, stepping flat-footed forward, his left foot stepping forward, his right dragging up to it.

"Hit me," he moved his head. "Try and hit me."

"I don't want to hit you."

"You won't get out of it that way. You're going to take a beating, see? Come on and lead at me."

"Cut it out," Nick said.

"All right, then, you bastard."

The little man looked down at Nick's feet. As he looked down the Negro, who had followed behind him as he moved away from the fire, set himself and tapped him across the base of the skull. He fell forward and Bugs dropped the cloth-wrapped blackjack on the grass. The little man lay there, his face in the grass. The Negro picked him up, his head hanging, and carried him to the fire. His face looked bad, the eyes open. Bugs laid him down gently.

"Will you bring me the water in the bucket, Mister Adams?" he said. "I'm afraid I hit him just a little hard."

The Negro splashed water with his hand on the man's face and pulled his ears gently. The eyes closed.

Bugs stood up.

"He's all right," he said. "There's nothing to worry about. I'm sorry, Mister Adams."

"It's all right." Nick was looking down at the little man. He saw the blackjack on the grass and picked it up. It had a flexible handle and was limber in his hand. Worn black leather with a handkerchief wrapped around the heavy end.

"That's a whalebone handle," the Negro smiled. "They don't make them any more. I didn't know how well you could take care of your self and, anyway, I didn't want you to hurt him or mark him up no more than he is."

The Negro smiled again.

"You hurt him yourself."

"I know how to do it. He won't remember nothing of it. I have to do it to change him when he gets that way."

Nick was still looking down at the little man, lying, his eyes closed in the firelight. Bugs put some wood on the fire.

"Don't you worry about him none, Mister Adams. I seen him like this plenty of times before."

"What made him crazy?" Nick asked.

"Oh, a lot of things," the Negro answered from the fire. "Would you like a cup of this coffee, Mister Adams?"

He handed Nick the cup and smoothed the coat he had placed under the unconscious man's head.

"He took too many beatings, for one thing," the Negro sipped the coffee. "But that just made him sort of simple. Then his sister was his manager and they was always being written up in the papers all about brothers and sisters and how she loved her brother and how he loved his sister, and then they got married in New York and that made a lot of unpleasantness."

"I remember about it."

"Sure. Of course they wasn't brother and sister no more than a rabbit, but there was a lot of people didn't like it either way and they commenced to have disagreements, and one day she just went off and never come back."

He drank the coffee and wiped his lips with the pink palm of his hand.

"He just went crazy. Will you have some more coffee, Mister Adams?"

"Thanks."

"I seen her a couple of times," the Negro went on. "She

was an awful good-looking woman. Looked enough like him to be twins. He wouldn't be bad-looking without his face all busted."

He stopped. The story seemed to be over.

"Where did you meet him?" asked Nick.

"I met him in jail," the Negro said. "He was busting people all the time after she went away and they put him in jail. I was in for cuttin' a man."

He smiled, and went on soft-voiced:

"Right away I liked him and when I got out I looked him up. He likes to think I'm crazy and I don't mind. I like to be with him and I like seeing the country and I don't have to commit no larceny to do it. I like living like a gentleman."

"What do you all do?" Nick asked.

"Oh, nothing. Just move around. He's got money."

"He must have made a lot of money."

"Sure. He spent all his money, though. Or they took it away from him. She sends him money."

He poked up the fire.

"She's a mighty fine woman," he said. "She looks enough like him to be his own twin."

The Negro looked over at the little man, lying breathing heavily. His blond hair was down over his forehead. His mutilated face looked childish in repose.

"I can wake him up any time now, Mister Adams. If you don't mind I wish you'd sort of pull out. I don't like to not be hospitable, but it might disturb him back again to see you. I hate to have to thump him and it's the only thing to do when he gets started. I have to sort of keep him away from people. You don't mind, do you, Mister Adams? No, don't thank me, Mister Adams. I'd have warned you about him but he seemed to have taken such a liking to you and I thought things were going to be all right. You'll hit a town about two miles up the track. Mancelona they call it. Good-bye. I wish we could ask you to stay the night but it's just out of the question. Would you like to take some of that ham and some bread with you? No? You better take a sandwich," all this in a low, smooth, polite nigger voice.

"Good. Well, good-bye, Mister Adams. Good-bye and good luck!"

Nick walked away from the fire across the clearing to the railway tracks. Out of the range of the fire he listened. The low soft voice of the Negro was talking. Nick could not hear the words. Then he heard the little man say, "I got an awful headache, Bugs."

"You'll feel better, Mister Francis," the Negro's voice soothed. "Just you drink a cup of this hot coffee."

Nick climbed the embankment and started up the track. He found he had a ham sandwich in his hand and put it in his pocket. Looking back from the mounting grade before the track curved into the hills he could see the firelight in the clearing.

DAVID LEAVITT

Territory

NEIL'S MOTHER, MRS. Campbell, sits on her lawn chair behind a card table outside the food co-op. Every few minutes, as the sun shifts, she moves the chair and table several inches back so as to remain in the shade. It is a hundred degrees outside, and bright white. Each time someone goes in or out of the co-op a gust of air-conditioning flies out of the automatic doors, raising dust from the cement.

Neil stands just inside, poised over a water fountain, and watches her. She has on a sun hat, and a sweatshirt over her tennis dress; her legs are bare, and shiny with cocoa butter. In front of her, propped against the table, a sign proclaims: MOTHERS, FIGHT FOR YOUR CHILDREN'S RIGHTS—SUPPORT A NON-NUCLEAR FUTURE. Women dressed exactly like her pass by, notice the sign, listen to her brief spiel, finger pamphlets, sign petitions or don't sign petitions, never give money. Her weary eyes are masked by dark glasses. In the age of Reagan, she has declared, keeping up the causes of peace and justice is a futile, tiresome, and unrewarding effort; it is therefore an effort fit only for mothers to keep up. The sun bounces off the window glass through which Neil watches her. His own reflection lines up with her profile.

* * *

Later that afternoon, Neil spreads himself out alongside the pool and imagines he is being watched by the shirtless Chicano gardener. But the gardener, concentrating on his pruning, is neither seductive nor seducible. On the lawn, his mother's large Airedales—Abigail, Lucille, Fern—amble, sniff, urinate. Occasionally, they accost the gardener, who yells at them in Spanish.

After two years' absence, Neil reasons, he should feel nostalgia, regret, gladness upon returning home. He closes his eyes and tries to muster the proper background music for the cinematic scene of return. His rhapsody, however, is interrupted by the noises of his mother's trio—the scratchy cello, whining violin, stumbling piano—as she and Lillian Havalard and Charlotte Feder plunge through Mozart. The tune is cheery, in a Germanic sort of way, and utterly inappropriate to what Neil is trying to feel. Yet it *is* the music of his adolescence; they have played it for years, bent over the notes, their heads bobbing in silent time to the metronome.

It is getting darker. Every few minutes, he must move his towel so as to remain within the narrowing patch of sunlight. In four hours, Wayne, his lover of ten months and the only person he has ever imagined he could spend his life with, will be in this house, where no lover of his has ever set foot. The thought fills him with a sense of grand terror and curiosity. He stretches, tries to feel seductive, desirable. The gardener's shears whack at the ferns; the music above him rushes to a loud, premature conclusion. The women laugh and applaud themselves as they give up for the day. He hears Charlotte Feder's full nasal twang, the voice of a fat woman in a pink pants suit—odd, since she is a scrawny, arthritic old bird, rarely clad in anything other than tennis shorts and a blouse. Lillian is the fat woman in the pink pants suit; her voice is thin and warped by too much crying. Drink in hand, she calls out from the porch, "Hot enough!" and waves. He lifts himself up and nods to her.

The women sit on the porch and chatter; their voices blend with the clink of ice in glasses. They belong to a small circle of ladies all of whom, with the exception of Neil's mother, are widows and divorcées. Lillian's husband left her twenty-two years ago, and sends her a check every month to live on; Charlotte has been divorced twice as long as she was married, and has a daughter serving a long sentence for terrorist acts committed when she was nineteen. Only Neil's mother has a husband, a distant sort of husband, away often on business. He is away on business now. All of them feel betrayed—by husbands, by children, by history.

Neil closes his eyes, tries to hear the words only as sounds. Soon, a new noise accosts him: his mother arguing with the gardener in Spanish. He leans on his elbows and watches them; the syllables are loud, heated, and compressed, and seem on the verge of explosion. But the argument ends happily; they shake hands. The gardener collects his check and walks out the gate without so much as looking at Neil.

He does not know the gardener's name; as his mother has reminded him, he does not know most of what has gone on since he moved away. Her life has gone on, unaffected by his absence. He flinches at his own egoism, the egoism of sons.

"Neil! Did you call the airport to make sure the plane's coming in on time?"

"Yes," he shouts to her. "It is."

"Good. Well, I'll have dinner ready when you get back."

"Mom—"

"What?" The word comes out in a weary wail that is more of an answer than a question.

"What's wrong?" he says, forgetting his original question.

"Nothing's wrong," she declares in a tone that indicates that everything is wrong. "The dogs have to be fed, dinner has to be made, and I've got people here. Nothing's wrong."

"I hope things will be as comfortable as possible when Wayne gets here."

"Is that a request or a threat?"

"Mom—"

Behind her sunglasses, her eyes are inscrutable. "I'm tired," she says. "It's been a long day. I . . . I'm anxious to meet Wayne. I'm sure he'll be wonderful, and we'll all have a wonderful, wonderful time. I'm sorry. I'm just tired."

She heads up the stairs. He suddenly feels an urge to cover himself; his body embarrasses him, as it has in her presence since the day she saw him shirtless and said with delight, "Neil! You're growing hair under your arms!"

Before he can get up, the dogs gather round him and begin to sniff and lick at him. He wriggles to get away from them, but Abigail, the largest and stupidest, straddles his stomach and nuzzles his mouth. He splutters and, laughing, throws her off. "Get away from me, you goddamn dogs," he shouts, and swats at them. They are new dogs, not the dog of his childhood, not dogs he trusts.

He stands, and the dogs circle him, looking up at his face expectantly. He feels renewed terror at the thought that Wayne will be here so soon: Will they sleep in the same room? Will they make love? He has never had sex in his parents' house. How can he be expected to be a lover here, in this place of his childhood, of his earliest shame, in this household of mothers and dogs?

"Dinnertime! Abbylucyferny, Abbylucyferny, dinnertime!" His mother's litany disperses the dogs, and they run for the door.

"Do you realize," he shouts to her, "that no matter how much those dogs love you they'd probably kill you for the leg of lamb in the freezer?"

Neil was twelve the first time he recognized in himself something like sexuality. He was lying outside, on the grass, when Rasputin—the dog, long dead, of his childhood—began licking his face. He felt a tingle he did not recognize, pulled off his shirt to give the dog access to more of him. Rasputin's tongue tickled coolly. A wet nose started to sniff down his body, toward his bathing suit. What he felt frightened him, but he couldn't bring himself to push the dog away. Then his mother called out, "Dinner," and Rasputin was gone, more interested in food than in him.

It was the day after Rasputin was put to sleep, years later, that Neil finally stood in the kitchen, his back turned to his parents, and said, with unexpected ease, "I'm a homosexual." The words seemed insufficient, reductive. For years, he had believed his sexuality to be detachable from the essential him, but now he realized that it was part of him. He had the sudden, despairing sensation that though the words had been easy to say, the fact of their having been aired was incurably damning. Only then, for the first time, did he admit that they were true, and he shook and wept in regret for what he would not be for his mother, for having failed her. His father hung back, silent; he was absent for that moment as he was mostly absent—a strong absence. Neil always thought of him sitting on the edge of the bed in his underwear, captivated by something on television. He said, "It's O.K., Neil." But his mother was resolute; her lower lip didn't quaver. She had enormous reserves of strength to which she only gained access at moments like this one. She hugged him from behind, wrapped him in the childhood smells of perfume and brownies, and whispered, "It's O.K., honey." For once, her words seemed as inadequate as his. Neil felt himself shrunk to an embarrassed adolescent, hating her sympathy, not wanting her to touch him. It was the way he would feel from then on whenever he was in her presence—even now, at twenty-three, bringing home his lover to meet her.

All through his childhood, she had packed only the most nutritious lunches, had served on the PTA, had volunteered at the children's library and at his school, had organized a successful campaign to ban a racist history textbook. The day after he told her, she located and got in touch with an organization called the Coalition of Parents of Lesbians and Gays. Within a year, she was president of it. On weekends, she and the other mothers drove their station wagons to San Francisco, set up their card tables in front of the Bulldog Baths, the Liberty Baths, passed out literature to men in leather and denim who were loath to admit they even had mothers. These men, who would habitually do violence to each other, were strangely cowed by the suburban ladies with their informational booklets, and bent their heads. Neil was a sophomore in college then, and lived in San Francisco. She brought him pamphlets detailing the dangers of bathhouses and back rooms, enemas and poppers, wordless sex in alleyways. His excursion into that world had been brief and lamentable, and was over. He winced at the thought that she knew all his sexual secrets, and vowed to move to the East Coast to escape her. It was not very different from the days when she had campaigned for a better playground, or tutored the Hispanic children in the audiovisual room. Those days, as well, he had run away from her concern. Even today, perched in front of the co-op, collecting signatures for nuclear disarmament, she was quintessentially a mother. And if the lot of mothers was to expect nothing in return, was the lot of sons to return nothing?

Driving across the Dumbarton Bridge on his way to the airport, Neil thinks, I have returned nothing; I have simply returned. He wonders if she would have given birth to him had she known what he would grow up to be.

Then he berates himself: Why should he assume himself to be the cause of her sorrow? She has told him that her life is full of secrets. She has changed since he left home—grown thinner, more rigid, harder to hug. She has given up baking, taken up tennis; her skin has browned and tightened. She is no longer the woman who hugged him and kissed him, who said, "As long as you're happy, that's all that's important to us."

The flats spread out around him; the bridge floats on purple and green silt, and spongy bay fill, not water at all. Only ten miles north, a whole city has been built on gunk dredged up from the bay.

He arrives at the airport ten minutes early, to discover that the plane has landed twenty minutes early. His first view of Wayne is from behind, by the baggage belt. Wayne looks as he always looks—slightly windblown—and is wearing the ratty leather jacket he was wearing the night they met. Neil sneaks up on him and puts his hands on his shoulders; when Wayne turns around, he looks relieved to see him.

They hug like brothers; only in the safety of Neil's mother's car do they dare to kiss. They recognize each other's smells, and grow comfortable again. "I never imagined I'd actually see you out here," Neil says, "but you're exactly the same here as there."

"It's only been a week."

They kiss again. Neil wants to go to a motel, but Wayne

insists on being pragmatic. "We'll be there soon. Don't worry."

"We could go to one of the bathhouses in the city and take a room for a couple of aeons," Neil says. "Christ, I'm hard up. I don't even know if we're going to be in the same bedroom."

"Well, if we're not," Wayne says, "we'll sneak around. It'll be romantic."

They cling to each other for a few more minutes, until they realize that people are looking in the car window. Reluctantly, they pull apart. Neil reminds himself that he loves this man, that there is a reason for him to bring this man home.

He takes the scenic route on the way back. The car careers over foothills, through forests, along white four-lane highways high in the mountains. Wayne tells Neil that he sat next to a woman on the plane who was once Marilyn Monroe's psychiatrist's nurse. He slips his foot out of his shoe and nudges Neil's ankle, pulling Neil's sock down with his toe.

"I have to drive," Neil says. "I'm very glad you're here."

There is a comfort in the privacy of the car. They have a common fear of walking hand in hand, of publicly showing physical affection, even in the permissive West Seventies of New York—a fear that they have admitted only to one another. They slip through a pass between two hills, and are suddenly in residential Northern California, the land of expensive ranch-style houses.

As they pull into Neil's mother's driveway, the dogs run barking toward the car. When Wayne opens the door, they jump and lap at him, and he tries to close it again. "Don't worry. Abbylucyferny! Get in the house, damn it!"

His mother descends from the porch. She has changed into a blue flower-print dress, which Neil doesn't recognize. He gets out of the car and halfheartedly chastises the dogs. Crickets chirp in the trees. His mother looks radiant, even beautiful, illuminated by the headlights, surrounded by the now quiet dogs, like a Circe with her slaves. When she walks over to Wayne, offering her hand, and says, "Wayne, I'm Barbara," Neil forgets that she is his mother.

"Good to meet you, Barbara," Wayne says, and reaches

out his hand. Craftier than she, he whirls her around to kiss her cheek.

Barbara! He is calling his mother Barbara! Then he remembers that Wayne is five years older than he is. They chat by the open car door, and Neil shrinks back—the embarrassed adolescent, uncomfortable, unwanted.

So the dreaded moment passes and he might as well not have been there. At dinner, Wayne keeps the conversation smooth, like a captivated courtier seeking Neil's mother's hand. A faggot son's sodomist—such words spit into Neil's head. She has prepared tiny meatballs with fresh coriander, fettucine with pesto. Wayne talks about the street people in New York; El Salvador is a tragedy; if only Sadat had lived; Phyllis Schlafly—what can you do?

"It's a losing battle," she tells him. "Every day I'm out there with my card table, me and the other mothers, but I tell you, Wayne, it's a losing battle. Sometimes I think us old ladies are the only ones with enough patience to fight."

Occasionally, Neil says something, but his comments seem stupid and clumsy. Wayne continues to call her Barbara. No one under forty has ever called her Barbara as long as Neil can remember. They drink wine; he does not.

Now is the time for drastic action. He contemplates taking Wayne's hand, then checks himself. He has never done anything in her presence to indicate that the sexuality he confessed to five years ago was a reality and not an invention. Even now, he and Wayne might as well be friends, college roommates. Then Wayne, his savior, with a single, sweeping gesture, reaches for his hand, and clasps it, in the midst of a joke he is telling about Saudi Arabians. By the time he is laughing, their hands are joined. Neil's throat contracts; his heart begins to beat violently. He notices his mother's eyes flicker, glance downward; she never breaks the stride of her sentence. The dinner goes on, and every taboo nurtured since childhood falls quietly away.

She removes the dishes. Their hands grow sticky; he cannot tell which fingers are his and which Wayne's. She clears the rest of the table and rounds up the dogs.

"Well, boys, I'm very tired, and I've got a long day ahead

of me tomorrow, so I think I'll hit the sack. There are extra towels for you in Neil's bathroom, Wayne. Sleep well."

"Good night, Barbara," Wayne calls out. "It's been wonderful meeting you."

They are alone. Now they can disentangle their hands.

"No problem about where we sleep, is there?"

"No," Neil says. "I just can't imagine sleeping with someone in this house."

His leg shakes violently. Wayne takes Neil's hand in a firm grasp and hauls him up.

Later that night, they lie outside, under redwood trees, listening to the hysteria of the crickets, the hum of the pool cleaning itself. Redwood leaves prick their skin. They fell in love in bars and apartments, and this is the first time that they have made love outdoors. Neil is not sure he has enjoyed the experience. He kept sensing eyes, imagined that the neighborhood cats were staring at them from behind a fence of brambles. He remembers he once hid in this spot when he and some of the children from the neighborhood were playing sardines, remembers the intoxication of small bodies packed together, the warm breath of suppressed laughter on his neck. "The loser had to go through the spanking machine," he tells Wayne.

"Did you lose often?"

"Most of the time. The spanking machine never really hurt—just a whirl of hands. If you moved fast enough, no one could actually get you. Sometimes, though, late in the afternoon, we'd get naughty. We'd chase each other and pull each other's pants down. That was all. Boys and girls together!"

"Listen to the insects," Wayne says, and closes his eyes.

Neil turns to examine Wayne's face, notices a single, small pimple. Their lovemaking usually begins in a wrestle, a struggle for dominance, and ends with a somewhat confusing loss of identity—as now, when Neil sees a foot on the grass, resting against his leg, and tries to determine if it is his own or Wayne's.

From inside the house, the dogs begin to bark. Their yelps

grow into alarmed falsettos. Neil lifts himself up. "I wonder if they smell something," he says."

"Probably just us," says Wayne.

"My mother will wake up. She hates getting waked up."

Lights go on in the house; the door to the porch opens.

"What's wrong, Abby? What's wrong?" his mother's voice calls softly.

Wayne clamps his hand over Neil's mouth. "Don't say anything," he whispers.

"I can't just—" Neil begins to say, but Wayne's hand closes over his mouth again. He bites it, and Wayne starts laughing.

"What was that?" Her voice projects into the garden. "Hello?" she says.

The dogs yelp louder. "Abbylucyferny, it's O.K., it's O.K." Her voice is soft and panicked. "Is anyone there?" she asks loudly.

The brambles shake. She takes a flashlight, shines it around the garden. Wayne and Neil duck down; the light lands on them and hovers for a few seconds. Then it clicks off and they are in the dark—a new dark, a darker dark, which their eyes must readjust to.

"Let's go to bed, Abbylucyferny," she says gently. Neil and Wayne hear her pad into the house. The dogs whimper as they follow her, and the lights go off.

Once before, Neil and his mother had stared at each other in the glare of bright lights. Four years ago, they stood in the arena created by the headlights of her car, waiting for the train. He was on his way back to San Francisco, where he was marching in a Gay Pride Parade the next day. The train station was next door to the food co-op and shared its parking lot. The co-op, familiar and boring by day, took on a certain mystery in the night. Neil recognized the spot where he had skidded on his bicycle and broken his leg. Through the glass doors, the brightly lit interior of the store glowed, its rows and rows of cans and boxes forming their own horizon, each can illuminated so that even from outside Neil could read the labels. All that was missing was the ladies in tennis dresses and sweatshirts, pushing their carts past bins of nuts and dried fruits.

"Your train is late," his mother said. Her hair fell loosely on her shoulders, and her legs were tanned. Neil looked at her and tried to imagine her in labor with him—bucking and struggling with his birth. He felt then the strange, sexless love for women which through his whole adolescence he had mistaken for heterosexual desire.

A single bright light approached them; it preceded the low, haunting sound of the whistle. Neil kissed his mother, and waved goodbye as he ran to meet the train. It was an old train, with windows tinted a sort of horrible lemon-lime. It stopped only long enough for him to hoist himself on board, and then it was moving again. He hurried to a window, hoping to see her drive off, but the tint of the window made it possible for him to make out only vague patches of light—street lamps, cars, the co-op.

He sank into the hard, green seat. The train was almost entirely empty; the only other passenger was a dark-skinned man wearing bluejeans and a leather jacket. He sat directly across the aisle from Neil, next to the window. He had rough skin and a thick mustache. Neil discovered that by pretending to look out the window he could study the man's reflection in the lemon-lime glass. It was only slightly hazy—the quality of a bad photograph. Neil felt his mouth open, felt sleep closing in on him. Hazy red and gold flashes through the glass pulsed in the face of the man in the window, giving the curious impression of muscle spasms. It took Neil a few minutes to realize that the man was staring at him, or, rather, staring at the back of his head—staring at his staring. The man smiled as though to say, I know exactly what you're staring at, and Neil felt the sickening sensation of desire rise in his throat.

Right before they reached the city, the man stood up and sat down in the seat next to Neil's. The man's thigh brushed deliberately against his own. Neil's eyes were watering; he felt sick to his stomach. Taking Neil's hand, the man said, "Why so nervous, honey? Relax."

Neil woke up the next morning with the taste of ashes in his mouth. He was lying on the floor, without blankets or sheets or pillows. Instinctively, he reached for his pants, and as he pulled them on came face to face with the man from the train. His name was Luis; he turned out to be a dog groomer. His apartment smelled of a dog.

"Why such a hurry?" Luis said.

"The parade. The Gay Pride Parade. I'm meeting some friends to march."

"I'll come with you," Luis said. "I think I'm too old for these things, but why not?"

Neil did not want Luis to come with him, but he found it impossible to say so. Luis looked older by day, more likely to carry diseases. He dressed again in a torn T-shirt, leather jacket, bluejeans. "It's my everyday apparel," he said, and laughed. Neil buttoned his pants, aware that they had been washed by his mother the day before. Luis possessed the peculiar combination of hypermasculinity and effeminacy which exemplifies faggotry. Neil wanted to be rid of him, but Luis's mark was on him, he could see that much. They would become lovers whether Neil liked it or not.

They joined the parade midway. Neil hoped he wouldn't meet anyone he knew; he did not want to have to explain Luis, who clung to him. The parade was full of shirtless men with oiled, muscular shoulders. Neil's back ached. There were floats carrying garishly dressed prom queens and cheerleaders, some with beards, some actually looking like women. Luis said, "It makes me proud, makes me glad to be what I am." Neil supposed that by darting into the crowd ahead of him he might be able to lose Luis forever, but he found it difficult to let him go; the prospect of being alone seemed unbearable.

Neil was startled to see his mother watching the parade, holding up a sign. She was with the Coalition of Parents of Lesbians and Gays; they had posted a huge banner on the wall behind them proclaiming: OUR SONS AND DAUGHTERS, WE ARE PROUD OF YOU. She spotted him; she waved, and jumped up and down.

"Who's that woman?" Luis asked.

"My mother. I should go say hello to her."

"O.K.," Luis said. He followed Neil to the side of the

parade. Neil kissed his mother. Luis took off his shirt, wiped his face with it, smiled.

"I'm glad you came," Neil said.

"I wouldn't have missed it, Neil. I wanted to show you I cared."

He smiled, and kissed her again. He showed no intention of introducing Luis, so Luis introduced himself.

"Hello, Luis," Mrs. Campbell said. Neil looked away. Luis shook her hand, and Neil wanted to warn his mother to wash it, warned himself to check with a V.D. clinic first thing Monday.

"Neil, this is Carmen Bologna, another one of the mothers," Mrs. Campbell said. She introduced him to a fat Italian woman with flushed cheeks, and hair arranged in the shape of a clamshell.

"Good to meet you, Neil, good to meet you," said Carmen Bologna. "You know my son, Michael? I'm so proud of Michael! He's doing so well now. I'm proud of him, proud to be his mother I am, and your mother's proud, too!"

The woman smiled at him, and Neil could think of nothing to say but "Thank you." He looked uncomfortably toward his mother, who stood listening to Luis. It occurred to him that the worst period of his life was probably about to begin and he had no way to stop it.

A group of drag queens ambled over to where the mothers were standing. "Michael! Michael!" shouted Carmen Bologna, and embraced a sticklike man wrapped in green satin. Michael's eyes were heavily dosed with green eyeshadow, and his lips were painted pink.

Neil turned and saw his mother staring, her mouth open. He marched over to where Luis was standing, and they moved back into the parade. He turned and waved to her. She waved back; he saw pain in her face, and then, briefly, regret. That day, he felt she would have traded him for any other son. Later, she said to him, "Carmen Bologna really was proud, and, speaking as a mother, let me tell you, you have to be brave to feel such pride."

Neil was never proud. It took him a year to dump Luis, another year to leave California. The sick taste of ashes was still in his mouth. On the plane, he envisioned his mother sitting alone in the dark, smoking. She did not leave his mind until he was circling New York staring down at the dawn rising over Queens. The song playing in his earphones would remain hovering on the edges of his memory, always associated with her absence. After collecting his baggage, he took a bus into the city. Boys were selling newspapers in the middle of highways, through the windows of stopped cars. It was seven in the morning when he reached Manhattan. He stood for ten minutes on East Thirty-fourth Street, breathed the cold air, and felt bubbles rising in his blood.

Neil got a job as a paralegal—a temporary job, he told himself. When he met Wayne a year later, the sensations of that first morning returned to him. They'd been up all night, and at six they walked across the park to Wayne's apartment with the nervous, deliberate gait of people aching to make love for the first time. Joggers ran by with their dogs. None of them knew what Wayne and he were about to do, and the secrecy excited him. His mother came to mind, and the song, and the whirling vision of Queens coming alive below him. His breath solidified into clouds, and he felt happier than he had ever felt before in his life.

The second day of Wayne's visit, he and Neil go with Mrs. Campbell to pick up the dogs at the dog parlor. The grooming establishment is decorated with pink ribbons and photographs of the owner's champion pit bulls. A fat, middle-aged woman appears from the back, leading the newly trimmed and fluffed Abigail, Lucille, and Fern by three leashes. The dogs struggle frantically when they see Neil's mother, tangling the woman up in their leashes. "Ladies, behave!" Mrs. Campbell commands, and collects the dogs. She gives Fern to Neil and Abigail to Wayne. In the car on the way back, Abigail begins pawing to get on Wayne's lap.

"Just push her off," Mrs. Campbell says. "She knows she's not supposed to do that."

"You never groomed Rasputin," Neil complains.

"Rasputin was a mutt."

"Rasputin was a beautiful dog, even if he did smell."

"Do you remember when you were a little kid, Neil, you used to make Rasputin dance with you? Once you tried to dress him up in one of my blouses."

"I don't remember that," Neil says.

"Yes. I remember," says Mrs. Campbell. "Then you tried to organize a dog beauty contest in the neighborhood. You wanted to have runners-up—everything."

"A dog beauty contest?" Wayne says.

"Mother, do we have to—"

"I think it's a mother's privilege to embarrass her son," Mrs. Campbell says, and smiles.

When they are about to pull into the driveway, Wayne starts screaming, and pushes Abigail off his lap. "Oh, my God!" he says. "The dog just pissed all over me."

Neil turns around and sees a puddle seeping into Wayne's slacks. He suppresses his laughter, and Mrs. Campbell hands him a rag.

"I'm sorry, Wayne," she says. "It goes with the territory."

"This is really disgusting," Wayne says, swatting at himself with the rag.

Neil keeps his eyes on his own reflection in the rearview mirror and smiles.

At home, while Wayne cleans himself in the bathroom, Neil watches his mother cook lunch—Japanese noodles in soup. "When you went off to college," she says, "I went to the grocery store. I was going to buy you ramen noodles, and I suddenly realized you weren't going to be around to eat them. I started crying right then, blubbering like an idiot."

Neil clenches his fists inside his pockets. She has a way of telling him little sad stories when he doesn't want to hear them—stories of dolls broken by her brothers, lunches stolen by neighborhood boys on the way to school. Now he has joined the ranks of male children who have made her cry.

"Mama, I'm sorry," he says.

She is bent over the noodles, which steam in her face. "I didn't want to say anything in front of Wayne, but I wish you had answered me last night. I was very frightened—and worried."

"I'm sorry," he says, but it's not convincing. His fingers prickle. He senses a great sorrow about to be born.

"I lead a quiet life," she says. "I don't want to be a disciplinarian. I just don't have the energy for these—shenanigans. Please don't frighten me that way again."

"If you were so upset, why didn't you say something?"

"I'd rather not discuss it. I lead a quiet life. I'm not used to getting woken up late at night. I'm not used—"

"To my having a lover?"

"No, I'm not used to having other people around, that's all. Wayne is charming. A wonderful young man."

"He likes you, too."

"I'm sure we'll get along fine."

She scoops the steaming noodles into ceramic bowls. Wayne returns, wearing shorts. His white, hairy legs are a shocking contrast to hers, which are brown and sleek.

"I'll wash those pants, Wayne," Mrs. Campbell says. "I have a special detergent that'll take out the stain."

She gives Neil a look to indicate that the subject should be dropped. He looks at Wayne, looks at his mother; his initial embarrassment gives way to a fierce pride—the arrogance of mastery. He is glad his mother knows that he is desired, glad it makes her flinch.

Later, he steps into the back yard; the gardener is back, whacking at the bushes with his shears. Neil walks by him in his bathing suit, imagining he is on parade.

That afternoon, he finds his mother's daily list on the kitchen table:

TUESDAY

7:00—breakfast
Take dogs to groomer
Groceries (?)

Campaign against Draft—4-7

Buy underwear
Trios—2:00

Spaghetti
Fruit
Asparagus if sale
Peanuts
Milk

Doctor's Appointment (make)
Write Cranston/Hayakawa
re disarmament

Handi-Wraps
Mozart
Abigail
Top Ramen
Pedro

Her desk and trash can are full of such lists; he remembers them from the earliest days of his childhood. He had learned to read from them. In his own life, too, there have been endless lists—covered with check marks and arrows, at least one item always spilling over onto the next day's agenda. From September to November, "Buy plane ticket for Christmas" floated from list to list to list.

The last item puzzles him: Pedro. Pedro must be the gardener. He observes the accretion of names, the arbitrary specifics that give a sense of his mother's life. He could make a list of his own selves: the child, the adolescent, the promiscuous faggot son, and finally the good son, settled, relatively successful. But the divisions wouldn't work; he is today and will always be the child being licked by the dog, the boy on the floor with Luis; he will still be everything he is ashamed of. The other lists—the lists of things done and undone—tell their own truth: that his life is measured more properly in objects than in stages. He knows himself as "jump rope," "book," "sunglasses," "underwear."

"Tell me about your family, Wayne," Mrs. Campbell says that night, as they drive toward town. They are going to see an Esther Williams movie at the local revival house: an underwater musical, populated by mermaids, underwater Rockettes.

"My father was a lawyer," Wayne says. "He had an office in Queens, with a neon sign. I think he's probably the only lawyer in the world who had a neon sign. Anyway, he died when I was ten. My mother never remarried. She lives in Queens. Her great claim to fame is that when she was twenty-two she went on 'The $64,000 Question.' Her category was mystery novels. She made it to sixteen thousand before she got tripped up."

"When I was about ten, I wanted you to go on 'Jeopardy,' " Neil says to his mother. "You really should have, you know. You would have won."

"You certainly loved 'Jeopardy,' " Mrs. Campbell says. "You used to watch it during dinner. Wayne, does your mother work?"

"No," he says. "She lives off investments."

"You're both only children," Mrs. Campbell says. Neil wonders if she is ruminating on the possible connection between that coincidence and their "alternative life style."

The movie theater is nearly empty. Neil sits between Wayne and his mother. There are pillows on the floor at the front of the theater, and a cat is prowling over them. It casts a monstrous shadow every now and then on the screen, disturbing the sedative effect of water ballet. Like a teen-ager, Neil cautiously reaches his arm around Wayne's shoulder. Wayne takes his hand immediately. Next to them, Neil's mother breathes in, out, in, out. Neil timorously moves his other arm and lifts it behind his mother's neck. He does not look at her, but he can tell from her breathing that she senses what he is doing. Slowly, carefully, he lets his hand drop on her shoulder; it twitches spasmodically, and he jumps, as if he had received an electric shock. His mother's quiet breathing is broken by a gasp; even Wayne notices. A sudden brightness on the screen illuminates the panic in her eyes, Neil's arm frozen above her, about to fall again. Slowly, he lowers his arm until his fingertips touch her skin, the fabric of her dress. He has gone too far to go back now; they are all too far.

Wayne and Mrs. Campbell sink into their seats, but Neil

remains stiff, holding up his arms, which rest on nothing. The movie ends, and they go on sitting just like that.

"I'm old," Mrs. Campbell says later, as they drive back home. "I remember when those films were new. Your father and I went to one on our first date. I loved them, because I could pretend that those women underwater were flying—they were so graceful. They really took advantage of Technicolor in those days. Color was something to appreciate. You can't know what it was like to see a color movie for the first time, after years of black-and-white. It's like trying to explain the surprise of snow to an East Coaster. Very little is new anymore, I fear."

Neil would like to tell her about his own nostalgia, but how can he explain that all of it revolves around her? The idea of her life before he was born pleases him. "Tell Wayne how you used to look like Esther Williams," he asks her.

She blushes. "I was told I looked like Esther Williams, but really more like Gene Tierney," she says. "Not beautiful, but interesting. I like to think I had a certain magnetism."

"You still do," Wayne says, and instantly recognizes the wrongness of his comment. Silence and a nervous laugh indicate that he has not yet mastered the family vocabulary.

When they get home, the night is once again full of the sound of crickets. Mrs. Campbell picks up a flashlight and calls the dogs. "Abbylucyferny, Abbylucyferny," she shouts, and the dogs amble from their various corners. She pushes them out the door to the back yard and follows them. Neil follows her. Wayne follows Neil, but hovers on the porch. Neil walks behind her as she tramps through the garden. She holds out her flashlight, and snails slide from behind bushes, from under rocks, to where she stands. When the snails become visible, she crushes them underfoot. They make a wet, cracking noise, like eggs being broken.

"Nights like this," she says, "I think of children without pants on, in hot South American countries. I have nightmares about tanks rolling down our street."

"The weather's never like this in New York," Neil says. "When it's hot, it's humid and sticky. You don't want to go outdoors."

"I could never live anywhere else but here. I think I'd die. I'm too used to the climate."

"Don't be silly."

"No, I mean it," she says. "I have adjusted too well to the weather."

The dogs bark and howl by the fence. "A cat, I suspect," she says. She aims her flashlight at a rock, and more snails emerge—uncountable numbers, too stupid to have learned not to trust light.

"I know what you were doing at the movie," she says.

"What?"

"I know what you were doing."

"What? I put my arm around you."

"I'm sorry, Neil," she says. "I can only take so much. Just so much."

"What do you mean?" he says. "I was only trying to show affection."

"Oh, affection—I know about affection."

He looks up at the porch, sees Wayne moving toward the door, trying not to listen.

"What do you mean?" Neil says to her.

She puts down the flashlight and wraps her arms around herself. "I remember when you were a little boy," she says. "I remember, and I have to stop remembering. I wanted you to grow up happy. And I'm very tolerant, very understanding. But I can only take so much."

His heart seems to have risen into his throat. "Mother," he says, "I think you know my life isn't your fault. But for God's sake, don't say that your life is my fault."

"It's not a question of fault," she says. She extracts a Kleenex from her pocket and blows her nose. "I'm sorry, Neil. I guess I'm just an old woman with too much on her mind and not enough to do." She laughs halfheartedly. "Don't worry. Don't say anything," she says. "Abbylucyferny, Abbylucyferny, time for bed!"

He watches her as she walks toward the porch, silent and regal. There is the pad of feet, the clinking of dog tags as the dogs run for the house.

* * *

He was twelve the first time she saw him march in a parade. He played the tuba, and as his elementary-school band lumbered down the streets of their then small town she stood on the sidelines and waved. Afterward, she had taken him out for ice cream. He spilled some on his red uniform, and she swiped at it with a napkin. She had been there for him that day, as well as years later, at that more memorable parade; she had been there for him every day.

Somewhere over Iowa, a week later, Neil remembers this scene, remembers other days, when he would find her sitting in the dark, crying. She had to take time out of her own private sorrow to appease his anxiety. "It was part of it," she told him later. "Part of being a mother."

"The scariest thing in the world is the thought that you could unknowingly ruin someone's life," Neil tells Wayne. "Or even change someone's life. I hate the thought of having such control I'd make a rotten mother."

"You're crazy," Wayne says. "You have this great mother, and all you do is complain. I know people whose mothers have disowned them."

"Guilt goes with the territory," Neil says.

"Why?" Wayne asks, perfectly seriously.

Neil doesn't answer. He lies back in his seat, closes his eyes, imagines he grew up in a house in the mountains of Colorado, surrounded by snow—endless white snow on hills. No flat places, and no trees; just white hills. Every time he has flown away, she has come into his mind, usually sitting alone in the dark, smoking. Today she is outside at dusk, skimming leaves from the pool.

"I want to get a dog," Neil says.

Wayne laughs. "In the city? It'd suffocate."

The hum of the airplane is druglike, dazing. "I want to stay with you a long time," Neil says.

"I know." Imperceptibly, Wayne takes his hand.

"It's very hot there in the summer, too. You know, I'm not thinking about my mother now."

"It's O.K."

For a moment, Neil wonders what the stewardess or the old woman on the way to the bathroom will think, but then he laughs and relaxes.

Later, the plane makes a slow circle over New York City, and on it two men hold hands, eyes closed, and breathe in unison.

CARSON McCULLERS

A Domestic Dilemma

On Thursday Martin Meadows left the office early enough to make the first express bus home. It was the hour when the evening lilac glow was fading in the slushy streets, but by the time the bus had left the mid-town terminal the bright city night had come. On Thursdays the maid had a half-day off and Martin liked to get home as soon as possible, since for the past year his wife had not been—well. This Thursday he was very tired and, hoping that no regular commuter would single him out for conversation, he fastened his attention to the newspaper until the bus had crossed the George Washington Bridge. Once on 9-W Highway Martin always felt that the trip was halfway done, he breathed deeply, even in cold weather when only ribbons of draught cut through the smoky air of the bus, confident that he was breathing country air. It used to be that at this point he would relax and begin to think with pleasure of his home. But in this last year nearness brought only a sense of tension and he did not anticipate the journey's end. This evening Martin kept his face close to the window and watched the barren fields and lonely lights of passing townships. There was a moon, pale on the dark earth and areas of late, porous snow; to Martin the countryside seemed vast and somehow desolate that evening. He took his hat from the rack and put his folded newspaper in the pocket of his overcoat a few minutes before time to pull the cord.

The cottage was a block from the bus stop, near the river but not directly on the shore; from the living-room window you could look across the street and opposite yard and see the Hudson. The cottage was modern, almost too white and new on the narrow plot of yard. In summer the grass was soft and bright and Martin carefully tended a flower border and a rose trellis. But during the cold, fallow months the yard was bleak and the cottage seemed naked. Lights were on that evening in all the rooms in the little house and Martin hurried up the front walk. Before the steps he stopped to move a wagon out of the way.

The children were in the living room, so intent on play that the opening of the front door was at first unnoticed. Martin stood looking at his safe, lovely children. They had opened the bottom drawer of the secretary and taken out the Christmas decorations. Andy had managed to plug in the Christmas tree lights and the green and red bulbs glowed with out-of-season festivity on the rug of the living room. At the moment he was trying to trail the bright cord over Marianne's rocking horse. Marianne sat on the floor pulling off an angel's wings. The children wailed a startling welcome. Martin swung the fat little baby girl up to his shoulder and Andy threw himself against his father's legs.

"Daddy, Daddy, Daddy!"

Martin set down the little girl carefully and swung Andy a few times like a pendulum. Then he picked up the Christmas tree cord.

"What's all this stuff doing out? Help me put it back in the drawer. You're not to fool with the light socket. Remember I told you that before. I mean it, Andy."

The six-year-old child nodded and shut the secretary drawer. Martin stroked his fair soft hair and his hand lingered tenderly on the nape of the child's frail neck.

"Had supper yet, Bumpkin?"

"It hurt. The toast was hot."

The baby girl stumbled on the rug and, after the first surprise of the fall, began to cry; Martin picked her up and carried her in his arms back to the kitchen.

"See Daddy," said Andy. "The toast—"

Emily had laid the children's supper on the uncovered porcelain table. There were two plates with the remains of cream-of-wheat and eggs and silver mugs that had held milk. There was also a platter of cinnamon toast, untouched except for one tooth-marked bite. Martin sniffed the bitten piece and nibbled gingerly. Then he put the toast into the garbage pail. "Hoo-phui— What on earth!"

Emily had mistaken the tin of cayenne for the cinnamon.

"I like to have burnt up," Andy said. "Drank water and ran outdoors and opened my mouth. Marianne didn't eat none."

"Any," corrected Martin. He stood helpless, looking around the walls of the kitchen. "Well, that's that, I guess," he said finally. "Where is your mother now?"

"She's up in you alls' room."

Martin left the children in the kitchen and went up to his wife. Outside the door he waited for a moment to still his anger. He did not knock and once inside the room he closed the door behind him.

Emily sat in the rocking chair by the window of the pleasant room. She had been drinking something from a tumbler and as he entered she put the glass hurriedly on the floor behind the chair. In her attitude there was confusion and guilt which she tried to hide by a show of spurious vivacity.

"Oh, Marty! You home already? The time slipped up on me. I was just going down—" She lurched to him and her kiss was strong with sherry. When he stood unresponsive she stepped back a pace and giggled nervously.

"What's the matter with you? Standing there like a barber pole. Is anything wrong with you?"

"Wrong with *me?*" Martin bent over the rocking chair and picked up the tumbler from the floor. "If you could only realize how sick I am—how bad it is for all of us."

Emily spoke in a false, airy voice that had become too familiar to him. Often at such times she affected a slight English accent, copying perhaps some actress she admired. "I haven't the vaguest idea what you mean. Unless you are referring to the glass I used for a spot of sherry. I had a finger of sherry—maybe two. But what is the crime in that, pray tell me? I'm quite all right. Quite all right."

"So anyone can see."

As she went into the bathroom Emily walked with careful gravity. She turned on the cold water and dashed some on her face with her cupped hands, then patted herself dry with the corner of a bath towel. Her face was delicately featured and young, unblemished.

"I was just going down to make dinner." She tottered and balanced herself by holding to the door frame.

"I'll take care of dinner. You stay up here. I'll bring it up."

"I'll do nothing of the sort. Why, whoever heard of such a thing?"

"Please," Martin said.

"Leave me alone. I'm quite all right. I was just on the way down—"

"Mind what I say."

"Mind your grandmother."

She lurched toward the door, but Martin caught her by the arm. "I don't want the children to see you in this condition. Be reasonable."

"Condition!" Emily jerked her arm. Her voice rose angrily. "Why, because I drink a couple of sherries in the afternoon you're trying to make me out a drunkard. Condition! Why, I don't even touch whiskey. As well you know. *I* don't swill liquor at bars. And that's more than you can say. I don't even have a cocktail at dinnertime. I only sometimes have a glass of sherry. What, I ask you, is the disgrace of that? Condition!"

Martin sought words to calm his wife. "We'll have a quiet supper by ourselves up here. That's a good girl." Emily sat on the side of the bed and he opened the door for a quick departure. "I'll be back in a jiffy."

As he busied himself with the dinner downstairs he was lost in the familiar question as to how this problem had come upon his home. He himself had always enjoyed a good drink. When they were still living in Alabama they had served long drinks or cocktails as a matter of course. For years they had drunk one or two—possibly three drinks before dinner, and at bedtime a long nightcap. Evenings before holidays they might get a buzz on, might even become a little tight. But alcohol had never seemed a problem to him, only a bothersome expense that with the increase in the family they could scarcely afford. It was only after his company had transferred him to New York that Martin was aware that certainly his wife was drinking too much. She was tippling, he noticed, during the day.

The problem acknowledged, he tried to analyze the source. The change from Alabama to New York had somehow disturbed her; accustomed to the idle warmth of a small Southern town, the matrix of the family and cousinship and childhood friends, she had failed to accommodate herself to the stricter, lonelier mores of the North. The duties of motherhood and housekeeping were onerous to her. Homesick for Paris City, she had made no friends in the suburban town. She read only magazines and murder books. Her interior life was insufficient without the artifice of alcohol. The revelations of incontinence insidiously undermined his previous conceptions of his wife. There were times of unexplainable malevolence, times when the alcoholic fuse caused an explosion of unseemly anger. He encountered a latent coarseness in Emily, inconsistent with her natural simplicity. She lied about drinking and deceived him with unsuspected stratagems.

Then there was an accident. Coming home from work one evening about a year ago, he was greeted with screams from the children's room. He found Emily holding the baby, wet and naked from her bath. The baby had been dropped, her frail, frail skull striking the table edge, so that a thread of blood was soaking into the gossamer hair. Emily was sobbing and intoxicated. As Martin cradled the hurt child, so infinitely precious at that moment, he had an affrighted vision of the future.

The next day Marianne was all right. Emily vowed that never again would she touch liquor, and for a few weeks she was sober, cold and downcast. Then gradually she began—not whiskey or gin—but quantities of beer, or sherry, or outlandish liqueurs; once he had come across a hatbox of empty crème de menthe bottles. Martin found a dependable maid who managed the household competently. Virgie was also from Alabama and Martin had never dared tell Emily the wage scale customary in New York. Emily's drinking was entirely secret now, done before he reached the house. Usually the effects were almost imperceptible—a looseness of movement or the heavy-lidded eyes. The times of irresponsibilities, such as the cayenne-pepper toast, were rare, and Martin could dismiss his worries when Virgie was at the house. But, nevertheless, anxiety was always latent, a threat of indefined disaster that underlay his days.

"Marianne!" Martin called, for even the recollection of that time brought the need for reassurance. The baby girl, no longer hurt, but no less precious to her father, came into the kitchen with her brother. Martin went on with the preparations for the meal. He opened a can of soup and put two chops in the frying pan. Then he sat down by the table and took his Marianne on his knees for a pony ride. Andy watched them, his fingers wobbling the tooth that had been loose all that week.

"Andy-the-candyman!" Martin said. "Is that old critter still in your mouth? Come closer, let Daddy have a look."

"I got a string to pull it with." The child brought from his pocket a tangled thread. "Virgie said to tie it to the tooth and tie the other end of the doorknob and shut the door real suddenly."

Martin took out a clean handkerchief and felt the loose tooth carefully. "That tooth is coming out of my Andy's mouth tonight. Otherwise I'm awfully afraid we'll have a tooth tree in the family."

"A what?"

"A tooth tree," Martin said. "You'll bite into something and swallow that tooth. And the tooth will take root in poor Andy's stomach and grow into a tooth tree with sharp little teeth instead of leaves."

"Shoo, Daddy," Andy said. But he held the tooth firmly between his grimy little thumb and forefinger. "There ain't any tree like that. I never seen one."

"There *isn't* any tree like that and I never *saw* one."

Martin tensed suddenly. Emily was coming down the stairs. He listened to her fumbling footsteps, his arm embracing the little boy with dread. When Emily came into the room he saw from her movements and her sullen face that she had again been at the sherry bottle. She began to yank open drawers and set the table.

"Condition!" she said in a furry voice. "You talk to me like that. Don't think I'll forget. I remember every dirty lie you say to me. Don't you think for a minute that I forget."

"Emily!" he begged. "The children—"

"The children—yes! Don't think I don't see through your dirty plots and schemes. Down here trying to turn my own children against me. Don't think I don't see and understand."

"Emily! I beg you—please go upstairs."

"So you can turn my children—my very own children—" Two large tears coursed rapidly down her cheeks. "Trying to turn my little boy, my Andy, against his own mother."

With drunken impulsiveness Emily knelt on the floor before the startled child. Her hands on his shoulders balanced her. "Listen, my Andy—you wouldn't listen to any lies your father tells you? You wouldn't believe what he says? Listen, Andy, what was your father telling you before I came downstairs?" Uncertain, the child sought his father's face. "Tell me. Mama wants to know."

"About the tooth tree."

"What?"

The child repeated the words and she echoed them with unbelieving terror. "The tooth tree!" She swayed and renewed her grasp on the child's shoulder. "I don't know what you're talking about. But listen, Andy, Mama is all right, isn't she? The tears were spilling down her face and Andy drew back from her, for he was afraid. Grasping the table edge, Emily stood up.

"See! You have turned my child against me."

Marianne began to cry, and Martin took her in his arms.

"That's all right, you can take *your* child. You have always shown partiality from the very first. I don't mind, but at least you can leave me my little boy."

Andy edged close to his father and touched his leg. "Daddy," he wailed.

Martin took the children to the foot of the stairs. "Andy, you take up Marianne and Daddy will follow you in a minute."

"But Mama?" the child asked, whispering.

"Mama will be all right. Don't worry."

Emily was sobbing at the kitchen table, her face buried in the crook of her arm. Martin poured a cup of soup and set it before her. Her rasping sobs unnerved him; the vehemence of her emotion, irrespective of the source, touched in him a strain of tenderness. Unwillingly he laid his hand on her dark hair. "Sit up and drink the soup." Her face as she looked up at him was chastened and imploring. The boy's withdrawal or the touch of Martin's hand had turned the tenor of her mood.

"Ma-Martin," she sobbed. "I'm so ashamed."

"Drink the soup."

Obeying him, she drank between gasping breaths. After a second cup she allowed him to lead her up to their room. She was docile now and more restrained. He laid her nightgown on the bed and was about to leave the room when a fresh round of grief, the alcoholic tumult, came again.

"He turned away. My Andy looked at me and turned away."

Impatience and fatigue hardened his voice, but he spoke warily. "You forget that Andy is still a little child—he can't comprehend the meaning of such scenes."

"Did I make a scene? Oh, Martin, did I make a scene before the children?"

Her horrified face touched and amused him against his will. "Forget it. Put on your nightgown and go to sleep."

"My child turned away from me. Andy looked at his mother and turned away. The children—"

She was caught in the rhythmic sorrow of alcohol. Martin withdrew from the room saying: "For God's sake go to sleep. The children will forget by tomorrow."

As he said this he wondered if it was true. Would the scene glide so easily from memory—or would it root in the unconscious to fester in the after-years? Martin did not know, and the last alternative sickened him. He thought of Emily, foresaw the morning-after humiliation: the shards of memory, the lucidities that glared from the obliterating darkness of shame. She would call the New York office twice—possibly three or four times. Martin anticipated his own embarrassment, wondering if the others at the office could possibly suspect. He felt that his secretary had divined the trouble long ago and that she pitied him. He suffered a moment of rebellion against his fate; he hated his wife.

Once in the children's room he closed the door and felt secure for the first time that evening. Marianne fell down on the floor, picked herself up and calling: "Daddy, watch me," fell again, got up, and continued the falling-calling routine. Andy sat in the child's low chair, wobbling the tooth. Martin ran the water in the tub, washed his own hands in the lavatory, and called the boy into the bathroom.

"Let's have another look at that tooth." Martin sat on the toilet, holding Andy between his knees. The child's mouth gaped and Martin grasped the tooth. A wobble, a quick twist and the nacreous milk tooth was free. Andy's face was for the first moment split between terror, astonishment, and delight. He mouthed a swallow of water and spat into the lavatory. "Look, Daddy! It's blood. Marianne!"

Martin loved to bathe his children, loved inexpressibly the tender, naked bodies as they stood in the water so exposed. It was not fair of Emily to say that he showed partiality. As Martin soaped the delicate boy-body of his son he felt that further love would be impossible. Yet he admitted the difference in the quality of his emotions for the two children. His love for his daughter was graver, touched with a strain of melancholy, a gentleness that was akin to pain. His pet names for the little boy were the absurdities of daily inspiration—he called the little girl always Marianne, and his voice as he spoke it was a caress. Martin patted dry the fat baby stomach and the sweet little genital fold. The washed child faces were radiant as flower petals, equally loved.

"I'm putting the tooth under my pillow. I'm supposed to get a quarter."

"What for?"

"You know, Daddy. Johnny got a quarter for his tooth."

"Who puts the quarter there?" asked Martin. "I used to think the fairies left it in the night. It was a dime in my day, though."

"That's what they say in kindergarten."

"Who does put it there?"

"Your parents," Andy said. "You!"

Martin was pinning the cover on Marianne's bed. His daughter was already asleep. Scarcely breathing. Martin bent over and kissed her forehead, kissed again the tiny hand that lay palm-upward, flung in slumber beside her head.

"Good night, Andy-man."

The answer was only a drowsy murmur. After a minute Martin took out his change and slid a quarter underneath the pillow. He left a night light in the room.

As Martin prowled about the kitchen making a late meal, it occurred to him that the children had not once mentioned their mother or the scene that must have seemed to them incomprehensible. Absorbed in the instant—the tooth, the bath, the quarter—the fluid passage of child-time had borne these weightless episodes like leaves in the swift current of a shallow stream while the adult enigma was beached and forgotten on the shore. Martin thanked the Lord for that.

But his own anger, repressed and lurking, arose again. His youth was being frittered by a drunkard's waste, his very manhood subtly undermined. And the children, once the immunity of incomprehension passed—what would it be like in a year or so? With his elbows on the table he ate his food brutishly, untasting. There was no hiding the truth—soon there would be gossip in the office and in the town; his wife was a dissolute woman. Dissolute. And he and his children were bound to a future of degradation and slow ruin.

Martin pushed away from the table and stalked into the living room. He followed the lines of a book with his eyes but his mind conjured miserable images: he saw his children drowned in the river, his wife a disgrace on the public street. By bedtime the dull, hard anger was like a weight upon his chest and his feet dragged as he climbed the stairs.

The room was dark except for the shafting light from the

half-opened bathroom door. Martin undressed quietly. Little by little, mysteriously, there came in him a change. His wife was asleep, her peaceful respiration sounding gently in the room. Her high-heeled shoes with the carelessly dropped stockings made to him a mute appeal. Her underclothes were flung in disorder on the chair. Martin picked up the girdle and the soft, silk brassière and stood for a moment with them in his hands. For the first time that evening he looked at his wife. His eyes rested on the sweet forehead, the arch of the fine brow. The brow had descended to Marianne, and the tilt at the end of the delicate nose. In his son he could trace the high cheekbones and pointed chin. Her body was full-bosomed, slender and undulant. As Martin watched the tranquil slumber of his wife the ghost of the old anger vanished. All thoughts of blame or blemish were distant from him now. Martin put out the bathroom light and raised the window. Careful not to awaken Emily he slid into the bed. By moonlight he watched his wife for the last time. His hand sought the adjacent flesh and sorrow paralleled desire in the immense complexity of love.

BERNARD MALAMUD

The Magic Barrel

NOT LONG AGO there lived in uptown New York, in a small, almost meager room, though crowded with books, Leo Finkle, a rabbinical student in the Yeshivah University. Finkle, after six years of study, was to be ordained in June and had been advised by an acquaintance that he might find it easier to win himself a congregation if he were married. Since he had no present prospects of marriage, after two tormented days of turning it over in his mind, he called in Pinye Salzman, a marriage broker whose two-line advertisement he had read in the *Forward*.

The matchmaker appeared one night out of the dark fourth-floor hallway of the graystone rooming house where Finkle lived, grasping a black, strapped portfolio that had been worn thin with use. Salzman, who had been long in the business, was of slight but dignified build, wearing an old hat, and an overcoat too short and tight for him. He smelled frankly of fish, which he loved to eat, and although he was missing a few teeth, his presence was not displeasing, because of an amiable manner curiously contrasted with mournful eyes. His voice, his lips, his wisp of beard, his bony fingers were animated, but give him a moment of repose and his mild blue eyes revealed a depth of sadness, a characteristic that put Leo a little at ease although the situation, for him, was inherently tense.

He at once informed Salzman why he had asked him to come, explaining that his home was in Cleveland, and that but for his parents, who had married comparatively late in life, he was alone in the world. He had for six years devoted himself almost entirely to his studies, as a result of which, understandably, he had found himself without time for a social life and the company of young women. Therefore he thought it the better part of trial and error—of embarrassing fumbling—to call in an experienced person to advise him on these matters. He remarked in passing that the function of the marriage broker was ancient and honorable, highly approved in the Jewish community, because it made practical the necessary without hindering joy. Moreover, his own parents had been brought together by a matchmaker. They had made, if not a financially profitable marriage—since neither had possessed any worldly goods to speak of—at least a successful one in the sense of their everlasting devotion to each other. Salzman listened in embarrassed surprise, sensing a sort of apology. Later, however, he experienced a glow of pride in his work, an emotion that had left him years ago, and he heartily approved of Finkle.

The two went to their business. Leo had led Salzman to the only clear place in the room, a table near a window that overlooked the lamp-lit city. He seated himself at the matchmaker's side but facing him, attempting by an act of will to suppress the unpleasant tickle in his throat. Salzman eagerly unstrapped his portfolio and removed a loose rubber band from a thin packet of much-handled cards. As he flipped through them, a gesture and sound that physically hurt Leo, the student pretended not to see and gazed steadfastly out the window. Although it was still February, winter was on its last legs, signs of which he had for the first time in years begun to notice. He now observed the round white moon, moving high in the sky through a cloud menagerie, and watched with half-open mouth as it penetrated a huge hen, and dropped out of her like an egg laying itself. Salzman, though pretending through eyeglasses he had just slipped on, to be engaged in scanning the writing on the cards, stole occasional glances at the young man's distinguished face, noting with pleasure the long, severe scholar's nose, brown eyes heavy with learning, sensitive yet ascetic lips, and a certain, almost hollow quality of the dark cheeks. He gazed around at shelves upon shelves of books and let out a soft, contented sigh.

When Leo's eyes fell upon the cards, he counted six spread out in Salzman's hand.

"So few?" he asked in disappointment.

"You wouldn't believe me how much cards I got in my office," Salzman replied. "The drawers are already filled to the top, so I keep them now in a barrel, but is every girl good for a new rabbi?"

Leo blushed at this, regretting all he had revealed of himself in a curriculum vitae he had sent to Salzman. He had thought it best to acquaint him with his strict standards and specifications, but in having done so, felt he had told the marriage broker more than was absolutely necessary.

He hesitantly inquired, "Do you keep photographs of your clients on file?"

"First comes family, amount of dowry, also what kind promises," Salzman replied, unbuttoning his tight coat and settling himself in the chair. "After comes pictures, rabbi."

"Call me Mr. Finkle. I'm not yet a rabbi."

Salzman said he would, but instead called him doctor, which he changed to rabbi when Leo was not listening too attentively.

Salzman adjusted his horn-rimmed spectacles, gently cleared his throat and read in an eager voice the contents of the top card:

"Sophie P. Twenty-four years. Widow one year. No children. Educated high school and two years college. Father promises eight thousand dollars. Has wonderful wholesale business. Also real estate. On the mother's side comes teachers, also one actor. Well known on Second Avenue."

Leo gazed up in surprise. "Did you say a widow?"

"A widow don't mean spoiled, rabbi. She lived with her husband maybe four months. He was a sick boy she made a mistake to marry him."

"Marrying a widow has never entered my mind."

"This is because you have no experience. A widow, especially if she is young and healthy like this girl, is a wonderful person to marry. She will be thankful to you the rest of her life. Believe me, if I was looking now for a bride, I would marry a widow."

Leo reflected, then shook his head.

Salzman hunched his shoulders in an almost imperceptible gesture of disappointment. He placed the card down on the wooden table and began to read another:

"Lily H. High school teacher. Regular. Not a substitute. Has savings and new Dodge car. Lived in Paris one year. Father is successful dentist thirty-five years. Interested in professional man. Well Americanized family. Wonderful opportunity.

"I knew her personally," said Salzman. "I wish you could see this girl. She is a doll. Also very intelligent. All day you could talk to her about books and theyater and what not. She also knows current events."

"I don't believe you mentioned her age?"

"Her age?" Salzman said, raising his brows. "Her age is thirty-two years."

Leo said after a while, "I'm afraid that seems a little too old."

Salzman let out a laugh. "So how old are you, rabbi?"

"Twenty-seven."

"So what is the difference, tell me, between twenty-seven and thirty-two? My own wife is seven years older than me. So what did I suffer?—Nothing. If Rothschild's daughter wants to marry you, would you say on account her age, no?"

"Yes," Leo said dryly.

Salzman shook off the no in the yes. "Five years don't mean a thing. I give you my word that when you will live with her for one week you will forget her age. What does it mean five years—that she lived more and knows more than somebody who is younger? On this girl, God bless her, years are not wasted. Each one that it comes makes better the bargain."

"What subject does she teach in high school?"

"Languages. If you heard the way she speaks French, you will think it is music. I am in the business twenty-five years, and I recommend her with my whole heart. Believe me, I know what I'm talking, rabbi."

"What's on the next card?" Leo said abruptly.

Salzman reluctantly turned up the third card:

"Ruth K. Nineteen years. Honor student. Father offers thirteen thousand cash to the right bridegroom. He is a medical doctor. Stomach specialist with marvelous practice. Brother-in-law owns own garment business. Particular people."

Salzman looked as if he had read his trump card.

"Did you say nineteen?" Leo asked with interest.

"On the dot."

"Is she attractive?" He blushed. "Pretty?"

Salzman kissed his finger tips. "A little doll. On this I give you my word. Let me call the father tonight and you will see what means pretty."

But Leo was troubled. "You're sure she's that young?"

"This I am positive. The father will show you the birth certificate."

"Are you positive there isn't something wrong with her?" Leo insisted.

"Who says there is wrong?"

"I don't understand why an American girl her age should go to a marriage broker."

A smile spread over Salzman's face.

"So for the same reason you went, she comes."

Leo flushed. "I am pressed for time."

Salzman, realizing he had been tactless, quickly explained. "The father came, not her. He wants she should have the best, so he looks around himself. When we will locate the right boy he will introduce him and encourage. This makes a better marriage than if a young girl without experience takes for herself. I don't have to tell you this."

"But don't you think this young girl believes in love?" Leo spoke uneasily.

Salzman was about to guffaw but caught himself and said soberly, "Love comes with the right person, not before."

Leo parted dry lips but did not speak. Noticing that Salzman had snatched a glance at the next card, he cleverly asked, "How is her health?"

"Perfect," Salzman said, breathing with difficulty. "Of course, she is a little lame on her right foot from an auto accident that it happened to her when she was twelve years, but nobody notices on account she is so brilliant and also beautiful."

Leo got up heavily and went to the window. He felt curiously bitter and upbraided himself for having called in the marriage broker. Finally, he shook his head.

"Why not?" Salzman persisted, the pitch of his voice rising.

"Because I detest stomach specialists."

"So what do you care what is his business? After you marry her do you need him? Who says he must come every Friday night in your house?"

Ashamed of the way the talk was going, Leo dismissed Salzman, who went home with heavy, melancholy eyes.

Though he had felt only relief at the marriage broker's departure, Leo was in low spirits the next day. He explained it as arising from Salzman's failure to produce a suitable bride for him. He did not care for his type of clientele. But when Leo found himself hesitating whether to seek out another matchmaker, one more polished than Pinye, he wondered if it could be—his protestations to the contrary, and although he honored his father and mother—that he did not, in essence, care for the matchmaking institution? This thought he quickly put out of mind yet found himself still upset. All day he ran around in the woods—missed an important appointment, forgot to give out his laundry, walked out of a Broadway cafeteria without paying and had to run back with the ticket in his hand; had even not recognized his landlady in the street when she passed with a friend and courteously called out, "A good evening to you, Doctor Finkle." By nightfall, however, he had regained sufficient calm to sink his nose into a book and there found peace from his thoughts.

Almost at once there came a knock on the door. Before Leo could say enter, Salzman, commercial cupid, was standing in the room. His face was gray and meager, his expression hungry, and he looked as if he would expire on his feet. Yet the marriage broker managed, by some trick of the muscles, to display a broad smile.

"So good evening, I am invited?"

Leo nodded, disturbed to see him again, yet unwilling to ask the man to leave.

Beaming still, Salzman laid his portfolio on the table. "Rabbi, I got for you tonight good news."

"I've asked you not to call me rabbi. I'm still a student."

"Your worries are finished. I have for you a first-class bride."

"Leave me in peace concerning this subject." Leo pretended lack of interest.

"The world will dance at your wedding."

"Please, Mr. Salzman, no more."

"But first must come back my strength," Salzman said weakly. He fumbled with the portfolio straps and took out of the leather case an oily paper bag, from which he extracted a hard, seeded roll and a small, smoked white fish. With a quick motion of his hand he striped the fish out of its skin and began ravenously to chew. "All day in a rush," he muttered.

Leo watched him eat.

"A sliced tomato you have maybe?" Salzman hesitantly inquired.

"No."

The marriage broker shut his eyes and ate. When he had finished he carefully cleaned up the crumbs and rolled up the remains of the fish, in the paper bag. His spectacled eyes roamed the room until he discovered, amid some piles of books, a one-burner gas stove. Lifting his hat he humbly asked, "A glass tea you got, rabbi?"

Conscience-stricken, Leo rose and brewed the tea. He served it with a chunk of lemon and two cubes of lump sugar, delighting Salzman.

After he had drunk his tea, Salzman's strength and good spirits were restored.

"So tell me, rabbi," he said amiably, "you considered some more the three clients I mentioned yesterday?"

"There was no need to consider."

"Why not?"

"None of them suits me."

"What then suits you?"

Leo let it pass because he could give only a confused answer.

Without waiting for a reply, Salzman asked, "You remember this girl I talked to you—the high school teacher?"

"Age thirty-two?"

But, surprisingly, Salzman's face lit in a smile. "Age twenty-nine."

Leo shot him a look. "Reduced from thirty-two?"

"A mistake," Salzman avowed. "I talked today with the dentist. He took me to his safety deposit box and showed me the birth certificate. She was twenty-nine years last August. They made her a party in the mountains where she went for her vacation. When her father spoke to me the first time I forgot to write the age and I told you thirty-two, but now I remember this was a different client, a widow."

"The same one you told me about? I thought she was twenty-four?"

"A different. Am I responsible that the world is filled with widows?"

"No, but I'm not interested in them, nor for that matter, in school teachers."

Salzman pulled his clasped hands to his breast. Looking at the ceiling he devoutly exclaimed, "Yiddishe kinder, what can I say to somebody that he is not interested in high school teachers? So what then you are interested?"

Leo flushed but controlled himself.

"In what else will you be interested," Salzman went on, "if you not interested in this fine girl that she speaks four languages and has personally in the bank ten thousand dollars? Also her father guarantees further twelve thousand. Also she has new car, wonderful clothes, talks on all subjects, and she will give you a first-class home and children. How near do we come in our life to paradise?"

"If she's so wonderful, why wasn't she married ten years ago?"

"Why?" said Salzman with a heavy laugh. "—Why? Because she is *partikiler.* This is why. She wants the *best.*"

Leo went silent, amused at how he had entangled himself. But Salzman had aroused his interest in Lily H., and he began seriously to consider calling on her. When the marriage broker observed how intently Leo's mind was at work on the facts he had supplied, he felt certain they would soon come to an agreement.

Late Saturday afternoon, conscious of Salzman, Leo Finkle walked with Lily Hirschorn along Riverside Drive. He walked briskly and erectly, wearing with distinction the black fedora he had that morning taken with trepidation out of the dusty hat box on his closet shelf, and the heavy black Saturday coat he had thoroughly whisked clean. Leo also owned a walking stick, a present from a distant relative, but quickly put temptation aside and did not use it. Lily, petite and not unpretty, had on something signifying the approach of spring. She was au courant, animatedly, with all sorts of subjects, and he weighed her words and found her surprisingly sound—score another for Salzman, who he uneasily sensed to be somewhere around, hiding perhaps high in a tree along the street, flashing the lady signals with a pocket mirror; or perhaps a cloven-hoofed Pan, piping nuptial ditties as he danced his invisible way before them, strewing wild buds on the walk and purple grapes in their path, symbolizing fruit of a union, though there was of course still none.

Lily startled Leo by remarking, "I was thinking of Mr. Salzman, a curious figure, wouldn't you say?"

Not certain what to answer, he nodded.

She bravely went on, blushing, "I for one am grateful for his introducing us. Aren't you?"

He courteously replied, "I am."

"I mean," she said with a little laugh—and it was all in good taste, or at least gave the effect of being not in bad—"do you mind that we came together so?"

He was not displeased with her honesty, recognizing that she meant to set the relationship aright, and understanding that it took a certain amount of experience in life, and courage, to want to do it quite that way. One had to have some sort of past to make that kind of beginning.

He said that he did not mind. Salzman's function was traditional and honorable—valuable for what it might achieve, which, he pointed out, was frequently nothing.

Lily agreed with a sigh. They walked on for a while and she said after a long silence, again with a nervous laugh, "Would you mind if I asked you something a little bit personal? Frankly, I find the subject fascinating." Although Leo shrugged, she went on half embarrassedly, "How was it that you came to your calling? I mean was it a sudden passionate inspiration?"

Leo, after a time, slowly replied, "I was always interested in the Law."

"You saw revealed in it the presence of the Highest?"

He nodded and changed the subject. "I understand that you spent a little time in Paris, Miss Hirschorn?"

"Oh, did Mr. Salzman tell you, Rabbi Finkle?" Leo winced but she went on, "It was ages ago and almost forgotten. I remember I had to return for my sister's wedding."

And Lily would not be put off. "When," she asked in a trembly voice, "did you become enamored of God?"

He stared at her. Then it came to him that she was talking not about Leo Finkle, but of a total stranger, some mystical figure, perhaps even passionate prophet that Salzman had dreamed up for her—no relation to the living or dead. Leo trembled with rage and weakness. The trickster had obviously sold her a bill of goods, just as he had him, who'd expected to become acquainted with a young lady of twenty-nine, only to behold, the moment he laid eyes upon her strained and anxious face, a woman past thirty-five and aging rapidly. Only his self-control had kept him this long in her presence.

"I am not," he said gravely, "a talented religious person," and in seeking words to go on, found himself possessed by shame and fear. "I think," he said in a strained manner, "that I came to God not because I loved Him, but because I did not."

This confession he spoke harshly because its unexpectedness shook him.

Lily wilted. Leo saw a profusion of loaves of bread go flying like ducks high over his head, not unlike the winged loaves by which he had counted himself to sleep last night. Mercifully, then, it snowed, which he would not put past Salzman's machinations.

He was infuriated with the marriage broker and swore he would throw him out of the room the minute he reappeared. But Salzman did not come that night, and when Leo's anger had subsided, an unaccountable despair grew in its place. At first he thought this was caused by his disappointment in Lily, but before long it became evident that he had involved himself with Salzman without a true knowledge of his own intent. He gradually realized—with an emptiness that seized him with six hands—that he had called in the broker to find him a bride because he was incapable of doing it himself. This terrifying insight he had derived as a result of his meeting and conversation with Lily Hirschorn. Her probing questions had somehow irritated him into revealing—to himself more than her—the true nature of his relationship to God, and from that it had come upon him, with shocking force, that apart from his parents, he had never loved anyone. Or perhaps it went the other way, that he did not love God so well as he might, because he had not loved man. It seemed to Leo that his whole life stood starkly revealed and he saw himself for the first time as he truly was—unloved and loveless. This bitter but somehow not fully unexpected revelation brought him to a point of panic, controlled only by extraordinary effort. He covered his face with his hands and cried.

The week that followed was the worst of his life. He did not eat and lost weight. His beard darkened and grew ragged. He stopped attending seminars and almost never opened a book. He seriously considered leaving the Yeshivah, although he was deeply troubled at the thought of the loss of all his years of study—saw them like pages torn from a book, strewn over the city—and at the devastating effect of this decision upon his parents. But he had lived without knowledge of himself, and never in the Five Books and all the Commentaries—mea culpa—had the truth been revealed to him. He did not know where to turn, and in all this desolating loneliness there was no *to whom,* although he often thought of Lily but not once could bring himself to go downstairs and make the call. He became touchy and irritable, especially with his landlady, who asked him all manner of personal questions; on the other hand, sensing his own disagreeableness, he waylaid her on the stairs and apologized abjectly, until mortified, she ran from him. Out of this, however, he drew the consolation that he was a Jew and that a Jew suffered. But gradually, as the long and terrible week drew to a close, he regained his composure and some idea of purpose in life: to go on as planned. Although he was imperfect, the ideal was not. As for his quest of a bride, the thought of continuing afflicted him with anxiety and heartburn, yet perhaps with this new knowledge of himself he would be more successful than in the past. Perhaps love would now come to him and a bride to that love. And for this sanctified seeking who needed a Salzman?

The marriage broker, a skeleton with haunted eyes, returned that very night. He looked, withal, the picture of frustrated expectancy—as if he had steadfastly waited the week at Miss Lily Hirschorn's side for a telephone call that never came.

Casually coughing, Salzman came immediately to the point: "So how did you like her?"

Leo's anger rose and he could not refrain from chiding the matchmaker: "Why did you lie to me, Salzman?"

Salzman's pale face went dead white, the world had snowed on him.

"Did you not state that she was twenty-nine?" Leo insisted.

"I give you my word—"

"She was thirty-five, if a day. *At least* thirty-five."

"Of this don't be too sure. Her father told me—"

"Never mind. The worst of it was that you lied to her."

"How did I lie to her, tell me?"

"You told her things about me that weren't true. You made me out to be more, consequently less than I am. She had in mind a totally different person, a sort of semimystical Wonder Rabbi."

"All I said, you was a religious man."

"I can imagine."

Salzman sighed. "This is my weakness that I have," he confessed. "My wife says to me I shouldn't be a salesman, but when I have two fine people that they would be wonderful to be married, I am so happy that I talk too much." He smiled wanly. "This is why Salzman is a poor man."

Leo's anger left him. "Well, Salzman, I'm afraid that's all."

The marriage broker fastened hungry eyes on him.

"You don't want any more a bride?"

"I do," said Leo, "but I have decided to seek her in a different way. I am no longer interested in an arranged marriage. To be frank, I now admit the necessity of premarital love. That is, I want to be in love with the one I marry."

"Love?" said Salzman, astounded. After a moment he remarked, "For us, our love is our life, not for the ladies. In the ghetto they—"

"I know, I know," said Leo. "I've thought of it often. Love, I have said to myself, should be a by-product of living and worship rather than its own end. Yet for myself I find it necessary to establish the level of my need and fulfill it."

Salzman shrugged but answered, "Listen, rabbi, if you want love, this I can find for you also. I have such beautiful clients that you will love them the minute your eyes will see them."

Leo smiled unhappily. "I'm afraid you don't understand."

But Salzman hastily unstrapped his portfolio and withdrew a manila packet from it.

"Pictures," he said, quickly laying the envelope on the table.

Leo called after him to take the pictures away, but as if on the wings of the wind, Salzman had disappeared.

March came. Leo had returned to his regular routine. Although he felt not quite himself yet—lacked energy—he was making plans for a more active social life. Of course it would cost something, but he was an expert in cutting corners; and when there were no corners left he would make circles rounder. All the while Salzman's pictures had lain on the table, gathering dust. Occasionally as Leo sat studying, or enjoying a cup of tea, his eyes fell on the manila envelope, but he never opened it.

The days went by and no social life to speak of developed with a member of the opposite sex—it was difficult, given the circumstances of his situation. One morning Leo toiled up the stairs to his room and stared out the window at the city. Although the day was bright his view of it was dark. For some time he watched the people in the street below hurrying along and then turned with a heavy heart to his little room. On the table was the packet. With a sudden relentless gesture he tore it open. For a half-hour he stood by the table in a state of excitement, examining the photographs of the ladies Salzman had included. Finally, with a deep sigh he put them down. There were six, of varying degrees of attractiveness, but look at them long enough and they all became Lily Hirschorn: all past their prime, all starved behind bright smiles, not a true personality in the lot. Life, despite their frantic yoohooings, had passed them by; they were pictures in a brief case that stank of fish. After a while, however, as Leo attempted to return the photographs into the envelope, he found in it another, a snapshot of the type taken by a machine for a quarter. He gazed at it a moment and let out a cry.

Her face deeply moved him. Why, he could at first not say. It gave him the impression of youth—spring flowers, yet age—a sense of having been used to the bone, wasted; this came from the eyes, which were hauntingly familiar, yet absolutely strange. He had a vivid impression that he had met her before, but try as he might he could not place her although he could almost recall her name, as if he had read it in her own handwriting. No, this couldn't be; he would have remembered her. It was not, he affirmed, that she had an extraordinary beauty—no, though her face was attractive; enough it was that *something* about her moved him. Feature for feature, even some of the ladies of the photographs could do better; but she leaped forth to his heart—had *lived,* or wanted to—more than just wanted, perhaps regretted how she had lived—had somehow deeply suffered: it could be seen in the depths of those reluctant eyes, and from the way the light enclosed and shone from her, and within her, opening realms of possibility: this was her own. Her he desired. His head ached and eyes narrowed with the intensity of his gazing, then as if an obscure fog had blown up in the mind, he experienced fear of her and was aware that he had received an impression, somehow, of evil. He shuddered, saying softly, it is thus with us all. Leo brewed some tea in a small pot and sat sipping it without sugar, to calm himself. But before he had finished drinking, again with excitement he examined the face and found it good: good for Leo Finkle. Only such a one could understand him and help him seek whatever he was seeking. She might, perhaps, love him. How she had happened to be among the discards in Salzman's barrel he could never guess, but he knew he must urgently go find her.

Leo rushed downstairs, grabbed up the Bronx telephone book, and searched for Salzman's home address. He was not listed, nor was his office. Neither was he in the Manhattan book. But Leo remembered having written down the address on a slip of paper after he had read Salzman's advertisement in the "personals" column of the *Forward.* He ran up to his room and tore through his papers, without luck. It was exasperating. Just when he needed the matchmaker he was nowhere to be found. Fortunately Leo remembered to look in his wallet. There on a card he found his name written and a Bronx address. No phone number was listed, the reason—Leo now recalled—he had originally communicated with Salzman by letter. He got on his coat, put a hat on over his skull cap and hurried to the subway station. All the way to the far end of the Bronx he sat on the edge of his seat. He was more than once tempted to take out the picture and see if the girl's face was as he remembered it, but he refrained, allowing the snapshot to remain in his inside coat pocket, content to have her so close. When the train pulled into the station he was waiting at the door and bolted out. He quickly located the street Salzman had advertised.

The building he sought was less than a block from the subway, but it was not an office building, not even a loft, nor a store in which one could rent office space. It was a very old tenement house. Leo found Salzman's name in pencil on a soiled tag under the bell and climbed three dark flights to his apartment. When he knocked, the door was opened by a thin, asthmatic, gray-haired woman, in felt slippers."

"Yes?" she said, expecting nothing. She listened without listening. He could have sworn he had seen her, too, before but knew it was an illusion.

"Salzman—does he live here? Pinye Salzman," he said, "the matchmaker?"

She stared at him a long minute. "Of course."

He felt embarrassed. "Is he in?"

"No." Her mouth, though left open, offered nothing more.

"The matter is urgent. Can you tell me where his office is?"

"In the air." She pointed upward.

"You mean he has no office?" Leo asked.

"In his socks."

He peered into the apartment. It was sunless and dingy, one large room divided by a half-open curtain, beyond which he could see a sagging metal bed. The near side of a room was crowded with rickety chairs, old bureaus, a three-legged table, racks of cooking utensils, and all the apparatus of a kitchen. But there was no sign of Salzman or his magic barrel, probably also a figment of the imagination. An odor of frying fish made Leo weak to the knees.

"Where is he?" he insisted. "I've got to see your husband."

At length she answered, "So who knows where he is? Every time he thinks a new thought he runs to a different place. Go home, he will find you."

"Tell him Leo Finkle."

She gave no sign she had heard.

He walked downstairs, depressed.

But Salzman, breathless, stood waiting at his door.

Leo was astounded and overjoyed. "How did you get here before me?"

"I rushed."

"Come inside."

They entered. Leo fixed tea, and a sardine sandwich for Salzman. As they were drinking he reached behind him for the packet of pictures and handed them to the marriage broker.

Salzman put down his glass and said expectantly, "You found somebody you like?"

"Not among these."

The marriage broker turned away.

"Here is the one I want." Leo held forth the snapshot.

Salzman slipped on his glasses and took the picture into his trembling hand. He turned ghastly and let out a groan.

"What's the matter?" cried Leo.

"Excuse me. Was an accident this picture. She isn't for you."

Salzman frantically shoved the manila packet into his portfolio. He thrust the snapshot into his pocket and fled down the stairs.

Leo, after momentary paralysis, gave chase and cornered the marriage broker in the vestibule. The landlady made hysterical outcries but neither of them listened.

"Give me back the picture, Salzman."

"No." The pain in his eyes was terrible.

"Tell me who she is then."

"This I can't tell you. Excuse me."

He made to depart, but Leo, forgetting himself, seized the matchmaker by his tight coat and shook him frenziedly.

"Please," sighed Salzman. *"Please."*

Leo ashamedly let him go. "Tell me who she is," he begged. "It's very important for me to know."

"She is not for you. She is a wild one—wild, without shame. This is not a bride for a rabbi."

"What do you mean wild?"

"Like an animal. Like a dog. For her to be poor was a sin. This is why to me she is dead now."

"In God's name, what do you mean?"

"Her I can't introduce to you," Salzman cried.

"Why are you so excited?"

"Why, he asks," Salzman said, bursting into tears. "This is my baby, my Stella, she should burn in hell."

* * *

Leo hurried up to bed and hid under the covers. Under the covers he thought his life through. Although he soon fell asleep he could not sleep her out of his mind. He woke, beating his breast. Though he prayed to be rid of her, his prayers went unanswered. Through days of torment he endlessly struggled not to love her; fearing success, he escaped it. He then concluded to convert her to goodness, himself to God. The idea alternately nauseated and exalted him.

He perhaps did not know that he had come to a final decision until he encountered Salzman in a Broadway cafeteria. He was sitting alone at a rear table, sucking the bony remains of a fish. The marriage broker appeared haggard, and transparent to the point of vanishing.

Salzman looked up at first without recognizing him. Leo had grown a pointed beard and his eyes were weighted with wisdom.

"Salzman," he said, "love has at last come to my heart."

"Who can love from a picture?" mocked the marriage broker.

"It is not impossible."

"If you can love her, then you can love anybody. Let me show you some new clients that they just sent me their photographs. One is a little doll."

"Just her I want," Leo murmured.

"Don't be a fool, doctor. Don't bother with her."

"Put me in touch with her, Salzman," Leo said humbly. "Perhaps I can be of service."

Salzman had stopped eating and Leo understood with emotion that it was now arranged.

Leaving the cafeteria, he was, however, afflicted by a tormenting suspicion that Salzman had planned it all to happen this way.

Leo was informed by letter that she would meet him on a certain corner, and she was there one spring night, waiting under a street lamp. He appeared, carrying a small bouquet of violets and rosebuds. Stella stood by the lamp post, smoking. She wore white with red shoes, which fitted his expectations, although in a troubled moment he had imagined the dress red, and only the shoes white. She waited uneasily and shyly. From afar he saw that her eyes—clearly her father's—were filled with desperate innocence. He pictured, in her, his own redemption. Violins and lit candles revolved in the sky. Leo ran forward with flowers outthrust.

Around the corner, Salzman, leaning against a wall, chanted prayers for the dead.

GLORIA NAYLOR

Kiswana Browne

FROM THE WINDOW of her sixth-floor studio apartment, Kiswana could see over the wall at the end of the street to the busy avenue that lay just north of Brewster Place. The late-afternoon shoppers looked like brightly clad marionettes as they moved between the congested traffic, clutching their packages against their bodies to guard them from sudden bursts of the cold autumn wind. A portly mailman had abandoned his cart and was bumping into indignant window-shoppers as he puffed behind the cap that the wind had snatched from his head. Kiswana leaned over to see if he was going to be successful, but the edge of the building cut him off from her view.

A pigeon swept across her window, and she marveled at its liquid movements in the air waves. She placed her dreams on the back of the bird and fantasized that it would glide forever in transparent silver circles until it ascended to the center of the universe and was swallowed up. But the wind died down, and she watched with a sigh as the bird beat its wings in awkward, frantic movements to land on the corroded top of a fire escape on the opposite building. This brought her back to earth.

Humph, it's probably sitting over there crapping on those folks' fire escape, she thought. Now, that's a safety hazard. . . . And her mind was busy again, creating flames and smoke and frustrated tenants whose escape was being hindered because they were slipping and sliding in pigeon shit. She watched their cussing, haphazard descent on the fire escapes until they had all reached the bottom. They were milling around, oblivious to their burning apartments, angrily planning to march on the mayor's office about the pigeons. She materialized placards and banners for them, and they had just reached the corner, boldly sidestepping fire hoses and broken glass, when they all vanished.

A tall copper-skinned woman had met this phantom parade at the corner, and they had dissolved in front of her long, confident strides. She plowed through the remains of their faded mists, unconscious of the lingering wisps of their presence on her leather bag and black fur-trimmed coat. It took a few seconds for this transfer from one realm to another to reach Kiswana, but then suddenly she recognized the woman.

"Oh, God, it's Mama!" She looked down guiltily at the forgotten newspaper in her lap and hurriedly circled random job advertisements.

By this time Mrs. Browne had reached the front of Kiswana's building and was checking the house number against a piece of paper in her hand. Before she went into the building she stood at the bottom of the stoop and carefully inspected the condition of the street and the adjoining property. Kiswana watched this meticulous inventory with growing annoyance but she involuntarily followed her mother's slowly rotating head, forcing herself to see her new neighborhood through the older woman's eyes. The brightness of the unclouded sky seemed to join forces with her mother as it highlighted every broken stoop railing and missing brick. The afternoon sun glittered and cascaded across even the tiniest fragments of broken bottle, and at that very moment the wind chose to rise up again, sending unswept grime flying into the air, as a stray tin can left by careless garbage collectors went rolling noisily down the center of the street.

Kiswana noticed with relief that at least Ben wasn't sitting in his usual place on the old garbage can pushed against the far wall. He was just a harmless old wino, but Kiswana knew her mother only needed one wino or one teenager with a reefer within a twenty-block radius to decide that her daughter was living in a building seething with dope factories and hang-outs for derelicts. If she had seen Ben, nothing would have made her believe that practically every apartment contained a family, a Bible, and a dream that one day enough could be scraped from those meager Friday night paychecks to make Brewster Place a distant memory.

As she watched her mother's head disappear into the building, Kiswana gave silent thanks that the elevator was broken. That would give her at least five minutes' grace to straighten up the apartment. She rushed to the sofa bed and hastily closed it without smoothing the rumpled sheets and blanket or removing her nightgown. She felt that somehow the tangled bedcovers would give away the fact that she had not slept alone last night. She silently apologized to Abshu's memory as she heartlessly crushed his spirit between the steel springs of the couch. Lord, that man was sweet. Her toes curled involuntarily at the passing thought of his full lips moving slowly over her instep. Abshu was a foot man, and he always started his lovemaking from the bottom up. For that reason Kiswana changed the color of the polish on her toenails every week. During the course of their relationship she had gone from shades of red to brown and was now into the purples. I'm gonna have to start mixing them soon, she thought aloud as she turned from the couch and raced into the bathroom to remove any traces of Abshu from there. She took up his shaving cream and razor and threw them into the bottom drawer of her dresser beside her diaphragm. Mama wouldn't dare pry into my drawers right in front of me, she thought as she slammed the drawer shut. Well, at least not the *bottom* drawer. She may come up with some sham excuse for opening the top drawer, but never the bottom one.

When she heard the first two short raps on the door, her eyes took a final flight over the small apartment, desperately seeking out any slight misdemeanor that might have to be defended. Well, there was nothing she could do about the crack in the wall over that table. She had been after the landlord to fix it for two months now. And there had been no time to sweep the rug, and everyone knew that off-gray always looked dirtier than it really was. And it was just too damn bad about the kitchen. How was she expected to be out job-hunting every day and still have time to keep a kitchen that looked like her mother's, who didn't even work and still had someone come in twice a month for general cleaning. And besides . . .

Her imaginary argument was abruptly interrupted by a second series of knocks, accompanied by a penetrating, "Melanie, Melanie, are you there?"

Kiswana strode toward the door. She's starting before she even gets in here. She knows that's not my name anymore.

She swung the door open to face her slightly flushed mother. "Oh, hi, Mama. You know, I thought I heard a knock, but I figured it was for the people next door, since no one hardly ever calls me Melanie." Score one for me, she thought.

"Well, it's awfully strange you can forget a name you answered to for twenty-three years," Mrs. Browne said, as she moved past Kiswana into the apartment. "My, that was a long climb. How long has your elevator been out? Honey, how do you manage with your laundry and groceries up all those steps? But I guess you're young, and it wouldn't bother you as much as it does me." This long string of questions told Kiswana that her mother had no intentions of beginning her visit with another argument about her new African name.

"You know I would have called before I came, but you don't have a phone yet. I didn't want you to feel that I was snooping. As a matter of fact, I didn't expect to find you home at all. I thought you'd be out looking for a job." Mrs. Browne had mentally covered the entire apartment while she was talking and taking off her coat.

"Well, I got up late this morning. I thought I'd buy the afternoon paper and start early tomorrow."

"That sounds like a good idea." Her mother moved toward the window and picked up the discarded paper and glanced over the hurriedly circled ads. "Since when do you have experience as a fork-lift operator?"

Kiswana caught her breath and silently cursed herself for her stupidity. "Oh, my hand slipped—I meant to circle file clerk." She quickly took the paper before her mother could see that she had also marked cutlery salesman and chauffeur.

"You're sure you weren't sitting here moping and day-dreaming again?" Amber specks of laughter flashed in the corner of Mrs. Browne's eyes.

Kiswana threw her shoulders back and unsuccessfully tried to disguise her embarrassment with indignation.

"Oh, God, Mama! I haven't done that in years—it's for kids. When are you going to realize that I'm a woman now?" She sought desperately for some womanly thing to do and settled for throwing herself on the couch and crossing her legs in what she hoped looked like a nonchalant arc.

"Please, have a seat," she said, attempting the same tones and gestures she'd seen Bette Davis use on the late movies.

Mrs. Browne, lowering her eyes to hide her amusement, accepted the invitation and sat at the window, also crossing her legs. Kiswana saw immediately how it should have been done. Her celluloid poise clashed loudly against her mother's quiet dignity, and she quickly uncrossed her legs. Mrs. Browne turned her head toward the window and pretended not to notice.

"At least you have a halfway decent view from here. I was wondering what lay beyond that dreadful wall—it's the boulevard. Honey, did you know that you can see the trees in Linden Hills from here?"

Kiswana knew that very well, because there were many lonely days that she would sit in her gray apartment and stare at those trees and think of home, but she would rather have choked than admit that to her mother.

"Oh, really, I never noticed. So how is Daddy and things at home?"

"Just fine. We're thinking of redoing one of the extra bedrooms since you children have moved out, but Wilson insists that he can manage all that work alone. I told him that he doesn't really have the proper time or energy for all that. As it is, when he gets home from the office, he's so tired he can hardly move. But you know you can't tell your father anything. Whenever he starts complaining about how stubborn you are, I tell him the child came by it honestly. Oh, and your brother was by yesterday,'' she added, as if it had just occurred to her.

So that's it, thought Kiswana. That's why she's here.

Kiswana's brother, Wilson, had been to visit her two days ago, and she had borrowed twenty dollars from him to get her winter coat out of layaway. That son-of-a-bitch probably ran straight to Mama—and after he swore he wouldn't say anything. I should have known, he was always a snotty-nosed sneak, she thought.

''Was he?'' she said aloud. ''He came by to see me, too, earlier this week. And I borrowed some money from him because my unemployment checks hadn't cleared in the bank, but now they have and everything's just fine.'' There, I'll beat you to that one.

''Oh, I didn't know that,'' Mrs. Browne lied. ''He never mentioned you. He had just heard that Beverly was expecting again, and he rushed over to tell us.''

Damn. Kiswana could have strangled herself.

''So she's knocked up again, huh?'' she said irritably.

Her mother started. ''Why do you always have to be so crude?''

''Personally, I don't see how she can sleep with Willie. He's such a dishrag.''

Kiswana still resented the stance her brother had taken in college. When everyone at school was discovering their blackness and protesting on campus, Wilson never took part; he had even refused to wear an Afro. This had outraged Kiswana because, unlike her, he was dark-skinned and had the type of hair that was thick and kinky enough for a good ''Fro.'' Kiswana had still insisted on cutting her own hair, but it was so thin and fine-textured, it refused to thicken even after she washed it. So she had to brush it up and spray it with lacquer to keep it from lying flat. She never forgave Wilson for telling her that she didn't look African, she looked like an electrocuted chicken.

''Now that's some way to talk. I don't know why you have an attitude against your brother. He never gave me a restless night's sleep, and now he's settled with a family and a good job."

"He's an assistant to an assistant junior partner in a law firm. What's the big deal about that?"

"The job has a future, Melanie. And at least he finished school and went on for his law degree."

"In other words, not like me, huh?"

"Don't put words into my mouth, young lady. I'm perfectly capable of saying what I mean."

Amen, thought Kiswana.

"And I don't know why you've been trying to start up with me from the moment I walked in. I didn't come here to fight with you. This is your first place away from home, and I just wanted to see how you were living and if you're doing all right. And I must say, you've fixed this apartment up very nicely."

"Really, Mama?" She found herself softening in the light of her mother's approval.

"Well, considering what you had to work with." This time she scanned the apartment openly.

"Look, I know it's not Linden Hills, but a lot can be done with it. As soon as they come and paint, I'm going to hang my Ashanti print over the couch. And I thought a big Boston Fern would go well in that corner, what do you think?"

"That would be find, baby. You always had a good eye for balance."

Kiswana was beginning to relax. There was little she did that attracted her mother's approval. It was like a rare bird, and she had to tread carefully around it lest it fly away.

"Are you going to leave that statue out like that?"

"Why, what's wrong with it? Would it look better somewhere else?"

There was a small wooden reproduction of a Yoruba goddess with large protruding breasts on the coffee table.

"Well," Mrs. Browne was beginning to blush, "it's just that it's a bit suggestive, don't you think? Since you live alone now, and I know you'll be having male friends stop by, you wouldn't want to be giving them any ideas. I mean, uh, you know, there's no point in putting yourself in any unpleasant situations because they may get the wrong impressions and uh, you know, I mean, well . . ." Mrs. Browne stammered on miserably.

Kiswana loved it when her mother tried to talk about sex. It was the only time she was at a loss for words.

"Don't worry, Mama." Kiswana smiled. "That wouldn't bother the type of men I date. Now maybe if it had big feet . . ." And she got hysterical, thinking of Abshu.

Her mother looked at her sharply. "What sort of gibberish is that about feet? I'm being serious, Melanie."

"I'm sorry, Mama." She sobered up. "I'll put it away in the closet," she said, knowing that she wouldn't.

"Good," Mrs. Browne said, knowing that she wouldn't either. "I guess you think I'm too picky, but we worry about you over here. And you refuse to put in a phone so we can call and see about you."

"I haven't refused, Mama. They want seventy-five dollars for a deposit, and I can't swing that right now."

"Melanie, I can give you the money."

"I don't want you to be giving me money—I've told you that before. Please, let me make it by myself."

"Well, let me lend it to you, then."

"No!"

"Oh, so you can borrow money from your brother, but not from me."

Kiswana turned her head from the hurt in her mother's eyes. "Mama, when I borrow from Willie, he makes me pay him back. You never let me pay you back," she said into her hands.

"I don't care. I still think it's downright selfish of you to be sitting over here with no phone, and sometimes we don't hear from you in two weeks—anything could happen—especially living among these people."

Kiswana snapped her head up. "What do you mean, *these people*. They're my people and yours, too, Mama—we're all black. But maybe you've forgotten that over in Linden Hills."

"That's not what I'm talking about, and you know it. These streets—this building—it's so shabby and rundown. Honey, you don't have to live like this."

"Well, this is how poor people live."

"Melanie, you're not poor."

"No, Mama, *you're* not poor. And what you have and I have are two totally different things. I don't have a husband in real estate with a five-figure income and a home in Linden Hills—*you* do. What I have is a weekly unemployment check and an overdrawn checking account at United Federal. So this studio on Brewster is all I can afford."

"Well, you could afford a lot better," Mrs. Browne snapped, "if you hadn't dropped out of college and had to resort to these dead-end clerical jobs."

"Uh-huh, I knew you'd get around to that before long." Kiswana could feel the rings of anger begin to tighten around her lower backbone, and they sent her forward onto the couch. "You'll never understand, will you? Those bourgie schools were counterrevolutionary. My place was in the streets with my people, fighting for equality and a better community."

"Counterrevolutionary!" Mrs. Browne was raising her voice. "Where's your revolution now, Melanie? Where are all those black revolutionaries who were shouting and demonstrating and kicking up a lot of dust with you on that campus? Huh? They're sitting in wood-paneled offices with their degrees in mahogany frames, and they won't even drive their cars past this street because the city doesn't fix potholes in this part of town."

"Mama," she said, shaking her head slowly in disbelief, "how can you—a black woman—sit there and tell me that what we fought for during the Movement wasn't important just because some people sold out?"

"Melanie, I'm not saying it wasn't important. It was damned important to stand up and say that you were proud of what you were and to get the vote and other social opportunities for every person in this country who had it due. But you kids thought you were going to turn the world upside down, and it just wasn't so. When all the smoke had cleared, you found yourself with a fistful of new federal laws and a country still full of obstacles for black people to fight their way over—

just because they're black. There was no revolution, Melanie, and there will be no revolution."

"So what am I supposed to do, huh? Just throw up my hands and not care about what happens to my people? I'm not supposed to keep fighting to make things better?"

"Of course, you can. But you're going to have to fight within the system, because it and these so-called 'bourgie' schools are going to be here for a long time. And that means that you get smart like a lot of your old friends and get an important job where you can have some influence. You don't have to sell out, as you say, and work for some corporation, but you could become an assemblywoman or a civil liberties lawyer or open a freedom school in this very neighborhood. That way you could really help the community. But what help are you going to be to these people on Brewster while you're living hand-to-mouth on file-clerk jobs waiting for a revolution? You're wasting your talents, child."

"Well, I don't think they're being wasted. At least I'm here in day-to-day contact with the problems of my people. What good would I be after four or five years of a lot of white brainwashing in some phony, prestige institution, huh? I'd be like you and Daddy and those other educated blacks sitting over there in Linden Hills with a terminal case of middle-class amnesia."

"You don't have to live in a slum to be concerned about social conditions, Melanie. Your father and I have been charter members of the NAACP for the last twenty-five years."

"Oh, God!" Kiswana threw her head back in exaggerated disgust. "That's being concerned? That middle-of-the-road, Uncle Tom dumping ground for black Republicans!"

"You can sneer all you want, young lady, but that organization has been working for black people since the turn of the century, and it's still working for them. Where are all those radical groups of yours that were going to put a Cadillac in every garage and Dick Gregory in the White House? I'll tell you where."

I knew you would, Kiswana thought angrily.

"They burned themselves out because they wanted too much

too fast. Their goals weren't grounded in reality. And that's always been your problem."

"What do you mean, my problem? I know exactly what I'm about."

"No, you don't. You constantly live in a fantasy world—always going to extremes—turning butterflies into eagles, and life isn't about that. It's accepting what is and working from that. Lord, I remember how worried you had me, putting all that lacquered hair spray on your head. I thought you were going to get lung cancer—trying to be what you're not."

Kiswana jumped up from the couch. "Oh, God, I can't take this anymore. Trying to be something I'm not—trying to be something I'm not, Mama! Trying to be proud of my heritage and the fact that I was of African descent. If that's being what I'm not, then I say fine. But I'd rather be dead than be like you—a white man's nigger who's ashamed of being black!"

Kiswana saw streaks of gold and ebony light follow her mother's flying body out of the chair. She was swung around by the shoulders and made to face the deadly stillness in the angry woman's eyes. She was too stunned to cry out from the pain of the long fingernails that dug into her shoulders, and she was brought so close to her mother's face that she saw her reflection, distorted and wavering, in the tears that stood in the older woman's eyes. And she listened in that stillness to a story she had heard from a child.

"My grandmother," Mrs. Browne began slowly in a whisper, "was a full-blooded Iroquois, and my grandfather a free black from a long line of journeymen who had lived in Connecticut since the establishment of the colonies. And my father was a Bajan who came to this country as a cabin boy on a merchant mariner."

"I know all that," Kiswana said, trying to keep her lips from trembling.

"Then, know this." And the nails dug deeper into her flesh. "I am alive because of the blood of proud people who never scraped or begged or apologized for what they were. They lived asking only one thing of this world—to be allowed to be. And I learned through the blood of these people that black isn't beautiful and it isn't ugly—black is! It's not kinky hair and it's not straight hair—it just is.

"It broke my heart when you changed your name. I gave you my grandmother's name, a woman who bore nine children and educated them all, who held off six white men with a shotgun when they tried to drag one of her sons to jail for 'not knowing his place.' Yet you needed to reach into an African dictionary to find a name to make you proud.

"When I brought my babies home from the hospital, my ebony son and my golden daughter, I swore before whatever gods would listen—those of my mother's people or those of my father's people—that I would use everything I had and could ever get to see that my children were prepared to meet this world on its own terms, so that no one could sell them short and make them ashamed of what they were or how they looked—whatever they were or however they looked. And Melanie, that's not being white or red or black—that's being a mother."

Kiswana followed her reflection in the two single tears that moved down her mother's cheeks until it blended with them into the woman's copper skin. There was nothing and then so much that she wanted to say, but her throat kept closing up every time she tried to speak. She kept her head down and her eyes closed, and thought, Oh, God, just let me die. How can I face her now?

Mrs. Browne lifted Kiswana's chin gently. "And the one lesson I wanted you to learn is not to be afraid to face anyone, not even a crafty old lady like me who can outtalk you." And she smiled and winked.

"Oh, Mama, I . . ." and she hugged the woman tightly.

"Yeah, baby." Mrs. Browne patted her back. "I know."

She kissed Kiswana on the forehead and cleared her throat. "Well, now, I better be moving on. It's getting late, there's dinner to be made, and I have to get off my feet—these new shoes are killing me."

Kiswana looked down at the beige leather pumps. "Those are really classy. They're English, aren't they?"

"Yes, but, Lord, do they cut me right across the instep."

She removed the shoe and sat on the couch to massage her foot.

Bright red nail polish glared at Kiswana through the stockings. "Since when do you polish your toenails?" she gasped. "You never did that before."

"Well . . ." Mrs. Browne shrugged her shoulders, "your father sort of talked me into it, and, uh, you know, he likes it and all, so I thought, uh, you know, why not, so . . ." And she gave Kiswana an embarrassed smile.

I'll be damned, the young woman thought, feeling her whole face tingle. Daddy's into feet! And she looked at the blushing woman on her couch and suddenly realized that her mother had trod through the same universe that she herself was now traveling. Kiswana was breaking no new trails and would eventually end up just two feet away on that couch. She stared at the woman she had been and was to become.

"But I'll never be a Republican," she caught herself saying aloud.

"What are you mumbling about, Melanie?" Mrs. Browne slipped on her shoe and got up from the couch.

She went to get her mother's coat. "Nothing, Mama. It's really nice of you to come by. You should do it more often."

"Well, since it's not Sunday, I guess you're allowed at least one lie."

They both laughed.

After Kiswana had closed the door and turned around, she spotted an envelope sticking between the cushions of her couch. She went over and opened it up; there was seventy-five dollars in it.

"Oh, Mama, darn it!" She rushed to the window and started to call to the woman, who had just emerged from the building, but she suddenly changed her mind and sat down in the chair with a long sigh that caught in the upward draft of the autumn wind and disappeared over the top of the building.

FLANNERY O'CONNOR

Everything That Rises Must Converge

HER DOCTOR HAD told Julian's mother that she must lose twenty pounds on account of her blood pressure, so on Wednesday nights Julian had to take her downtown on the bus for a reducing class at the Y. The reducing class was designed for working girls over fifty, who weighed from 165 to 200 pounds. His mother was one of the slimmer ones, but she said ladies did not tell their age or weight. She would not ride the buses by herself at night since they had been integrated, and because the reducing class was one of her few pleasures, necessary for her health, and *free*, she said Julian could at least put himself out to take her, considering all she did for him. Julian did not like to consider all she did for him, but every Wednesday night he braced himself and took her.

She was almost ready to go, standing before the hall mirror, putting on her hat, while he, his hands behind him, appeared pinned to the door frame, waiting like Saint Sebastian for the arrows to begin piercing him. The hat was new and had cost her seven dollars and a half. She kept saying, "Maybe I shouldn't have paid that for it. No, I shouldn't have. I'll take it off and return it tomorrow. I shouldn't have bought it."

Julian raised his eyes to heaven. "Yes, you should have bought it," he said. "Put it on and let's go." It was a hideous hat. A purple velvet flap came down on one side of it and stood up on the other; the rest of it was green and looked like a cushion with the stuffing out. He decided it was less comical than jaunty and pathetic. Everything that gave her pleasure was small and depressed him.

She lifted the hat one more time and set it down slowly on top of her head. Two wings of gray hair protruded on either side of her florid face, but her eyes, sky-blue, were as innocent and untouched by experience as they must have been when she was ten. Were it not that she was a widow who had struggled fiercely to feed and clothe and put him through school and who was supporting him still, "until he got on his feet," she might have been a little girl that he had to take to town.

"It's all right, it's all right," he said. "Let's go." He opened the door himself and started down the walk to get her going. The sky was a dying violet and the houses stood out darkly against it, bulbous liver-colored monstrosities of a uniform ugliness though no two were alike. Since this had been a fashionable neighborhood forty years ago, his mother persisted in thinking they did well to have an apartment in it. Each house had a narrow collar of dirt around it in which sat, usually, a grubby child. Julian walked with his hands in his pockets, his head down and thrust forward and his eyes glazed with the determination to make himself completely numb during the time he would be sacrificed to her pleasure.

The door closed and he turned to find the dumpy figure, surmounted by the atrocious hat, coming toward him. "Well," she said, "you only live once and paying a little more for it, I at least won't meet myself coming and going."

"Some day I'll start making money," Julian said gloomily—he knew he never would—"and you can have one of those jokes whenever you take the fit." But first they would move. He visualized a place where the nearest neighbors would be three miles away on either side.

"I think you're doing fine," she said, drawing on her gloves. "You've only been out of school a year. Rome wasn't built in a day."

She was one of the few members of the Y reducing class who arrived in hat and gloves and who had a son who had been to college. "It takes time," she said, "and the world is in such a mess. This hat looked better on me than any of the others, though when she brought it out I said, 'Take that thing back. I wouldn't have it on my head,' and she said, 'Now wait till you see it on,' and when she put it on me, I said, 'We-ull,' and she said, 'If you ask me, that hat does something for you and you do something for the hat, and besides,' she said, 'with that hat, you won't meet yourself coming and going.' "

Julian thought he could have stood his lot better if she had been selfish, if she had been an old hag who drank and screamed at him. He walked along, saturated in depression, as if in the midst of his martyrdom he had lost his faith. Catching sight of his long, hopeless, irritated face, she stopped suddenly with a grief-stricken look, and pulled back on his arm. "Wait on me," she said. "I'm going back to the house and take this thing off and tomorrow I'm going to return it. I was out of my head. I can pay the gas bill with the seven-fifty."

He caught her arm in a vicious grip. "You are not going to take it back," he said. "I like it."

"Well," she said, "I don't think I ought . . ."

"Shut up and enjoy it," he muttered, more depressed than ever.

"With the world in the mess it's in," she said, "it's a wonder we can enjoy anything. I tell you, the bottom rail is on the top."

Julian sighed.

"Of course," she said, "if you know who you are, you can go anywhere." She said this every time he took her to the reducing class. "Most of them in it are not our kind of people," she said, "but I can be gracious to anybody. I know who I am."

"They don't give a damn for your graciousness," Julian said savagely. "Knowing who you are is good for one generation only. You haven't the foggiest idea where you stand now or who you are."

She stopped and allowed her eyes to flash at him. "I most

certainly do know who I am," she said, "and if you don't know who you are, I'm ashamed of you."

"Oh hell," Julian said.

"Your great-grandfather was a former governor of this state," she said. "Your grandfather was a prosperous landowner. Your grandmother was a Godhigh."

"Will you look around you," he said tensely, "and see where you are now?" and he swept his arm jerkily out to indicate the neighborhood, which the growing darkness at least made less dingy.

"You remain what you are," she said. "Your great-grandfather had a plantation and two hundred slaves."

"There are no more slaves," he said irritably.

"They were better off when they were," she said. He groaned to see that she was off on that topic. She rolled onto it every few days like a train on an open track. He knew every stop, every junction, every swamp along the way, and knew the exact point at which her conclusion would roll majestically into the station: "It's ridiculous. It's simply not realistic. They should rise, yes, but on their own side of the fence."

"Let's skip it," Julian said.

"The ones I feel sorry for," she said, "are the ones that are half white. They're tragic."

"Will you skip it?"

"Suppose we were half white. We would certainly have mixed feelings."

"I have mixed feelings now," he groaned.

"Well let's talk about something pleasant," she said. "I remember going to Grandpa's when I was a little girl. Then the house had double stairways that went up to what was really the second floor—all the cooking was done on the first. I used to like to stay down in the kitchen on account of the way the walls smelled. I would sit with my nose pressed against the plaster and take deep breaths. Actually the place belonged to the Godhighs but your grandfather Chestny paid the mortgage and saved it for them. They were in reduced circumstances," she said, "but reduced or not, they never forgot who they were."

"Doubtless that decayed mansion reminded them," Julian

muttered. He never spoke of it without contempt or thought of it without longing. He had seen it once when he was a child before it had been sold. The double stairways had rotted and been torn down. Negroes were living in it. But it remained in his mind as his mother had known it. It appeared in his dreams regularly. He would stand on the wide porch, listening to the rustle of oak leaves, then wander through the high-ceilinged hall into the parlor that opened onto it and gaze at the worn rugs and faded draperies. It occurred to him that it was he, not she, who could have appreciated it. He preferred its threadbare elegance to anything he could name and it was because of it that all the neighborhoods they had lived in had been a torment to him—whereas she had hardly known the difference. She called her insensitivity "being adjustable."

"And I remember the old darky who was my nurse, Caroline. There was no better person in the world. I've always had a great respect for my colored friends," she said. "I'd do anything in the world for them and they'd . . ."

"Will you for God's sake get off that subject?" Julian said. When he got on a bus by himself, he made it a point to sit down beside a Negro, in reparation as it were for his mother's sins.

"You're mighty touchy tonight," she said. "Do you feel all right?"

"Yes I feel all right," he said. "Now lay off."

She pursed her lips. "Well, you certainly are in a vile humor," she observed. "I just won't speak to you at all."

They had reached the bus stop. There was no bus in sight and Julian, his hands still jammed in his pockets and his head thrust forward, scowled down the empty street. The frustration of having to wait on the bus as well as ride on it began to creep up his neck like a hot hand. The presence of his mother was borne in upon him as she gave a pained sigh. He looked at her bleakly. She was holding herself very erect under the preposterous hat, wearing it like a banner of her imaginary dignity. There was in him an evil urge to break her spirit. He suddenly unloosed his tie and pulled it off and put it in his pocket.

She stiffened. "Why must you look like *that* when you take

me to town?" she said. "Why must you deliberately embarrass me?"

"If you'll never learn where you are," he said, "you can at least learn where I am."

"You look like a—thug," she said.

"Then I must be one," he murmured.

"I'll just go home," she said. "I will not bother you. If you can't do a little thing like that for me . . ."

Rolling his eyes upward, he put his tie back on. "Restored to my class," he muttered. He thrust his face toward her and hissed, "True culture is in the mind, the *mind,*" he said, and tapped his head, "the mind."

"It's in the heart," she said, "and in how you do things and how you do things is because of who you *are.*"

"Nobody in the damn bus cares who you are."

"I care who I am," she said icily.

The lighted bus appeared on top of the next hill and as it approached, they moved out into the street to meet it. He put his hand under her elbow and hoisted her up on the creaking step. She entered with a little smile, as if she were going into a drawing room where everyone had been waiting for her. While he put in the tokens, she sat down on one of the broad front seats for three which faced the aisle. A thin woman with protruding teeth and long yellow hair was sitting on the end of it. His mother moved up beside her and left room for Julian beside herself. He sat down and looked at the floor across the aisle where a pair of thin feet in red and white canvas sandals were planted.

His mother immediately began a general conversation meant to attract anyone who felt like talking. "Can it get any hotter?" she said and removed from her purse a folding fan, black with a Japanese scene on it, which she began to flutter before her.

"I reckon it might could," the woman with the protruding teeth said, "but I know for a fact my apartment couldn't get no hotter."

"It must get the afternoon sun," his mother said. She sat forward and looked up and down the bus. It was half filled.

Everybody was white. "I see we have the bus to ourselves," she said. Julian cringed.

"For a change," said the woman across the aisle, the owner of the red and white canvas sandals. "I come on one the other day and they were thick as fleas—up front and all through."

"The world is in a mess everywhere," his mother said. "I don't know how we've let it get in this fix."

"What gets my goat is all those boys from good families stealing automobile tires," the woman with the protruding teeth said. "I told my boy, I said you may not be rich but you been raised right and if I ever catch you in any such mess, they can send you on to the reformatory. Be exactly where you belong."

"Training tells," his mother said. "Is your boy in high school?"

"Ninth grade," the woman said.

"My son just finished college last year. He wants to write but he's selling typewriters until he gets started," his mother said.

The woman leaned forward and peered at Julian. He threw her such a malevolent look that she subsided against the seat. On the floor across the aisle there was an abandoned newspaper. He got up and got it and opened it out in front of him. His mother discreetly continued the conversation in a lower tone but the woman across the aisle said in a loud voice, "Well that's nice. Selling typewriters is close to writing. He can go right from one to the other."

"I tell him," his mother said, "that Rome wasn't built in a day."

Behind the newspaper Julian was withdrawing into the inner compartment of his mind where he spent most of his time. This was a kind of mental bubble in which he established himself when he could not bear to be a part of what was going on around him. From it he could see out and judge but in it he was safe from any kind of penetration from without. It was the only place where he felt free of the general idiocy of his fellows. His mother had never entered it but from it he could see her with absolute clarity.

The old lady was clever enough and he thought that if she

had started from any of the right premises, more might have been expected of her. She lived according to the laws of her own fantasy world, outside of which he had never seen her set foot. The law of it was to sacrifice herself for him after she had first created the necessity to do so by making a mess of things. If he had permitted her sacrifices, it was only because her lack of foresight had made them necessary. All of her life had been a struggle to act like a Chestny without the Chestny goods, and to give him everything she thought a Chestny ought to have; but since, said she, it was fun to struggle, why complain? And when you had won, as she had won, what fun to look back on the hard times! He could not forgive her that she had enjoyed the struggle and that she thought *she* had won.

What she meant when she said she had won was that she had brought him up successfully and had sent him to college and that he had turned out so well—good looking (her teeth had gone unfilled so that his could be straightened), intelligent (he realized he was too intelligent to be a success), and with a future ahead of him (there was of course no future ahead of him). She excused his gloominess on the grounds that he was still growing up and his radical ideas on his lack of practical experience. She said he didn't yet know a thing about "life," that he hadn't even entered the real world—when already he was as disenchanted with it as a man of fifty.

The further irony of all this was that in spite of her, he had turned out so well. In spite of going to only a third-rate college, he had, on his own initiative, come out with a first-rate education; in spite of growing up dominated by a small mind, he had ended up with a large one; in spite of all her foolish views, he was free of prejudice and unafraid to face facts. Most miraculous of all, instead of being blinded by love for her as she was for him, he had cut himself emotionally free of her and could see her with complete objectivity. He was not dominated by his mother.

The bus stopped with a sudden jerk and shook him from his meditation. A woman from the back lurched forward with little steps and barely escaped falling in his newspaper as she righted herself. She got off and a large Negro got on. Julian kept his paper lowered to watch. It gave him a certain satisfaction to see injustice in daily operation. It confirmed his view that with a few exceptions there was no one worth knowing within a radius of three hundred miles. The Negro was well dressed and carried a briefcase. He looked around and then sat down on the other end of the seat where the woman with the red and white canvas sandals was sitting. He immediately unfolded a newspaper and obscured himself behind it. Julian's mother's elbow at once prodded insistently into his ribs. "Now you see why I won't ride on these buses by myself," she whispered.

The woman with the red and white canvas sandals had risen at the same time the Negro sat down and had gone further back in the bus and taken the seat of the woman who had got off. His mother leaned forward and cast her an approving look.

Julian rose, crossed the aisle, and sat down in the place of the woman with the canvas sandals. From this position, he looked serenely across at his mother. Her face had turned an angry red. He stared at her, making his eyes the eyes of a stranger. He felt his tension suddenly lift as if he had openly declared war on her.

He would have liked to get in conversation with the Negro and to talk with him about art or politics or any subject that would be above the comprehension of those around them, but the man remained entrenched behind his paper. He was either ignoring the change of seating or had never noticed it. There was no way for Julian to convey his sympathy.

His mother kept her eyes fixed reproachfully on his face. The woman with the protruding teeth was looking at him avidly as if he were a type of monster new to her.

"Do you have a light?" he asked the Negro.

Without looking away from his paper, the man reached in his pocket and handed him a packet of matches.

"Thanks, ' Julian said. For a moment he held the matches foolishly. A NO SMOKING sign looked down upon him from over the door. This alone would not have deterred him; he had no cigarettes. He had quit smoking some months before because he could not afford it. "Sorry," he muttered and handed back the matches. The Negro lowered the paper and gave him an annoyed look. He took the matches and raised the paper again.

His mother continued to gaze at him but she did not take advantage of his momentary discomfort. Her eyes retained their battered look. Her face seemed to be unnaturally red, as if her blood pressure had risen. Julian allowed no glimmer of sympathy to show on his face. Having got the advantage, he wanted desperately to keep it and carry it through. He would have liked to teach her a lesson that would last her a while, but there seemed no way to continue the point. The Negro refused to come out from behind his paper.

Julian folded his arms and looked stolidly before him, facing her but as if he did not see her, as if he had ceased to recognize her existence. He visualized a scene in which, the bus having reached their stop, he would remain in his seat and when she said, "Aren't you going to get off?" he would look at her as at a stranger who had rashly addressed him. The corner they got off on was usually deserted, but it was well lighted and it would not hurt her to walk by herself the four blocks to the Y. He decided to wait until the time came and then decide whether or not he would let her get off by herself. He would have to be at the Y at ten to bring her back, but he could leave her wondering if he was going to show up. There was no reason for her to think she could always depend on him.

He retired again into the high-ceilinged room sparsely settled with large pieces of antique furniture. His soul expanded momentarily but then he became aware of his mother across from him and the vision shriveled. He studied her coldly. Her feet in little pumps dangled like a child's and did not quite reach the floor. She was training on him an exaggerated look of reproach. He felt completely detached from her. At that moment he could with pleasure have slapped her as he would have slapped a particularly obnoxious child in his charge.

He began to imagine various unlikely ways by which he could teach her a lesson. He might make friends with some distinguished Negro professor or lawyer and bring him home to spend the evening. He would be entirely justified but her blood pressure would rise to 300. He could not push her to the extent of making her have a stroke, and moreover, he had never been successful at making any Negro friends. He had tried to strike up an acquaintance on the bus with some of the better types, with ones that looked like professors or ministers or lawyers. One morning he had sat down next to a distinguished-looking dark brown man who had answered his questions with a sonorous solemnity but who had turned out to be an undertaker. Another day he had sat down beside a cigar-smoking Negro with a diamond ring on his finger, but after a few stilted pleasantries, the Negro had rung the buzzer and risen, slipping two lottery tickets into Julian's hand as he climbed over him to leave.

He imagined his mother lying desperately ill and his being able to secure only a Negro doctor for her. He toyed with that idea for a few minutes and then dropped it for a momentary vision of himself participating as a sympathizer in a sit-in demonstration. This was possible but he did not linger with it. Instead, he approached the ultimate horror. He brought home a beautiful suspiciously Negroid woman. Prepare yourself, he said. There is nothing you can do about it. This is the woman I've chosen. She's intelligent, dignified, even good, and she's suffered and she hasn't thought it *fun.* Now persecute us, go ahead and persecute us. Drive her out of here, but remember, you're driving me too. His eyes were narrowed and through the indignation he had generated, he saw his mother across the aisle, purple-faced, shrunken to the dwarf-like proportions of her moral nature, sitting like a mummy beneath the ridiculous banner of her hat.

He was tilted out of his fantasy again as the bus stopped. The door opened with a sucking hiss and out of the dark a large, gaily dressed, sullen-looking colored woman got on with a little boy. The child, who might have been four, had on a short plaid suit and a Tyrolean hat with a blue feather in it. Julian hoped that he would sit down beside him and that the woman would push in beside his mother. He could think of no better arrangement.

As she waited for her tokens, the woman was surveying the seating possibilities—he hoped with the idea of sitting where she was least wanted. There was something familiar-looking about her but Julian could not place what it was. She was a giant of a woman. Her face was set not only to meet opposition but to seek it out. The downward tilt of her large lower lip was like a warning sign: DON'T TAMPER WITH ME. Her bulging figure was encased in a green crepe dress and her feet overflowed in red shoes. She had on a hideous hat. A purple velvet flap came down on one side of it and stood up on the other; the rest of it was green and looked like a cushion with the stuffing out. She carried a mammoth red pocketbook that bulged throughout as if it were stuffed with rocks.

To Julian's disappointment, the little boy climbed up on the empty seat beside his mother. His mother lumped all children, black and white, into the common category, "cute," and she thought little Negroes were on the whole cuter than little white children. She smiled at the little boy as he climbed on the seat.

Meanwhile the woman was bearing down upon the empty seat beside Julian. To his annoyance, she squeezed herself into it. He saw his mother's face change as the woman settled herself next to him and he realized with satisfaction that this was more objectionable to her than it was to him. Her face seemed almost gray and there was a look of dull recognition in her eyes, as if suddenly she had sickened at some awful confrontation. Julian saw that it was because she and the woman had, in a sense, swapped sons. Though his mother would not realize the symbolic significance of this, she would feel it. His amusement showed plainly on his face.

The woman next to him muttered something unintelligible to herself. He was conscious of a kind of bristling next to him, muted growling like that of an angry cat. He could not see anything but the red pocketbook upright on the bulging green thighs. He visualized the woman as she had stood waiting for her tokens—the ponderous figure, rising from the red shoes upward over the solid hips, the mammoth bosom, the haughty face, to the green and purple hat.

His eyes widened.

The vision of the two hats, identical, broke upon him with the radiance of a brilliant sunrise. His face was suddenly lit with joy. He could not believe that Fate had thrust upon his mother such a lesson. He gave a loud chuckle so that she would look at him and see that he saw. She turned her eyes on him slowly. The blue in them seemed to have turned a bruised purple. For a moment he had an uncomfortable sense of her innocence, but it lasted only a second before principle rescued him. Justice entitled him to laugh. His grin hardened until it said to her as plainly as if he were saying aloud: Your punishment exactly fits your pettiness. This should teach you a permanent lesson.

Her eyes shifted to the woman. She seemed unable to bear looking at him and to find the woman preferable. He became conscious again of the bristling presence at his side. The woman was rumbling like a volcano about to become active. His mother's mouth began to twitch slightly at one corner. With a sinking heart, he saw incipient signs of recovery on her face and realized that this was going to strike her suddenly as funny and was going to be no lesson at all. She kept her eyes on the woman and an amused smile came over her face as if the woman were a monkey that had stolen her hat. The little Negro was looking up at her with large fascinated eyes. He had been trying to attract her attention for some time.

"Carver!" the woman said suddenly. "Come heah!"

When he saw that the spotlight was on him at last, Carver drew his feet up and turned himself toward Julian's mother and giggled.

"Carver!" the woman said. "You heah me? Come heah!"

Carver slid down from the seat but remained squatting with his back against the base of it, his head turned slyly around toward Julian's mother, who was smiling at him. The woman reached a hand across the aisle and snatched him to her. He righted himself and hung backwards on her knees, grinning at Julian's mother. "Isn't he cute?" Julian's mother said to the woman with the protruding teeth.

"I reckon he is," the woman said without conviction.

The Negress yanked him upright but he eased out of her grip and shot across the aisle and scrambled, giggling wildly, onto the seat beside his love.

"I think he likes me," Julian's mother said, and smiled at the woman. It was the smile she used when she was being particularly gracious to an inferior. Julian saw everything lost. The lesson had rolled off her like rain on a roof.

The woman stood up and yanked the little boy off the seat as if she were snatching him from contagion. Julian could feel the rage in her at having no weapon like his mother's smile. She gave the child a sharp slap across his leg. He howled once and then thrust his head into her stomach and kicked his feet against her shins. "Behave," she said vehemently.

The bus stopped and the Negro who had been reading the newspaper got off. The woman moved over and set the little boy down with a thump between herself and Julian. She held him firmly by the knee. In a moment he put his hands in front of his face and peeped at Julian's mother through his fingers.

'I see yoooooooo!" she said and put her hand in front of her face and peeped at him.

The woman slapped his hand down. "Quit yo' foolishness," she said, "before I knock the living Jesus out of you!"

Julian was thankful that the next stop was theirs. He reached up and pulled the cord. The woman reached up and pulled it at the same time. Oh my God, he thought. He had the terrible intuition that when they got off the bus together, his mother would open her purse and give the little boy a nickel. The gesture would be as natural to her as breathing. The bus stopped and the woman got up and lunged to the front, dragging the child, who wished to stay on, after her. Julian and his mother got up and followed. As they neared the door, Julian tried to relieve her of her pocketbook.

"No," she murmured, "I want to give the little boy a nickel."

"No!" Julian hissed. "No!"

She smiled down at the child and opened her bag. The bus door opened and the woman picked him up by the arm and descended with him, hanging at her hip. Once in the street she set him down and shook him.

Julian's mother had to close her purse while she got down the bus step but as soon as her feet were on the ground, she opened it again and began to rummage inside. "I can't find but a penny," she whispered, "but it looks like a new one."

"Don't do it!" Julian said fiercely between his teeth. There was a streetlight on the corner and she hurried to get under it so that she could better see into her pocketbook. The woman was heading off rapidly down the street with the child still hanging backward on her hand.

"Oh little boy!" Julian's mother called and took a few quick steps and caught up with them just beyond the lamppost. "Here's a bright new penny for you," and she held out the coin, which shone bronze in the dim light.

The huge woman turned and for a moment stood, her shoulders lifted and her face frozen with frustrated rage, and stared at Julian's mother. Then all at once she seemed to explode like a piece of machinery that had been given one ounce of pressure too much. Julian saw the black fist swing out with the red pocketbook. He shut his eyes and cringed as he heard the woman shout, "He don't take nobody's pennies!" When he opened his eyes, the woman was disappearing down the street with the little boy staring wide-eyed over her shoulder. Julian's mother was sitting on the sidewalk.

"I told you not to do that," Julian said angrily. "I told you not to do that!"

He stood over her for a minute, gritting his teeth. Her legs were stretched out in front of her and her hat was on her lap. He squatted down and looked her in the face. It was totally expressionless. "You got exactly what you deserved," he said. "Now get up."

He picked up her pocketbook and put what had fallen out back in it. He picked the hat up off her lap. The penny caught his eye on the sidewalk and he picked that up and let it drop before her eyes into the purse. Then he stood up and leaned over and held his hands out to pull her up. She remained immobile. He sighed. Rising above them on either side were black apartment buildings, marked with irregular rectangles of light. At the end of the block a man came out of a door and walked off in the opposite direction. "All right," he said, "suppose somebody happens by and wants to know why you're sitting on the sidewalk?"

She took the hand and, breathing hard, pulled heavily up on it and then stood for a moment, swaying slightly as if the spots of light in the darkness were circling around her. Her eyes, shadowed and confused, finally settled on his face. He did not try to conceal his irritation. "I hope this teaches you a lesson," he said. She leaned forward and her eyes raked his face. She seemed trying to determine his identity. Then, as if she found nothing familiar about him, she started off with a headlong movement in the wrong direction.

"Aren't you going on to the Y?" he asked.

"Home," she muttered.

"Well, are we walking?"

For answer she kept going. Julian followed along, his hands behind him. He saw no reason to let the lesson she had had go without backing it up with an explanation of its meaning. She might as well be made to understand what had happened to her. "Don't think that was just an uppity Negro woman," he said. "That was the whole colored race which will no longer take your condescending pennies. That was your black double. She can wear the same hat as you, and to be sure," he added gratuitously (because he thought it was funny), "it looked better on her than it did on you. What all this means," he said, "is that the old world is gone. The old manners are obsolete and your graciousness is not worth a damn." He thought bitterly of the house that had been lost for him. "You aren't who you think you are," he said.

She continued to plow ahead, paying no attention to him. Her hair had come undone on one side. She dropped her pocketbook and took no notice. He stooped and picked it up and handed it to her but she did not take it.

"You needn't act as if the world had come to an end," he said, "because it hasn't. From now on you've got to live in a new world and face a few realities for a change. Buck up," he said, "it won't kill you."

She was breathing fast.

"Let's wait on the bus," he said.

"Home," she said thickly.

"I hate to see you behave like this," he said. "Just like a child. I should be able to expect more of you." He decided to stop where he was and make her stop and wait for a bus. "I'm not going any farther," he said, stopping. "We're going on the bus."

She continued to go on as if she had not heard him. He took a few steps and caught her arm and stopped her. He looked into her face and caught his breath. He was looking into a face he had never seen before. "Tell Grandpa to come get me," she said.

He stared, stricken.

"Tell Caroline to come get me," she said.

Stunned, he let her go and she lurched forward again, walking as if one leg were shorter than the other. A tide of darkness seemed to be sweeping her from him. "Mother!" he cried. "Darling, sweetheart, wait!" Crumpling, she fell to the pavement. He dashed forward and fell at her side, crying, "Mamma, Mamma!" He turned her over. Her face was fiercely distorted. One eye, large and staring, moved slightly to the left as if it had become unmoored. The other remained fixed on him, raked his face again, found nothing and closed.

"Wait here, wait here!" he cried and jumped up and began to run for help toward a cluster of lights he saw in the distance ahead of him. "Help, help!" he shouted, but his voice was thin, scarcely a thread of sound. The lights drifted farther away the faster he ran and his feet moved numbly as if they carried him nowhere. The tide of darkness seemed to sweep him back to her, postponing from moment to moment his entry into the world of guilt and sorrow.

KATHERINE ANNE PORTER

The Jilting of Granny Weatherall

SHE FLICKED HER wrist neatly out of Doctor Harry's pudgy careful fingers and pulled the sheet up to her chin. The brat ought to be in knee breeches. Doctoring around the country with spectacles on his nose! "Get along now, take your school books and go. There's nothing wrong with me."

Doctor Harry spread a warm paw like a cushion on her forehead where the forked green vein danced and made her eyelids twitch. "Now, now, be a good girl, and we'll have you up in no time."

"That's no way to speak to a woman nearly eighty years old just because she's down. I'd have you respect your elders, young man."

"Well, Missy, excuse me." Doctor Harry patted her cheek. "But I've got to warn you, haven't I? You're a marvel, but you must be careful or you're going to be good and sorry."

"Don't tell me what I'm going to be. I'm on my feet now, morally speaking. It's Cornelia. I had to go to bed to get rid of her."

Her bones felt loose, and floated around in her skin, and Doctor Harry floated like a balloon around the foot of the bed. He floated and pulled down his waistcoat and swung his glasses on a cord. "Well, stay where you are, it certainly can't hurt you."

"Get along and doctor your sick," said Granny Weatherall. "Leave a well woman alone. I'll call for you when I want you. . . . Where were you forty years ago when I pulled through milk-leg and double pneumonia? You weren't even born. Don't let Cornelia lead you on," she shouted, because Doctor Harry appeared to float up to the ceiling and out. "I pay my own bills, and I don't throw my money away on nonsense!"

She meant to wave good-bye, but it was too much trouble. Her eyes closed of themselves, it was like a dark curtain drawn around the bed. The pillow rose and floated under her, pleasant as a hammock in a light wind. She listened to the leaves rustling outside the window. No, somebody was swishing newspapers: no, Cornelia and Doctor Harry were whispering together. She leaped broad awake, thinking they whispered in her ear.

"She was never like this, *never* like this!" "Well, what can we expect?" "Yes, eighty years old. . . ."

Well, and what if she was? She still had ears. It was like Cornelia to whisper around doors. She always kept things secret in such a public way. She was always being tactful and kind. Cornelia was dutiful; that was the trouble with her. Dutiful and good: "So good and dutiful," said Granny, "that I'd like to spank her." She saw herself spanking Cornelia and making a fine job of it.

"What'd you say, Mother?"

Granny felt her face tying up in hard knots.

"Can't a body think, I'd like to know?"

"I thought you might want something."

"I do. I want a lot of things. First off, go away and don't whisper."

She lay and drowsed, hoping in her sleep that the children would keep out and let her rest a minute. It had been a long day. Not that she was tired. It was always pleasant to snatch a minute now and then. There was always so much to be done, let me see: tomorrow.

Tomorrow was far away and there was nothing to trouble about. Things were finished somehow when the time came; thank God there was always a little margin over for peace:

then a person could spread out the plan of life and tuck in the edges orderly. It was good to have everything clean and folded away, with the hair brushes and tonic bottles sitting straight on the white embroidered linen: the day started without fuss and the pantry shelves laid out with rows of jelly glasses and brown jugs and white stone-china jars with blue whirligigs and words painted on them: coffee, tea, sugar, ginger, cinnamon, allspice: and the bronze clock with the lion on top nicely dusted off. The dust that lion could collect in twenty-four hours! The box in the attic with all those letters tied up, well, she'd have to go through that tomorrow. All those letters—George's letters and John's letters and her letters to them both—lying around for the children to find afterwards made her uneasy. Yes, that would be tomorrow's business. No use to let them know how silly she had been once.

While she was rummaging around she found death in her mind and it felt clammy and unfamiliar. She had spent so much time preparing for death there was no need for bringing it up again. Let it take care of itself now. When she was sixty she had felt very old, finished, and went around making farewell trips to see her children and grandchildren, with a secret in her mind: This is the very last of your mother, children! Then she made her will and came down with a long fever. That was all just a notion like a lot of other things; but it was lucky too, for she had once for all got over the idea of dying for a long time. Now she couldn't be worried. She hoped she had better sense now. Her father had lived to be one hundred and two years old and had drunk a noggin of strong hot toddy on his last birthday. He told the reporters it was his daily habit, and he owed his long life to that. He had made quite a scandal and was very pleased about it. She believed she'd just plague Cornelia a little.

"Cornelia! Cornelia!" No footsteps, but a sudden hand on her cheek. "Bless you, where have you been?"

"Here, Mother."

"Well, Cornelia, I want a noggin of hot toddy."

"Are you cold, darling?"

"I'm chilly, Cornelia. Lying in bed stops the circulation. I must have told you that a thousand times."

Well, she could just hear Cornelia telling her husband that Mother was getting a little childish and they'd have to humor her. The thing that most annoyed her was that Cornelia thought she was deaf, dumb, and blind. Little hasty glances and tiny gestures tossed around her and over her head saying, "Don't cross her, let her have her way, she's eighty years old," and she sitting there as if she lived in a thin glass cage. Sometimes Granny almost made up her mind to pack up and move back to her own house where nobody could remind her every minute that she was old. Wait, wait, Cornelia, till your own children whisper behind your back!

In her day she had kept a better house and had got more work done. She wasn't too old yet for Lydia to be driving eighty miles for advice when one of the children jumped the track, and Jimmy still dropped in and talked things over: "Now, Mammy, you've a good business head, I want to know what you think of this? . . ." Old. Cornelia couldn't change the furniture around without asking. Little things, little things! They had been so sweet when they were little. Granny wished the old days were back again with the children young and everything to be done over. It had been a hard pull, but not too much for her. When she thought of all the food she had cooked, and all the clothes she had cut and sewed, and all the gardens she had made—well, the children showed it. There they were, made out of her, and they couldn't get away from that. Sometimes she wanted to see John again and point to them and say, Well, I didn't do so badly, did I? But that would have to wait. That was for tomorrow. She used to think of him as a man, but now all the children were older than their father, and he would be a child beside her if she saw him now. It seemed strange and there was something wrong in the idea. Why, he couldn't possibly recognize her. She had fenced in a hundred acres once, digging the post holes herself and clamping the wires with just a negro boy to help. That changed a woman. John would be looking for a young woman with the peaked Spanish comb in her hair and the painted fan. Digging post holes changed a woman. Riding country roads in the winter when women had their babies was another thing: sitting up nights with sick horses and sick negroes and sick children and hardly ever losing one. John, I hardly ever lost one of them! John would see that in a minute, that would be something he could understand, she wouldn't have to explain anything!

It made her feel like rolling up her sleeves and putting the whole place to rights again. No matter if Cornelia was determined to be everywhere at once, there were a great many things left undone on this place. She would start tomorrow and do them. It was good to be strong enough for everything, even if all you made melted and changed and slipped under your hands, so that by the time you finished you almost forgot what you were working for. What was it I set out to do? she asked herself intently, but she could not remember. A fog rose over the valley, she saw it marching across the creek swallowing the trees and moving up the hill like an army of ghosts. Soon it would be at the near edge of the orchard, and then it was time to go in and light the lamps. Come in, children, don't stay out in the night air.

Lighting the lamps had been beautiful. The children huddled up to her and breathed like little calves waiting at the bars in the twilight. Their eyes followed the match and watched the flame rise and settle in a blue curve, then they moved away from her. The lamp was lit, they didn't have to be scared and hang on to mother any more. Never, never, never more. God, for all my life I thank Thee. Without Thee, my God, I could never have done it. Hail, Mary, full of grace.

I want you to pick all the fruit this year and see that nothing is wasted. There's always someone who can use it. Don't let good things rot for want of using. You waste life when you waste good food. Don't let things get lost. It's bitter to lose things. Now, don't let me get to thinking, not when I am tired and taking a little nap before supper. . . .

The pillow rose about her shoulders and pressed against her heart and the memory was being squeezed out of it: oh, push down the pillow, somebody: it would smother her if she tried to hold it. Such a fresh breeze blowing and such a green day with no threats in it. But he had not come, just the same. What does a woman do when she has put on the white veil and set out the white cake for a man and he doesn't come?

She tried to remember. No, I swear he never harmed me but in that. He never harmed me but in that . . . and what if he did? There was the day, the day, but a whirl of dark smoke rose and covered it, crept up and over into the bright field where everything was planted so carefully in orderly rows. That was hell, she knew hell when she saw it. For sixty years she had prayed against remembering him and against losing her soul in the deep pit of hell, and now the two things were mingled in one and the thought of him was a smoky cloud from hell that moved and crept in her head when she had just got rid of Doctor Harry and was trying to rest a minute. Wounded vanity, Ellen, said a sharp voice in the top of her mind. Don't let your wounded vanity get the upper hand of you. Plenty of girls get jilted. You were jilted, weren't you? Then stand up to it. Her eyelids wavered and let in streamers of blue-gray light like tissue paper over her eyes. She must get up and pull the shades down or she'd never sleep. She was in bed again and the shades were not down. How could that happen? Better turn over, hide from the light, sleeping in the light gave you nightmares. "Mother, how do you feel now?" and a stinging wetness on her forehead. But I don't like having my face washed in cold water!

Hapsy? George? Lydia? Jimmy? No, Cornelia, and her features were swollen and full of little puddles. "They're coming, darling, they'll all be here soon." Go wash your face, child, you look funny.

Instead of obeying, Cornelia knelt down and put her head on the pillow. She seemed to be talking but there was no sound. "Well, are you tongue-tied? Whose birthday is it? Are you going to give a party?"

Cornelia's mouth moved urgently in strange shapes. "Don't do that, you bother me, daughter."

"Oh, no, Mother. Oh, no. . . ."

Nonsense. It was strange about children. They disputed your every word. "No what, Cornelia?"

"Here's Doctor Harry."

"I won't see that boy again. He just left five minutes ago."

"That was this morning, Mother. It's night now. Here's the nurse."

"This is Doctor Harry, Mrs. Weatherall. I never saw you look so young and happy!"

"Ah, I'll never be young again—but I'd be happy if they'd let me lie in peace and get rested."

She thought she spoke up loudly, but no one answered. A warm weight on her forehead, a warm bracelet on her wrist, and a breeze went on whispering, trying to tell her something. A shuffle of leaves in the everlasting hand of God, He blew on them and they danced and rattled. "Mother, don't mind, we're going to give you a little hypodermic." "Look here, daughter, how do ants get in this bed? I saw sugar ants yesterday." Did you send for Hapsy too?

It was Hapsy she really wanted. She had to go a long way back through a great many rooms to find Hapsy standing with a baby on her arm. She seemed to herself to be Hapsy also, and the baby on Hapsy's arm was Hapsy and himself and herself, all at once, and there was no surprise in the meeting. Then Hapsy melted from within and turned flimsy as gray gauze and the baby was a gauzy shadow, and Hapsy came up close and said, "I thought you'd never come," and looked at her very searchingly and said, "You haven't changed a bit!" They leaned forward to kiss, when Cornelia began whispering from a long way off, "Oh, is there anything you want to tell me? Is there anything I can do for you?"

Yes, she had changed her mind after sixty years and she would like to see George. I want you to find George. Find him and be sure to tell him I forgot him. I want him to know I had my husband just the same and my children and my house like any other woman. A good house too and a good husband that I loved and fine children out of him. Better than I hoped for even. Tell him I was given back everything he took away and more. Oh, no, oh, God, no, there was something else besides the house and the man and the children. Oh, surely they were not all? What was it? Something not given back. . . . Her breath crowded down under her ribs and grew into a monstrous frightening shape with cutting edges; it bored up into her head, and the agony was unbelievable: Yes, John, get the Doctor now, no more talk, my time has come.

When this one was born it should be the last. The last. It should have been born first, for it was the one she had truly wanted. Everything came in good time. Nothing left out, left over. She was strong, in three days she would be as well as ever. Better. A woman needed milk in her to have her full health.

"Mother, do you hear me?"

"I've been telling you—"

"Mother, Father Connolly's here."

"I went to Holy Communion only last week. Tell him I'm not so sinful as all that."

"Father just wants to speak to you."

He could speak as much as he pleased. It was like him to drop in and inquire about her soul as if it were a teething baby, and then stay on for a cup of tea and a round of cards and gossip. He always had a funny story of some sort, usually about an Irishman who made his little mistakes and confessed them, and the point lay in some absurd thing he would blurt out in the confessional showing his struggles between native piety and original sin. Granny felt easy about her soul. Cornelia, where are your manners? Give Father Connolly a chair. She had her secret comfortable understanding with a few favorite saints who cleared a straight road to God for her. All as surely signed and sealed as the papers for the new Forty Acres. Forever . . . heirs and assigns forever. Since the day the wedding cake was not cut, but thrown out and wasted. The whole bottom dropped out of the world, and there she was blind and sweating with nothing under her feet and the walls falling away. His hand had caught her under the breast, she had not fallen, there was the freshly polished floor with the green rug on it, just as before. He had cursed like a sailor's parrot and said, "I'll kill him for you." Don't lay a hand on him, for my sake leave something to God. "Now, Ellen, you must believe what I tell you. . . ."

So there was nothing, nothing to worry about any more, except sometimes in the night one of the children screamed in a nightmare, and they both hustled out shaking and hunting for the matches and calling, "There, wait a minute, here we are!" John, get the doctor now. Hapsy's time has come.

But there was Hapsy standing by the bed in a white cap. "Cornelia, tell Hapsy to take off her cap. I can't see her plain."

Her eyes opened very wide and the room stood out like a picture she had seen somewhere. Dark colors with the shadows rising toward the ceiling in long angles. The tall black dresser gleamed with nothing on it but John's picture, enlarged from a little one, with John's eyes very black when they should have been blue. You never saw him, so how do you know how he looked? But the man insisted the copy was perfect, it was very rich and handsome. For a picture, yes, but it's not my husband. The table by the bed had a linen cover and a candle and a crucifix. The light was blue from Cornelia's silk lampshades. No sort of light at all, just frippery. You had to live forty years with kerosene lamps to appreciate honest electricity. She felt very strong and she saw Doctor Harry with a rosy nimbus around him.

"You look like a saint, Doctor Harry, and I vow that's as near as you'll ever come to it."

"She's saying something."

"I heard you, Cornelia. What's all this carrying-on?"

"Father Connolly's saying—"

Cornelia's voice staggered and bumped like a cart in a bad road. It rounded corners and turned back again and arrived nowhere. Granny stepped up in the cart very lightly and reached for the reins, but a man sat beside her and she knew him by his hands, driving the cart. She did not look in his face, for she knew without seeing, but looked instead down the road where the trees leaned over and bowed to each other and a thousand birds were singing a Mass. She felt like singing too, but she put her hand in the bosom of her dress and pulled out a rosary, and Father Connolly murmured Latin in a very solemn voice and tickled her feet. My God, will you stop that nonsense? I'm a married woman. What if he did run away and leave me to face the priest by myself? I found another a whole world better. I wouldn't have exchanged my husband for anybody except St. Michael himself, and you may tell him that for me with a thank you in the bargain.

Light flashed on her closed eyelids, and a deep roaring shook her. Cornelia, is that lightning? I hear thunder. There's going to be a storm. Close all the windows. Call the children in. . . . "Mother, here we are, all of us." "Is that you, Hapsy?" "Oh, no, I'm Lydia. We drove as fast as we could." Their faces drifted above her, drifted away. The rosary fell out of her hands and Lydia put it back. Jimmy tried to help, their hands fumbled together, and Granny closed two fingers around Jimmy's thumb. Beads wouldn't do, it must be something alive. She was so amazed her thoughts ran round and round. So, my dear Lord, this is my death and I wasn't even thinking about it. My children have come to see me die. But I can't, it's not time. Oh, I always hated surprises. I wanted to give Cornelia the amethyst set—Cornelia, you're to have the amethyst set, but Hapsy's to wear it when she wants, and, Doctor Harry, do shut up. Nobody sent for you. Oh, my dear Lord, do wait a minute. I meant to do something about the Forty Acres, Jimmy doesn't need it and Lydia will later on, with that worthless husband of hers. I meant to finish the altar cloth and send six bottles of wine to Sister Borgia for her dyspepsia. I want to send six bottles of wine to Sister Borgia, Father Connolly, now don't let me forget.

Cornelia's voice made short turns and tilted over and crashed. "Oh, Mother, oh, Mother, oh, Mother. . . ."

"I'm not going, Cornelia. I'm taken by surprise. I can't go."

You'll see Hapsy again. What about her? "I thought you'd never come." Granny made a long journey outward, looking for Hapsy. What if I don't find her? What then? Her heart sank down and down, there was no bottom to death, she couldn't come to the end of it. The blue light from Cornelia's lampshade drew into a tiny point in the center of her brain, it flickered and winked like an eye, quietly it fluttered and dwindled. Granny lay curled down within herself, amazed and watchful, staring at the point of light that was herself; her body was now only a deeper mass of shadow in an endless darkness and this darkness would curl around the light and swallow it up. God, give a sign!

For the second time there was no sign. Again no bridegroom and the priest in the house. She could not remember any other sorrow because this grief wiped them all away. Oh, no, there's nothing more cruel than this—I'll never forgive it. She stretched herself with a deep breath and blew out the light.

JEAN STAFFORD

The Liberation

ON THE DAY Polly Bay decided to tell her Uncle Francis and his sister, her Aunt Jane, that in a week's time she was leaving their house and was going East to be married and to live in Boston, she walked very slowly home from Nevilles College, where she taught, dreading the startled look in their eyes and the woe and the indignation with which they would take her news. Hating any derangement of the status quo, her uncle, once a judge, was bound to cross-examine her intensively, and Aunt Jane, his perfect complement, would bolster him and baffle her. It was going to be an emotional and argumentative scene; her hands, which now were damp, would presently be dripping. She shivered with apprehension, fearing her aunt's asthma and her uncle's polemic, and she shook with rebellion, knowing how they would succeed in making her feel a traitor to her family, to the town, and to Colorado, and, obscurely, to her country.

Uncle Francis and Aunt Jane, like their dead kinsmen, Polly's father and her grandfather and her great-grandmother, had a vehement family and regional pride, and they counted it virtue in themselves that they had never been east of the Mississippi. They had looked on the departures of Polly's sisters and her cousins as acts of betrayal and even of disobedience. They had been distressed particularly by removals to the East, which were, they felt, iconoclastic and, worse, rude; how, they marveled, could this new generation be so ungrateful to those intrepid early Bays who in the forties had toiled in such peril and with such fortitude across the plains in a covered wagon and who with such perseverance had put down the roots for their traditions in this town that they had virtually made? Uncle Francis and Aunt Jane had done all in their power—through threats and sudden illnesses and cries of "Shame!"—to prevent these desertions, but nevertheless, one by one, the members of the scapegrace generation had managed to fly, cut off without a penny, scolded to death, and spoken of thereafter as if they were unredeemed, treasonous, and debauched. Polly was the last, and her position, therefore, was the most uncomfortable of all; she and her aunt and uncle were the only Bays left in Adams, and she knew that because she was nearly thirty they had long ago stopped fearing that she, too, might go. As they frequently told her, in their candid way, they felt she had reached "a sensible age"—it was a struggle for them not to use the word "spinster" when they paid her this devious and crushing compliment. She knew perfectly well, because this, too, they spoke of, that they imagined she would still be teaching *Immensee* in German I years after they were dead, and would return each evening to the big, drafty house where they were born, and from which they expected to be carried in coffins ordered for them by Polly from Leonard Harper, the undertaker, whose mealy mouth and shifty eye they often talked about with detestation as they rocked and rocked through their long afternoons.

Polly had been engaged to Robert Fair for five months now and had kept his pretty ring in the desk in her office at college; she had not breathed a word to a soul. If she had spoken out when she came back from the Christmas holidays in her sister's Boston house, her uncle and aunt, with a margin of so much time for their forensic pleas before the college year was over, might have driven her to desperate measures; she might have had to flee, without baggage, in the middle of the night on a bus. Not wanting to begin her new life so haphazardly, she had guarded her secret, and had felt a hypocrite.

But she could not keep silent any longer; she had to tell

them and start to pack her bags. She did not know how to present her announcement—whether to disarm them with joy or to stun them with a voice of adamant intention. Resenting the predicament, which so occupied her that her love was brusquely pushed aside, and feeling years younger than she was—an irritable adolescent, nerve-racked by growing pains—she now snatched leaves from the springtime bushes and tore them into shreds. It was late May and the purple lilacs were densely in blossom, offering their virtuous fragrance on the wind; the sun was tender on the yellow willow trees; the mountain range was blue and fair and free of haze. But Polly's senses were not at liberty today to take in these demure delights; she could not respond today at all to the flattering fortune that was to make her a June bride; she could not remember of her fiancé anything beyond his name, and, a little ruefully and a little cynically, she wondered if it was love of him or boredom with freshmen and with her aunt and uncle that had caused her to get engaged to him.

Although she loitered like a school child, she had at last to confront the house behind whose drawn blinds her aunt and uncle awaited her return, innocent of the scare they were presently to get and anticipating the modest academic news she brought each day to serve them with their tea. She was so unwilling that when she came in sight of the house she sat down on a bench at a trolley stop, under the dragging branches of a spruce tree, and opened the book her uncle had asked her to bring from the library. It was *The Heart of Midlothian.* She read with distaste; her uncle's pleasures were different from her own.

Neither the book, though, nor the green needles could hide from her interior eye that house where she had lived for seven years, since her father had died; her mother had been dead for many years and her sisters had long been gone—Fanny to Washington and Mary to Boston—but she had stayed on, quiet and unquestioning. Polly was an undemanding girl and she liked to teach and she had not been inspired to escape; she had had, until now, no reason to go elsewhere although, to be sure, these years had not been exclusively agreeable. For a short time, she had lived happily in an apartment by herself, waking each morning to the charming novelty of being her own mistress. But Uncle Francis and Aunt Jane, both widowed and both bereft of their heartless children, had cajoled her and played tricks upon her will until she had consented to go and live with them. It was not so much because she was weak as it was because they were so extremely strong that she had at last capitulated out of fatigue and had brought her things in a van to unpack them, sighing, in two wallpapered rooms at the top of the stout brown house. This odious house, her grandfather's, was covered with broad, unkempt shingles; it had a turret, and two bow windows within which begonia and heliotrope fed on the powerful mountain sun. Its rooms were huge, but since they were gorged with furniture and with garnishments and clumps and hoards of artifacts of Bays, you had no sense of space in them and, on the contrary, felt cornered and nudged and threatened by hanging lamps with dangerous dependencies and by the dark, bucolic pictures of Polly's forebears that leaned forward from the walls in their insculptured brassy frames.

The house stood at the corner of Oxford Street and Pine, and at the opposite end of the block, at the corner of Pine and Plato (the college had sponsored the brainy place names), there was another one exactly like it. It had been built as a wedding present for Uncle Francis by Polly's grandfather, and here Uncle Francis and his wife, Aunt Lacy, had reared an unnatural daughter and two unnatural sons, who had flown the coop, as he crossly said, the moment they legally could; there was in his tone the implication that if they had gone before they had come of age, he would have haled them back, calling on the police if they offered to resist. Uncle Francis had been born litigious; he had been predestined to arraign and complain, to sue and sentence.

Aunt Jane and Uncle Richard had lived in Grandpa's house, and their two cowed, effeminate sons had likewise vanished when they reached the age of franchise. When both Uncle Richard and Aunt Lacy had been sealed into the Bay plot, Uncle Francis had moved down the street to be with his sister for the sake of economy and company, taking with him his legal library, which, to this day, was still in boxes in the back hall, in spite of the protests of Mildred, their truculent housekeeper. Uncle Francis had then, at little cost, converted his own house into four inconvenient apartments, from which he derived a shockingly high income. A sign over the front door read, "The Bay Arms."

Polly's parents' red brick house, across the street from Uncle Francis's—not built but bought for them, also as a wedding present—had been torn down. And behind the trolley bench on which she sat there was the biggest and oldest family house of all, the original Bay residence, a vast grotesquerie of native stone, and in it, in the beginning of Polly's life, Great-grandmother had imperiously lived, with huge, sharp diamonds on her fichus and her velvet, talking without pause of red Indians and storms on the plains, because she could remember nothing else. The house was now a historical museum; it was called, not surprisingly, the Bay. Polly never looked at it without immediately remembering the intricate smell of the parlor, which had in it moss, must, belladonna, dry leaves, wet dust, oil of peppermint, and something that bound them all together—a smell of tribal history, perhaps, or the smell of a house where lived a half-cracked and haughty old woman who had come to the end of the line.

In those early days, there had been no other houses in this block, and the Bay children had had no playmates except each other. Four generations sat down to Sunday midday dinner every week at Great-grandmother's enormous table; the Presbyterian grace was half as long as a sermon; the fried rabbit was dry. On Christmas Eve, beneath a towering tree in Grandpa's house, sheepish Uncle Richard, as Santa Claus, handed round the presents while Grandpa sat in a central chair like a king on a throne and stroked his proud goatee. They ate turkey on Thanksgiving with Uncle Francis and Aunt Lacy, shot rockets and pinwheels off on the Fourth of July in Polly's family's back yard. Even now, though one of the houses was gone and another was given over to the display of minerals and wagon wheels, and though pressed-brick bungalows had sprung up all along the block, Polly never entered the street without the feeling that she came into a zone restricted for the use of her blood kin, for there lingered in it some energy, some air, some admonition that this was the territory of Bays and that Bays and ghosts of Bays were, and forever would be, in residence. It was easy for her to vest the wind in the spruce tree with her great-grandmother's voice and to hear it say, "Not a one of you knows the sensation of having a red Indian arrow whiz by your sunbonnet with wind enough to make the ribbons wave." On reflection, she understood the claustrophobia that had sent her sisters and cousins all but screaming out of town; horrified, she felt that her own life had been like a dream of smothering.

She was only pretending to read Walter Scott and the sun was setting and she was growing cold. She could not postpone any longer the discharge of the thunderbolt, and at last she weakly rose and crossed the street, feeling a convulsion of panic grind in her throat like a hard sob. Besides the panic, there was a heavy depression, an ebbing away of self-respect, a regret for the waste of so many years. Generations should not be mingled for daily fare, she thought; they are really contemptuous of one another, and the strong individuals, whether they belong to the older or the younger, impose on the meek their creeds and opinions, and, if they are strong enough, brook no dissent. Nothing can more totally subdue the passions than familial piety. Now Polly saw, appalled and miserably ashamed of herself, that she had never once insisted on her own identity in this house. She had dishonestly, supinely (thinking, however, that she was only being polite), allowed her aunt and uncle to believe that she was contented in their house, in sympathy with them, and keenly interested in the minutiae that preoccupied them: their ossifying arteries and their weakening eyes, their dizzy spells and migrant pains, their thrice-daily eucharist of pills and drops, the twinges in their old, uncovered bones. She had never disagreed with them, so how could they know that she did not, as they did, hate the weather? They assumed that she was as scandalized as they by Uncle Francis's tenants' dogs and children. They had no way of knowing that she was bored nearly to frenzy by their vicious quarrels with Mildred over the way she cooked their food.

In the tenebrous hall lined with closed doors, she took off her gloves and coat, and, squinting through the shadows, saw in the mirror that her wretchedness was plain in her drooping lips and her frowning forehead; certainly there was no sign at all upon her face that she was in love. She fixed her mouth into a bogus smile of courage, she straightened out her brow; with the faintest heart in the world she entered the dark front parlor, where the windows were always closed and the shades drawn nearly to the sill. A coal fire on this mild May day burned hot and blue in the grate.

They sat opposite each other at a round, splayfooted table under a dim lamp with a beaded fringe. On the table, amid the tea things, there was a little mahogany casket containing the props with which, each day, they documented their reminiscences of murders, fires, marriages, bankruptcies, and of the triumphs and the rewards of the departed Bays. It was open, showing cracked photographs, letters sallow-inked with age, flaccid and furry newspaper clippings, souvenir spoons flecked with venomous green, little white boxes holding petrified morsels of wedding cake. As Polly came into the room, Aunt Jane reached out her hand and, as if she were pulling a chance from a hat, she picked a newspaper clipping out of the box and said, "I don't think you have ever told Polly the story of the time you were in that train accident in the Royal Gorge. It's such a yarn."

Her uncle heard Polly then and chivalrously half rose from his chair; tall and white-haired, he was distinguished, in a dour way, and dapper in his stiff collar and his waistcoat piped with white. He said, "At last our strayed lamb is back in the fold." The figure made Polly shiver.

"How late you are!" cried Aunt Jane, thrilled at this small deviation from routine. "A department meeting?" If there had been a department meeting, the wreck in the Royal Gorge might be saved for another day.

But they did not wait for her answer. They were impelled, egocentrically and at length, to tell their own news, to explain why it was that they had not waited for her but had begun their tea. Uncle Francis had been hungry, not having felt quite himself earlier in the day and having, therefore, eaten next to nothing at lunch, although the soufflé that Mildred had made was far more edible than customary. He had several new symptoms and was going to the doctor tomorrow; he spoke with infinite peace of mind. Painstakingly then, between themselves, they discussed the advisability of Aunt Jane's making an appointment at the beauty parlor for the same hour Uncle Francis was seeing Dr. Wilder; they could in this way share a taxi. And what was the name of that fellow who drove the Town Taxi whom they both found so cautious and well-mannered? Bradley, was it? They might have him drive them up a little way into the mountains for the view; but, no, Francis might have got a bad report and Jane might be tired after her baking under the dryer. It would be better if they came straight home. Sometimes they went on in this way for hours.

Polly poured herself a cup of tea, and Aunt Jane said, as she had said probably three thousand times in the past seven years, "You may say what you like, there is simply nothing to take the place of a cup of tea at the end of the day."

Uncle Francis reached across the table and took the newspaper clipping from under his sister's hand. He adjusted his glasses and glanced at the headlines, smiling. "There was a great deal of comedy in that tragedy," he said.

"Tell Polly about it," said Aunt Jane. Polly knew the details of this story by heart—the number of the locomotive and the name of the engineer and the passengers' injuries, particularly her uncle's, which, though minor, had been multitudinous.

Amazing herself, Polly said, "Don't!" And, amazed by her, they stared.

"Why, Polly, what an odd thing to say!" exclaimed Aunt Jane. "My dear, is something wrong?"

She decided to take them aback without preamble—it was the only way—and so she said, "Nothing's wrong. Everything's right at last. I am going to be married ten days from today to a teacher at Harvard and I am going to Boston to live."

They behaved like people on a stage; Aunt Jane put her

teacup down, rattling her spoon, and began to wring her hands; Uncle Francis, holding his butter knife as it were a gavel, glared.

"What are you talking about, darling?" he cried. "Married? What do you mean?"

Aunt Jane wheezed, signaling her useful asthma, which, however, did not oblige her. "Boston!" she gasped. "What ever for?"

Polly returned her uncle's magisterial look, but she did so obliquely, and she spoke to her cuffs when she said, "I mean 'married,' the way you were married to Aunt Lacy and the way Aunt Jane was married to Uncle Richard. I am in love with a man named Robert Fair and *he* is with *me* and we're going to be married."

"How lovely," said Aunt Jane, who, sight unseen, hated Robert Fair.

"Lovely perhaps," said Uncle Francis the magistrate, "and perhaps not. You might, if you please, do us the honor of enlightening us as to the qualifications of Mr. Fair to marry and export you. To the best of my knowledge, I have never heard of him."

"I'm quite sure we don't know him," said Aunt Jane; she coughed experimentally, but her asthma was still in hiding.

"No, you don't know him," Polly said. "He has never been in the West." She wished she could serenely drink her tea while she talked, but she did not trust her hand. Fixing her eyes on a maidenhair fern in a brass jardiniere on the floor, she told them how she had first met Robert Fair at her sister Mary's cottage in Edgartown the summer before.

"You never told us," said Uncle Francis reprovingly. "I thought you said the summer had been a mistake. Too expensive. Too hot. I thought you agreed with Jane and me that summer in the East was hard on the constitution." (She had: out of habit she had let them deprecate the East, which she had loved at first sight, had allowed them to tell her that she had had a poor time when, in truth, she had never been so happy.)

Shocked by her duplicity, Aunt Jane said, "We ought to have suspected something when you went back to Boston for

Christmas with Mary instead of resting here beside your own hearth fire."

Ignoring this sanctimonious accusation, Polly continued, and told them as much of Robert Fair as she thought they deserved to know, eliding some of his history—for there was a divorce in it—but as she spoke, she could not conjure his voice or his face, and he remained as hypothetical to her as to them, a circumstance that alarmed her and one that her astute uncle sensed.

"You don't seem head over heals about this Boston fellow," he said.

"I'm nearly thirty," replied his niece. "I'm not sixteen. Wouldn't it be unbecoming at my age if I *were* lovesick?" She was by no means convinced of her argument, for her uncle had that effect on her; he could make her doubt anything—the testimony of her own eyes, the judgments of her own intellect. Again, and in vain, she called on Robert Fair to materialize in this room that was so hostile to him and, through his affection, bring a persuasive color to her cheeks. She did not question the power of love nor did she question, specifically, the steadfastness of her own love, but she did observe, with some dismay, that, far from conquering all, love lazily sidestepped practical problems; it was no help in this interview; it seemed not to cease but to be temporarily at a standstill.

Her uncle said, "Sixteen, thirty, sixty, it makes no difference. It's true I wouldn't like it if you were wearing your heart on your sleeve, but, my Lord, dear, I don't see the semblance of a light in your eye. You look quite sad. Doesn't Polly strike you as looking downright blue, Jane? If Mr. Fair makes you so doleful, it seems to me you're better off with us."

"It's not a laughing matter," snapped Aunt Jane, for Uncle Francis, maddeningly, had chuckled. It was a way he had in disputation; it was intended to enrage and thereby rattle his adversary. He kept his smile, but for a moment he held his tongue while his sister tried a different tack. "What I don't see is why you have to go to Boston, Polly," she said.

"Couldn't he teach Italian at Nevilles just as well as at Harvard?"

Their chauvinism was really staggering. When Roddy, Uncle Francis's son, went off to take a glittering job in Brazil, Aunt Jane and his father had nearly reduced this stalwart boy to kicks and tears by reiterating that if there had been anything of worth or virtue in South America, the grandparent Bays would have settled there instead of in the Rocky Mountains.

"I don't think Robert would like it here," said Polly.

"What wouldn't he like about it?" Aunt Jane bridled. "I thought our college had a distinguished reputation. Your great-grandfather, one of the leading founders of it, was a man of culture, and unless I am sadly misinformed, his humanistic spirit is still felt on the campus. Did you know that his critical study of Isocrates is *highly* esteemed among classical scholars?"

"I mean I don't think he would like the West," said Polly, rash in her frustration.

She could have bitten her tongue out for the indiscretion, because her jingoistic uncle reddened instantly and menacingly, and he banged on the table and shouted, "How does he know he doesn't like the West? You've just told us he's never been farther west than Ohio. How does he dare to presume to damn what he doesn't know?"

"I didn't say he damned the West. I didn't even say he didn't like it. I said *I* thought he wouldn't."

"Then *you* are presuming," he scolded. "I am impatient with Easterners who look down their noses at the West and call us crude and barbaric. But Westerners who renounce and denounce and derogate their native ground are worse."

"Far worse," agreed Aunt Jane. "What can have come over you to turn the man you intend to marry against the land of your forebears?"

Polly had heard it all before. She wanted to clutch her head in her hands and groan with helplessness; even more, she wished that this were the middle of next week.

"We three are the last left of the Bays in Adams," pursued Aunt Jane, insinuating a quaver into her firm, stern voice.

"And Francis and I will not last long. You'll only be burdened and bored with us a little while longer."

"We have meant to reward you liberally for your loyalty," said her uncle. "The houses will be yours when we join our ancestors."

In the dark parlor, they leaned toward her over their cups of cold tea, so tireless in their fusillade that she had no chance to deny them or to defend herself. Was there to be, they mourned, at last not one Bay left to lend his name and presence to municipal celebrations, to the laying of cornerstones and the opening of fairs? Polly thought they were probably already fretting over who would see that the grass between the family graves was mown.

Panicked, she tried to recall how other members of her family had extricated themselves from these webs of casuistry. Now she wished that she had more fully explained her circumstances to Robert Fair and had told him to come and fetch her away, for he, uninvolved, could afford to pay the ransom more easily than she. But she had wanted to spare him such a scene as this; they would not have been any more reticent with him; they would have, with this same arrogance—and this underhandedness—used their advanced age and family honor to twist the argument away from its premise.

Darkness had shrunk the room to the small circle where they sat in the thin light of the lamp; it seemed to her that their reproaches and their jeremiads took hours before they recommenced the bargaining Aunt Jane had started.

Reasonably, in a judicious voice, Uncle Francis said, "There is no reason at all, if Mr. Fair's attainments are as you describe, that he can't be got an appointment to our Romance Language Department. What is the good of my being a trustee if I can't render such a service once in a way?"

As if this were a perfectly wonderful and perfectly surprising solution, Aunt Jane enthusiastically cried, "But of course you can! That would settle everything. Polly can eat her cake and have it, too. Wouldn't you give them your house, Francis?"

"I'd propose an even better arrangement. Alone here, Jane,

you and I would rattle. Perhaps we would move into one of my apartments and the Robert Fairs could have this house. Would that suit you?"

"It would, indeed it would," said Aunt Jane. "I have been noticing the drafts here more and more."

"I don't ask you to agree today, Polly," said Uncle Francis. "But think it over. Write your boy a letter tonight and tell him what your aunt and I are willing to do for him. The gift of a house, as big a house as this, is not to be scoffed at by young people just starting out."

Her "boy," Robert, had a tall son who in the autumn would enter Harvard. "Robert has a house," said Polly, and she thought of its dark-green front door with the brilliant brass trimmings; on Brimmer Street, at the foot of Beacon Hill, its garden faced the Charles. Nothing made her feel more safe and more mature than the image of that old and handsome house.

"He could sell it," said her indomitable aunt.

"He could rent it," said her practical uncle. "That would give you additional revenue."

The air was close; it was like the dead of night in a sealed room and Polly wanted to cry for help. She had not hated the West till now, she had not hated her relatives till now; indeed, till now she had had no experience of hate at all. Surprising as the emotion was—for it came swiftly and authoritatively—it nevertheless cleared her mind and, outraged, she got up and flicked the master switch to light up the chandelier. Her aunt and uncle blinked. She did not sit down again but stood in the doorway to deliver her valediction. "I don't want Robert to come here because I don't want to live here any longer. I want to live my own life."

"Being married is hardly living one's own life," said Aunt Jane.

At the end of her tether now, Polly all but screamed at them, "We *won't* live here and that's that! You talk of my presuming, but how can *you* presume to boss not only me but a man you've never even seen? I don't want your houses! I hate these houses! It's true—I hate, I despise, I abominate the West!"

So new to the articulation of anger, she did it badly and ashamed to death, began to cry. Though they were hurt, they were forgiving, and both of them rose and came across the room, and Aunt Jane, taking her in a spidery embrace, said, "There. You go upstairs and have a bath and rest and we'll discuss it later. Couldn't we have some sherry, Francis? It seems to me that all our nerves are unstrung."

Polly's breath toiled against her sobs, but all the same she took her life in her hands and said, "There's nothing further to discuss. I am leaving. I am not coming back."

Now, for the first time, the old brother and sister exchanged a look of real anxiety; they seemed, at last, to take her seriously; each waited for the other to speak. It was Aunt Jane who hit upon the new gambit. "I mean, dear, that we will discuss the wedding. You have given us very short notice but I daresay we can manage."

"There is to be no wedding," said Polly. "We are just going to be married at Mary's house. Fanny is coming up to Boston."

"Fanny has known all along?" Aunt Jane was insulted. "And all this time you've lived under our roof and sat at our table and never told *us* but told your sisters, who abandoned you?"

"Abandoned me? For God's sake, Aunt Jane, they had their lives to lead!"

"Don't use that sort of language in this house, young lady," said Uncle Francis.

"I apologize. I'm sorry. I am just so sick and tired of—"

"Of course you're sick and tired," said the adroit old woman. "You've had a heavy schedule this semester. No wonder you're all nerves and tears."

"Oh, it isn't that! Oh, leave me alone!"

And, unable to withstand a fresh onslaught of tears, she rushed to the door. When she had closed it upon them, she heard her aunt say, "I simply can't believe it. There must be some way out. Why, Francis, we would be left altogether *alone*," and there was real terror in her voice.

Polly locked the door to her bedroom and dried her eyes and bathed their lids with witch hazel, the odor of which made her think of her Aunt Lacy, who, poor simple creature, had had to die to escape this family. Polly remembered that every autumn Aunt Lacy had petitioned Uncle Francis to let her take her children home for a visit to her native Vermont, but she had never been allowed to go. Grandpa, roaring, thumping his stick, Uncle Francis bombarding her with rhetoric and using the word "duty" repeatedly, Polly's father scathing her with sarcasm, Aunt Jane slyly confusing her with red herrings had kept her an exhausted prisoner. Her children, as a result, had scorned their passive mother and had wounded her, and once they finally escaped, they had not come back—not for so much as a visit. Aunt Lacy had died not having seen any of her grandchildren; in the last years of her life she did nothing but cry. Polly's heart ached for the plight of that gentle, frightened woman. How lucky *she* was that the means of escape had come to her before it was too late! In her sister's Boston drawing room, in a snowy twilight, Robert Fair's proposal of marriage had seemed to release in her an inexhaustible wellspring of life; until that moment she had not known that she was dying, that she was being killed—by inches, but surely killed—by her aunt and uncle and by the green yearlings in her German classes and by the dogmatic monotony of the town's provincialism. She shuddered to think of her narrow escape from wasting away in these arid foothills, never knowing the cause or the name of her disease.

Quiet, herself again, Polly sat beside the window and looked out at the early stars and the crescent moon. Now that she had finally taken her stand, she was invulnerable, even though she knew that the brown sherry was being put ceremoniously on a tray, together with ancestral Waterford glasses, and though she knew that her aunt and uncle had not given up—that they had, on the contrary, just begun. And though she knew that for the last seven days of her life in this house she would be bludgeoned with the most splenetic and most defacing of emotions, she knew that the worst was over; she knew that she would survive, as her sisters and her cousins had survived. In the end, her aunt and uncle only *seemed* to survive; dead on their feet for most of their lives, they had no personal history; their genesis had not been individual—it had only been a part of a dull and factual plan. And they had been too busy honoring their family to love it, too busy defending the West even to look at it. For all their pride in their surroundings, they had never contemplated them at all but had sat with the shades drawn, huddled under the steel engravings. They and her father had lived their whole lives on the laurels of their grandparents; their goal had already been reached long before their birth.

The mountains had never looked so superb to her. She imagined a time, after Uncle Francis and Aunt Jane were dead, when the young Bays and their wives and husbands might come back, free at last to admire the landscape, free to go swiftly through the town in the foothills without so much as a glance at the family memorials and to gain the high passes and the peaks and the glaciers. They would breathe in the thin, lovely air of summits, and in their mouths there would not be a trace of the dust of the prairies where, as on a treadmill, Great-grandfather Bay's oxen plodded on and on into eternity.

The next days were for Polly at once harrowing and delightful. She suffered at the twilight hour (the brown sherry had become a daily custom, and she wondered if her aunt and uncle naïvely considered getting her drunk and, in this condition, persuading her to sign an unconditional indenture) and all through dinner as, by turns self-pitying and contentious, they sought to make her change her mind. Or, as they put it, "come to her senses." At no time did they accept the fact that she was going. They wrangled over summer plans in which she was included; they plotted anniversary speeches in the Bay museum; one afternoon Aunt Jane even started making a list of miners' families among whom Polly was to distribute Christmas baskets.

But when they were out of her sight and their nagging voices were out of her hearing, they were out of her mind, and in it, instead, was Robert Fair, in his rightful place. She graded examination papers tolerantly, through a haze; she packed her new clothes into her new suitcases and emptied her writing desk completely. On these starry, handsome nights, her dreams were charming, although, to be sure, she sometimes woke from them to hear the shuffle of carpet slippers on the floor below her as her insomniac aunt or uncle paced. But before sadness or rue could overtake her, she burrowed into the memory of her late dream.

The strain of her euphoria and her aunt's and uncle's antipodean gloom began at last to make her edgy, and she commenced to mark the days off on her calendar and even to reckon the hours. On the day she met her classes for the last time and told her colleagues goodbye and quit the campus forever, she did not stop on the first floor of the house but went directly to her room, only pausing at the parlor door to tell Aunt Jane and Uncle Francis that she had a letter to get off. Fraudulently humble, sighing, they begged her to join them later on for sherry. "The days are growing longer," said Aunt Jane plaintively, "but they are growing fewer."

Polly had no letter to write. She had a letter from Robert Fair to read, and although she knew it by heart already, she read it again several times. He shared her impatience; his students bored him, too; he said he had tried to envision her uncle's house, so that he could imagine her in a specific place, but he had not been able to succeed, even with the help of her sister. He wrote, "The house your malicious sister Mary describes could not exist. Does Aunt Jane *really* read Ouida?"

She laughed aloud. She felt light and purged, as if she had finished a fever. She went to her dressing table and began to brush her hair and to gaze, comforted, upon her young and loving face. She was so lost in her relief that she was pretty, and that she was going to be married and was going away, that she heard neither the telephone nor Mildred's feet upon the stairs, and the housekeeper was in the room before Polly had turned from her pool.

"It's your sister calling you from Boston," said Mildred with ice-cold contempt; she mirrored her employers. "I heard those operators back East giving themselves *some* airs with their la-di-da way of talking."

Clumsy with surprise and confusion (Mary's calls to her were rare and never frivolous), and sorry that exigency and not calm plan took her downstairs again, she reeled into that smothering front hall where hat trees and cane stands stood like people. The door to the parlor was closed, but she knew that behind it Aunt Jane and Uncle Francis were listening.

When Mary's far-off, mourning voice broke to Polly the awful, the impossible, the unbelievable news that Robert Fair had died that morning of the heart disease from which he had intermittently suffered for some years, Polly, wordless and dry-eyed, contracted into a nonsensical, contorted position and gripped the telephone as if this alone could keep her from drowning in the savage flood that had come from nowhere.

"Are you there, Polly? Can you hear me, darling?" Mary's anxious voice came louder and faster. "Do you want me to come out to you? Or can you come on here now?"

"I can't come now," said Polly. "There's nothing you can do for me." There had always been rapport between these sisters, and it had been deeper in the months since Robert Fair had appeared upon the scene to rescue and reward the younger woman. But it was shattered; the bearer of ill tidings is seldom thanked. "How can you help me?" Polly demanded, shocked and furious. "You can't bring him back to life."

"I can help bring you back to life," her sister said. "You must get out of *there*, Polly. It's more important now than ever."

"Do you think that was why I was going to marry him? Just to escape this house and this town?"

"No, no! Control yourself! We'd better not try to talk any more now—you call me when you can."

The parlor door opened, revealing Uncle Francis with a glass of sherry in his hand.

"Wait, Mary! Don't hang up!" Polly cried. There was a facetious air about her uncle; there was something smug. "I'll get the sleeper from Denver tonight," she said.

When she hung up, her uncle opened the door wider to welcome her to bad brown sherry; they had not turned on the lights, and Aunt Jane, in the twilight, sat in her accustomed place.

"Poor angel," said Uncle Francis.

"I am so sorry, so very sorry," said Aunt Jane.

When Polly said nothing but simply stared at their impassive faces, Uncle Francis said, "I think I'd better call up Wilder. You ought to have a sedative and go straight to bed."

"I'm going straight to Boston," said Polly.

"But why?" said Aunt Jane.

"Because he's there. I love him and he's there."

They tried to detain her; they tried to force the sherry down her throat; they told her she must be calm and they asked her to remember that at times like this one needed the love and the support of one's blood kin.

"I am going straight to Boston," she repeated, and turned and went quickly up the stairs. They stood at the bottom, calling to her: "You haven't settled your affairs. What about the bank?" "Polly, get hold of yourself! It's terrible, I'm heartbroken for you, but it's not the end of the world."

She packed nothing; she wanted nothing here—not even the new clothes she had bought in which to be a bride. She put on a coat and a hat and gloves and a scarf and put all the money she had in her purse and went downstairs again. Stricken but diehard, they were beside the front door.

"Don't go!" implored Aunt Jane.

"You need us now more than ever!" her uncle cried.

"And we need you. Does that make no impression on you, Polly? Is your heart that cold?"

She paid no attention to them at all and pushed them aside and left the house. She ran to the station to get the last train to Denver, and once she had boarded it, she allowed her grief to overwhelm her. She felt chewed and mauled by the niggling hypochondriacs she had left behind, who had fussily tried to appropriate even her own tragedy. She felt sullied by their disrespect and greed.

How lonely I have been, she thought. And then, not fully knowing what she meant by it but believing in it faithfully, she said half aloud, "I am not lonely now."

RICHARD WRIGHT

Almos' a Man

DAVE STRUCK OUT across the fields, looking homeward through paling light. Whut's the usa talkin wid em niggers in the field? Anyhow, his mother was putting supper on the table. Them niggers can't understan nothing. One of these days he was going to get a gun and practice shooting, then they couldn't talk to him as though he were a little boy. He slowed, looking at the ground. Shucks, Ah ain scareda them even ef they are biggern me! Aw, Ah know whut Ahma do. Ahm going by ol Joe's sto n git that Sears Roebuck catlog n look at them guns. Mebbe Ma will lemme buy one when she gits mah pay from ol man Hawkins. Ahma beg her to gimme some money. Ahm ol ernough to hava gun. Ahm seventeen. Almos a man. He strode, feeling his long loose-jointed limbs. Shucks, a man oughta hava little gun aftah he done worked hard all day.

He came in sight of Joe's store. A yellow lantern glowed on the front porch. He mounted steps and went through the screen door, hearing it bang behind him. There was a strong smell of coal oil and mackerel fish. He felt very confident until he saw fat Joe walk in through the rear door, then his courage began to ooze.

"Howdy, Dave! Whutcha want?"

"How yuh, Mistah Joe? Aw. Ah don wanna buy nothing.

Ah just wanted t see ef yuhd lemme look at tha catlog erwhile."

'Sure! You wanna see it here?"

"Nawsuh. Ah wans t take it home wid me. Ah'll bring it back termorrow when Ah come in from the fiels."

"You plannin on buying something?"

"Yessuh."

"Your ma lettin you have your own money now?"

"Shucks. Mistah Joe, Ahm gittin t be a man like anybody else!"

Joe laughed and wiped his greasy white face with a red bandanna.

"Whut you plannin on buyin?"

Dave looked at the floor, scratched his head, scratched his thigh, and smiled. Then he looked up shyly.

"Ah'll tell yuh, Mistah Joe, ef yuh promise yuh won't tell."

"I promise."

"Waal, Ahma buy a gun."

"A gun? Whut you want with a gun?"

"Ah wanna keep it."

"You ain't nothing but a boy. You don't need a gun."

"Aw, lemme have the catlog, Mistah Joe. Ah'll bring it back."

Joe walked through the rear door. Dave was elated. He looked around at barrels of sugar and flour. He heard Joe coming back. He craned his neck to see if he was bringing the book. Yeah, he's got it. Gawddog, he's got it!

"Here, but be sure you bring it back. It's the only one I got."

"Sho, Mistah Joe."

"Say, if you wanna buy a gun, why don't you buy one from me? I gotta gun to sell."

"Will it shoot?"

"Sure it'll shoot."

"Whut kind is it?"

"Oh, it's kinda old . . . a left-hand Wheeler. A pistol. A big one."

"Is it got bullets in it?"

"It's loaded."

"Kin Ah see it?"

"Where's your money?"

"Whut yuh wan fer it?"

"I'll let you have it for two dollars."

"Just two dollahs? Shucks, Ah could buy tha when Ah git mah pay."

"I'll have it here when you want it."

"Awright, suh. Ah be in fer it."

He went through the door, hearing it slam again behind him. Ahma git some money from Ma n buy me a gun! Only two dollahs! He tucked the thick catalogue under his arm and hurried.

"Where yuh been, boy?" His mother held a steaming dish of black-eyed peas.

"Aw, Ma, Ah jus stopped down the road t talk wid the boys."

"Yuh know bettah than t keep suppah waitin."

He sat down, resting the catalogue on the edge of the table.

"Yuh git up from there and git to the well n wash yosef! Ah ain feedin no hogs in mah house!"

She grabbed his shoulder and pushed him. He stumbled out of the room, then came back to get the catalogue.

"Whut this?"

"Aw, Ma, it's jusa catlog."

"Who yuh git it from?"

"From Joe, down at the sto."

"Waal, thas good. We kin use it in the outhouse."

"Naw, Ma." He grabbed for it. "Gimme ma catlog, Ma."

She held onto it and glared at him.

"Quit hollerin at me! Whut's wrong wid yuh? Yuh crazy?"

"But Ma, please. It ain mine! It's Joe's! He tol me t bring it back t im termorrow."

She gave up the book. He stumbled down the back steps, hugging the thick book under his arm. When he had splashed water on his face and hands, he groped back to the kitchen and fumbled in a corner for the towel. He bumped into a chair; it clattered to the floor. The catalogue sprawled at his feet. When he had dried his eyes he snatched up the book and held it again under his arm. His mother stood watching him.

"Now, ef yuh gonna act a fool over that ol book, Ah'll take it n burn it up."

"Naw, Ma, please."

"Waal, set down n be still!"

He sat down and drew the oil lamp close. He thumbed page after page, unaware of the food his mother set on the table. His father came in. Then his small brother.

"Whutcha got there, Dave?" his father asked.

"Jusa catlog," he answered, not looking up.

"Yeah, here they is!" His eyes glowed at blue-and-black revolvers. He glanced up, feeling sudden guilt. His father was watching him. He eased the book under the table and rested it on his knees. After the blessing was asked, he ate. He scooped up peas and swallowed fat meat without chewing. Buttermilk helped to wash it down. He did not want to mention money before his father. He would do much better by cornering his mother when she was alone. He looked at his father uneasily out of the edge of his eye.

"Boy, how come yuh don quit foolin wid tha book n eat yo suppah?"

"Yessuh."

"How you n old man Hawkins gitten erlong?"

"Suh?"

"Can't yuh hear? Why don yuh lissen? Ah ast yuh how wuz yuh n ol man Hawkins gittin erlong?"

"Oh, swell, Pa. Ah plows mo lan than anybody over there."

"Waal, yuh oughta keep yo mind on whut yuh doin."

"Yessuh."

He poured his plate full of molasses and sopped it up slowly with a chunk of cornbread. When his father and brother had left the kitchen, he still sat and looked again at the guns in the catalogue, longing to muster courage enough to present his case to his mother. Lawd, ef Ah only had tha pretty one! He could almost feel the slickness of the weapon with his fingers. If he had a gun like that he would polish it and keep it shining so it would never rust. N Ah'd keep it loaded, by Gawd!

"Ma?" His voice was hesitant.

"Hunh?"

"Ol man Hawkins give yuh mah money yit?"

"Yeah, but ain no usa yuh thinking bout throwin nona it erway. Ahm keepin tha money sos yuh kin have cloes to go to school this winter."

He rose and went to her side with the open catalogue in his palms. She was washing dishes, her head bent low over a pan. Shyly he raised the book. When he spoke, his voice was husky, faint.

"Ma, Gawd knows Ah wans one of these."

"One of whut?" she asked, not raising her eyes.

"One of these," he said again, not daring even to point. She glanced up at the page, then at him with wide eyes.

"Nigger, is yuh gone plumb crazy?"

"Aw, Ma—"

"Git outta here! Don yuh talk t me bout no gun! Yuh a fool!"

"Ma, Ah kin buy one fer two dollahs."

"Not ef Ah knows it, yuh ain!"

"But yuh promised me one—"

"Ah don care whut Ah promised! Yuh ain nothing but a boy yit!"

"Ma, ef yuh lemme buy one Ah'll *never* ast yuh fer nothing no mo."

"Ah to yuh to git outta here! Yuh ain gonna toucha penny of tha money fer no gun! Thas how come Ah has Mistah Hawkins t pay yo wages t me, cause Ah knows yuh ain got no sense."

"But, Ma, we needa gun. Pa ain got no gun. We needa gun in the house. Yuh kin never tell whut might happen."

"Now don yuh try to maka fool outta me, boy! Ef we did hava gun, yuh wouldn't have it!"

He laid the catalogue down and slipped his arm around her waist.

"Aw, Ma, Ah done worked hard alla summer n ain ast yuh fer nothin, is Ah, now?"

"Thas whut yuh spose t do!"

"But Ma, Ah wans a gun. Yuh kin lemme have two dollahs outta mah money. Please, Ma. I kin give it to Pa . . . Please, Ma! Ah loves yuh, Ma."

When she spoke her voice came soft and low.

"Whut yuh wan wida gun, Dave? Yuh don need no gun. Yuh'll git in trouble. N ef yo pa jus thought Ah let yuh have money t buy a gun he'd hava fit."

"Ain nothin wrong, Ma. Ahm almos a man now. Ah wans a gun."

'Who gonna sell yuh a gun?"

"Ol Joe at the sto."

"N it don cos but two dollahs?"

"Thas all, Ma. Jus two dollahs. Please, Ma."

She was stacking the plates away; her hands moved slowly, reflectively. Dave kept an anxious silence. Finally, she turned to him.

"Ah'll let yuh git tha gun ef yuh promise me one thing."

"Whut's tha, Ma?"

"Yuh bring it straight back t me, yuh hear? It be fer Pa."

"Yessum! Lemme go now, Ma."

She stooped, turned slightly to one side, raised the hem of her dress, rolled down the top of her stocking, and came up with a slender wad of bills.

"Here," she said. "Lawd knows yuh don need no gun. But yer pa does. Yuh bring it right back t me, yuh hear? Ahma put it up. Now ef yuh don, Ahma have yuh pa lick yuh so hard yuh won fergit it."

"Yessum."

He took the money, ran down the steps, and across the yard.

"Dave! Yuuuuh Daaaaave!"

He heard, but he was not going to stop now. "Naw, Lawd!"

The first movement he made the following morning was to reach under his pillow for the gun. In the gray light of dawn he held it loosely, feeling a sense of power. Could kill a man with a gun like this. Kill anybody, black or white. And if he were holding his gun in his hand, nobody could run over him; they would have to respect him. It was a big gun, with a long barrel and a heavy handle. He raised and lowered it in his hand, marveling at its weight.

He had not come straight home with it as his mother had asked; instead he had stayed out in the fields, holding the weapon in his hand, aiming it now and then at some imaginary foe. But he had not fired it; he had been afraid that his father might hear. Also he was not sure he knew how to fire it.

To avoid surrendering the pistol he had not come into the house until he knew that they were all asleep. When his mother had tiptoed to his bedside late that night and demanded the gun, he had first played possum; then he had told her that the gun was hidden outdoors, that he would bring it to her in the morning. Now he lay turning it slowly in his hands. He broke it, took out the cartridges, felt them, and then put them back.

He slid out of bed, got a long strip of old flannel from a trunk, wrapped the gun in it, and tied it to his naked thigh while it was still loaded. He did not go in to breakfast. Even though it was not yet daylight, he started for Jim Hawkins' plantation. Just as the sun was rising he reached the barns where the mules and plows were kept.

"Hey! That you, Dave?"

He turned. Jim Hawkins stood eyeing him suspiciously.

"What're yuh doing here so early?"

"Ah didn't know Ah wuz gittin up so early, Mistah Hawkins. Ah wuz fixin t hitch up ol Jenny n take her t the fiels."

"Good. Since you're so early, how about plowing that stretch down by the woods?"

"Suits me, Mistah Hawkins."

"O.K. Go to it!"

He hitched Jenny to a plow and started across the fields. Hot dog! This was just what he wanted. If he could get down by the woods, he could shoot his gun and nobody would hear. He walked behind the plow, hearing the traces creaking, feeling the gun tied tight to his thigh.

When he reached the woods, he plowed two whole rows before he decided to take out the gun. Finally, he stopped, looked in all directions, then untied the gun and held it in his hand. He turned to the mule and smiled.

"Know whut this is, Jenny? Naw, yuh wouldn know! Yuhs jusa ol mule! Anyhow, this is a gun, n it kin shoot, by Gawd!"

He held the gun at arm's length. Whut t hell, Ahma shoot this thing! He looked at Jenny again.

"Lissen here, Jenny! When Ah pull this ol trigger, Ah don wan yuh t run n acka fool now!"

Jenny stood with head down, her short ears pricked straight. Dave walked off about twenty feet, held the gun far out from him at arm's length, and turned his head. Hell, he told himself, Ah ain afraid. The gun felt loose in his fingers; he waved it wildly for a moment. Then he shut his eyes and tightened his forefinger. Bloom! The report half deafened him and he thought his right hand was torn from his arm. He heard Jenny whinnying and galloping over the field, and he found himself on his knees, squeezing his fingers hard between his legs. His hand was numb; he jammed it into his mouth, trying to warm it, trying to stop the pain. The gun lay at his feet. He did not quite know what had happened. He stood up and stared at the gun as though it were a living thing. He gritted his teeth and kicked the gun. Yuh almos broke mah arm! He turned to look for Jenny; she was far over the fields, tossing her head and kicking wildly.

"Hol on there, ol mule!"

When he caught up with her she stood trembling, walling her big white eyes at him. The plow was far away; the traces had broken. Then Dave stopped short, looking, not believing. Jenny was bleeding. Her left side was red and wet with blood. He went closer. Lawd, have mercy! Wondah did Ah shoot this mule? He grabbed for Jenny's mane. She flinched, snorted, whirled, tossing her head.

"Hol on now! Hol on."

Then he saw the hole in Jenny's side, right between the ribs. It was round, wet, red. A crimson stream streaked down the front leg, flowing fast. Good Gawd! Ah wuzn't shootin at tha mule. He felt panic. He knew he had to stop that blood, or Jenny would bleed to death. He had never seen so much blood in all his life. He chased the mule for half a mile, trying to catch her. Finally she stopped, breathing hard, stumpy tail half arched. He caught her mane and led her back to where the plow and gun lay. Then he stooped and grabbed handfuls of damp black earth and tried to plug the bullet hole. Jenny shuddered, whinnied, and broke from him.

"Hol on! Hol on now!"

He tried to plug it again, but blood came anyhow. His fingers were hot and sticky. He rubbed dirt into his palms, trying to dry them. Then again he attempted to plug the bullet hole, but Jenny shied away, kicking her heels high. He stood helpless. He had to do something. He ran at Jenny; she dodged him. He watched a red stream of blood flow down Jenny's leg and form a bright pool at her feet.

"Jenny . . . Jenny," he called weakly.

His lips trembled. She's bleeding t death! He looked in the direction of home, wanting to go back, wanting to get help. But he saw the pistol lying in the damp black clay. He had a queer feeling that if he only did something, this would not be; Jenny would not be there bleeding to death.

When he went to her this time, she did not move. She stood with sleepy, dreamy eyes; and when he touched her she gave a low-pitched whinny and knelt to the ground, her front knees slopping in blood.

"Jenny . . . Jenny . . ." he whispered.

For a long time she held her neck erect; then her head sank, slowly. Her ribs swelled with a mighty heave and she went over.

Dave's stomach felt empty, very empty. He picked up the gun and held it gingerly between his thumb and forefinger. He buried it at the foot of a tree. He took a stick and tried to cover the pool of blood with dirt—but what was the use? There was Jenny lying with her mouth open and her eyes walled and glassy. He could not tell Jim Hawkins he had shot his mule. But he had to tell him something. Yeah, Ah'll tell em Jenny started gittin wil n fell on the joint of the plow. . . . But that would hardly happen to a mule. He walked across the field slowly, head down.

It was sunset. Two of Jim Hawkins' men were over near the edge of the woods digging a hole in which to bury Jenny. Dave was surrounded by a knot of people, all of whom were looking down at the dead mule.

"I don't see how in the world it happened," said Jim Hawkins for the tenth time.

The crowd parted and Dave's mother, father, and small brother pushed into the center.

"Where Dave?" his mother called.

"There he is," said Jim Hawkins.

His mother grabbed him.

"Whut happened, Dave? Whut yuh done?"

"Nothin."

"C mon, boy, talk," his father said.

Dave took a deep breath and told the story he knew nobody believed.

"Waal," he drawled. "Ah brung ol Jenny down here sos Ah could do mah plowin. Ah plowed bout two rows, just like yuh see." He stopped and pointed at the long rows of upturned earth. "Then somethin musta been wrong wid ol Jenny. She wouldn ack right a-tall. She started snortin n kickin her heels. Ah tried t hol her, but she pulled erway, rearin n goin on. Then when the point of the plow was stickin up in the air, she swung erroun n twisted herself back on it . . . She stuck herself n started t bleed. N fo Ah could do anything, she wuz dead."

"Did you ever hear of anything like that in all your life?" asked Jim Hawkins.

There were white and black standing in the crowd. They murmured. Dave's mother came close to him and looked hard into his face. "Tell the truth, Dave," she said.

"Looks like a bullet hole to me," said one man.

"Dave, whut yuh do wid the gun?" his mother asked.

The crowd surged in, looking at him. He jammed his hands into his pockets, shook his head slowly from left to right, and backed away. His eyes were wide and painful.

"Did he hava gun?" asked Jim Hawkins.

"By Gawd, Ah tol yuh that wuz a gun wound," said a man, slapping his thigh.

His father caught his shoulders and shook him till his teeth rattled.

"Tell whut happened, yuh rascal! Tell whut . . ."

Dave looked at Jenny's stiff legs and began to cry.

"Whut yuh do wid tha gun?" his mother asked.

"Whut wuz he doin wida gun?" his father asked.

"Come on and tell the truth," said Hawkins. "Ain't nobody going to hurt you . . ."

His mother crowded close to him.

"Did yuh shoot tha mule, Dave?"

Dave cried, seeing blurred white and black faces.

"Ahh ddinn gggo tt sshooot hher . . . Ah ssswear ffo Gawd Ahh ddin. . . . Ah wuz a-tryin t sssee ef the old gggun would sshoot—"

"Where yuh git the gun from?" his father asked.

"Ah got it from Joe, at the sto."

"Where yuh git the money?"

"Ma give it t me."

"He kept worryin me, Bob. Ah had t. Ah tol im t bring the gun right back t me . . . it was fer yuh, the gun."

"But how yuh happen to shoot that mule?" asked Jim Hawkins.

"Ah wuzn shootin at the mule, Mistah Hawkins. The gun jumped when Ah pulled the trigger . . . n fo Ah knowed anythin Jenny was there a-bleedin."

Somebody in the crowd laughed. Jim Hawkins walked close to Dave and looked into his face.

"Well, looks like you have bought you a mule, Dave."

"Ah swear fo Gawd, Ah didn go t kill the mule, Mistah Hawkins!"

"But you killed her!"

All the crowd was laughing now. They stood on tiptoe and poked heads over one another's shoulders.

"Well, boy, looks like yuh done bought a dead mule! Hahaha!"

"Ain tha ershame."

"Hohohohoho."

Dave stood, head down, twisting his feet in the dirt.

"Well, you needn't worry about it, Bob," said Jim Hawkins to Dave's father. "Just let the boy keep on working and pay me two dollars a month."

"Whut yuh wan fer yo mule, Mistah Hawkins?"

Jim Hawkins screwed up his eyes.

"Fifty dollars."

"Whut yuh do wid tha gun?" Dave's father demanded.

Dave said nothing.

"Yuh wan me t take a tree lim n beat yuh till yuh talk!"

"Nawsuh!"

"Whut yuh do wid it?"

"Ah throwed it erway."

"Where?"

"Ah . . . Ah throwed it in the creek."

"Waal, c mon home. N firs thing in the mawnin git to tha creek n fin tha gun."

"Yessuh."

"What yuh pay fer it?"

"Two dollahs."

"Take tha gun n git yo money back n carry it t Mistah Hawkins, yuh hear? N don fergit Ahma lam you black bottom good fer this! Now march yoself on home, suh!"

Dave turned and walked slowly. He heard people laughing. Dave glared, his eyes welling with tears. Hot anger bubbled in him. Then he swallowed and stumbled on.

That night Dave did not sleep. He was glad that he had gotten out of killing the mule so easily, but he was hurt. Something hot seemed to turn over inside him each time he remembered how they had laughed. He tossed on his bed, feeling his hard pillow. N Pa says he's gonna beat me . . . He remembered other beatings, and his back quivered. Naw, naw, Ah sho don wan im t beat me tha way no mo. Dam em all! Nobody ever gave him anything. All he did was work. They treat me like a mule, n then they beat me. He gritted his teeth. N Ma had t tell on me.

Well, if he had to, he would take old man Hawkins that two dollars. But that meant selling the gun. And he wanted to keep that gun. Fifty dollars for a dead mule.

He turned over, thinking how he had fired the gun. He had an itch to fire it again. Ef other men kin shoota gun, by Gawd, Ah kin! He was still, listening. Mebbe they all sleepin now. The house was still. He heard the soft breathing of his brother. Yes, now! He would go down and get that gun and see if he could fire it! He eased out of bed and slipped into overalls.

The moon was bright. He ran almost all the way to the edge of the woods. He stumbled over the ground, looking for the spot where he had buried the gun. Yeah, here it is. Like a hungry dog scratching for a bone, he pawed it up. He puffed his black cheeks and blew dirt from the trigger and barrel. He broke it and found four cartridges unshot. He looked around; the fields were filled with silence and moonlight. He clutched the gun stiff and hard in his fingers. But, as soon as he wanted to pull the trigger, he shut his eyes and turned his head. Naw, Ah can't shoot wid mah eyes closed n mah head turned. With effort he held his eyes open; then he squeezed. *Blooooom!* He was stiff, not breathing. The gun was still in his hands. Dammit, he'd done it. He fired again. *Blooooom!* He smiled. *Blooooom! Blooooom! Click, click.* There! It was empty. If anybody could shoot a gun, he could. He put the gun into his hip pocket and started across the fields.

When he reached the top of a ridge he stood straight and proud in the moonlight, looking at Jim Hawkins' big white house, feeling the gun sagging in his pocket. Lawd, ef Ah had just one mo bullet Ah'd taka shot at tha house. Ah'd like t scare ol man Hawkins jusa little . . . Jusa enough t let im know Dave Glover is a man.

To his left the road curved, running to the tracks of the Illinois Central. He jerked his head, listening. From far off came a faint *hoooof-hoooof; hoooof-hoooof; hoooof-hoooof. . . .* That's number eight. He took a swift look at Jim Hawkins' house, he thought of Pa, of Ma, of his little brother, and the boys. He thought of the dead mule and heard hoooof-hoooof; hoooof-hoooof; hoooof-hoooof . . . He stood rigid. Two dollahs a mont. Les see now . . . Tha means it'll take bout two years. Shucks! Ah'll be dam!

He started down the road, toward the tracks. Yeah, here she comes! He stood beside the track and held himself stiffly. Here she comes, erroun the ben . . . C mon, yuh slow poke! C mon! He had his hand on his gun; something quivered in his stomach. Then the train thundered past, the gray and brown box cars rumbling and clinking. He gripped the gun tightly;

then he jerked his hand out of his pocket. Ah betcha Bill wouldn't do it! Ah betcha . . . The cars slid past, steel grinding upon steel. Ahm ridin yuh ternight, so hep me Gawd! He was hot all over. He hesitated just a moment; then he grabbed, pulled atop of a car, and lay flat. He felt his pocket; the gun was still there. Ahead the long rails were glinting in the moonlight, stretching away, away to somewhere, somewhere where he could be a man . . .

Notes on the Stories

I. FIRST PERSON VOICES

"Cathedral," by Raymond Carver

Raymond Carver was born in Oregon in 1939 and has lived most of his life in the West. He is the author of three volumes of short stories, *Will You Please Be Quiet, Please?*, *What We Talk About When We Talk About Love*, and *Cathedral.*

"Cathedral," like many of Carver's stories, concerns characters in the midstream of American culture. It's narrated by a man of modest achievements and aspirations. His voice is affable and idiomatic, but as the story opens we can hear signs of his anxiousness over an upcoming visit to his house by a blind man, a friend of his wife's. During the blind man's visit, however, he undergoes a change that's reflected in his voice. What is it?

"The Writer in the Family," by E. L. Doctorow

E. L. Doctorow was born in the Bronx during the Depression, and he lives today in the suburbs of New York City. He is the author of one collection of stories, *Lives of the Poets*, and six novels, among them *Welcome to Hard Times*, *The Book of Daniel*, *Ragtime*, and most recently, *World's Fair.*

"The Writer in the Family" is narrated by a man looking back on his childhood, who tells of a family drama that was instigated by the death of his father. In the way he puts together the chronology of events, he seems to be searching in his memory for the meaning of it all, and the story concludes with a finality that indicates he has found it. In his voice we can hear the odd mixture of nostalgia and bitterness. Is he satisfied, looking back?

"Rock Springs," by Richard Ford

Richard Ford, a native Mississippian, has written three novels: *A Piece of My Heart, The Ultimate Good Luck,* and *The Sportswriter.*

"Rock Springs" is the story of a man whose life history is full of bad decisions and bad breaks, and who can't seem to get himself on the right track. He yearns for something more, "a better shake in things," as he puts it, for himself and his young daughter. Though we can't sympathize with him in some of his actions—at the beginning of the story he steals a car, for example—through the earnest sincerity in his voice we feel his desperation and his rock-bottom goodness. And so we come to the story's provocative questions: Is the man's emptiness of his own making? Or is it true for some people, that no matter what they do, there are no happy endings?

"Hiding," by Susan Minot

Susan Minot grew up in Massachusetts and lives in New York City. This story is taken from *Monkeys,* her first book, a novel in the form of interrelated short stories.

"Hiding" is narrated by a little girl, the second oldest of six children in a suburban family. In her voice, we can recognize the signs of a vivacious and perceptive child, but, too, we can hear signs of insecurity. She often uses "we" instead of "I," speaking collectively for all of the children. What does that suggest about her? Where does her nervousness come from?

"Wants," by Grace Paley

Grace Paley was born in New York, where she still lives. Her short stories, written over the past thirty years, have been collected in three volumes, *The Little Disturbances of Man, Enormous Changes at the Last Minute,* and *Later the Same Day.*

In "Wants," a woman runs into her ex-husband on the steps of the public library, and their chance encounter sets off in her a cryptic self-evaluation. Her voice is sharp and urban, wise and wise-guy, a little vituperative, a little sad. What does she think of herself?

"An Amateur's Guide to the Night," by Mary Robison

Mary Robison is the author of two short story collections, *Days* and *An Amateur's Guide to the Night.* She has also written a novel, *Oh!*

In the voice of "An Amateur's Guide to the Night," we hear the regionalism of the contemporary American Midwest. Lindy, the narrator, is about to graduate from high school, and we can hear the strain of this crucial moment. She lives with her odd family. She's a bit of a dreamer. Her main interest is in looking through a telescope at the night sky. What's really on her mind? Is it something larger than graduation and closer to home than Mars?

"Dead Reckoning," by Bob Shacochis

Bob Shacochis was born in Virginia. A former Peace Corps volunteer and a graduate of the Iowa Writers' Workshop, he received the American Book Award for first fiction in 1985 for his collection *Easy in the Islands,* from which this story is taken.

"Dead Reckoning" is the tale of a young woman who, during a period of uncertainty in her life, falls in love with a willful and inflexible man, a sailor. The story is told in a straightforward chronological fashion, and in a voice redolent of newfound confidence and alertness. We sense the events of the story have changed this young woman. In what way? How did it happen?

"Why I Live at the P.O.," by Eudora Welty

Eudora Welty was born in Jackson, Mississippi, in 1909 and has lived most of her life in the Deep South. Her many works of fiction include *The Robber Bridegroom, A Curtain of Green,* and *The Wide Net.* She is also the author of a memoir, *One Writer's Beginnings.*

"Why I Live at the P.O.," like much of Eudora Welty's fiction, depicts the rural South. In the voice of the narrator, an adult woman living at home with the eccentric members of her family, we hear the peculiar idiom of her time and place, and we also hear the strain of someone at odds with those around her. Is it right for her to move out? Or has she been overreactive and insecure?

II. DIRECTED VOICES

"Haircut," by Ring Lardner (1885–1933)

Ring Lardner was born in Niles, Michigan, and spent many years as a sportswriter and columnist in Chicago. His short stories, known for their biting satire, are collected in many volumes, among them *You Know Me Al*, *How to Write Short Stories*, and *The Love Nest and Other Stories*.

The narrator of "Haircut," a small town barber, tells us a story he thinks is funny. Is it? Imagining ourselves stuck in the barber's chair, listening to the man's voice just a few inches from our ear, how do we feel about his story? How do we feel about him?

"It's Six A.M. Do You Know Where You Are?" by Jay McInerney

Jay McInerney made a celebrated literary debut with his novel *Bright Lights, Big City*. His second book is *Ransom*.

"It's Six A.M." is the story of a young man at a trendy rock and roll club in New York who is in the midst of sampling all of the city's transient pleasures. The voice, of someone speaking to himself, is sassy and clever and hip. But there's a cynicism in there, too. What's he so cynical about? The "you" address invites us to put ourselves in the young man's place. How does that affect our response to the story?

"The Kid's Guide to Divorce," by Lorrie Moore

This story comes from Lorrie Moore's collection *Self-Help*. She has also written *Anagrams*, a novel.

"The Kid's Guide to Divorce" speaks at us in the voice of a child as if we, too, were children. The speaker is mischievous, full of the know-it-all condescension of an adolescent, but does she really know as much as she thinks she does? Is there some greater seriousness in this story that the speaker reveals unwittingly?

"Pal Joey," by John O'Hara (1905–1970)

John O'Hara is best known for his novels about the social habits of the American middle class, including *From the Terrace*, *Butterfield 8*, and *Appointment in Samarra*, but he was as well a prolific writer of short stories, many of which were posthumously collected and published in a 1985 volume, *The Stories of John O'Hara*.

"Pal Joey" is written in the form of a letter from a musician on the road to his friend back home. What do we think of someone who would write a letter like this, with its misuse of words, its misspellings, its vulgar sexism, and its logic twisted to be self-serving? What sort of friendship does this letter reveal? And, invited as we are to be on the receiving end of the letter, how do we feel not being able to write back?

III. THIRD PERSON VOICES

"Silent Snow, Secret Snow," by Conrad Aiken (1889–1973)

Conrad Aiken was best known as a poet, but he also wrote short stories, novels, and literary criticism. In his work he often dealt with the inner workings of the mind, and this story is a clear example of his interest in psychopathology.

"Silent Snow, Secret Snow" is about the onset of madness in a young boy. In spite of the insidious nature of the subject, however, the voice is both lyrical and erudite. What are we to conclude from the fact that the narrator explains the boy's thoughts to us with a linguistic sophistication that is far beyond the boy's own power to express himself? And what are all those lovely metaphors and nearly musical sentences doing in there? In other words, what are we to make of the difference between what is happening to the boy, and what he thinks is happening?

"Sunshine and Shadow," by Ann Beattie

Ann Beattie is often cited as the writer who best depicted the generation of Americans who came to adulthood in the 1970s. Her novels include *Chilly Scenes of Winter, Falling in Place,* and *Love, Always.* This story is from her collection, *The Burning House.*

"Sunshine and Shadow," like much of Ann Beattie's work, is full of references to the rebellion of the sixties and reflective of the blander, self-interest-dominated culture that followed. The story is about a couple trying to patch things up after the man's infidelity. The narrator lets us in on the confused thoughts of both major characters as they wonder whether to pursue selfish impulses or generous ones. Should they part? Or should they stay together and work things out? The voice is a tricky one. Does it cultivate our sympathy for the characters? Or does it enjoin us to be critical?

"The Enormous Radio," by John Cheever (1912–1982)

John Cheever was the author of five novels, including *The Wapshot Chronicle,* his first, which won the National Book Award in 1958. He is best remembered, however, for his more than 100 short stories, many of which were collected in 1978 in *The Stories of John Cheever,* a book that not only won the Pulitzer Prize but became that rarity of rarities among short story collections, a bestseller.

From the opening sentence of "The Enormous Radio," when the main characters are mildly deprecated by a clever stereotype, the narrator puts us at an odd distance from them, allowing us to share in his air of supremacy. Though the story is grounded in the familiar details of real life, it is nonetheless focused on a queer, supernatural chain of events. In the end, the characters come to judge themselves more harshly than they did initially. Once they do that, can we maintain our distance? Does the voice maintain its snide implications after all? Or has an introspective irony crept in?

"Was," by William Faulkner (1897–1962)

William Faulkner, the author of more than twenty novels chronicling the changing culture of the American South between the middle of the nineteenth century and the middle of the twentieth, is widely held to be among the, if not *the*, greatest of American writers. His books include *The Sound and The Fury, As I Lay Dying, Light in August, Absalom, Absalom,* and *Go Down, Moses,* from which this story is taken.

On the one hand, "Was" is an intricate and difficult story about relations between neighboring families in the antebellum rural South, resonant with the profound tragedy of slavery and the equally profound Southern tradition of the autonomous family. On the other hand, it is a slapstick comedy, complete with a cast of fiercely eccentric characters, a wacky chase, and a ridiculous courtship. The narrator, employing tortuous sentences, complicated syntax, and regional jargon, presents everything, explains nothing. There's nothing given especial weight. Jokes are delivered with the same offhand bluntness as, say, a description of the forest. In the voice is an unflagging intensity, a challenge. We're called upon to recognize that within the confines of the small lives of the story's characters can be witnessed the large consequences of history and culture.

"The Battler," by Ernest Hemingway (1899–1961)

Ernest Hemingway remains the most celebrated and perhaps the most influential American writer of the twentieth century. His lean, forthright prose, startlingly original when it first came to public light in the 1920s, has by now spawned countless imitations. Among his books are *In Our Time,* the collection of stories from which "The Battler" is taken, *The Sun Also Rises, A Farewell to Arms, For Whom the Bell Tolls,* and *The*

Old Man and the Sea. He was awarded the Nobel Prize for Literature in 1954.

"The Battler" is the story of young Nick Adams, a recurring character in Hemingway's early fiction, and his brief, surprising, and subtly troubling encounter with strangers in the woods. We're privy to Nick's thoughts; at least, the narrator presents the situation as Nick perceives it. But Nick is on his guard, naive and nervous, and he observes things without analyzing them, the way people do in unfamiliar situations. He notices things one at a time and lets the details of the situation envelop him. What does Nick make of what happens? Is he changed by it? Can we tell?

"Territory," by David Leavitt

David Leavitt is a graduate of Yale. His first collection of stories, *Family Dancing,* from which this story is taken, was published when he was just twenty-three. He is also the author of a novel, *The Lost Language of Cranes.*

"Territory" is the story of a young man who is staying in his mother's home and anticipating the visit of his homosexual lover, whom he will introduce to his mother for the first time. Narrated primarily through the perceptions of Neil, the main character, the story focuses on his anxiety over the impending encounter. The voice, quiet, circumspect, and even a little trembly, evokes an image of Neil as a thoughtful but uncertain fellow. What is he uncertain about? Does his lover's visit help him overcome his unease? In the story's final line, the narrator abandons its translation of Neil's thoughts and becomes an outside observer. Does this shift urge us toward any conclusions about Neil? Does the voice change as well?

"A Domestic Dilemma," by Carson McCullers (1917–1967)

Carson McCullers's first novel, *The Heart is a Lonely Hunter,* about the friendship between a young girl and a mute man in a small Southern town, was published when the author was just twenty-three. Her other well-known works include *Reflections in a Golden Eye, The Member of the Wedding,* and a novella, *The Ballad of the Sad Cafe.*

"A Domestic Dilemma" is something of an oddity in McCullers's work, taking place in the suburbs of New York City, but its subject, the cruel difficulties of love, is one she often explored. In this story a man is tormented by his wife's inability to give up drinking. It is narrated almost exclusively through his perceptions and thoughts. The voice is full of weariness and exasperation. What are we led to believe in the end about the man's inner conflict? Is it resolvable?

"The Magic Barrel," by Bernard Malamud (1914–1986)

During his lifetime, Bernard Malamud was a winner of the Pulitzer Prize, and he twice won the National Book Award, once for *The Magic Barrel,* the collection of stories from which this story is taken. His novels include *The Natural, The Assistant, The Fixer, Dubin's Lives,* and *God's Grace.*

In "The Magic Barrel" we find the wry invocation of myth that characterizes much of Malamud's work. The story concerns the relationship between a lonely man who seems to be of a pragmatic turn of mind and the matchmaker he hires to find him a wife. The voice of the story mingles the traditionally this-is-just-a-story tone of a fable-spinner with the diligently observant, concretely detailed one of a realist, and in it is an echo of the story's interesting questions: Do dreams and realities co-exist? Is this what life is about?

"Kiswana Browne," by Gloria Naylor

Gloria Naylor's first book, *The Women of Brewster Place,* from which "Kiswana Browne" is taken, is a novel in the form of seven interrelated stories. For it, she received the American Book Award in 1983. She is also the author of a second novel, *Linden Hills.*

In Kiswana Browne, the title character, a young black woman trying to make it on her own, is visited in her apartment by her doting, worried mother. Though we get all of the story's information through the perceptions of Kiswana, the narrator maintains an apparent objectivity, relating Kiswana's thoughts and observations in a voice that is scantly emotional. Kiswana's reactions to her mother change as the story moves along, and we witness the change unfolding, step-by-step.

"Everything That Rises Must Converge," by Flannery O'Connor (1925–1964)

Flannery O'Connor, a native Georgian, wrote two novels, *Wise Blood* and *The Violent Bear It Away,* but her finest work is contained in her short stories, known for their unflinching examination of stunted, unpleasant characters.

In its cool scorn and its grim, scarifying humor, "Everything That Rises Must Converge," the story of a doltish mother and her intellectually pretentious adult son, is an example of O'Connor at her most pitiless. The voice of the story is spiny and mocking, and the story itself proceeds to a cruel conclusion. Do we sympathize with the characters at the end?

"The Jilting of Granny Weatherall," by Katherine Anne Porter (1890–1980)

Katherine Anne Porter is known as one of the finest stylists in American fiction, in spite of a relatively small body of work. Her one full-length novel was *Ship of Fools*. Her *Collected Stories*, published in 1965, received a Pulitzer Prize and the National Book Award.

"The Jilting of Granny Weatherall" concerns a bedridden old woman whose life is waning. So weak that she cannot even adjust her pillows, she can't busy herself; she's at the mercy of her own thoughts, unable to block out either her memories or her knowledge that death is near. The narrator of the story alternates revelations of what's going on in the woman's mind with the chronicle of what's going on in her bedroom. As the story proceeds, the voice seems to gather speed, rushing almost coldly to the story's conclusion. What does the hurry suggest?

"The Liberation," by Jean Stafford (1915–1979)

Jean Stafford was the author of several novels, among them *The Mountain Lion*, *Bad Characters*, and *The Catherine Wheel*. In 1970 she won the Pulitzer Prize for Literature for her volume of collected short stories.

"The Liberation" concerns a woman's decision, at the age of thirty, to leave the Western town of her upbringing and the home of her tyrannically possessive aunt and uncle in order to marry a man who lives in the East. The haughty, judgmental voice of the narrator emphasizes the limited lives of the aunt and uncle, and leads us to judge them poorly ourselves. But how do we feel about the young woman? Is she doing the right thing?

"Almos' a Man," by Richard Wright (1908–1960)

Richard Wright, a black novelist and essayist, for many years an avowed communist, and ultimately an expatriate, was the first important black American writer militantly to attack racism. His books include *Native Son*, *Black Boy*, *The Outsider*, and a posthumously published collection of stories, *Eight Men*, from which this story is taken.

"Almos' a Man," the story of an adolescent's desire to be treated seriously as an adult, takes place in the rural Jim Crow South. The narrator of the story alternately speaks with the cool erudition of a sophisticated observer and the crude vernacular of Dave, the main character. The contrasting qualities in the voice allow us to feel the huge gap between the repressively limited world that Dave lives in and the larger world beyond. But although there is a historical and cultural context within which we view Dave's plight, the story is not simply a didactic portrayal of racism. Can we sympathize with him in everything he chooses to do? Does his becoming a man depend entirely on outside forces, on others?